California

An A

Compiled and Edited by
Z Publishing House

2018

Table of Contents

Foreword, or How This Series Came to Be

There is a troubling catch-22 that exists in the world of publishing: in order to be published—at least by any of the major houses—you must already have been published. The logic works like this: Publishing houses want to sell books. What easier way to sell books than by publishing authors who already have amassed large followings of readers to whom they can market? Inevitably, this cycle leaves the aspiring author with the pressing question of where to begin. Sure, the dramatic rise of self-publishing platforms has enabled everyone to put their writing out there, which is great, but it does come with its own set of problems. Namely, when everyone actually does put their writing out there, as has happened, the question now becomes: Where are the readers to begin? With the oversaturation of the market, readers could spend entire lifetimes buying and reading self-published books and still not find that one author with whom they truly resonate. On Amazon alone, for instance, a new book is uploaded every five minutes, and that number is only set to rise as more and more people take advantage of the self-empowering platforms available to writers today.

The good news is that readers want to discover new talent. This we learned firsthand after beginning Z Publishing in November of 2015. What started as a small Facebook group designed to bring independent writers together on a shared platform of exposure soon transcended into a wave of newfound appreciation for independent writing. Within a few short months, Z Publishing had amassed tens of thousands of followers across social media. Once we knew the idea had struck a chord with a growing group of people, we took the next step and launched Z Publishing's own website in March of 2016. Publishing articles from writers of a multitude of genres—including travel, fiction, politics, lifestyle, and poetry—the website garnered more support from readers and writers alike, and our following continued to grow.

Furthering upon our mission to promote the work of talented wordsmiths across the nation, we began a series called America's Best Emerging Poets, through which we showcased our favorite up-and-coming poets on a state-by-state basis. After the success of our first series, we decided to open submissions to prose writers as well. Thus began our Emerging Writers series, a collection of short writings from a wide variety of genres—including literary fiction, mystery, and narrative nonfiction—through which we hope to offer our readers a quick and efficient way to discover new local talent and perhaps entirely new genres that otherwise may have been too daunting to explore.

While working on this series, and as our base of physical retailers has expanded, we've also been able to take perhaps the most significant step forward in our publishing evolution, and we now proudly offer solo-author book deals. To make the selections on who to offer these deals to, we will take into account reader reviews, so if there are any writings within this book that you particularly enjoy, be sure to give them a mention in your Amazon review!

Now that you know a bit about how this series came to be, we'd like to thank you for taking the time to explore this edition of the Emerging Writers series. We hope you enjoy this publication, and we look forward to hearing your thoughts regarding how, together, we can build the publishing house of the future.

-The Z Publishing Team

Eenie Meenie Miney
Ariel Castagna

Angelo had found the lamp at a yard sale. His plan was to repurpose it as a gravy boat. But as he was suds-ing it up in his kitchen sink, the lamp began to shake. It lifted itself out of Angelo's hands and hovered in midair. The spout spurted green and purple sparks that ignited together and gave birth to the spirit of an ancient genie.

"Greetings mortal," the apparition's voice boomed. "I am Elymas, sworn resident of the Lamp of Nod. You have released me, and I am now indebted to you in the sum of three wishes."

"Are you serious?" Angelo spewed with excitement.

"Quite."

"Can I have a ukulele?"

"You can have anything from this realm or another."

"Make it out of chocolate." Angelo closed his eyes and held his hands out.

Elymas had dealt with humans before and knew that it sometimes took them a while to make up their minds. "Do not feel rushed. I shall not return to my confines until your desires are materialized."

"I already told you: I want a chocolate ukulele."

". . . Yes. You did say that. But your response came hastily, and out of courtesy," Elymas said 'courtesy,' but he really meant 'pity,' "I'd like to reemphasize—"

"It ain't hasty, bro. I've been thinking about this my whole life. "Angelo's options might have been limitless, but his time was not. "Bring the strings."

This feat was a waste of Elymas' power, but he was bound by forces even greater than his own.

When the instrument appeared in Angelo's hands, he twanged a couple of chords from "Lady Marmalade" and gave a whole new meaning to the phrase "mocha-chocolata-ya-ya."

Elymas hoped that there would be a period of self-reflection before the following wishes were cast, but they came swiftly.

"Okay, next: I want a Netflix reboot of *David the Gnome*."

"I implore you," Elymas pressed the palms of his hands together. "Please allow me to explain how this arrangement is supposed to work."

"Rules are simple. I ask for things and you make them happen."

"Yes, but you can have *anything*. You can use this moment to benefit your life, your existence, your race at large."

"Wish three: You know cup holders?"

Finally. A chance to get really creative. Elymas spun his hands, one over the other until a cloud of smoke sprouted out from them. It grew and swirled into a tornado that swallowed Angelo up and shooed him outside into his driveway. When the scene evaporated, the genie and the mortal were standing outside next to Angelo's new car.

"What the heck is this?" he asked.

"This," Elymas drew a powerful breath, "is your custom, gold-plated, convertible Ferrari. With an eight-cylinder engine, leather seats fitted with detachable fur-liners— both materials garnered from endangered animals that died of natural causes and Darwinist principles, jetpack-powered speed boosters, an in-car theater system with surround sound speakers and VR headset technology, cruise control, a thermostat that will allow you to adjust the internal temperature up to the tenth desired degree, a private chauffer who has been sworn to serve you for the rest of his temporal life (or the next twenty years, whichever is longer), gas mileage that's unheard of in this dimension, a retractable kitchenette along with a custom brisket smoker, and twenty-six," Elymas snapped his fingers and twenty-six slots jutted out from the frame of the vehicle, "count them, twenty-six cup holders."

Angelo was far less impressed by the creation. "You gotta be the worst genie this world has ever seen."

"You wished for cup holders. I commanded cupholders."

"Dude, I can *buy* a car that has cup holders in it," said Angelo. "I wanted a cup holder attached to my pants."

Train Stop and Train Starts
Nicolette Nodine

The hunk of metal came wheezing into the southern Oregon station and slowed to a halt. Parts of it rattled and whined, but Casey's train always managed to get back home to unravel its mechanical bones.

Casey was the proud, strong boned conductor; this was his train. And proud Casey had been the conductor for some odd amount of years maybe 15, maybe 17. He ducked under every cabin door and got down on one knee every time he checked a child's ticket. When he smiled, 3 or 4 dark brown lines would appear at the corner of his eyes, and the warm, heavy palm of his hand would always find its way to cover his heart whenever he gave way to a chuckle. Casey wore a red and white pinstriped shirt, navy blue suspenders and a neatly placed tie under his uniform blue blazer. He wore this nearly every day for the past some odd years maybe 15, maybe 17. He felt young enough to keep a short, neatly trimmed beard but he thought perhaps when he reached his sixties he'd start shaving every day before work. Casey had no intention of retiring any time soon.

As his darling train rolled into the southern station, he made sure to prepare a piping hot cup of cocoa for his train doctor, sweet Georgia.

"She don't sound too good today Georgia. I hope you're feelin' mighty lively because I got a feelin' she's gonna drain you." Casey stepped onto the platform, handing her the routine cup of hot cocoa.

"Well good news, I'm in great spirits today, Casey. The sun's out, almost reached 30 this morning and I'm feelin' mighty fine!" She replied in her usual soft southern way and sipped cautiously.

Sweet Georgia was a silly sort of woman. Divorced in her early 40s, children all grown, she went back to college and decided she wanted to be a train mechanic for no reason at all. She'd been following Casey and his train for ten years now, fixing her up whenever she came back to southern Oregon. Sweet Georgia had the prominent stature of a woman, strong limbs, and tall grace, with a southern twang she picked up from the movies. Every time she laughed, her white teeth made the snow look dull, and she waved at every train leaving or coming home.

Sweet Georgia readjusted her blue-gray, floppy hat, takes one last sip of the hot cocoa and hands the empty cup to Casey as she begins to work on the train.

Breadths of white and blue covered everything at the station, the train, the snow. Everything was crisp and glistening. Casey in his deep blue uniform stood tall on the wooden platform, with both hands in his pocket. Sometimes for no reason at all, he'd lay one of his hands gently on his chest and sigh in a Sunday morning kind of way.

He sighed and thought about sweet Georgia and how she was the only one who could make him happy to hear a hiccup in his train's engine. He thought about how he traveled up and down the North West several times a month but never truly went anywhere. He wondered how sweet Georgia would like the beaches in Mexico.

"Well, well, well it looks like you were right. She's being pretty stubborn. She mus' be tired. She's been givin' it her all for maybe fifteen or seventeen years, hasn't she? She ain't getting out of here till tomorrow morning, at the earliest."

"I better make an announcement huh?" Casey asked.

There was clearly no one left at the station except for a few custodial employees. The place was nearly silent.

A giggle slipped out of sweet Georgia's mouth as she wiped her forehead and looked around. Casey opened the loudspeaker box and with the 3 or 4 deep brown lines at the crease of his eyes, smiled and said, "I'm sorry folks for the inconvenience but my train seems to be taking a sick day. See ya'll here bright 'n early tomorrow mornin'."

He closed up the loudspeaker box and walked back to sweet Georgia, shrugging his large shoulders.

"That ol' train otta take a break anyhow," sweet Georgia crooned, "do you like Mexican food? I'm starving."

Oceans
William R. Hincy

With her feet spread in the stirrups and her knees pressed together, Mary's legs resembled the tentacles of a squid floating lifelessly along a deep-sea current. Her face was blue, almost green—the way it looked when she had a stomachache.

Wading to her side—"Is everything all right?"

"I'm okay," she muttered breathlessly, taking my hand and pressing it against her chest.

The hospital gown she was wearing was patterned with small green fish at regular intervals and was so loose on her that it revealed large seas of flesh at the openings, including the pale, cold patch she was pressing my hand against. Her dark eyes were hollow; a black wing of her raven hair cast down over the side of her face like a veil.

"Just leave it," she said, pulling away the moment my free hand reached to brush away the hair. "It's fine."

The ultrasound technician, a dark-skinned woman named Balianne, drew the curtain closed. Moving with militaristic precision, she took two steps to the counter along the wall, removed the lid from a jar of condoms, set it in an exact position next to the jar, withdrew a condom in a black wrapper with gold lettering, and then reclosed the jar with her free hand. With one step and one deft motion of the hand, she had torn the wrapper of the condom open and stepped on a lever, popping the lid to the trashcan open in which she discarded the wrapper. Two quick steps later she was at the ultrasound machine. Swaying rhythmically, she picked up a plastic bottle of ultrasound gel and squeezed a dollop of it on the inside of the condom. She drew the ultrasound transducer out of the holster and began to unroll the condom over the submarine-shaped transducer.

"I expect you'll recognize how this feels," she said, neither coldly nor humorously. "Only this can't cause you any problems."

After the condom was fully unrolled, she squeezed a precise line of gel over the top edge of the transducer. The image on the ultrasound machine brightened, and a second later the probe disappeared beneath Mary's gown.

Even though the ultrasound machine produced no sound it seemed like the rippling images on the monitor were emitting vibrations on a frequency too low for the human ear to hear but powerful enough you felt them in your chest. Focused on the monitor, we were traveling through the deepest depths of the ocean, the way science had imagined it to be before it had ever been glimpsed. Desolate, black— completely incapable of supporting life. An underwater wasteland threatening to suffocate any life that dare impregnate its depths. The ocean after science had vanquished the Kraken and the sea serpent, and with ardor declared the giant squid a similar myth. The ocean when there were no glowing specters who could ignite the membranes in their angelic bodies and illuminate the darkness by just their presence—all-power life willing itself into existence before there was even will.

Mary had stopped looking at the barrenness on the monitor; she was now staring at her belly beneath the hospital gown, her black eyes wet and bottomless. Her grip slackened; letting go, her hand slipped down to her side and her fingers coiled like boiled lobster-tails.

As we all sank down into the darkness of the room, as the weight of the ocean buried us, as our eyes bulged from their sockets, ready to burst, all that was left to do was stare up at the last ounces of water where light still played, swaying in the waves, dancing with the shadows. How shameful is it to feel relieved, even for a moment, that there is no Kraken to fear—that something doesn't exist, that it has, in fact, never lived, so you can continue on thinking and believing and acting the same way you always have? How heartbreakingly lifeless would the ocean be if we probed its depths again today and found it as faceless as had previously been described? Just how unimportant would our lives feel if we discovered that the belly of creation was that utterly empty?

Creekside
An Excerpt
Jeanne O'Halloran

There were twelve of us children in the house—five girls, four boys, and a few of us that were somewhere in the middle. Our house was a little rickety, partly because of us, partly because Pa had never built a house before. They didn't live at home, Ma and Pa. They're what the nanny calls "hippies." They live in a van and drive all around the country. They come home sometimes, always to give us another sibling. They tried to do what Ma calls "that whole domestic thing," but she missed the open road so it didn't last long. So when they come, they don't stay for long. It's always a good day when they come home. They bring us gifts and teach us how to plant flowers and catch butterflies. Or if the day is rainy, like when Jack was born, Pa rolls around in the mud and collects worms with us—things Miss Agatha would never do.

He's an artist, Pa. He painted something new directly onto the walls anytime he was home. Miss Agatha didn't let us paint on the walls though—not even Olivia, who had Pa's gift. Olivia could paint, Gilly could sing, and Blu had magic fingers when he held his guitar. I liked to write. Olivia, Gilly, and Blu were all older than me and didn't have time for my stories, but the little ones loved them. Even Forrest would linger in the shadows as I narrated the adventures that came to me in dreams. He wasn't good at much though. Poor Forrest. He was prone to bad luck.

He was my favorite brother but I didn't dare tell him. I didn't dare hang out with him in front of the other kids, but every once in a while we'd sneak down to the creek and spend the day just the two of us. He and I shared the beautiful difference. That's what Ma called it anyway. Except only I knew this about Forrest. It didn't show with him as it did in me. He didn't let it show. He was too afraid, though he never told me why. This always scared me. He was five years my senior and I feared he saw something that I didn't yet. He was always afraid though, Forrest. Any creak in the house or shadow in the dark sent him away. No one spooked like Forrest did. The other kids, particularly the younger ones, called him "Fraidy Forrest." It was juvenile at best but it still got to him. In truth, everything did. The kids were just having fun, but all they did ate away at him—I could tell.

For some reason, I was the only one who knew anything about Forrest. Well, me and Ma. Forrest was Ma's favorite. He was her firstborn. I didn't know what that had to do with anything but Miss Agatha said it's important.

Sometime around early March, we had one of those days when we were able to sit by the creek without being disturbed by the rest of the horde. Forrest was happily trying—and failing—to skip rocks against the current. I had tried a few times in the past to ask him, only he's so afraid. It's never worked before, but I thought maybe it would when he was in such good spirits. Yet, seeing him smile like that was a rarity I didn't want to steal. I debated internally for a few moments, watching him search for flattened river stones. *Maybe in his concentration he won't notice I'm askin'.*

"Hey, Forrest?"

He turned to me, still ankle deep in the water, "Yeah, Rahl?"

"Why do you hide it?" I decided to build up to it, rather than slap him in the face with my skepticism and judgment.

He stared at me, looking almost pained, "I don't really have a choice."

This confused me, "Why not? Everyone knows about me."

"That's different," he turned away from me then.

"How?" Forrest didn't respond. He just stood there in the creek, turning a pebble over and over in his fingers. "Forrest?"

Forrest looked in my direction but refused to meet my eyes. He was looking past me rather than at me, and still did not answer. I looked away this time, ashamed that I upset him, "I'm sorry." He nodded, accepting my apology, and went back to skipping rocks.

Forrest, Olivia, and Blu all went to the high school in town, while the rest of us old enough attended the charter up the road. Two weeks after I killed Forrest's spirit by the creek, the older kids began to get excited about homecoming—Olivia and Blu that was. Forrest, however, moped around the house until the night of the dance. That night, Billy Summers, whose family owned the property just on the other side of the creek from us, showed up at the front door to pick up Olivia. I opened the door to the stocky boy wearing his letter jacket over his dress shirt. *Great choice, Olivia.* I thought to myself while holding back a laugh. Standing slightly behind him was his younger sister Maybrie. I had assumed she was Blu's date; but for some reason, this didn't feel quite right. Blu was only in the ninth grade and Maybrie was in the eleventh with Olivia. I didn't know much about high school culture, but I did know that older girls didn't go for younger boys. And she was a pretty thing, standing there in an olive dress that flowed delicately over her thin frame. Surely she would have had no trouble finding a date her own age. And she looked nervous, fiddling with the hem of her sleeve. There was no way a girl this typically pretty would be so nervous to dance with a scrawny boy of fourteen.

Olivia came bounding down the stairs—interrupting my train of thought—as I rudely stood in the doorway staring at them. "Hey, Billy!" She was grinning ear to ear, clearly excited to have a date with *the* Billy Summers. I had to resist the urge to gag. Olivia then caught sight of Maybrie and shouted up the stairs, "Forrest! Maybrie's here!"

My stomach dropped and my eyes locked on the pretty girl on the porch. The realization made me sick. Forrest came down looking somehow more nervous than his date. He glanced from Maybrie to me and his brows knit together, clearly confused by my visible anger. Not anger really—betrayal, but how can betrayal show on your face? Knowing I was only bound to scare my brother even further, I ducked into the kitchen to collect Miss Agatha. She had been cleaning up from dinner but abandoned the endeavor to take photos for Ma and Pa. I climbed up onto the kitchen island and began eating directly from a bowl of potatoes, listening to the group in the entryway. I'd surely get in trouble for this, but I was too upset to bother with Miss Agatha's stupid rules.

The Mysteries
An Excerpt
After Nardo di Cione's "The Annunciate Virgin"
Ethan Chua

Maria Sanchez Asuncion was born in General Santos hospital, with the noonday heat of Manila still streaming humid and sticky through the windows. Her mother, Gabriela Dela Rosa Asuncion, held a shell-bead rosary in her right hand as she contracted, each push coupled with a squeeze of the beads, a *susmaryosep*, a knee-bent gasp, a pale clinic scream. This was to be Gabriela's second and final pregnancy, as prophesied by tea leaves and various members of the order of St. Padre de Pio, so the mother took no chances with her child's flickering life. She was thus flanked by both a Catholic priest and a chaplain from the Iglesia ni Cristo; though she knew there was only one God (one Holy Spirit, one Only Begotten Son), she also figured approaching said God through several holy channels would do more good than harm.

As Gabriela pushed for a final time, sweat trickling in half-evaporate rivulets down her forehead, she clenched the rosary in her palm and cracked one of its beads. Then, rivered down by blood and placenta, the soon-to-be-christened Maria exited her mother's womb and screamed. At that, both chaplain and priest rushed to be the first to dab holy water on her forehead, only to be stopped by the doctor's stern gaze. He severed the umbilical cord connecting child to mother with a quick flash of the scalpel, though to Gabriela his movements seemed weighed with ceremonial intent.

Gabriela was the kind of woman who saw love as a series of carefully practiced rituals. When Tomas had started wooing her with the Cebu-acoustic bought cheap from Divisoria, crooning his way through the off notes of a bluesy *harana*, she hadn't fallen the first time. The brown boy with his tattered sando and fingers clunky as his chords did not charm her. But when he came by the window every Monday after, singing the only Parokya ni Edgar song he knew, she began to leave coffee cups unwashed and pans still marinating in adobo grease to lean an elbow against the sill and listen. Eventually, the Monday serenade became a habit, a blanket fuzzed around the shoulders to rest in, a Quiapo street from memory with the lamps gleaming like *tiyo*'s cigars. Until Gabriela opened the door and Tomas walked in and guitar propped by the highway kissed her, and this was for years how they would open their Mondays, with a kiss by the windowsill as regular as an October rosary.

Gabriela brought the same fervor of ritual to the birth of her Only Begotten Daughter, cutting short the quarrel of the chaplain and the priest to pray her every Thursday (and all November) prayer. In English she began: *I believe in God, the Father Almighty, Creator of Heaven and earth*, and she truly believed the Joyful Mysteries, for contained within them is the secret to a transcendent kind of joy, so she plumbed each word of the prayer for it, clapped each syllable against the walls of her cheek and the red roof of her tongue for those small jubilances. By the time the company reached the Finding of Jesus at the Temple, the chaplain could barely contain his annoyance at this distinctly Catholic ritual, mouthing all his references to the Virgin and hoping no one would notice. Neither Gabriela nor the priest did—the former because of her ardent recitation, the latter because the itch on his knee had revealed itself to be a mosquito bite which now throbbed and burnt through the whole *Hail Holy Queen*.

Maria spent her childhood in a small San Juan home with one bedroom and a kitchen, and though Gabriela feared the absence of a father would worm its way into her daughter's formative years (manifesting, perhaps, as a devil-colored pimple or an immutable bruise), such concerns turned out to be unfounded. Gabriela, however, knew the curses that often befell the houses of the annulled, had heard the fate of Maricel from Batangas whose son had grown an extra eye on his ninth birthday and could not be exorcised, not even by the Jesuits. So to safeguard her daughter from Satan's assortment of maladies, Gabriela regaled her child with bedtime stories lifted from the Bible, mostly Gospels, with the occasional Revelation when Maria stained the blankets and needed a good scaring back into shape. Maria thus grew up thinking Jesus, Peter, Paul, and all the other apostles were real people, who sometimes wandered Tomas Morato offering to magic water into wine or alms into endless bread, who must have once been children trapped within pale cradles, tracing figures on the drywall with their spit, shitting into diapers, crying at inopportune hours.

Gabriela spent most of those early years shaken, her carefully calibrated routine thrown apart by the whims of an infant named after a queen. She could no longer rely on her morning coffee—the first time she tried leaving the baby to make it, Maria had nearly swallowed the eraser end of a pencil and Gabriela, screaming, left her coffee mid-stir and came back to find it lukewarm and congealing. Neither could she rely on her post-schoolteacher nap, because whenever she came home from work, Gabriela would find the bedsheets in disarray. Sometimes they would be piss-yellowed, sometimes they would be balled up in the corner of the bathroom, and once they were even hung flaglike from the house's only balustrade.

Worst of all, Maria slowly dismantled Gabriela's collection of devotional objects, a pious treasure trove near decades in the making. She would topple the portraits of St. Anthony de Padua (patron saint of lost things), St. Ignatius de Loyola (patron saint of soldiers), and St. Lorenzo Ruiz (patron saint of Filipinos) from their perches, sending their glass frames crash landing into the floor. Each time, Gabriela replaced the glass; each time, Gabriela placed the portraits on higher-up pieces of furniture; each time, Maria would be victorious and the shatters would resound through the house like suddenly stopped bells. Eventually, Gabriela suspended all her statues and porcelain Christs and Nazarenes and images and prayer cards from the ceiling with thin string, putting them far past Maria's reach. It looked, to visitors, like the Rapture had been taped and placed on freeze frame, all the personalities of Christendom wingless stopped on their free elevator rides to heaven.

When she got older, Maria could spend hours on end fixated on a particular suspended image, watching for the Manila sunlight's glint off Jesus's laddered ribs or Peter's upside-down lacquer cross. Sometimes she would reach out to touch them in an echo of her infant curiosity, but now that she was old enough to understand her mother's commands, each outstretching of her arms would be followed immediately by the sharp clap of a broomstick onto her shins, a harsh command in Gabriela's knifing voice, a reminder that Mary said yes to God, that the whole salvation of the world had hinged on the unquestioning obedience of a young woman and thank the Lord the woman wasn't you, *tigas-ulo* Maria, *ang-bastos-mo* Maria, *hay-naku* Maria, or we would all be burning in the *impyerno* right now and Satan's pitchfork would leave holes the size of buttons on your buttocks, believe me.

Maria grew up into grade school, wearing a gray backpack and the same checkerboard uniform each day except for PE days, waking up at six-thirty in the morning as her mother drove her to the gates of St. Pedro Poveda Academy. The Academy was an all-girls school run by a cadre of nuns who wore their habits to meetings both official and unofficial. Though Maria mostly behaved, sometimes she would doodle stick figures on the margins of her science notebook, or drop a pencil too loud on the floor, or ask a teacher what a *puta* was and whether she knew any, and each time she would receive a disciplinary infraction and be sent to the habited nuns for a good wood-ruler whipping. In Maria's eyes, only her mother had permission to chastise her in this way, and so she memorized the features of each nun that beat her for the record of her future vengeance—Sister Tessie's pinhole dimples, Sister Margarita's staccato brows, the callous on Sister Regina's pointer finger that swelled like an onion bulb. Whenever Maria got home after, she'd search for the floating statue of St. Martin de Porres (patron saint of justice) and list to him the grievances of the day. In the mornings that followed, Maria would saunter into class unbowed by the beatings, knowing that Jesus and Peter and Paul and Andrew and Bartholomew and the Zebedee brothers would one day visit St. Pedro Poveda Academy to smite those who had wronged her.

Months passed and the apostles never arrived, so Maria began worrying that she was committing some kind of grievous sin that deterred their entrance. But she reasoned to St. Martin that in the hierarchy of sins surely it was worse for a nun to beat a poor innocent girl with a wooden ruler than it was for a girl to call a nun *gago* behind her back; and surely it was worse for Alfonso from Ignatius across the street to tape a hand-mirror to his left shoe and look up the skirts of girls than it was for one of those girls to slap him; and surely it was worse for a teacher to sneak cigarettes into the bathroom than it was for a student to doodle in her science notebook and be caught for the fifth time this quarter. When Maria later learned from a classmate that Jesus and all his apostles had died several thousand years ago, she spent the entire afternoon distraught, crying into her lunchbox. Sister Sarah, the school counselor and one of the kinder nuns, sat beside her during dismissal to remind her that the kingdom of God was forthcoming. To that, Maria said she wished it were here now and didn't understand what was taking Jesus so long.

Behind the High School's Football Field
An Excerpt
Anna Miles

Behind the football field there was a barn, where the Future Farmers of America kept their livestock, and behind the barn was a rusting playground that used to be the main attraction of the park adjacent to the high school. The playground consisted of an old-fashioned swing set made of thin metal poles and a jungle gym made up of stacked hollow cubes. Now, the relic was covered on the park side by an overgrowth of waxy-leaved bushes and on the high school side with a chain link fence. Weeds snaked up in the spaces between the metal poles until it looked like the playground itself had grown up out of the ground. The city council had discussed removing the play equipment when they installed the high-tech plastic playground with the safe rubber padding at the base, but since the bushes around the original jungle gym were so thick and no one could see behind them anyway, they decided to spare the cost and leave the equipment to rot, forgotten, behind a poorly-mucked barn filled with cow manure.

They weren't allowed to leave the high school campus, and every possible exit, including the hidden fence that led to the old playground, was usually patrolled by a security guard in a bright orange vest. Security was very thorough, except during second period, when the guards had their required briefing in the staff lounge, when it was assumed that all students were safely in class listening to the morning announcements.

But Sadie wasn't in class during second period, and neither was Ryan Davidson, who was given a free period to devote to his "weight training" for baseball. Ryan was the star of the baseball team, but the real truth was, he hated baseball. He was the youngest in a family of five boys, and every one of them had played baseball, starting with their father who played in the minor leagues for two years before meeting Ryan's mother. He was then forced to take a job as a construction foreman, and forced to project his failed dreams onto his children. All of his brothers before him had played baseball in high school and then graduated to join their father in the construction field, and although Ryan's mother insisted playing baseball would help him get a scholarship for a good college, Ryan could not shake the feeling that baseball in high school was the first step toward manual labor after high school.

Sadie had fulfilled most of her credits by that time because she took a community college course her junior year to finish her last AP language requirement. Sadie had been the most advanced student in her class since the first grade, and since then the public school system had been struggling to figure out what to do with her. Her mother refused to move her up a grade because she said that a child's social development was just as important as her intellectual development, so for most of her education Sadie was put in a corner with a special book or a special lesson, and for a long time, until her teacher explained it to her, Sadie thought she was too stupid to learn with the other kids. She had gleaned most of what she could out of high school by her sophomore year, but Sadie still had to finish senior math and English, so she was stuck there until graduation. Without any other place to put her, the administration assigned her a TA job during second period. Sadie had Ms. Patterson for Honors English her sophomore year. Ms. Patterson trusted Sadie, and so after

Sadie checked in at the beginning of the period, she was allowed to leave the teacher's classroom with a hall pass and spend the rest of the period however she pleased.

The first time Sadie and Ryan met at the playground, it was late September, and it still felt like summer. The metal was so hot it burned marks into their skin when they touched it. They took turns rubbing their upper thighs against the lowest layer of jungle gym supports, seeing how long they could keep their skin in contact with the aluminum before the pain forced them to shy away.

The second time Sadie and Ryan met at the playground, it was mid-October, and the weeds on the ground had turned brittle and dry. They scooped up leaves in large handfuls and crinkled them between their fingers on top of each other's heads. Ryan smushed the crumbles into Sadie's straight brown hair and then trailed his hand down her face to her lips. Sadie closed her eyes and kissed his fingers. They tasted like the earth.

The third time Sadie and Ryan met at the playground, exactly one week had passed since the homecoming dance, and the equipment was still littered with pieces of tissue paper left over from the homecoming parade floats that had been stored in the barn. Ryan brought a blanket this time, which Sadie insisted they didn't need. He cleared a bundle of weeds from the corner behind the swing set and spread the blanket on the ground. They lay down on the blanket together. She took his hand. Ryan still had sunburn from riding in the parade, and he winced whenever Sadie touched him. She laughed when she branded a smiley face into his tomato-red shoulder, and he laughed when he made her real face smile, because when she smiled her eyes crinkled up and her cheeks got puffy, and Ryan couldn't help but kiss her when she let her teeth show through.

The fourth time Sadie and Ryan met at the playground, it was January and freezing, and Ryan wrapped Sadie in his down jacket and rubbed her hands together between his own.

The last time Sadie and Ryan met at the playground, school had been over for a week, and the dirt had been drenched by a series of summer storms. The sky was still drizzling, and Sadie sat on the edge of the jungle gym catching droplets on her tongue. Ryan sat on the ground, facing away from her, digging a tiny hole, the kind he imagined a worm digging to escape into the earth. Sadie picked up a sharp stick and brought it up to the metal pole of the swing set. She scratched a deep line into the metal. Without a word she grabbed Ryan by the hand and pulled him to the pole. She pointed out the line and handed him the stick. He scratched the word "peace" underneath Sadie's line, which she followed with the word "fear." He scratched in "water" and she scratched in "mud."

Skin.

Sweat.

Scratch

Fingertips.

Will you miss me when I'm gone?
Scratch

21

Power.

Submission.

Scratch

Understanding.

Confusion.

Scratch

Meaning.

Does anything really matter?

Scratch

You.

Me.

Scratch

Us.

Ryan carved in this last word and then took Sadie's chin in his hand. He kissed her with extreme caution, afraid she might disintegrate under the pressure of his lips.

What do you like about me? She asked.

You know, he said, I really don't know.

Sadie smiled and moved his hand away from her face. Taking the stick, still holding on to his hand, she scratched into the pole their final word. The only word that really meant anything.

Goodbye.

The Drake

An Excerpt

Marina Kapralau

My name is Ada, Adellaida Loboda. I live with my family in a rural town in central Ukraine.

Old people say many years ago dozens of white and black swans lived on the lake that gently rolls its waves about half a mile east from our big house with whitewashed walls. By the time my great-grandfather settled here after the World War II, though, the swan population was represented by only one graceful couple. The two birds brought lots of joy to the town residents for a long time, but one day, the pen came back from the warm lands alone. No one knew what happened to her mate. But the pen stayed loyal to him and kept coming back to the lake without a pair until one spring no white wings cast a shadow on the waters. Ducks and wild geese occupied the lake. But the name of the city remained the same—Lebedin, or Swan Town—and the legend of the bird loyalty still lives in the people's gossip.

I often wish my mama was like the swan from the local fable and never married again. Yet, she did. She even had another cygnet.

It is only 2 p.m., but regular blackouts make the wild '90s in our town so dark. A melting candle stub sheds a dim light on a few rye bread crumbs, an empty sugar-bowl and a cracked mug with stinky leftovers of tea, brewed from plum tree branches.

He looks at me from the kitchen table with his beady little eyes. The beads are deep and shiny even in the dim light, at the very bottom of them—all the despair of a fading life.

Just a few hours ago, the drake had pecked duckweed and dove for water lily stalks in the darkening lake. When frightened away by the barking of hunting dogs, the bird had rushed up, and an imprecise shot from my stepfather's gun hit his tail.

Now the drake's life is measured only by the distance from the kitchen table to the gas stove. I stand in between, by the sink, and do the dishes in a large washbowl. I am only nine and I can hardly reach up to it. Cheap soap doesn't dissolve, and all the dishes feel dirty even after they are washed. The bones in my hands ache from ice-cold water. Meticulously wiping cold palms on my mama's over-laundered apron, I slowly get closer and carefully touch the drake's black glossy quills. He doesn't scream, doesn't try to get away.

My teacher says ducks have a special layer of fat that makes their feathers waterproof, but the drake's feathers don't feel oily. I gently stroke him, then untie my long dirty-blond ponytail and run the fingers on my hair—the roots are slightly greasy all the time because my parents cannot afford good shampoo. They can't afford many things. Girls at my school have denim skirts and plenty of pocket money to buy that sour chewing gum with the little stickers inside. All I have plenty of is dandruff. Last month, my sister Anastasia brought home lice from kindergarten, so we had plenty of those too.

"Finish the dishes and go to your room." I jump and quickly snatch my hand from the drake's head. My stepfather walks into the kitchen with his mother gaiting behind him. They look so alike: same wide shoulders, same red hair, same pursed, thin lips, same frightening look in the sharp gray eyes.

His words—not evil, but indifferent and harsh—hit me like the shots from his gun. Only with me the shots never miss.

"I'm almost done, Papa. I'll just wipe these." I shrink under their looks. I reach for an aluminum mug from the pile of washed dishes and start rubbing it with a towel, as if trying to make a jinn appear in front of us.

I call my stepfather *"Papa,"* but I am only allowed to address his mother by her first name and surname—Amaliya Vladimirovna. "I am your friend and your older comrade, not your grandmother. You understand?" she often says.

I understand.

I think she doesn't like mama and me much because at dinner, when Amaliya is in charge of pouring soup, she always puts meat in Papa's and Anastasia's bowls, but never in mine and never in my mama's. That is, when we have meat, of course. She scolds us for everything, and I often hide Amaliya's glasses so she can see fewer of our faults.

Mama says I am a big girl already and should stop acting childish. She says I have to always think ahead and put myself in other people's shoes—then I will not be constantly yelled at.

Continuing to rub a shiny side of the mug, I close my eyes and imagine myself in Amaliya's trampled blue slippers.

I shuffle into the library and shout at my daughter-in-law for dusting her grandfather's portrait in a heavy mourning frame and the old oakwood bookshelves. Spit splatters around as I ask bitterly, "Hey, intelligentsia! Have nothing better to do? Those collectible books of yours belong at the scrapyard—they don't cost a ruble now!" I watch my daughter-in-law turning purple with anger.

Then I leave the library and walk through the forest in Papa's brown shabby hunting boots with a gun pressed to my right armpit; dead scarlet leaves rustle under the soles and a decoy rattles between my lips. I look up and pull the trigger. In a few minutes, the wounded drake beats its short wings in my hunting bag. I walk home and whistle cheerfully, because now my family will finally have meat for dinner. I wish they ate well every day, even that awkward stepdaughter of mine—the baggage I got along with my wife, as I often say to Amaliya Vladimirovna. Ah, that Ada girl, she is so clueless and clumsy. Who would like to kiss a girl like that? Who would want to play, or ride a bike with her? Well, obviously, not me!

I open my eyes and look down. A large tear falls from my cheek onto my left wool sock and disappears between the thick white threads.

I don't think I am very good at this, at putting myself in other people's shoes …

Nasty jangling sounds of a knife-sharpening machine break into the kitchen from the barn. I carefully wipe all the dishes and hang a kitchen towel and an apron on a nail above the sink, looking over my shoulder at the drake. Blood on his tail has already clotted and started to dry. I stroke the drake for the last time, pick up a new candle, and bury myself in books in my room as a distraction. The old volume that smells like time and oranges swishes with its yellowed pages, and opens at my favorite scene from *Les Misérables*—little Cosette carries a bucket to the woods in the dark. But my eyes fail me—the lines jump in some crazy dance. All I can think about is Amaliya's callused hands with swollen blue veins and red spots reaching out to the dumpy green drake's neck.

Papa has hunted ducks before and rabbits too, but they usually appeared in a steaming casserole. I have never seen them dying on the kitchen table before. No. We absolutely can't have this drake for dinner!

Rubbing my knees that still remember the last punishment for hiding Amaliya's glasses in my school backpack, I open the door. The raw buckwheat grains I had to stand on for the whole two hours yesterday left tiny dark spots on my skin. Furtively looking around, I sneak into the kitchen, grab the drake from the table, press the bird closer to my chest and rush across the yard into the neighbor's chicken coop. It smells awful here, and chickens look wary and cluck in a hostile way at us.

"Shoo, speckled!" I hiss at them.

Afraid that chickens might scratch the wounded drake, I put him in the highest nesting box of the coop and cover the opening with a plaque. My whisper sounds muffled and unreal inside the crooked coop, "You'll be safe here."

But he won't. Papa finds the drake in the neighbor's coop in an hour. Then he finds me in the old apple tree in the garden.

My stomach makes a couple of incredible somersaults as I fly through the corridor like a rag and land on my right side. A dull pain pierces through my belly. Thousands of feelings overwhelm me at once: fear, anger, humiliation, so I don't know right away whether I should retreat, run back at Papa with my fists clenched or cry. Fear becomes the winner in this wrestling match between my feelings. I curl up on the dusty rug like a May beetle grub we find during potato planting in spring. I wait for more smacks, but Papa just steps over me and walks away.

"Get away from her!" he growls at mama, who rushes into the corridor with Anya in her arms. Mama's fingers convulsively clench and unclench as she puts my little sister down on the rug and exits behind Papa. Anya awkwardly falls on her butt next to me; she combs my hair with her tiny plump hand and sings.

I cover my ears when the cracking sound is finally heard from the kitchen.

"Would you like me to leave him? Ada! Look at me! Yes or no?" Mama examines the bruises on my right arm, checking it for fractures with her eyes full of tears.

I stare back at her, puzzled, unprepared. What should I say? I can't put myself in your shoes, mommy. Please, don't make me! I am not a big enough girl yet!

Avoiding her pleading look, I focus all my attention on the corner of the living room, where Anya swarms with the toys that used to be mine. She just broke my favorite wooden mill. Ah, I so wish Anya didn't break my things and fart around our houseguests . . . But I love how she listens to my bedtime stories, so quietly . . . And how she smiles in her sleep . . .

I gaze at the pieces that five minutes ago were my old windmill. I stare at its wooden body and wide blades and suddenly imagine myself in the shoes of a stranger—of some other man who would come after Papa—black shoes, no laces.

I drag Anya through the corridor and make her stand with her knees on dried peas, or worse. . . buckwheat grains . . .

Mama sighs with relief when I exhale, "No, mommy."

Delilah
GC Philipp

She used to say it was fun. For a while, she loved it. On Tuesday nights she'd pull out of the driveway in her beat-up baby blue Jeep and head for The Headless Horseman. She used to say rock'n'roll made her want to give in to her dark. I hoped she'd listen to everything but that. She'd wave goodbye to the picket fence and parents who were too absent to realize any trouble she was in. Although she wasn't really in trouble, she just looked for it. She hungered for it so deeply that it became a hunt. I hoped she'd never improve as a hunter, I hoped her shot was off. For a while, it was. Three weeks ago her aim was dead on.

She closed the front door behind her quietly and walked to the car, the bounce in her step of a pretty girl who knows she's pretty. She wore white sneakers with white knee-high socks, a dusty pink skirt, and a white silk camisole. I knew the guys at the bar would like that. It would send undeniable tingling through their jeans. She was the chick they'd never be able to get in high school, the head of the cheer squad. She opened the door of the Jeep and swept herself in, careful to keep her legs closed, even when no one was around. She had no bag or wallet with her. She needed nothing, she was taken care of wherever she went. The only item she carried resided between her hip and the band of her underwear, a pale pink lipstick. Looking in the rear-view mirror, she popped open the cap of the lipstick and rolled it over her lips; it spread like warm butter. She clicked the lid back on and slipped it between her underwear and hip again. Using her finger, she rubbed off the imperfections, the wiggly edges. Putting her hand behind the passenger seat, she looked back, and put her car in reverse. She was on the road.

She pulled up to The Headless Horseman. The neon light above the worn wooden door flickered in a primary red. The parking lot was never full. She parked right in front of the door. She looked at herself in the rearview mirror again. She twirled her fingers through her curls and pushed all of her hair behind her ears. Her pearl earrings gleamed red. She opened the car door and stepped out. Legs closed.

She pulled open the wooden door with a loud creak. The loud slam behind her once she let it close attracted the glossy eyes sitting at the black velvet booths. The room was the same as every other day, the only things to change were the men. The floorboards were matte with scratches and treading. Her white sneakers seemed to float above the boards, untouchable. She scanned the room. In one of the velvet booths were a group of three men her father's age. They looked at her like they hadn't eaten or drank water in days. She walked to the bar and leaned on it to order a drink.

"Could I get a Cosmo, please?" she asked.

"You can have whatever you want, dear." The bartender chuckled.

She curved her back as she stood, and her skirt rose up the back of her legs, barely covering her underwear. One of the men from the booth stood up and walked towards the bar. The bartender walked to the switch by the door and turned off the neon sign. He locked the door.

Happy Birthday, Baby
An Excerpt
Michele Kilmer

The mother, who was looking in the mirror to check her carefully curated blonde perfection, told the daughter they were going on a birthday trip to Arizona to see the London Bridge.

The daughter, who in the mother's dazzling hazel eyes fell quite short of perfection with her reddish-brown hair and ink-blue eyes, was not happy about this surprise trip and wondered, rightly so, what the real reason for the trip was. Sensing the daughter's distrust, the mother acted hurt, even though she could not have cared less. The daughter felt bad and made a tepid but genuine effort to be excited; she was still fooled by the mother sometimes. This birthday, her thirteenth, was the last birthday this would be so.

The mother had moved out a year ago to the day. The daughter was glad then, thought it was the best birthday ever. Now, the mother was attempting to move back into the father's house. She missed the lifestyle the father could provide. She didn't however miss the daughter or the father.

The father had a talk with the daughter the night before the trip. He told her that she should really give the mother a chance. The daughter said that she'd already given her a million chances. The father told her not to exaggerate and that he believed the mother was doing her best this time. The daughter was not at all convinced. She wanted to hang out with her friends on her birthday. The father reminded her that her friends would be there when she got back, and he promised to let her have a sleepover and said that they could stay up all night if they wanted to. The daughter gave in.

When the mother came to pick up the daughter, she was two hours late and she was not in the silver Mercedes the father had given her. The mother was in the passenger seat of her best friend Jean's gold Datsun. The daughter couldn't stand Jean, or her ugly car. She gave the mother a nasty look and said under her breath that she thought that this was supposed to be a mother-daughter trip. The mother just rolled her eyes and looked at Jean as if to say, *I told you she was nasty.* Jean opened the trunk of the Datsun and started talking about how much she loved a good road trip and about the CB radio she just had installed. Neither woman said happy birthday to the daughter.

For the first several hours the mother and Jean talked as if the daughter wasn't there. The daughter was regretting leaving her Walkman in her suitcase, which was in the trunk, and hoped they would stop soon so she could get it out. The father had made her promise not to use it to ignore the mother on the trip, but when the daughter sneezed—and it scared the mother because she'd forgotten that the daughter was there, she didn't feel like she'd be breaking her promise.

They finally stopped at a roadside diner and Jean talked non-stop about the accident she'd been in a few years ago. It was a bad pile-up on I-5 in the middle of a freak snowstorm in Southern California—eighteen cars. She'd survived but had broken all the bones in her face, which got rearranged ever so slightly, and looked just off enough to make people wonder. She'd also lost her sense of smell so she couldn't taste food anymore. She only ordered food that felt good in her mouth, like pineapples, and cottage cheese. She said that everything else felt dry, especially scrambled eggs. They used to be her favorite, but now they just felt rough. She did like sunny-side up though; Jean said sunny side up went down pretty smooth.

The daughter didn't say a word throughout dinner, except to the waitress, who reminded her of a grandma, kind and plump. The daughter pushed around her side of mashed potatoes and pouted. It didn't bother the mother that the daughter didn't speak. She was too busy having second thoughts about bringing the daughter in the first place. She was starting to doubt this whole birthday bullshit. She really missed being seen at the club, and she couldn't get in the club if she wasn't living in the damn house with the father. The father really didn't know the mother at all; he'd been satisfied with the façade she'd created to snag a man like him and never felt a need to look underneath it. And when the mother thought about it for more than a moment, she knew the club was the only thing she liked about him. The mother lacked appreciation for the irony of her resentment towards the father.

The daughter counted all the black and white tiles of the diner floor on her way to the bathroom. The waitress was in there dabbing a wet paper towel at the back of her neck. Her eyes were a bright, watery, sky blue and she gave the daughter a wink in the mirror and told her she was a quiet one. The daughter just shrugged her shoulders and told the waitress that this was her worst birthday ever and went into the stall. Sitting there, the daughter thought about the quarters in her pocket and using them for the pay phone next to the cigarette machine. She wanted the father to come and get her but didn't make the call.

There was a piece of cherry pie on the table when the daughter got back. It had whipped cream with a little pink candle in it that was melting fast. She blew it out and the mother said *happy birthday, baby* in a syrupy voice and made an awkward attempt to give the daughter a squeeze. The daughter ignored the mother and scraped the whipped cream off the top. The mother told Jean that she didn't understand what kind of kid didn't like whipped cream. Jean rolled her eyes and pointed at the daughter behind her hand, like it was funny.

On the way out of the diner, the daughter caught sight of the waitress through the little windows in the swinging kitchen doors. She was surprised how little pressure the door needed to open, she ran up to the waitress and gave her a big hug. The waitress knew that it meant that maybe it wasn't the worst birthday after all. The daughter told herself to remember how soft the skin on the cheek of the watery-eyed waitress was.

Jean popped the trunk and sighed like she was really annoyed. The daughter pulled out her new Walkman and the three new tapes she'd gotten from the father earlier that day. When Jean closed the trunk, she told the daughter that she'd been awfully rude, she hadn't even said say thank you for the pie. The daughter glared at the mother and told Jean without looking at her that she did say thank you to the person who gave her the pie. The mother glared back and commanded the daughter to get in the car. Jean shook her head like she didn't understand kids these days.

Jean turned on the CB and said that they all had to come up with a handle before the daughter could get her Walkman going. Jean teased the mother and said her handle should be sweet pea, because so many people were sweet on her. The daughter rolled her eyes, sighed and clicked on the Thompson Twins. The mother laughed, forced a blush and pretended to be embarrassed, swatting at Jean's leg. The daughter lay down as best she could across the hump between the back seats. Under Jean's seat, the daughter spotted a white handle with the carved outline of a naked girl in red, like the one she'd been seeing on the backs of truckers' mud flaps. It was so small that it looked like a toy gun, but the daughter knew enough to know it was no toy.

When the car jerked to a stop, it woke the daughter up; her Walkman had gone quiet by then. She heard the mother tell Jean she couldn't believe they were actually here. It had been thirteen years since she had last seen him. The daughter now knew that whoever he was, he was the real reason for the trip. She pretended to be dead asleep when the mother tried to wake her. Jean said not to worry about the daughter; she could just sleep in the car. The mother checked her face in the mirror, puckered up, and refreshed her lipstick.

When the daughter heard the front door to wherever they were open and shut, and a dog's barking quiet down, she grabbed at the handle under the seat. She wanted to hold it. She popped Depeche Mode into the Walkman and started to wonder about the Father's Day. She wanted to tell him about the waitress, and about the mother's real reason for the trip. After all, it was the daughter who told the father about the mother cheating in the first place. He would probably tell the daughter that she was being too hard on the mother and that she'd had a hard life. The daughter didn't care anymore.

Unnatural Disasters
Lila Riesen

The first time I saw her was on television. I was immediately obsessed.

Perhaps haunted is a better word. The girl *haunted* me for days. Weeks. Until by chance, or perhaps not chance, I saw her again.

She wasn't an actress, or some pawn in some ridiculous lotion commercial promising younger skin in seconds—she was on CNN, nameless, standing in front of a blazing red fire. One of the lucky victims of Canberra's bushfires. It was bad that year. Over five hundred deaths in the ACT. I hadn't been to Australia yet, and to be honest, growing up in Indiana to a poor welder father didn't give me many options financially. Lack of stimuli around me drew me in further into external stimuli—particularly, disasters. Disasters of all sorts: plane crashes, hurricanes, tornadoes, fires, bank robberies, you name it. Hearing about a seismic earthquake was like waking up on Christmas morning. I couldn't wait to unwrap the facts and play with them, fantasize about them.

I remembered her because she didn't look panicked like the others. Her hair flew out behind her in a curly sheet of red, almost indistinguishable from the flames. She was carrying something. A small dictionary, perhaps. It didn't make any sense. Why would she carry a book, just a book, and leave the rest of her house to burn? What about pictures? Valuables? Perhaps a beloved pet?

Her face was so cold yet so real I felt as if I could reach through the television and touch it. She looked so bizarrely angelic, or devilish, that for a moment I thought I had been dreaming. DMV photographers don't have the most exciting of jobs, and I've been known to daydream more than the usual eighteen-something. It's cost me the odd one or two girlfriends, my career as a journalism student at IU, my mother.

DMW work. Fluorescent lights. Baggy eyes. Cigarette smoke. Hoosier talk. Old man with bifocals, sixteen-year-old overwrought douchebag, old woman with a faint mustache, tatted guy in overalls, old man, old woman, old man. Stand behind the line sir, look at the camera sir, brush your hair from your ears sir, keep a neutral face you old cranky geyser. Yes, I do know what the hell I'm doing, thanks very much. Flash. Repeat.

It was Valentine's Day, and I hadn't taken more than ten photos in three hours. Before the appearance of the girl with the flaming hair, I had been fretting over what to get Melody. Roses? They'd die. Chocolates? She'd eat them, and then complain that I'm trying to make her fat. A teddy bear? Laughable. We're not twelve, after all. I knew if I came home empty-handed, however, I would be girlfriendless for the first time in six months, and that scared me. I should've known it was coming, right? Melody losing interest? I'd dropped out of IU due to my obsession with the news. More like kicked out. Teachers don't like when you're on your phone during the lecture. The only thing was, I wasn't texting. I was seeing if that man made it out of that cave, if that hurricane claimed any more lives, if that plane was ever found, if the president withdrew his racial epithet slip. Melody was in the music school, a beautiful violinist. According to her handsome, twenty-eight-year-old professor (is that even legal?), she was "going places."

Right. Going places.

I got off work still thinking about the girl, not my girl, *the* girl, so much so that I could drown out triple-chinned Rowanda's girlish laughs as she flirted with our boss Clive Jive. Seriously. Clive Jive. Sounds like some sort of smooth talking, boogie dancing, fifty-five-year-old with a bad haircut, right? Actually, that's exactly on point. "How're ya going, slugger?" he asks me every day as I walk in to work. "How's the cam-er-ahh slugger?" he asks with a stupid, chipped tooth grin. "Better close the wind-ah in the back, slugger." I hate Hoosier accents. That's the advantage to being a news-watcher. I'm fantastic at accents. You'd never know I was a native Hoosier (except for the horrible haircut; we just don't have any Europeans here to do a good cut) just from looking at me. I was glued to the television from a young age. Mom and dad were rarely around. Too busy trying to *make it work*. Dad rationalizes mom leaving as 'if you have to force your relationship, it's probably poo, son.' That's how he deals with tragedy—sarcasm. Since my parents were spending all that time together away from me, figuring out they weren't meant for each other, I spent a lot of time by myself. I'd fall asleep to the sound of news anchors' droning voices, wondering what it'd be like to brave a wretched storm on a fishing boat in the ocean.

Dear Estrella
An Excerpt
Sheryl Kay

I don't think about you as often as I should. Thoughts of you come creeping up to me in odd ways; I'll smell dead grass in the sun, and that'll be you, sometimes, but not all the times. When I'm driving, it's nothing but grass, but if I'm walking, or if I'm barefoot and I can smell the warm grass and the blackness of the asphalt, then it's you. Sometimes I go down to the Salvation Army, where my father used to take us, sneaking us into the drop-off area and letting us pick toys before they could be priced and sold, and I think first, looking at the toys and the old VHS tapes, that I should get it as a gift for someone. And then I realize that the someone is you, and I don't get it. When I watch the fireworks from my balcony, I taste cherry and lemon and blue raspberry and I try not to cry, feeling the ghost of your hand slipping through my fingers. I can go days without thinking about you, weeks, and I'm sure there must have been a year where I didn't think about you and your bracelets and your laugh, but when I do think about you, it's all that I can think about. You consume me from beyond the grave, or wherever it was that you went when you disappeared.

When we were kids, I met you in the land without sidewalks, where our fathers lived in sun-drenched splendor, where the streets were called *Calle*, with names like *Margarita* and *Los Robles*, and all the men were long-limbed with calloused hands, and the women were soft and large and demanded that we call them auntie and gramma. In this land without sidewalks, all of the lawns were dried goldenrod and warm, and almost no-one owned an air conditioner; if they did, it hulked, crouching on a windowsill, and was as loud as a lawnmower. Windows and doors were left open to the breeze to come and go, the breeze and the barefooted children that we were.

Your father's house was across the street from my father's, and they worked together painting houses and standing in front of the Home Depot, smoking cigarettes and sipping from Coronas and Budweisers, throwing the empty bottles and cans into the back of my father's white pickup truck. We were friends by nature of us being so close, and both only children. We would crouch on the curb in front of my father's house when my godfather Eddie washed his truck next door, dropping leaves and bits of yellow grass into the sudsy water flowing past, and you'd suffer through playing Barbies with me, and I was in love with you for it. You'd laugh at me often, at how pale and white and small I was, and how I wasn't allowed to stay up and watch television after nine o'clock, when all the adult shows came on, and you'd feed me scraps of dialogue you remembered from those shows, racy jokes I didn't understand, wasn't allowed to understand, and once you let me try on your training bra and it had been too big for me, which was funny.

You were two years older than I was, and wise with all the things the fifth grade had to teach you; you wore short-shorts and your ears were pierced, really pierced, metal all the way through, and I had to make do with the glittery plastic baby earrings, the hard stickers that I never got to be even. You wore colorful metal bangles stacked high on each arm and I was in love with you, right up until you went missing.

In my memories of you, and the land without sidewalks, it is always summer, always overheated and long and sweaty, and the afternoons would all melt into a thousand hours spent getting sunburned and playing with you in the front lawns of our father's houses, running barefoot across the blistering black street, and pacing down the curbs, arms out for balance. No one could walk across the curbs as fast as you could, with so much skill. In my memory, you were so adult and so sure, I had a hard time believing that you weren't the President, or the Governor, that you were just some fifth-grader from the *Calles*, who wore thin-strapped tank tops and had dark freckles over your shoulders. I begged my mother to let me dress like that, to get my ears pierced, and the tyrant always denied me, and my father would always be too afraid to go against her; he would not return me to her on Mondays any older than I had been when she dropped me off on Fridays. If they had their way, I'd be a third-grader for the rest of my life.

On that Fourth of July, I found you at the park with the sidewalks where we all went to watch the fireworks. My father had a cooler and his good Mexican blanket with him, the one that Mom let him have in the divorce because they'd gotten it on their honeymoon in Baja, and she didn't want it in her house anymore. I had left my shoes and my lace-edged socks on the blanket, and with his blessing, we had run off to the playground there and ran wild and free in the sandbox, the two of us conquering all the other kids, kids that were pale and white like I was, but I wasn't one of them. I had you, and so I was great and special, and the two of us could have taken over countries that late afternoon, in that sandbox, and settled for claiming the monkey-bars as ours, and you didn't let anyone else play on them. I remember nothing but you, and you, and you, until the sunset, until after the sun had set, and I remember the first *boom* of the fireworks starting, how that sound shook everything to a stop.

My father and mother were both tall, six feet and above, and I hadn't gotten into my growth spurt yet. You were a head taller than me, and it had always made me feel even smaller than I already was, to have to glance up at your dark eyes and your pierced ears, but something about those fireworks made me grow. Until that year, I had always watched the fireworks, sitting on the Mexican blanket between my mother and father, overshadowed and babyish. But then, in the sandbox, with only you and the other kids—I felt tall then, one hundred thousand feet tall, like all I had to do was stretch out my neck and I could lick the glitter from the sky and it would taste like pop rocks—cherry, lemon, blue raspberry—and you tried to pull on my hand, tried to pull me away, and I couldn't hear the jangling of your bracelets over the sound of the sky being bombarded with colors. I dug my toes down into the sand, past the warm layer, down to where it was damp and cold, and didn't even glance at you, eating up the colors that rippled across the sky. I didn't even notice when you let go of my hand; I only noticed once the fireworks had disappeared that you had, too.

My father came to the sandbox after a while, when the crowds were thinning, the cooler and the Mexican blanket in his arms, and he got me up and settled on his shoulders. The top of his shaved head was sunburned and had a scab on it, from when he had been fixing some guy's roof, and a piece of tile had hit him. I floated from that high up, watching all of the families fold up blankets and collect empty chip bags, loading up vans and trucks for the trip back to the land without sidewalks.

As my father was putting the cooler and the blanket away, your father came up to us. He was missing a few teeth, and my father had always told me not to be alone with him, and I had never asked why. He asked if I had seen you, and I told him that you had been in the sandbox with me, but that you had gone.

He asked me if I had seen where you had gone because you weren't at the sandbox, and I had been embarrassed by his question, and hid my red face behind my hands and hair. My father had told your father to keep looking, that you had to be somewhere, and if anything, once everyone else had left, she would be waiting. Your father had said okay, and I couldn't look at him, keeping my eyes closed until my father had bundled me into the truck and we had gone back to the house.

In the morning, I woke up to the news that you had vanished.

Words didn't have the same weight to them, way back then. Words like *kidnapped* and *taken* meant little to nothing to me, just words that were used in the far-away places television shows occupied, television shows that I wasn't allowed to watch but sometimes my father left the TV going when he took a nap, and I could watch hiding in the hallway. *Missing* was for small Barbie shoes that always were lost, *vanished* was when Tuxedo Mask on Sailor Moon would throw down a smoke bomb, and would pull his cloak around him, and he was gone. But he would be back next week. You weren't back the next week, or the one after that.

Summer slowly slunk back towards school, and my father and mother were talking in the courtrooms about changing the custody agreement, which always made me sad. Your father and mother had never been in courtrooms; your mother had just left, and I thought maybe you had gone to live with her. They put a For Sale sign in your lawn, but I never saw anyone look at it.

One afternoon, a few weeks after you had gone, I left my father's house as he slept, sweating, on the couch in the front room. Barefoot, I went down the driveway to where the sidewalk wasn't, and I walked along the bleached-bone curb, arms out like airplane wings, looking down resolutely at my toes to keep my balance. I went past seven houses, all the way down the street corner, and I stopped where the sidewalk began. In my mind, you were somewhere out there, laughing and banging your bracelets together, and all I had to do was follow like I always did, and there you'd be, laughing and asking why I took so long. Perhaps you were one block away, or two, and all I had to do was keep on walking, but I'd never been past the street corner on my own before.

I stood there, where the sidewalk started, and the sun began to drip lower and lower, all yolky and yellow, and I was terrified. I was only in the third grade and my ears weren't pierced yet, and so at last I turned around and went back the way I'd come, all the way up the street, balancing on the curb, like we had done so many times before, but all those times you had been there behind me, telling me to go faster, to stop being afraid, to stop thinking that I'd fall, to stop being such a baby. I went slowly all the way back to my father's house, and once I was inside, I shut the door, and I locked it.

Frank
An Excerpt
Alicia Eileen Sage

Frank's most vivid memory constantly replayed in his mind like a favorite scene on a VCR tape—the film rolling back and forth until only that one scene could play across the screen.

The war, he thought. *Oh Jesus, oh Jesus, oh Jesus.*

He, seventeen and freezing, huddled behind a mound of mud. His fingers shivered as they held a tattered white letter typewritten by a nurse from Louisiana, "Claire." Frank's brother, Joe, had scavenged the letter from his front pocket and thrust it into those shivering fingers years (or perhaps moments) before.

"I think I might die," Joe said as he thrust the letter over, just before the blasts of bombs destroyed their eardrums with fear. "I guess you should know."

"We regret to inform you that your mother has died," Claire's typewriter showed no emotion, but smudged an "e" every so often. Maybe those were the typewriter's mourning tears.

In the spaces between the black letters—with the background sound of Joe breathing hurriedly in and out and the sweat and blood-soaked uniform itching—Frank saw his tiny Sicilian mother waving goodbye.

Joe rubbed his furry eyebrows, breathing in and out, in and out, in and out. *Oh Jesus, oh Jesus, oh Jesus.*

"Francisco! Guiseppe!" the nasally, aggravating voice of an Italian boy in their regiment screamed somewhere behind the mound in the middle of a rare audible moment.

Joe reacted immediately, springing up out of safety at his God-given, un-Americanized name. Frank irritably licked the plaque crust of his teeth. The Italian clung to the brothers because of the origin of the blood in their veins, but neither understood a word he said or knew his name.

Frank didn't even like him, in fact.

The plain black writing faded in and out of focus as he counted the seconds without Joe. *One one-thousand. Two one-thousand. Three one-thousand.* At four one thousand, Frank cautiously forged a trail up the mud wall with his nose to peek over. Joe, twenty and enviously, perfectly, athletically built, reached out into hell. Frank pushed up further to see the Italian flailing his arms and legs towards them distances away, too far away to be reaching out.

Frank wanted to huck a rock at Joe to make him come back. He called for Joe to *come back,* but the wall of sound enveloping them made even his own voice incomprehensible.

"Joe!" Frank thought he called.

He looked off into the apocalyptic, angrily searching to see if the sky were still blue. A brimming black dot dropped through the hazy clouds. Maybe a dead bird. *Dropping through.* Maybe a propelled dead bird.

The Italian still distances away.

"Joe, come back!"

A bomb! Oh, sweet Jesus, a grenade!

"Joe! Joe! Joe!"

Frank felt the tubes in his throat reverberating but only heard the most terrible thunder. Distances away still, but the grenade close.

"Guiseppe!"

Joe finally saw and stepped back. *Too late.*

Frank's eyes closed enough to half-way witness the grenade hit, and the flesh and organs once comprising the Italian spread across the weeping Earth. Something heavy flew over and something soft smacked at the hem of his hairline, painfully sticking there.

"Damn it, Joe!"

He turned, pulling the flying object off his face, completely deafened and slightly blinded. In bright white, he saw an ear in the pool of his palm. Color leaked in browns and reds as he stared up.

Joe clutched at the Earth around him in handfuls, screaming for the missing connection of his knees with his feet. His left boot laid right in eyesight, just out of hands reach.

Oh, Jesus.

"That's my boot!" Joe could be heard. "Frank, that's my boot!"

Frank's heartbeat terrified fists against his ribcage, and his lungs struggled to find the strength and time to breathe. *He could not breathe.*

"Frank!" Joe could be deafeningly heard.

Please God save us.

"Dad," Sarah's beautiful voice bloomed into the air with smoke, "God is not going to save us."

Frank still saw the whitened sky of hell for a moment.

Please.

"Dad."

Slowly, real blue filtered into his vision. There no longer was a war. Sarah's smoke suffocated the glass, blocking the cool air from outside. Frank shivered inside his empty house with his brown leather shoes tied tight, worn wool slacks hanging off sagging hips, and stained polyester jacket protecting tattered plaid shirt. Knick-knacks, pictures, Eileen, Sarah, garbage, change cluttered what used to be a warm living room. He felt as though his memories had taken the place of his furniture now because he lived so comfortably within them. His veiny, wrinkled hands clutched a handmade plywood sign painted with the word of God.

"I think God will save us," Frank heard himself say.

The cluck of the cuckoo clock given to him and Eileen as a wedding present echoed throughout the emptiness, touching the few still hanging family pictures with tender, wanting fingers. *Six clucks.* They, the elderly married couple, always left for the local farmers' market by 6:15, and it always took some time to put his sign in the car. She would desert him to buy fresh produce as the masses whispered around him, avoided him, and were saved by him. The two would reunite at the old Subaru to journey home where they would separate again: he to the couch to watch the television and the coming and going outside, and she to their bedroom to watch her own television and fall asleep before he came to bed.

Blue
Maya Rahman Rios

You are seven years old when you hold him for the first time. Babies are supposed to be cute. He's not, but you don't care. He looks like an old man—wrinkled forehead, eyes shut, and already disgruntled with the world, but you don't care. You can't wait to teach him how to play catch, surf a wave, do a backflip on the trampoline, not to get caught during Hot Lava Monster. When he grasps your finger in his tiny hand, a tear leaks down your cheek. Big boys aren't supposed to cry, but this is different.

You are thirty-six years old when you see her for the first time. She's got a face like from a movie and you can't look away as she stands in line to meet you and your coworkers at the event you spent weeks planning. The conversation is rehearsed in your head. *I love you guys so much; I listen every day on my commute. Oh, how nice, thank you so much for your support.* You hope she asks you for a picture with you. Just you. When she does, pride swells up in your chest like the ocean tattoo on your back.

You are fifteen years old when you have sex for the first time. You hold your breath the whole time and you are scared. The girl's older, a senior. It wasn't supposed to happen this way. She looks bored. Like she'd rather count the wood chips on the ground at the playground behind your house or hand-wash dirty underwear. It was supposed to be amazing. It was just … awkward. Kinda smelly. When she puts her clothes back on, you wish it never happened. You just try it again. And again. And again. Different girl each time. Just keep trying until it feels like it's supposed to.

You are ten years old when he starts to follow you everywhere. He likes to hold your hand. *You my big budder. I love you.* He lets you feed him and you're the first person he hugs when he gets home from preschool. You're the one he asks for when he wakes up crying. It happens often. *Night terrors?* Your parents speak in hushed whispers about him, but he just smiles. *You my big budder, Grey. I love you. I'm scared of the monsters I see at night, but I love you.* When he wakes up crying, you always tell him that you love him, too. You love him more than you thought you should, thought you could, thought you would. You wish you could have the nightmares instead of him, but you never tell anyone. Instead, you turn on his sound machine. He likes the waves the best.

You are seventeen years old when he tries the first time. A razor to the wrist. Your dad takes the door off the hinges and says nothing while your mother cries in the corner. Bandages on his wrist for three days, seventy-two hours, and then the smile returns, like nothing ever happened. You ask him why, but he says he doesn't remember. *Bad dream, probably. Not the kids at school? No. Have they teased you lately? No. Just remember to tell me if they—They aren't, Grey, I swear.* You know he's lying. You noticed the bruises on his ribs and his screams in the middle of the night, but he stopped asking for you. You miss it. A lot.

You are sixteen years old when his nightmares start. Like really start. No more shapeless monsters with sharp teeth or heavy breathing. Dreams of dying, falling. Starvation. Breath escaping from lungs as head is pushed underwater. He calls to you and you run to him, but he's crying and spitting and begging you not to tell anyone. *I'm fine. Only babies cry from their nightmares.* You want to tell him he's not a baby and that it's okay to cry. But he doesn't believe you. And you don't believe yourself. You're full of shit and you know it.

You are thirty-seven years old when you see her again. Another event, another meetup. She smiles at you, expects you not to remember, but you do. Your chest burns. Nerves. This never happens to you. You ask for her number, telling her that you need her advice on an upcoming bit for the show. She buys it. Five-nine-one, five-five-five, seven-seven-eight-six. You repeat the number in your head until it synchs with your breathing. It takes you three days to text her. You spent three days (72 hours) crafting the perfect message, but you'd never admit it.

You are twenty-one years old when he's successful. You weren't the one who found him. Your mom did. He was swinging from the rafters in his closet, his nicest tie tied tight around his neck. You can't get her scream out of your head. Or his face, blue like the ocean he always loved. You drink that night. A lot. You don't know how you got home. The alcohol rips you apart even further and you can't breathe. You think that this must have been how his nightmares were. Except he could wake up. You hate yourself. You could have saved him, you could have saved him if you'd picked him up from school, if you could just look those people in the eye and—

You are twenty-three years old when you start seeing him. Around corners, in mirrors, in windows. He smiles and waves at you. You smile and wave back, but blink until he goes away, until you start crying. Guilt rises in you again, like it has every day. The lights flicker and you see him in every room of every apartment you try to stay in, in the closets of every girl you've been with, in the passenger's seat of every car you pass. You ask your mom if she sees him, too. She doesn't. He's all of a sudden three years old again, following you everywhere like a well-trained dog. You get the ocean inked into your back and think of how he would have loved you for it. He watches you from outside the window of the tattoo parlor and smiles before fading from your vision forever.

You are thirty-four years old when you forget to visit him on his birthday. You spend the day at some chick's house and you forget. You forget to eat a slice of cake in his honor (Funfetti, naturally), you forget to drop off a balloon for him, you forget to sit down and tell him everything (everyone) you've done recently. You hate yourself. You run to the cemetery the next day and beg for his forgiveness. You press your hands to his headstone and cry, ignoring the subtle stares from the couple passing by. *I'm so sorry. I'm so, so sorry. I'll never forget again. I promise.* You never quite forgive yourself.

You are thirty-eight years old when you realize you're in love. She tells you she loves you in the middle of a deserted In-n-Out at 12:43 a.m. and it comes spilling out of you before you can stop it. *I love you, too.* You don't know how long it's been since you said that. It feels good to say it. It feels good to say it as she steals the last of your fries and sticks them balls deep in her vanilla milkshake. It feels good to say it as she kisses you for hours in her apartment after you tell her about him. It feels good to say it as you realize that this is what you craved for the past seventeen years. Her fingers trace your tattoo as she falls asleep, and you can finally breathe again.

Two Minutes
Alyssa Ahle

At 10:45 p.m. on a Wednesday, Night fell in love with Day. He had never met her, but he had often heard the stars speak admirably of her warmth and light. So Night sought advice from the Moon on how to approach Day without seeming too dark and menacing. The Moon decided to help and asked his wife the Sun to set up a date between the two of them.

At 6:42 p.m. on a Friday, Day and Night met for the first time at a café in the left-hand corner of the universe. Night wore a jet-black vest combo over a midnight blue shirt. Day wore a sundress that matched the deep blue sky on a lazy afternoon. The only time they had was the two-minute transition between their jobs, during sunrise and sunset when the Sun was one with the horizon. So they met for two minutes. And talked. They talked about their hopes and dreams, favorite books and television shows, the pros and cons of their occupations, and whether or not they could see each other again at sunrise. At 6:44 p.m. they paused their conversation and ordered sodas to go.

They met again at sunrise and resumed their conversation; Day showed Night how to bottle and preserve sunshine. Twelve hours later, at the stroke of sunset, Night took Day dancing on the Milky Way. On their fourth date, Day and Night flew kites together under the Northern Lights. For their fifth date, Night showed Day how to safely catch and release fireflies. Many two-minute dates followed. Thus began the infinite courtship of Night and Day.

The Evening Braised Red
An Excerpt
Mark Westphal

I love Chinese cuisine. I love smelling it. I love talking about it. I love preparing and cooking it. I love eating it. I am a connoisseur. I am an expert. I've been to China six times. I know the culinary style of a region by its taste alone. I can make the most niche of dishes at home and grow my own Sichuan Peppercorns. Yet, my restaurant of choice is Hong's Rooster Garden Restaurant, run by my good friend, Old Hong (who I have been avoiding giving a bag of peppercorns to that I owe him from a rather unlucky game of Mahjong).

I always act like it's not even that good of a place to eat, but it is an old favorite. You can't beat old favorites. Everything, all 56 items on the menu, is delicious despite questionable authenticity to the Hong's Cantonese roots. I have no usual item I like getting, and the atmosphere is always fairly quiet. Also, since most people buy takeout, which is a good option, there aren't very many people sitting around. The staff, who know me, always puts me in the most peaceful part of the restaurant on purpose to separate me from the hum of the kitchen fan and the range of the speakers playing Kenny G on loop. However, I'm still in a place where I can smell the oil to determine whether it is a good day to order any fried food, even though I hardly ever order it unless I really feel like disregarding my diet and throwing caution to the wind.

And I'm here today, at my usual time: 7:15. I'm guided to my seat with the usual low-rent fanfare and shy smile by the lady of the house, Hong Xiao Li. I sit down in my booth and immediately start talking to her.

"One glass of plum wine," I say, "and *not* chilled, please." Her head nods as she smiles and leaves me to examine the menu. I smell the oil. Not tonight. They didn't change it. Steamed spring onion and shrimp wontons it is then. It's always the better choice anyways; steamed dumplings are one of the finer things in life. I especially love the way Hong's makes them; the dough is never raw, yet it is delightfully translucent, still retaining a bite as well as a doughy taint that enhances the ginger-and-garlic-ridden filling to the point where it somehow gets sweet. I usually never order seafood from a restaurant due to uncertainty over its freshness and quality, but tonight I don't care. It just seems right.

She brings me my plum wine. It's cold to the touch, much to my disappointment, but it's been a long day and I didn't want to tell her to get me a new one. What a waste it would've been anyways. I order my dumplings. Then I order the Shanghai-Style Red Braised Pork, a favorite in the Hong family's recipe book, published three years ago and still not doing as well in sales as its contemporaries, which is unfortunate. The pork, however, is absolutely amazing. The flavors work beautifully and the glaze on the outside is perfect. It's a shame more people don't order it.

She smiles and nods again and leaves for the kitchen. I take a sip of my wine. It is cloyingly sweet, of course, but still fairly satisfying. I hear the door open and more people coming in. More muttering in mandarin starts emanating from the kitchen. The kitchen must not like these people. I divert my attention to the front, sacrificing my previously veiled position and shuffle myself over to the one spot of the booth in which I can see the rest of the store. It's four people, all standing up, assuming the position needed to order takeout; one is a child, two are parents, and the other is a woman, who is tall, athletically built, and packing heat. Must be a family, although your average family doesn't have a tough female bodyguard at their side. Probably another attempt at a mob takeover. I start wondering why a family like this wouldn't just stay at home, order takeout, and have the bodyguard take the food home. It would make more sense.

"What do you mean you guys don't have cream cheese rangoons?! Every Chinese restaurant has them!" The mother yells at the waitress who took my order earlier.

Hong Xiao Li, however, is not fazed by her outburst: "I'm sorry, it's not on our menu. I do recommend our fried crab wontons though—"

"Unacceptable! We deserve better than this!" Typical overprivileged family behavior. What's even worse about this conversation is that the supposed strong father mob figure is completely ignoring the fact that his shitheaded wife is harassing someone for no reason and is instead showing his son something on his smartphone. I hate having to look at stuff like this, but as someone whose curiosity always got the best of him throughout his life, I can't help but keep my tired eyes and hateful, judgmental ears open.

Hong Xiao Li looked intimidated: "I'm sorry, madam, really, please calm down—"

"Jesus, Nina listen to the woman and order the food already," the husband finally chimed in with all the tough guy attitude of a stoic bit of gristle.

"Don't tell me what to do!"

"Don't you remember we're in a hurry?" He retorted and tightly clutched his wife's arm menacingly. The bodyguard moved over to calm him down and break them up, looking slightly annoyed in the process, and subsequently, the mother named Nina calmed down after that too.

Then Nina finished ordering the takeout. An order of House Special Chow Mein. An order of the Vegetable Lo Mein (good choice, although the oyster sauce-marinated beef that the Hongs add to it is simply to die for if you're in the mood for beef), an order of Mongolian Beef (I guess these people aren't the type for Buddha's Delight). An order of egg rolls (judging from the fact that she ordered the House Special Chow Mein, I'm not surprised at this choice). Chicken Fried Rice, three large orders (Jesus Christ, how much do these people eat, and does *everything* they order have to have meat in it?). Finally, she wraps up this blasphemous order with an order of steamed vegetables from the low-calorie menu (which, if one knew how much chefs hate that loathsome little section of the takeout menu, you wouldn't order from it. No one wants three kinds of vegetables with no flavor whatsoever steamed way past the point where they should be unless they hate the children they feed them too).

At this time, another waitress brings me my pork, making my brain cells and stomach quiver with orgasmic anticipation as I smell the beauty that is the Shanghai-Style Red Braised Pork. I couldn't hesitate to dive into its salty beauty. And no, I didn't get any vegetables because this is my cheat day. Besides, the Luo Huan Zhai at this place pales in comparison to my homemade version. I make it with way less cornstarch and no baby corn (I'm not a fan of baby corn).

I hear Hong Xiao Li say "it'll be about 15-20 minutes," and the family takes a seat at the front of the store on the bench specifically designed for assholes and early birds to wait.

But going back to the question I had before about why they didn't call ahead, maybe I can fill in some blanks. I know these people out outspoken, talk to each other harshly, have no word filter even when they are around their young son, and have an extravagant-looking bodyguard, meaning that there is a possibility that they are indeed a family with an organized crime background. Judging by the way they dress, too, which I didn't pay attention to earlier, I'd say this theory still holds up. They had to have bought those painfully-obvious looking monkey suits with laundered money. My eyes don't deceive me when it comes to things like this.

I scoot back to the position I was in before. I didn't want them to see me staring at them and their child, after all. Minutes went by as I enjoyed my delectable pork, savoring every bite I took. Then the volume at the front of the house escalates. Somehow I knew it would happen. It's time to come to the front of the house to get some toothpicks.

This gives me a good opportunity to get a view of these people from up close. I grab a toothpick from the plastic container near the register. The bodyguard shifts her position to face me with her hand drifting lazily towards the inside of her coat. I wave hello at her specifically. Then the wife chimes in: "What are you looking at?"

"Nothing. Just getting a toothpick." I say.

"Well, you've spent a little too much time doing it." She says threateningly.

Tempting fate, I take another handful of toothpicks and say: "At least I put more effort into grabbing toothpicks than you do in ordering the best food on the menu."

I really don't know why I decided to say that; it wasn't even a good insult. The wife's stare became more and more intense as I started walking away, and I began to feel it. Then I heard a gun click. I figure that spinning around quickly and throwing my toothpicks out like ninja stars was just about the worst idea I could think of, so I keep walking, hoping that nothing tumultuous would happen.

Then two shots go off. None of them hit me. Tempting fate yet again, I slowly turn around to see who was holding the gun and, not at all to my surprise, it was the bodyguard, who just shot the wife, husband, and child in two shots. Very efficient. She starts to face towards me.

"Drop the toothpicks!" she yells. I drop the toothpicks.

Observer Anxiety
An Excerpt
Dean L. Shauger

The trip truly starts on Monday, a day and a half after it was originally set to begin, in North Carolina after we spent the previous night and most of the day packing all his belongings and cleaning out his house. This is, however, not the beginning of the story. The story begins a snowy Friday night in front of a large vortex sitting in the middle of the Chicago skyline. Or at least that is where the story should begin. It is in actuality a tale about a train ride and a young man stumbling through a strange city for a night. Like promised, the train ride was an uneventful way to start a night, which had only briefly started earlier at a pizza joint which had a nasty habit of building its pizzas backwards with the piping hot sauce layered over the cheese, then the toppings, and finally ending in a flaky crust. It was under all accounts exactly like a flight he, who was a part of myself existing in a past state of consciousness, had taken only two hours before which led to him getting stuck in the aforementioned strange city. Currently he was sitting in front of a bum who had a nasty habit of drinking, clinking various items along the metal handrails, talking to himself, and occasionally stinking of human urine and the salty smell of an unwashed body, while he, our narrator, scribbled notes along his arm because he had forgotten his notebook with his luggage, and observed the crowd of sadly uninteresting characters, all the while trying to seem as inconspicuous as possible.

This same man, the narrator, would later be stuck in a tightly-packed Prius, his knees pressed against the dashboard and four hours later pressed against the steering wheel, driving late into the night blinded by rain and the large wall of possessions that blocked off the rear window and everything that wasn't the foot and a half gap between the front of the car, the driver, and that crushing wall of everything his best friend owned. He might even have thought back to that mumbling bum with a rosy haze remembering exactly how he was able to spread his legs, stretch, and yawn, and he had the ability to talk to so many people he did not know that he never talked to in the first place, but that fantasy of talking to the boring passengers was all that was keeping him awake through the dark night—well that and the Red Bulls and the loud music that hammered through the labyrinth of clothes, television sets, and other knick-knacks. He thought back to the vortex and the people he saw there. Maybe he should have never left, maybe he should have stayed cramped in a different type of space with a few beers surrounded by people he could only faintly understand, people that he had no concern over, and who he had written off as simple noise.

The bar he found, in the moments after pressing himself into that oblong void, held its head high with a simple promise and motto *Chicago's most intimate bar.* The bar was able to add one more tagline, a promise that no one read but soon everyone became aware of, *we do not have the drinks you want instead we have everything that we promise will be close to what it is you are craving.* And in that sense they could not lie, for he, the narrator, sat at the cramped bar in a building so small its name couldn't be anything other than "The Matchbox," concerning himself solely with his quest to be drunk in a city he had never been to before after having seen the bulbous reflection of another universe sitting softly in the snow. It hadn't even been his idea to go see the void but was instead proposed by a girl who was several hundreds of miles away but who would be flying into the same city hours after he had landed in a way that promised they could never link up. So he sat with a beer in his hands, strangers pressing into him like a wall of knickknacks, bartenders rattling off drinks that were close to the Black and Tan that he so desperately craved, trying to drown himself in alcohol hoping it would help him find the words to describe and inevitably steal all the magic behind that bean-shaped galactic anomaly that sat in the middle of Millennium Park. Had the other who pressed back through that glassy void found, in his own world, his little matchbox to sit in and bide the time until the game began? Or had he, like our narrator, given up on understanding the people and drunkenly staggered back to the blue line to find the hotel that would transport him into a tomorrow where he would sit on a cramped flight with the promises of finding his best friend, a small red Prius, and a house full of belongings that needed to be packed?

Good Bye ground. Hello Sky.

Our man, the narrator, fell asleep in a small room in snowy Chicago to find himself waking again in the green embrace of North Carolina. He couldn't remember how he got here, but somehow he could remember that giant void sitting in Chicago, and that familiar face that peeked out. Three days, twelve hours and a trip to UPS would find him, again, cramped into that red Prius contemplating the footsteps in the snow that led to that rift but disappeared where it settled, still wondering whether or not it would have been safer to stay in the Matchbox. In less than four and a half days he would join me, the narrator, and our mutual friend in Austin where we would find the rest of the story together, but before he could find his way back to the present he is stuck in a world of transplants deep in the south partaking in melodrama that isn't his, but he is aware that even the cameraman is part of the action. He lets himself be dragged over Troutman, the small town stuck in the forest between cities and lakes like a void stuck in the snow, cataloging and collecting the stories of the strangers who'd been caught in the small town's pull unable to escape its event horizon until they too became relics of the south.

He, the narrator, knew his job. He had found his way to the south to retrieve his, our, best friend from becoming like the transplants who had left New York and California on the way to their new lives who got stuck in the Troutman singularity. Of course, the friend, Adam, had purposefully driven himself into the singularity thinking he could find his new life among the collapsing pull of all the transplants and lost ones who had been dragged and warped until they could only assume the world around them had always been trees and hunting grounds, forgetting the call of the cities and families to settle a land where there were no fences because the people couldn't be bothered to divvy up the land. Instead they built houses where they chose to be among biblical streets, only ever thinking twice to avoid the church on Judas Way, but he only ever lived on the event horizon where he was able to watch the world age and wonder how this town could be so rooted and lost in a time without time, only ever consuming those who got too close and slipped forever into the web, unable to remember the escape velocity or simply the course of their own trajectory. Adam lived with a hand on the safety line circling the black hole that was his ex-fiancée, feeling the alluring pull of his newest girlfriend, wondering if maybe the world didn't simply end in Troutman and that it would be easier to let go. It was here our narrator found him, here the young man grabbed his friend's hand and pulled him inch by inch until the black hole spit him out with all his possessions, until the black hole collapsed into a single flashing anomaly and slowly got eaten by the Void that had taken over the night as they raced from North Carolina in a car packed with possessions and knick-knacks, packed so tightly that the narrator had his knees pressed to the dashboard and found his mind drifting back to the snow-covered floor that rested under his little anomaly, wondering what would have happened if he just slipped past his event horizon, pushed gently past the glassy film and allowed the Void to swallow him. He wondered if anyone would have grabbed his hand to save him. He wondered if perhaps he should have stayed in the Matchbox till he got the courage built up to slink back over the snow and dive into a new world. Yet now the Void chased him into the dark, chewing up the road and spitting out lone lines of red lights, and the two of them slipped farther and farther into the night chasing the point where they could find the present and escape the prison of their past, driving farther and farther until they could find the open arms of Texas and finally step out of the car without having to worry about collapsing back into the Troutman singularity.

The true tragedy was that places like this still exist.

Nighthawks
Natasha Lelchuk

My mom named me Indigo for my eyes, which were bright blue when I was born, but they've since lost their color. Now they are gray like a forgotten dream, like the dust on the spine of the book nobody touches, like the ink that comes out of a pen when the cartridge is nearly empty.

It's a silly name, Indigo.

Indigo Marsden.

It's the name of a 1920s stage actress who is cast as Ophelia but doesn't make it to opening night because she dies in an ironic boating accident off the coast of Monaco. It's certainly not the name of an insomniac university student whose future looks more and more bleak with every passing day.

Tonight, the diner is nearly empty, the fryers quiet and the jukebox neglected. The clock ticks, almost the loudest sound in the room. I help myself to another cup of coffee, my third, my fourth, as the animatronic bird erupts from his house and shatters the silence of the room.

Cuckoo, cuckoo. It echoes off the walls of the room, the walls of my brain.

Four o'clock. Tonight, this morning, what does it matter? I've spent every night here for the past two weeks—or has it been three?—and every night I imagine that I am a figure in an Edward Hopper painting. I am a nighthawk, a creature of paint and canvas, and time has no place here.

Indigo Marsden is the kind of character you'd expect to see in an Edward Hopper painting. She belongs there, frozen in time, frozen in space. She can't see you, but you can see her. There isn't much detail to her face, but you know she has gray eyes. Gray like a forgotten dream.

I'd meant to work on an assignment tonight, a reading on Charles Darwin's effects on literature, but the pages lay forgotten on the table in front of me. Across the diner, somebody else sits at the counter. From my booth, I can only see his back, arched like a comma as he bends over a notebook, writing. He has dark hair, and dark eyes, too, I bet. I haven't seen them and can only imagine their color, but I feel right about this.

He's been here every night for the last two weeks, just like me. Maybe he's an insomniac as well. Maybe the light of the moon rouses him the way it does me and sends his thoughts spinning. Or maybe he's nocturnal, a passionate artist type, most productive at night. Some writers are like that. Maybe he's one of them.

He rolls his head to the side, scratching his neck. I follow the movements of his hand with my eyes. He doesn't drop the pen, doesn't flinch as it marks his skin with a black smudge. He writes with a basic ballpoint, nothing fancy, but you don't need an overpriced fountain pen to create something magical. Suddenly he does drop the pen, letting it fall softly on his notebook as he stretches his arms over his head. Despite the storm raging on outside, his arms are bare, revealing a lattice of tattoos, and his jacket lays over the back of a nearby chair. I wonder what kind of stories the tattoos tell.

Like I've done every night for the past two weeks, I imagine asking him. In my imagination I embody Indigo Marsden, fictional character, to the fullest: I am sweeping curves and sultry tones and the blue of my eyes could never be captured in a Crayola crayon. Edward Hopper, eat your heart out. Writer boy, eat your heart out. In my vision, I move silently across the diner, but he looks up nonetheless, looks over his shoulder at me and locks his gaze with mine. His eyes are dark like midnight, and endless.

We don't speak for a minute. We are frozen in time, his tattoos dancing on his arms, telling silent stories. Finally he moves, standing gracefully to his feet. He removes his jacket from the chair and lifts it over my shoulders. It is weightless. I am weightless.

"Indigo Marsden," I say. My voice is ethereal, formless. As quick as it came, it's gone.

He doesn't tell me his name. He never does. Instead he says, "You have beautiful eyes."

I don't blush or look away.

"I know," I say. Or sometimes I don't. Sometimes I disregard the compliment and ask what he's writing. *A play*, he says. Or *a sonnet*, or *I'm translating Proust*. The answer doesn't matter too much to me.

"But you're much more interesting than anything I could ever write," he says. And there the daydream ends.

It's not enough, because even my imagination has limits. His voice in my head isn't a voice—it's an amalgamation of the voices of the weatherman from channel 5 and Brandon Flowers from the Killers and my history professor. It's not real.

The clock strikes five, the bird cuckooing the hour, and I take another sip of my cooling coffee. I usually leave before sunrise, packing up my things and dropping some coins in the tip jar before sneaking out the door. The writer never notices me, always too engrossed in his notebook, in his words, in his own fictional world. But this morning, I wait. Sunrise begins to creep in through the windows, casting shadows on the walls, and I wait.

This morning I want something more. Something more than my sleepless dreams.

Another half hour goes by. Daywalkers, the kind of people who fall asleep at night, begin trickling in, ordering decaf coffee and breakfast specials. The scent of bacon frying fills my nostrils.

Someone sits down at the booth next to mine, but I don't let that distract me from the writer. Finally he recaps his pen, preparing to leave. I don't take my eyes off of him as I gather my things. Today I leave my tip on the table instead of dropping it in the jar. Then I follow the writer out the door.

Outside, the world erupts in color. The sky is blue today, not gray like my eyes. Yellow cabs speed past us, policemen in navy walk by, and a woman in red brushes past me, a Starbucks cup clutched in her hand. She isn't the sort of woman to drink diner coffee, but I am.

"Hey, are you following me?"

I freeze. This would never happen to Indigo Marsden, Hopper girl. But Indie Marsden—she didn't think this far ahead. My heart zooms in my chest. This isn't part of the daydream.

"I'm sorry," I say, and though the writer's eyes are as dark as I imagined, I can't stay to admire them. I spin on my heel and begin to walk away, in the opposite direction of my apartment, when I feel a hand on my arm.

"No, I'm sorry," he says, spinning me back around to face him. "I'm just kidding. I saw you in the diner."

I don't know what to say. I want to know when he had time to notice me. More than that, I want to know what he was writing, what kind of worlds he makes up to escape to when this one gets to be too much. Instead, I ask, "Are you an insomniac, too?"

"Yeah, I am," he says with a laugh. Paintings can't capture laughter, especially not a laugh as light as this one. "I've never met another one, actually." Then he holds out his hand. "I'm Jack."

I take it. My hand is small, too small for this. I almost regret the decision to follow him out, but his hand is warm, and it makes me feel okay. "Indie." I'm not Indigo Marsden now. I'm just Indie, and my voice shakes as I speak.

"Nice to meet you." He drops my hand and cocks his head to the side. "You headed this way?"

I nod. Now anticipation hums through my veins.

"What a coincidence. Me too." He starts walking, so I follow him. I don't know what to say, so I wait for him to speak. I am bad at conversations, at meeting strangers, at being Indie. "You live around here?"

"Just one stop east," I say. We're headed for the subway station; I can see it on the next block, the entrance crowded with suited men and high heeled women. When I leave before sunrise, I miss getting caught in rush hour, but today I'm sacrificing the convenience of an uncrowded ride for the possibilities of this conversation.

"Oh, I'm west," he says. I nod, but don't say anything else. As we get closer to the station, a sense of urgency overcomes me. Though we've both been at the diner every night for the last few weeks, there's a chance I might never see him again. If I don't ask now, I might never find out.

I manage to stay by him as we go down into the station and swipe through the turnstiles, but then we reach the point where we must part to go in opposite directions.

"I'll see you around, Indie," he says, turning to go right, and I know that this is it. I have to ask him now, if only to complete my Indigo daydream. I take a second to work up the courage, turning it over in my stomach and then—

"Wait," I call after him. He stops on the platform and looks back at me. "What were you working on?"

He grins at me, amused by the question. "Just math." Then he disappears around the corner, leaving me with nothing to do but stare after him and repeat the words in my head.

Just math.

Human Race: Library
Priscilla Lam

Afternoon. The sun is bright. It would be nice to stay out here but I must go print. Through the doors I go. Touch the magic door opener or will someone open the door for me? Walk past displays. There are books in glass cases. Does anyone bother to stop and read them? No. People walk past it. Someone worked hard to put this together. No one cares, no one ever does. But neither do I. No time to stop. I'm sure it's interesting. They call us the human race. Keep going. Keep going. The second door opens. There are people. Look down? Look in their eyes? Avoid eye contact. Why is it so busy in the afternoon? The air is musty. Too many in one place. Walk past front desk. Avoid eye contact. How is it to work in the library? They have time to get work done. Must be nice. Librarians help lost books find homes again. The gatekeepers of stories. Protectors. Organizers. Important job. The older librarians dedicated their lives to books. To stories. To people they meet through pages. Does anybody ask the librarians for help? Or are the librarians forgotten too? The human race. Keep going. Keep going. Stop? No. Move on. Move on. Everything moves fast. Printing. Look at the printer press. Does anyone notice it here in the library? Words on paper took longer to circulate. Slow machinery. Now it works fast like us. Keep moving. Print. Another display. New books. Always new books. What happens to old books. Have we lost them all? The more we try to save the more we lose. There is too much to know. I must print. Many faces at computers. I do not know them. I recognize them. Will these faces mean something to me in a year? There are faces that mean something to me now that did not before. How many times have I passed someone in the universe that would later mean so much? Take a seat. Many hands have been here. Germs. I do not sleep much. I hope I do not get sick. We transmit diseases without even touching the person. Invisible connections all around us. Login. Always forget password. Human race. Forget. Move on. I should write it down. I will later. Print essay. Are there mistakes I didn't see? Probably. Too tired to check. How many hours do we spend on things that don't matter? Too much time. Not enough time. Writing. Writing. Human race. Writing takes time. It is not a race if it is done well. Print. Login again. What is in a name? Our names are now number. 20538329. ID. Am I a number? Identification please? Yes, my name is 20538329. Print. Printer E. It works faster. Human race. Prints. Essay feels good. Warm. Heat is energy. Human Race. Keep going. Keep going. It is easy to feel lonely. Keep going. Keep going. We forget how to care about anything. We forget how to care about people. Human race. Someone is forgotten. I am forgotten. But maybe I do not want to be remembered. Conflicted. Like being alone but feel lonely. We are walking contradictions. Reflections of loneliness. Paper print. Extra time. Walk around the corner to see if there are empty seats. Groups of friends laugh. No one I know. Sit down by window. It is hot. Sun through the window. They never put the shades down. Heat. Energy. Motion. Human race. People walk by. You can see everyone from the library windows. They never know you're watching. Distracted. Should read for tomorrow. Never start early enough. Look around. It seems everyone has a place to belong. What does it feel like? It must feel nice. Does anyone really belong to anybody when we can't even belong to ourselves? Questions. No answers. Always in the void. Within and without. Can't focus here. Too loud. If I were laughing too it would be okay. Not laughing. Alone.

                    Round the
                            Corner
            Up the
                Stairs.
                    Second Floor.
            Quiet.

Easy to get lost in the library. Nooks and crannies. Easy to hide. Walk towards windows. Always someone in my seat. Walk further. Yes. Sit. Chair by window. Look down. They are all going to lunch. Food. Lunch rush. Keep going. Keep going. Human race. Book. Yes. I must read. Reading is a distraction. Book. *Ulysses* episode 5. Bloom. Begin.

His life isn't a bed of roses
Flowers of idleness
Petals too tired to
Walk on rose leaves
A yellow flower with flattened petals
I think of you so often you have no idea
Language of flowers.
They like it because no one can hear
No roses without thorns
A languid floating flower.

Close book. Race Begins. Rush to class. Bloom.

End.

Forever and Always, Luna
An Excerpt
Taylor Rivers

Setting: It is dusk in a small backyard of a bakery, its window cracked slightly open. There is an apartment adjoining it where the baker's family lives. Clotheslines, gardening tools, and old toys blanket the backyard lawn. The apartment possesses a set of rickety stairs, leading up to the only entrance of its second story.

At Rise: Behind this door, two girls are heard talking loudly. The elated JOSIE LEE who is visiting the irritated LUNA, the baker's daughter.

JOSIE LEE
I swear, you always get the neatest stuff.

A loud bump is heard in the room—as though a dresser fell.

LUNA
Give it back! Abuela gave me that! I told you, you can look at it, not run around with it!

JOSIE LEE
But every time I move with it, it changes color! I know, let's take it outside!

JOSIE LEE bursts open the second-story door, holding a large, shiny marble. Within it is a large star, ever-shifting. LUNA keeps close behind her. JOSIE LEE slams right into the railing. The marble slips from her hands and into the great, wide sky. Without a moment's hesitation, LUNA leaps several feet from the top of the staircase. She goes up, up, up until she catches the marble high in the sky. She starts floating down ever so gently. JOSIE LEE rushes down the stairs, as LUNA slowly falls.

JOSIE LEE
Holy cow! It's true—I thought the whole town must've been crazy, or fibbin' through their teeth. But it's really true!

LUNA
Josie Lee, how many times do you I have to tell you? You have to be more careful when handling other people's things.

JOSIE LEE
You can fly! As sure a cattle chews cud, you can fly!

LUNA
Actually I can only float.

JOSIE LEE

After all this time, why you haven't told me yet? We're not supposed to keep secrets from each other, especially spiffy ones like this.

LUNA
There wasn't gonna be a right time to tell you this. And there's nothing spiffy about something makes me a weirdo.

JOSIE LEE
All I'm sayin' is I'm disappointed, Lu-Lu.

LUNA
Disappointed?
(Lands on the ground, then rushes toward Josie Lee.)

I should be disappointed with you! I told a hundred times not to touch my nice things. You played with my doll, *poof*, its head is rolling across the floor. You read my favorite books, *bam*, they're somehow soaked with water. I can't trust you with anything. You're too much of a klutz!

JOSIE LEE
(Takes a step back.)
Maybe I shouldn't come over then.

LUNA
You're not gonna comeback now anyway. Admit it, you've only been coming over here to catch me flying.

JOSIE LEE
(Laughs, dryly.)
You really think I'm that crummy, don't you? You think I keep comin' to your house—to what, spy you flyin'? Just so I can chuckle 'bout it with the kids at school?

LUNA
Well, how am I to know what you and your school friends say when I'm not around?

JOSIE LEE
Just 'cause I go to that pigpen of a school don't mean I got any friends there! You aren't the only one they make fun of. They punch me and laugh at me every day! I like you, flyin' weirdo and all.

LUNA
Well gee, Josie Lee. I never thought about—I'm sorry for insulting you.

JOSIE LEE
Yeah, well, sometimes you gotta walk in someone else's boots for a while. That's what my Pappy says.

LUNA

It's just—

(Looks at the large marble in her hands.)

This means so much to me. Abuela gave me this the last time I saw her. Before she passed away.

JOSIE LEE

Yeah, well, you're sometimes right too, Luna. I shouldn't touch things that are so important. I'm sorry. I promise I won't tell anybody that I saw you—float.

LUNA

It doesn't matter anyhow, I'm running away. No point in staying in a town where even the adults look at me like some no-good monster.

JOSIE LEE

Stop pullin' my leg, Lu-Lu. Let's head back in.

(Heads towards the stairs.)

LUNA

I'm serious, Josie Lee. This was a long time coming. Almost losing this gift, I now know I need to leave real soon.

(Heads to the opposite end of the yard.)

Special Friend
Amethyst Hethcoat

Tracey's face, abnormally round and covered with drool, looks something like an ice cream scoop; wet and fragile, the pudgy mass might drip to the floor at any moment. Yet she is the prize for whom we both battle, Samuel and I: the golden cup validating the victor's noble heart and charitable yearnings. In short, the few hours we share with Tracey during this one, excruciatingly hot afternoon will absolve us of the moral transgressions we commit every other day. After all, instead of shooting hoops, hugging old men in animal suits, and munching on stale Western Bacon Cheeseburgers with Tracey, we could be in front of our laptops watching The Walking Dead or on our iPhones playing Words with Friends. So it's not like Samuel and I don't have better things to do. The Special Olympics, an annual adventure filled with sports and sunlight, allows philanthropic, progressive "normal" students like myself to bond with developmentally-challenged, mentally-handicapped "special" kids like Tracey; it's a way of giving back. Like the evangelical Christians who fly to Africa and upload pictures with emaciated youngsters, this is our domestic way of showcasing the fine morals our Protestant school has instilled within us. I smile extra huge at Tracey, trying very hard not to show my disgust. By now, the slime oozing from her open mouth has already pooled by her little light-up princess shoes.

"Hey, Tracey! Ready to have fun?" Anxiously, I wait for a response. Hands perched on my knees, I'm bent down to her level.

"She's non-verbal." Samuel smirks.

"So how do you suppose we communicate, huh?" Slightly ticked, my voice has risen, alarming Tracey whose animalistic instincts have prompted her to cover her ears and rock back and forth violently.

"Sweetheart, I'm sorry. How about we go see Mr. Waggles, the firefighting Dalmatian?" I take her hand and she starts crying. I let go, scared and confused.

"What the hell are you doing?" Samuel scolds. He snaps his fingers before pointing to his side. "Tracey, here!" Tracey wipes her snotty nose onto my pink and blue friendship tee and then runs to Samuel. With his arm draped around her contorted, toad-like shoulders, Samuel escorts Tracey to Waggles. Meanwhile, I'm abandoned, covered in snot and drool like a discarded hankie.

I don't know why, but Samuel seems to evoke this brand of unwavering adoration in all females, special or otherwise. There was a time when I, too, fell prey to the sandy-blonde locks that cascade perfectly across his forehead. His silky-smooth voice used to stir within my loins the fire about which my Bible teacher so frequently warned: the fire of lust, the devil's seed. For desire is tantamount to evil, especially when you're a woman. You're a port, merely a train to be boarded. Any kind of animalistic drive, connection to flesh, separates one further from the Savior.

"Michelle, you coming?" Like he even cares.

"Just a minute." I jog to the cleaning station where I lather antibacterial hand sanitizer not only on my hands but on my arms. While running to Samuel and Tracey, I don latex gloves as well.

"She doesn't have AIDS, you know." Tracey shakes her head, tightening her grip around Samuel's waist.

"Well, after she's through with you, she might."

"What's that supposed to mean?"

"Nothing. Just that you have a nasty habit of making girls fall in love with your oh-so-wholesome charm before spitting them out like ancient Juicy Fruit. I've heard you've been through more plaid skirts than a bagpiper."

"Michelle, we hooked up one time. That was so long ago, it's ridiculous. And if I remember, you didn't take much convincing."

"You remember wrong. You know the game and you just keep playing it."

"Anyway, rumor has it that you're a sexually-frustrated, obsessive-compulsive control freak who suffers from abandonment issues after your daddy's affair." I remove my latex gloves before slapping him across the face. Tracey rams her chubby, malformed fist into my stomach, almost imperceptibly pooched. Does she know? I wonder. Curled on the floor like a giant ringworm, I watch as Samuel hovers above not only me, but the seed he unknowingly spawned.

"Why'd you take off the glove?" he asks, head cocked to one side like a mischievous pug puppy.

"So I could feel your skin."

"Told you it feels better that way."

"Asshole." Tracey kicks me, rattling the fetus. Who knows whether it will be special? Samuel and his special friend walk arm in arm to the snow cone station, leaving me with nothing but my shame and pain. Mr. Waggles hops over me on his way to grab a hotdog. As I watch him take off the black and white spotted head, I realize: he is just a man.

55

Wings
An Excerpt
Cam Plunkett

The note Doctor Booker had left on the fridge was scarcely different from the one he had left just a month earlier, or the many others he had left over the years. He had been called away for work. He could not say where he was going. He did not know when he would be back. His wife and his son could call him any time and he would pick up unless he was working. When he learned when he would be back in Bethesda, he would let them know. He loved them both very much.

Doctor Booker had almost written "P.S. Good luck!" at the end, but thought it better not to draw attention to the importance of the day he would be gone. Now, stepping through the lobby of an unfamiliar building on the Duke University campus, the doctor checked his phone. Maybe he should have included the postscript. It was nearly seven in the morning. The sun was already peeking out above the few trees which were visible out the lobby windows. He had not received a call or text from home since he left for BWI late the previous night. In the past, his wife would phone him when she awoke to an empty bed, but within the past couple of years she had fallen out of that habit. His concern was irrelevant now, though. He did not have enough time to call home himself.

An imposing man clutched a rifle at rest in front of the elevator. He seemed to recognize the doctor's purpose immediately by the lack of surprise he showed at seeing an armed guard in a medical facility. The guard was already stepping aside when Doctor Booker flashed his badge. The elevator was empty. So, too, was the basement hallway, which provided access to a dozen instructional operating rooms and anatomy labs. Historical photographs dotted the hallway. Doctor Booker caught a glimpse of one beside the door to B4, which featured some sort of factory. Every room the doctor passed was vacated and dark, save for the meager attempt at a study lounge or break room in B8, where somebody had left a light on to illuminate empty couches and chairs.

Sterile white light pervaded room B9 at the Trent Semans Center when Doctor Booker entered, burning from the fluorescent bulbs that buzzed overhead. The floors were stainless steel, as were the bottom few feet of wall. Above that practical adornment, the drywall was painted Pepto-Bismol pink. Now this was an operating room. Too often Doctor Booker had been called out to the kinds of towns you could not find on an AAA atlas. At such places he would have to perform his examination at a dentist's office or within the cramped confines of some family physician's practice. Once, memorably, he had spent ten hours with a specimen in an abandoned igloo in an Alaskan area so remote it had no name. Here, though, he had every instrument and technology he needed, as well as several he did not need, but still felt compelled to use so as not to waste the opportunity. In the center of the operating room, the specimen lay on a wheeled metal table. She was face-down. It would have been impossible, really, for her to be lying any other way, for protruding from a slit down the center of her back was a pair of gigantic butterfly wings.

A man about Doctor Booker's age in green scrubs stood at the head of the specimen. He ducked his considerable height under one of the wings to approach the door. "You must be Doctor Booker," he said, nodding slightly in lieu of giving a handshake.

"I am. Are you on the team for the day?"

"Yes. I'm Doctor Collins. We've also got Doctor Hazel." He gestured to a woman standing behind the specimen's left wing, whose bouffant cap barely contained her dark, curly hair. "And Doctor Goins." A doughy man rubbing his hands at the wash station turned his head and gave a nod.

Doctor Booker recognized two of them. He had worked with Doctor Collins once in the early aughts, when each had gone by a different name. Dr. Hazel actually worked in the same research lab as he back in DC. But of course, none of them could acknowledge their recognition. "Good, good. Have you been waiting long?"

"No. You're right on time."

"Are we waiting on anybody else?"

"No."

"Alright. How's everybody feeling today? No trouble getting in?" The heads in the room bobbed slightly as they turned away from Doctor Booker, back towards their work. Nobody responded. "Let's begin, then." Doctor Booker made his way to the wash-station. "Do we know the specimen's story?" He said over the rush of water.

"I spoke with the lead for Retrievals. He said it looked like she had been clipped by a plane mid-flight. Some old lady saw her fall and called the cops. She probably thought it was a skydiving gone wrong or something. They found her, called HQ, Retrievals got her, set up the secure zone, and now we're here."

"So no."

"We won't know anything else until Investigations is finished."

"Just like always," Doctor Booker said. He wiggled damp fingers up into his latex gloves as he turned to face his team and his specimen. "Hazel, take a photo of the wings before we cut her. Do we know of any other abnormalities?"

"We don't know of any, no," answered Doctor Hazel as she raised a digital camera over her head. The shutter fired rapidly. She brought the camera down to inspect her image, then gave Doctor Booker a thumbs up.

"There's probably nothing, then. We will still have to do a thorough inspection, though, of course." The professional excitement in Doctor Booker's voice as he spoke these last words was tinged with some weariness. The thrill of performing an examination, peering directly into the places where the bizarre and extraordinary descended to the somatic reality of humanity, was still present. But after the examination, that thrill disappeared into a vacuum, while any knowledge gained in the process was forgotten or ignored. Examinations and Research had begun to feel like a vestigial remnant left over from a time when the Paranormal Branch of the CIA still looked upon the specimens they worked on with a sort of awe. In the past it was hoped that such creatures could provide keys to technological or scientific breakthroughs. Even when Doctor Booker entered the Paranormal branch as a twenty-seven-year-old recruit, there was a reverence for Examinations and Research. Now all of the money was funneled into Retrievals and Investigations—as if the CIA's only concern for these monsters was to prevent public awareness. In 17 years, Doctor Booker had never seen his research put into practice.

"That we will." Goins spoke for the first time.

"Do any of you have experience with Entomorphology?" said Doctor Booker.

Only Doctor Hazel nodded. That was to be expected. Their lab back in Bethesda was currently examining and cataloging the abominations left over by a deranged New Mexico man intent on inducing human pupation. But he himself had only handled two other such cases personally. They were not so common in America.

"That is alright. We will follow normal procedure. Let's make any surface observations before we cut into her." Doctor Booker nodded to Doctor Collins, who responded by jerkily raising a tape-recorder to his mouth.

The team surrounded the operating table, ducking under the wings as they passed the specimen's sides, while Doctor Collins recorded his observations.

Specimen NC-14. Specimen appears to be a young woman, Caucasian, in her late teens or early twenties. Observable external abnormality is a pair of wings, much like a butterfly's, extending from out the center of her back with a span of . . ." He checked a clipboard on the table beside him. "18 meters fully extended. The right wing is folded down and relatively intact. The left is torn and bent in several places. The wings appear anchored to her spine by way of cartilage protruding through a wound down the length of her back. The manifestation of the wound is consistent with that of an exit wound, implying the wings grew rapidly from within. The specimen has one large contusion down the front right side of her torso, as well as several small lacerations on her face, arms, and legs. Rigor Mortis has set in, though appears not to have affected the wings. Internal examination will begin now."

Doctor Booker held a scalpel above the specimen's seventh thoracic vertebrae. The skin was smooth. Though the girl's arms were a deep tan, her back was kind of pale which shone like porcelain under the fluorescent lights. Most of her hair had been chopped off, but what was left was full and voluminous. She had a slender frame, bony in a way that flowed in natural harmony with the gentle terrain of her musculature. She had probably been beautiful. As beautiful as Doctor Booker's wife had been on their honeymoon, and in much the same way: the lean legs, the petite frame, the perky butt, the smooth skin. Even the wings, though repulsively attached, had a beauty to them. They were segmented. The bottom portion was much larger than the top, though less ornate—a dappled, driftwood brown. The upper segments were a mellow golden color, framed by that same driftwood brown. In each window of gold was displayed a black circle, perfectly round. The wings were fringed with a centimeter of pure white. Something about the wings reminded Doctor Booker, again, of his wife.

He made an incision beside the seventh thoracic vertebrae, and the internal examination began.

58

Nia's Angel
Anresa D. Tyler

The young woman leaned against the old and rusted chain link fence, unnoticed by passersby on the cracked sidewalk and the elementary school children playing in the enormous yard. She was short, around five feet and a half, with a slightly muscular build that would put most people off. The black leather jacket she wore, along with her worn and torn dark wash jeans, would certainly do so. With her curly hair and caramel colored skin, she would, subconsciously, be given a bit of a berth. However, no one noticed her and that suited her just fine.

Besides, she had no use for others. Her gaze was focused on a young girl, maybe nine or ten years old, sitting alone on a bench in the yard. The girl seemed to be a loner, but the woman had no idea if that was by choice. The girl's head was down, her arms, contained in a large gray hoodie, crossed loosely over her hunched body with what seemed to be her homework in her lap. The woman's curiosity was soon abated as a group of five other school children circled the girl twice but, ultimately, didn't interact with her. The woman could see the girl's shoulders tense, as if in preparation of a confrontation but when the children left, the girl was still tense.

The woman sighed and stepped and materialized through the chain link fence. No one blinked an eye considering no one could see her. She stepped over to the bench the lonely girl was sitting on and sat down beside her. The girl looked over at the woman in what appeared to be shock but said nothing. She probably *was* shocked.

"My name is Hola," the woman said softly.

"I'm Nia," the girl replied softly. "You're an angel, aren't you?"

The woman smiled at the simple statement. Nia was a very unassuming and observant child. She must have seen when Hola went through the fence. If Hola was honest with herself, Nia had probably spotted her many times. Since Nia was still a child and needed some help, it enabled her to clearly see and hear Hola. Since no one ever interacted with Hola, it was probably safe to assume that Nia thought she wasn't quite human. Nia being a child allowed her to suspend her disbelief much easier than an adult would.

"You could say that," Hola replied with a smile. "Most people wouldn't have gotten it right on their first try." Nia shrugged and turned her head back toward her homework before looking up at her angel once more.

"Is that why I can see you but others can't?" Hola nodded. "Are you here for me?" Hola nodded again. "Why?"

Hola sighed softly before she answered Nia. "Because … it seems you need my help." Nia's expression didn't change and Hola had a feeling the child didn't quite understand the circumstances that brought Hola to her. Hola only barely understood them herself but she knew that it was her own decision to talk to Nia.

"The bullies," Nia stated it so firmly yet forlornly that, in Hola's mind, it had to be a fact. "They've been getting bolder toward me." The angel said nothing and let the little girl talk. Nia probably didn't have anyone to talk to who would truly understand and not pass judgment or tell her what to do outright.

"It's not like I'm not used to it," Nia continued when Hola didn't say anything. "I've been bullied since first grade."

"It doesn't get any easier," Hola said and looked sideways at her young charge. "You just get tougher."

"Is this a test?" Hola looked confused so Nia continued. "My momma says that God tests us sometimes."

"I suppose you could look at it that way." Hola wouldn't get into the intricacies of that particular subject. Nia looked down at her homework once more in despair. Hola sighed and slung her right arm around the girl. "You're doing great," she reassured the ten-year-old. Nia looked skeptical but Hola continued. "You're keeping your grades up and you don't start trouble. That seems pretty good to me."

Nia shrugged. "I guess."

"Talking to yourself?" a snide and uppity voice asked from behind the duo. Nia and Hola looked over their shoulders to see the same group of school children that was circling Nia earlier. The owner of the voice was a thin girl with cornrows and a stature slightly taller than Nia.

Hola raised her eyebrows at the new girl and sniffed dramatically. Although Nia didn't show any obvious signs, Hola could tell the young girl was holding in a smile. Nia said nothing and stood up, putting her homework and writing utensils away. For once, the girl did not look scared or tired. Instead, she looked determined, as if having her angel by her side somehow gave her a boost in strength.

The small group sniggered and laughed at this show of strength but the ring leader, the tall girl, looked a bit intimidated. "Well?" she demanded.

"What do you want, Niki?" Nia asked softly. However, Hola could see the fire in the girl's eyes.

"Easy, Nia," Hola said as she stood behind the young girl, still invisible and non-existent to the bullies. "Don't show them everything in one go."

Niki's nostrils flared and she stepped up to Nia, trying to use her size to intimidate her.

"Remember, you are wider than her," Hola reminded Nia. The girl was definitely stockier than Niki. "Don't let her think she has a size advantage. You have to make her see you as an equal in physical presence." She didn't think Nia understood all of her words, but she probably got the gist of what Hola meant. "Try not to get into a fight; there are too many for that. However, you can start by standing up for yourself. The longer this goes on, the less chance of the teachers and staff ignoring it."

Hola knew the teachers would often turn a blind eye on Nia. The girl was very intelligent and nice and, yet, the staff ignored her. No wonder she was able to see Hola so easily.

Nia did not blink and a staring contest ensued. Hola did not hide her wide, beaming grin as Niki blinked after a few moments. The tall girl looked at the shorter one in shock and stepped back two paces. The other kids looked dumbfounded and started to whisper. Niki, possibly sensing herself losing leadership, once again took charge of the situation.

"You're not even worth the effort, today." The jealous girl snorted and rolled her eyes, but her actions did not have the same bite as they had earlier. "We'll catch you later."

Nia said nothing as the group walked away. She waited until they were closer to the school building before turning back to Hola. "Thanks for being here with me."

Hola smiled at the girl. "That was all you," she said proudly. "Just remember, you are a better person than them, the bigger person. It isn't your job to pursue a fight with them, but it also isn't your job to back down from them either." Nia nodded in determination. "You'll get the hang of it. Have faith." Hola nodded at Nia and turned to walk away.

"Wait, where are you going?" Nia asked in a panic as she followed her savior.

"Don't worry." Hola tuned back to Nia and knelt down to look into the girl's brown eyes. "I'll always be around. Just because you can't see me doesn't mean I'm not there." Hola briefly hugged the girl before she stood up to her full height. "I expect great things from you," Hola continued as she walked backwards. "You just have to believe in yourself."

There was a determination in Nia's eyes and Hola nodded in satisfaction. The angel finally turned disappeared from view. Nia's life would not get much better. In fact, it would get worse before she got a break but Hola knew that if anyone deserved to be happy, then it was definitely Nia. "Good luck, kid."

The Canary
Moira S. Peckham

The cars stopped coming after the first rain of the season. At first, the Tillmans didn't notice. They started their days early and it wasn't unusual for the highway to stay quiet until seven or eight in the morning. But today was different: 10 a.m. rolled around and still not a single vehicle had passed Tillman Farm on its way to the coast. Miranda was the first to notice the uncanny silence when it was abruptly interrupted by a chopper flying low over the valley. It came from the west and when it disappeared over a hill at the far end of the valley, Miranda was struck by how well she could hear the family of towhees that roosted in the king oak by the farmhouse. Just as she was starting to feel uneasy, she spotted her six-year-old brother sprinting out of the house towards her, rain jacket billowing behind him.

"Miranda, did you see it? I've never seen one so low before!" Before Miranda could respond, Billy darted past her towards the highway, trying to get a longer look at the chopper. Miranda rushed after him, lunging to stop him from running out into the road.

"Billy! You have to be more careful! Cars don't stop on this road," she scolded gently.

"I wanted to see the copter," Billy sulked. "Besides, it's not like there are any cars anyway."

It was at this point that Miranda realized why she'd been feeling a creeping sense of unrest since she'd woken up that day. The noise of the highway had faded to nothing. Billy was right: there were no cars.

"Stay there," Miranda commanded, pointing at the shoulder next to the road. Billy obliged and Miranda cautiously stepped out onto the asphalt. It felt wrong, like she was breaking a fundamental rule. She looked both ways out of habit, to the west where the chopper had come from, the coast, and east towards the ridge behind which it had disappeared. Silence.

"Let's go get Dad." Billy nodded and took his sister's hand as they walked back down their driveway.

When Miranda and Billy approached the barn next to the house, they heard the high-pitched buzzing of a chainsaw. It was the most comforting sound Miranda had heard all day. Around the corner, their father, Tomas, was taking apart an oak tree that had fallen over in the storm, cleanly sawing through branch after branch until he could attack the main trunk. When he saw his children, Tomas stopped and took off his visor, wiping the sweat away from his forehead.

"You bring me coffee?" He said with a grin before noticing the looks on his children's faces. "What is it?"

"Dad, have you noticed anything weird about this morning? About how quiet it is?" Miranda probed.

"Not really. I've been under the visor all morning. You think firewood just manifests itself in the stove?"

"Daddy, listen!" Billy cried. "What can you hear?"

Tomas paused, noticing for the first time how silent the morning was.

"Not a single car has driven past this morning," Miranda said. "You know how weird that is for this time of year."

"Not that I'm upset that those inland assholes aren't coming here but you're right. That *is* odd," Tomas mused. "Let's see if the news said anything."

Inside the house, Miranda sat down at the computer to check the news but none of the pages loaded. She checked the router. Everything looked fine.

Tomas felt unease rising in his chest. "I'm going to call around. See if anyone knows anything." He went to pick up the phone and started dialing before he noticed that the line was dead.

"I don't like this," Tomas said. "Let's walk up the road as far as we can go and see if we can figure out what's going on. East." He turned to Billy. "Go get your bike." Billy cheered and went to get his bike from behind the house.

The journey started slowly, as Billy kept racing ahead to look at things and comment on them loudly to his family behind him. To the six-year-old, this was a great adventure. The 41 was forbidden territory and to be able to fly around it on his bike offered a rare taste of freedom. The sound of his laughter cut through the silence of the highway, winding like a river of black ice up into the hills.

When the Tillmans rounded the bend in the road that began the ascent into the hills that bracketed the eastern end of the valley, they heard the faint roar of a helicopter on the wind. Less than a mile further along the highway, they caught the first glimpse of what was blocking their path. Billy saw it first, pedaling faster to get a better look. As they rounded a sharp curve they saw it: a roadblock made of barbed wire and iron, and behind it a pair of tanks and people dressed in green. The helicopter rested between the tanks, its rotor spinning loudly. On top of the steep cliff, they could see what looked like a row of snipers' nests, some still under construction. One of the people in green noticed the family and ran to the helicopter, and it began to ascend once again, away from the barricade and the family.

With that, the chopper flew briskly back towards the coast, over the farms. From this vantage point, Miranda could see that there were groups of people putting what looked like small antennas on the tops of all the hills in the valley.

Tomas eyed the sniper posts above them. "We need to go home. Billy, you can ride down the hill if you promise to stay where I can see you." Billy let out a whoop and took off, following the helicopter back towards the farm.

When the Tillmans arrived back home, the light was fading from the sky, and it had begun to rain. Billy was asleep in Tomas's arms; Miranda put Billy's bike by the front door. She was standing there, staring down the driveway at the 41, when she saw the headlights: a single car pulling into their driveway. She called out to her father and he ran to join her, rifle in his hand, eyes wild.

"Miranda, go in the back." She nodded, backing away from the door as a hulking military hummer ground to a halt in front of their house and a woman about Tomas's age wearing blue coast guard fatigues stepped out and approached him as he stood at the open door, gun cocked.

"My name is Lieutenant Markum. There's no need for that," she gestured towards the rifle trained on her. "I expect you have some questions but for now I think you might want to sit down and just listen." Tomas lowered the gun and stepped back from the door, gesturing inside.

Billy couldn't go back to sleep. His dad and the lady in blue were talking too loudly. Some of the words he understood: safety, need, California, dead, agriculture (he was proud of that one). Then he heard a word he didn't understand that clung to

63

his mind like a spider in a dark corner. He got up and padded down the hall to Miranda's room, where she was sitting on her bed, staring at her feet. She looked up when he came in. Billy approached cautiously and asked:

"Miranda, what's a quarantine?"

Shadowcrest Manor
An Excerpt
Michaela Bishop

July 12, 1801 Charleston, South Carolina

A soft cold breeze flowed throughout the whole house, it carried the scent of the Sea Island cotton and seawater, taking away the smell of dust and stillness. Shadowrest Manor was to become our new home here in Charleston. The manor had been vacant for a while since its last owner had passed away, and leaving no will or surviving heir, the plantation was shut down. The outside was a little bit weather-damaged however, Father is having the whole house repainted a colonial white, the front columns will be a nice off-white to balance the main color. The painters are coming tomorrow to do the whole house inside and out. They are even going to repaint the servants' quarters too.

Some of our servants back in England decided to stay on with us but most were let go. Betsey was our nanny when we were younger and now she is the head maid and she still helps the four of us whenever we need it. Antony is the best cook my family has ever had and he is one of the most understanding people I have ever met. He has always been there for me whenever I needed to talk about my family.

Mother and Father are so excited to open the plantation again and to start a new chapter in our lives. We left London a month ago and I am happy about the move, but this place does not feel like home, yet.

"Rosie, come upstairs and see our new room. I think you will like it," my twin sister Jessamine said from the doorway. "I know you miss London, but this will be good for everyone."

"I know but I cannot help but miss the view from my window."

"Then come upstairs, you might find that you like this new view better."

I turned away from the window and walked with Jessie up to our new room and I fell in love. The room was big enough for the two of us to share, as we have for most of our lives. We each had brought our bed frames and most of our furniture from our old home. Jessamine and I used to have bookshelves in our bedroom but in the new house we have a full library that Father had stocked for my use. I also insisted that we bring a vanity that was made especially for our great-grandmother, it was handcrafted by a suitor of hers when she first entered society. In the corner of the room are a set of double doors that led out onto the wrap around balcony. Mother said that my sisters and I can decorate our side however we wanted, I suggested that we put some tables and chairs out there so we could enjoy the view while we entertain guests or for our own use whenever we want to. From the balcony, I could see the ships coming into port from the far reaches of the world. It reminded me of my old bedroom view. In London, I could see the sun set upon the river Thames, but this view is better.

"Rosalind, Jessamine. Come downstairs, we must go to town to pick up the new drapery for the main rooms and the bedrooms," Mother said as she stood in the doorway. Victoria and Juliette had their own separate rooms and the two of them are more particular about their styles so they always need to be present when new décor was being picked out.

Jessamine and I went along with Mother and our sisters to town. I would have rather been at home reading in the library, however today the library was being re-polished and painted this afternoon. While Mother and my sisters walked into the dress boutique and I stayed outside looking at my new surroundings, a young gentleman walked up to me.

"Good morning, Miss. I have never seen you around here. Have you just arrived in our fair city?" the gentleman asked.

"A good morning to you too. My family and I have moved here quite recently."

"Where did you come from and where are you living?"

"We came from London. We moved into Shadowrest Manor."

"Rosalind, come here," Mother said tersely. "Who is that you are speaking with?"

"A young man I have just met."

"What is your name young man?" Mother said to Daniel.

"I am Daniel Blackwood, Ma'am."

"Have you lived in Charleston long?" Mother asked.

"Born and bred. I would not think of living anywhere else."

"Well, it was nice to meet you. My daughters and I must be going now. Come, girls."

"It was wonderful to meet you, Rosalind. I hope to see you again," Daniel said as he kissed my hand goodbye.

"Goodbye, Daniel."

As we got into the carriage, Mother expressed her happiness at my meeting Daniel.

"He is from the Blackwood's. They are a very prestigious family around here."

"Mother, how did you know that?" Victoria asked.

"When your father and I came here to first see Shadowrest Manor, we met with some of other families and they talked about the Blackwood family. They have been here for generations, they are one of the most influential families around here. However, no one has really seen any of the family except for Daniel."

"That's strange," Juliette stated.

"No, it is not. Some family patriarchs do not like to socialize with other families who are of a lower social status than them." Mother explained.

"I did not like him. He had a weird feeling about him," Jessamine said. "He seemed to attentive to you, Rosie."

"He was being friendly, Jessie. You are so suspicious," Juliette teased. My sister was right, Daniel was being friendly towards the new family who had just moved into town. Jessamine is only being paranoid, she has been nervous since we arrived here about a month ago. She tends to think the worse out of people she does not know. Daniel does seem like a person that we can trust, his green eyes seem trustworthy.

July 15th, 1801

My parents decided to throw a ball at our plantation to show off all the renovations my parents put into the house and they invited many influential families to join us. So, to prepare, I went with some of the servants to *supervise* getting food and supplies. Mother and Father just wanted me out of the house while the rest of the staff was decorating the whole house and I guess I was in the way of some of the servants.

"Miss Rosalind, are you coming?" Betsey asked breaking me from my thoughts of being back at the plantation reading one of my new books.

"Yes, Betsey. Where are we to next?"

"Your mother wants us to go to the butcher and get the best piece of meat we can find."

"Don't you mean Antony?" I asked.

"True, he doesn't trust the butchers here yet. Antony did want to supervise the butcher cutting the meat however he needed to watch the new kitchen servants preparing the beginning courses. I swear, I love that man but he can be the most demanding cook I have ever worked with."

As Betsey and I were laughing about Antony's mannerisms, I spotted Daniel walking towards us.

"Greetings Daniel, how is your day?" As I talked with Daniel, Betsey went on to finish the list of supplies we needed to get.

"Wonderful now that I have found you, Rosalind. What are you doing on this fine day?"

"My family is hosting a ball so I went along with the servants to purchase the supplies. Would you like to attend? I am sure that there is more than enough room for one more person."

"Yes, I would love to attend. When shall I be by?"

"Tomorrow evening at six o'clock. I hope to see you there."

Then I went into the carriage and was taken home. When I arrived, the whole house had been cleaned and my sisters were all upstairs trying on their new dresses for the party.

"Mother, while I was out I saw Daniel and invited him to the party tomorrow night."

"That is wonderful dear, we would love to have him join us. I will just let Gertie know that there will be one more for dinner," Mother said as she walked out of the room. I was relieved that Mother is not mad at me for inviting Daniel at the last minute. I hope everything goes well tomorrow night ....

Overexposure
Avery Cardosi

I wasn't happy. My strawberry gloss smile is stretched from ear to ear like a taut clothespin line, and my eyes are crinkled up in some imitation of a laugh; but I remember that night. I wasn't happy. I hold the photo on my outstretched palms, fingers spread so one doesn't accidently slip and leave an oily ripple of me across its still-water surface. On the backside, someone with alcohol infused handwriting had scribbled "Pregame!!!!" When I first saw it, I remember desperately wanting to White-Out the messy caption, to bury the four exclamation points beneath layers of chaste liquid latex. I thought the inscription only seemed to accentuate the juvenility of the image it accompanied, like a little girl covered in her mother's burgundy lipstick and pearls. What I don't remember was when I forgot that the writing was there at all. How could I remember when the photo had found a permanent home in the deepest drawer of my desk? It had lain undisturbed on an old class syllabus and the carcasses of a few unfortunate grass bugs until my Eureka in search of a functioning pen.

I remember the scene it captured, it wasn't taken long ago. Five months, maybe six, the blurry time shoved uncomfortably between Thanksgiving and Christmas. Lucky for us four, our SoCal winters brought sunscreen instead of snow, so we could still squeeze into shorts and Brandy Melville crop tops for frat parties without looking too desperate. From under a protective layer of Sienna #5 my pixel counterpart stared up at me, face squished beside the dark forest of Lara's hair, Ale's bangle covered arms, and Maddie's ever reddening cheeks. Maddie could only have been a glass or two of Moscato into the night because her skin was still a shade between rosy and flushed. I remember two minutes after the shutter snapped closed Maddie sat down in a kitchen chair with her fourth glass of wine still half full and cried. She sputtered ugly, exposed sobs and swayed back and forth as she struggled to stay afloat in the flood of salt and booze. She missed Max, she said. She cried because he was a missing limb that she kept trying to use after a dirty amputation, one that left thick scar tissue to build and numb the site where he used to be. She said tonight was the night she was going to find a new boy, or at least a tourniquet to stop the bleeding. She needed a pair of new lips to be the anesthesia she never got. We tried to comfort her, but Maddie had burst her stitches before she could even leave the waiting room. We left her slumped on the couch with quiet condolences in her ears and mascara smeared under her eyes. We tried to be quiet when we shut the front door.

I remember telling Lara I felt bad about leaving Maddie, and she said something sympathetic under the weight of the vodka she chased with apple juice and her half-closed eyes. I didn't hear what Lara said, but I understood. She couldn't afford to miss this party. Lara needed a boy too, but she needed one who would stick around after the blanket covered explorations where through, where she crossed canyons and summited mountains I had never seen. She needed a boy who wouldn't just take what he wanted and creep out before the sun had a chance to see them in the same bed. I remember after the click of the camera she smiled her brightest and laughed her loudest and did everything you are supposed to do to get a stumbling somebody to drape his arm around you and ask if you're having a good time. She stayed by his side the whole night, drinking and dancing with me and Ale from all the way across the room. I didn't see him leave the next morning, but I heard the creaks of regret on the stairs and the slam of finality that always comes with a closing door. I pretended I couldn't hear Lara's tears when she woke up beside the indent of another mistake.

Ale didn't have to ignore her quiet sobs, because she hadn't heard anything over the sound of her own midnight sins. Ale never went to parties looking for a somebody, just a warm body. She kissed them with all the passion worthy of a silver screen and couldn't care less. She was a good-times girl in all her glory, which meant she needed to forget the skeletons that had followed her out of the closet. She carried a bottle of buffer wherever she went, she poured me my first shot of Grey Goose paint stripper and told me to "drink up and catch up," she needed someone to dance with. She moved with the ease of a gin and tonic and locked eyes with every pretty girl in the room. Three hours after the Polaroid developed she was clawing at her own throat, looking for a way to quell her body's rebellion. I remember trying to hold her long bangs out of her face as she was filled and emptied over and over with weekend mistakes and too much of a good thing. I crouched beside her on the cold plastic floor of the real world and told her to press her fingers to the side of her throat, so she wouldn't scratch her insides with her nails as she pumped her own stomach.

I wish I didn't know to do that, but before Maddie and Lara and Ale had yelled up the stairs for me to come down and make memories we could pin on our walls, I was googling how many calories there were in one shot, two shots, three shots. I had saved up my allowance all week for tonight, because I knew sometimes drunk me forgot that she looked best dressed in hunger pains. But just in case she did forget, I had an undo button at the back of my throat that could control-alt-delete some of the glitches in my self-control. I spent most of the party on the stairs alone because dancing made my stomach move to all the wrong beats. I remember feeling simply too big to exist, and I promised for the hundredth time that I would never let myself feel full until there was less of me.

I wasn't happy then, and I wasn't happy in the snapshots of any weekend night I shoved into the crypt of my desk without so much as a departing prayer. Maybe none of us were happy when the flash went off and we gritted our teeth into big girl smiles, but it made a very pretty picture.

Wives
Leah Francesca Christianson

The men in my husband's family yelled. When we visited San Luis Obispo for the holidays, the house would already be wheezing, struggling to contain excess air and sound. On our drive up from Los Angeles, I'd be lulled into calmness by the dancing trees, the unassuming air, the light applied with a cotton ball. We would pull up to the house, and the shouts would be leaking out into the street.

The yells differed depending on the time of day. In the morning, men were dogs, barking and scratching at each other. A light sleeper at best, I'd jerk awake before six to different strains of conversation—even a cup of coffee couldn't be offered at a volume appropriate for humans. As the day geared up, so did they, volumes rising with the sun. By midday, their voices held chainsaws. At night, they became engines needing oil. Polishers on rough surfaces. Gears irreparably jammed.

Harry did not yell. He was a silent bear lumbering through the family zoo, patting people on the back and completing unsung tasks, like replacing toilet paper and mincing garlic. Mostly though, our daughter kept him occupied with her games and pretending. Despite only seeing his family a few times a year, Harry preferred playing with Bryn to hee-hawing with his brothers and uncles. I loved him for that.

Sometimes, I'd wake in the middle of the night to him standing at the window. When he noticed my alertness, he pointed at the ceiling, then at the walls, loosening a mischievous smile. I took this to mean he was reveling in the quiet; breathing in air that wasn't polluted with hot breath. But when I asked what he was thinking, the playfulness faded away. Silent answers must have lurked within him, but when I failed at guessing the question, he retreated to a place I was not invited.

Born and raised in Colorado, Harry's mother declared an intolerance for shoveling her driveway once she turned sixty. She bought the house without seeing it in person. This turned out to be an auspicious gamble, and her lottery home became the gathering point for the entire family. Some may find it strange that a single woman could transfer a family's traditions to a new place. Those people have not met Jill.

During our last visit, Jill sat me down. Harry had left twenty minutes before to take Bryn to wade in tide pools. I realized, as more men filed into rank, that I was under siege.

"Sherry, we need to talk," Jill began, speaking slowly.

"We're worried about Harry," barked Uncle Rick.

"Why?" I asked. When this unleashed a chorus of sputters, I gleaned that they thought the answer was obvious.

"He doesn't talk! He barely speaks anymore!" This cry came from Harry's brother, Manuel. Manuel was a pear-shaped man with the habit of popping his hip while standing, giving him an unmistakably feminine stance. He was the only one who seemed aware of his family's volume, making an effort not only to lower his voice but to actually ask me questions with it. He would call me Sherry Pie after some wine.

"What do you mean, 'he doesn't talk anymore'?" I asked, hurt that Manuel was ignoring our former camaraderie.

"I find it hard to believe that you haven't noticed," said Jill. "My son. Doesn't speak. Anymore."

"That's ridiculous!" Cloudy with confusion, I could not come up with a better retort. "I don't even know what you mean. Of course, he still speaks. As much as he always has."

The toolshed erupted. Perturbed, I headed for the balcony, slamming the door behind me. In the distance, I could see a stripe of ocean. Somewhere near it, my husband and daughter played in shallow water, hopping around crustaceans and letting their fingers grow wrinkled from salt. But from where I stood, the water didn't move at all. I took solace in that.

Jill approached. We both waited.

"We're just concerned," she said.

"Because he's what? Quieter?"

"It's more than that," said Jill, swiveling towards me.

"What are you implying?" I asked. Although my marriage was creeping up on the five-year mark, I never outgrew my fear of Jill. She was an intense woman with a gray stare and a German pallor that, despite years on the West Coast, had not darkened a shade.

"You know perfectly well," she said, letting the words fall from her gash of a mouth.

Years after Harry and I divorced and Bryn began dividing her parental time between weeks and ends, she still spoke wistfully of the tide pools at Grammy Jill's house. With our custody agreement dictating shared holidays, I'd claimed Christmas early on, thinking I was saving Bryn from the holiday squawk.

After Harry remarried, she protested more.

"Didn't you love how … together it all felt?"

"What do you mean, 'together'?"

Bryn—five when we split, nine at present moment—didn't have the words to explain what she meant. But I understood. She missed the synchronized howling, the churn and scrape of a day with Harry's family. Her family.

"You liked that?"

"You didn't?"

Thinking she was kidding, I told Bryn I was saving her from premature deafness. This did not go over well.

"It's not fair," Bryn began to wail. "Everyone else gets to go. We don't even do anything."

Something heavy dropped from my throat to my knees. Rather than fight her— Bryn drew her temper from a bottomless well—I called Harry.

"I mean, sure," he said, tinted with surprise. "We'd love it. But. Is this what you want?"

It wasn't about what I wanted, I reminded him, trying to keep martyrdom out of my voice. As Bryn and I wound our way up the coast, the trees scratched their heads, wondering what I was doing in territory I'd surrendered.

We heard the ruckus before Jill's house slid into view. Bryn hopped out of the car before I parked. The family was strewn about, seated on the lawn or meandering around the balcony, grilling and fishing drinks out of sweaty coolers. Greetings sang out. Harry's new wife stood as I walked up, her dark hair glinting red in the sun. Bryn hugged her first.

"Come in for a bit," Harry said with a shine I did not recognize. I wanted to refuse but could think of no good reason.

We migrated to the balcony. Together, the men roared. Harry sang along, slapping backs and wrapping his arms around his brothers. His clothes and haircut had not changed, yet he seemed an entirely different person. Harry's new wife joined in too. She had a baked-in grin, eyes permanently crinkled into mischief. Jill radiated with quiet joy.

"Sherry Pie," Manuel smiled, friendliness returned. "Have a drink."

While I sipped, I saw Harry whisper something in his wife's ear. She laughed loudly, then chewed her lips shut. She placed her hand upon her cheek, blocking her mouth from even the most skilled lip reader. Harry's ears reddened and he nuzzled into her neck. It felt intrusive to watch but I couldn't look away.

I left soon after.

As Jill's house shrunk in my rear-view mirror, I allowed myself one last float through that life, pausing at the table where Bryn spilled an entire bottle of maple syrup, the sand permanently stuck between floorboards, the trees that bent backwards, the pottery from Monterey holding homegrown persimmons. The noise that flickered until it burned out.

Here for You
An Excerpt
Trish Caragan

Prom is supposed to be a time where couples dance—which, at a moment like this, hasn't been something I dwelled on—or hang out and jump along with their friends, hip hop music blaring from the speakers. The choice of music is something I can write a checkmark next to. Everything else, well, gets a strikethrough because they're not going to happen. Gwen and Elizabeth have dates. Never have I ever thought that I'd go to prom with my sister. My friends told me that I shouldn't be surprised that I'm going with Natalie, especially since we used to be so close. Really, I think I'm more surprised that Natalie's the one I'm hanging out with at prom.

And I still remember the night at the beach. Of all the people who'd even know that I was there, it was Natalie. I'm surprised but not surprised at all.

Gwen rests her head on her prom date's shoulder while Elizabeth interlocks her arm into her date's own. I just walk beside Natalie. Maybe this moment would've been more fun if Natalie were more open to trending, contemporary music, but I still try to make the most of it. After all, she ... saved me last night.

As we scrunch our way into the crowd, we begin to bounce along with everybody else. Although the rap song bleeds my ears, and the bobbing bodies around me crush me, I continue shaking my body around. Every couple shimmies too close to me, squeezing and suffocating me. One of my classmates bumps his shoulder against mine. When he turns around, he apologizes, but for something that doesn't have to do with bumping into me.

"Sorry about what happened with Joel," he says.

I stand there, mouth opened but words unreleased. I should thank him, but for some reason, I can't. It seems like everybody has heard him because a bunch of people turn to me, looking at me as if I've been slapped for no good reason. Some even walk up to me and share their condolences.

"I can tell he really loved you," one girl says.

"I'm sorry about your loss," another girl says.

"You meant a lot to him," a boy, someone who I recognize as one of the boys Joel used to hang out with during one of the classes we didn't have together, tells me.

Others place their hand on my shoulders, telling me sorry. Some hug me. I hug them back, only to restrain myself from pushing them away and telling them to please, please stop apologizing. I don't deserve to hear "sorry."

In this crowd of swaying bodies, I'm the only one who's not moving.

"Are you okay?" Natalie asks me. She's also, to my surprise, bobbing along to the music that she always complains about. Must be her attempt to have fun. All for me.

I don't look at her or say anything. Instead I run away. Natalie calls my name, but I don't bother to turn back. I know if I do, I'll want to run back to her or even Gwen or Elizabeth. In the darkness, I crash against some chairs, almost falling down. I find a bathroom, thrust the door open, and then search for an open stall. None are available.

My hands curl into a fist. I want to bang on each stall door and beg everyone to please get out because I'm about to cry, and I'm already as weak as it is. But I don't want to irritate anyone. I already irritate myself. Nobody wants to see the awful person that I am.

Don't cry, Erika. You'll just drag everyone's attention towards you.

When a girl leaves the sink, I walk towards it and lean my head back, making sure no tears leak out of my eyes. I take out my eyeliner and darken thick lines underneath my eyes. At the corner I shade a wing-tip, pressing my eyeliner pencil until black liquid soaks onto my skin. I stare at the time on my phone: 9:48 p.m. Just an hour and twelve minutes before this stupid night is over. Maybe after tonight the apologies will disappear. Hopefully. I glance back at the bathroom door and watch girls enter into bathroom. My hopes rise when I see girls with blonde hair, only for them to vanish when I realize they're not my sister. Even though Natalie and I don't have the same relationship anymore—which makes me sadder than hearing all these condolences—I still hope she finds me.

Rocky
An Excerpt
Renee Bulda

I am Rocky. Yesterday I was Jean-Paul, but today I am Rocky. Or at least, that's what I told the pretty coffee shop barista when she asked for my name.

I fingered the little tins of mints at the front of the counter while she wrote my order on the cup. She had big, loopy handwriting that was almost unreadable.

"You want one of those?" She said, gesturing slightly at the mints with her sharpie. She was trying to catch my eye.

"No, thanks." I looked anywhere but at her.

"So that's one grande Americano, two pumps of hazelnut, room for cream?" She finished the question expectantly, sharpie poised over the cup. I nodded, darting my gaze up to her face, then back at her hands. There was a tarnished silver ring on her right thumb, emblazoned with an upside-down star. Or right side up, whichever way you looked at it. I tried to concentrate on that star, but it didn't matter. My eyes only met hers for half a moment, but half a moment was all it took. Her eyes flashed and six numbers entered my head. *05-24-2022*. It would probably be an accident. A car crash. A stupid stunt at a party. She was only eighteen or nineteen.

"Here's your change, would you like your receipt?"

I took the change and answered with, "All things written must come to pass." I smiled slightly at her confused look and walked away, taking a seat on one of the chairs to wait for my coffee. The cushion sunk under my weight, thin enough for me to feel the frame of the chair beneath me. The arms were faux leather, and cracked from countless hands resting on them every day, every week. I thought about all those people. I thought about their numbers. There are so many numbers in my head, it's a wonder they don't spill out of my mouth when I open it. I stroked one armrest, the ridges of my palms catching on the cracks. The middle-aged woman in the chair next to me watched my hand for a few moments before shifting her weight away and looking in another direction.

". . . Rocky?"

I stood, took my coffee with a small smile and walked out, the bell above the door singing farewell. The streets were crowded, the sky white, the air crisp with early morning. Men and women dressed for work dragged briefcases and attachés behind them. A few truant teens wandered the streets, loving their freedom. I used to play hooky, too. I couldn't stand knowing the numbers of my classmates, my friends. Better not to have friends. Better to wander. Better to find a new city every week, a new name every other day. Then I wouldn't grow attached, wouldn't try to fix it or prevent it. In the past I tried to help. All I ever got from that was cold shoulders and questions about my sanity.

A family standing by the window of a toy shop caught my eye. They were probably doing some Christmas window the shopping, the parents finding out what their children wanted most. The boy was gesturing wildly as his parents laughed at his excitement. I caught the boy's eye as I passed. He looked about seven years old, the same age I was when I realized what I could do. Numbers flashed in my head. I smiled. He would have a long life.

A homeless man stepped in front of me, asking for spare change. I ignored his pleas. He persisted until the light turned and I stepped onto the street, lost in the throng of people, head bowed, eyes downcast, counting the cracks in the sidewalk. I headed for the shabby motel where I was staying this week. Cockroach infested, water stained walls, and faded curtains that did nothing to keep the light out. It had been my home for the past three years. Not that motel, but that room, in dozens of different motels. When the location changed, at least the familiarity didn't.

I set my coffee on the shaky wooden table. It was the only piece of furniture besides the couch. I went into the bathroom and set my hands on the sides of the yellowed sink and leaned forward toward the mirror, so close my nose was almost touching the glass.

An old man stared back at me. He was, in fact, much younger than he looked. Gaunt and hollow. The corners of his mouth pulled at a steep angle towards the ground. There were permanent creases on his forehead, and between his thick brows. His eyes sunk deep into their sockets, trying to hide from what they could see. They were blue and dull.

And no matter how I hard I tried, or how long I looked, they never flashed back at me. No numbers attached to my face. I wasn't even sure I wanted to know them.

Then it wasn't my eyes I was seeing, but my mother's, which had been a much brighter blue than mine. I started remembering everything about her. Gloriously sharp cheekbones and elegant hands that were always moving, doing something. Her nose had been longer, her face a bit narrower, but there was no mistaking her beauty.

I had a sudden need to call the place I left behind, to check in, even though I no longer called it home.

I didn't own a phone. I had to rush out of the motel and down the street to the nearest payphone. I pushed the change from my morning coffee through the slot and punched the keys. The phone rang. And rang. And rang.

"Damn," I cursed, just as the voicemail picked up. I had forgotten about the time difference. It was the middle of the day where they were. With everyone at work or school, no one was going to pick up the phone. I slammed the phone into its cradle, the plastic almost cracking.

My coffee was cold by the time I got back. I dumped it out the window.

It's becoming tougher to live like this. Even though it's familiar, even though I could do it for the rest of my life, it gets harder and harder to live without purpose, without a plan. All I know is run and hide, close my eyes and pretend I'm not cursed. I keep wishing that there is a reason why I can do what I do, some special destiny I have to fulfill. Or rather, I wish there was some way to save them.

But that didn't work the last time. I couldn't save my mother. Why would it work now?

Someone was cursing from the street below. My abandoned coffee must have found a head to land on. I just shut the window.

It seemed unusually crowded on the streets this morning. I kept bumping shoulders with everyone, and had my toes stepped on more than a few times with less than a few sorry's.

A girl bumped into me, hard enough to make her stumble.

"Sorry," I said, reaching out a hand to steady her. She shied away, sparing me a heavy look, her eyes flashing, before speeding in the opposite direction, moving so

76

fast she was almost running. I found four numbers floating in my head. Not six, four. Not a date, but a time.

I followed. It took a second to find her, then I caught a glimpse of a plaid skirt bouncing around a corner. From the back, she looked like an ordinary schoolgirl. Long brown hair, knee-high socks, dark blue blazer. But at this moment she wasn't very ordinary. Today, she was going to die.

She glanced over her shoulder, eyes skimming through the crowd behind her. When she saw me, they widened, her hands clenched into fists, and she took off.

"Come on!" I started sprinting. It was easy enough to follow her now, she left a pathway of confused city folk in her wake.

Red Velvet
Dani Neiley

Nothing as bewildering had happened before at Bluebird Bakery. The cinnamon roll recipe, written on a notecard in Bessie Bluebird's own hand, had been passed on since the 1900s; it even survived the infamous kitchen fire of '72, safely nestled among the ashes, only the edges singed, but now it was missing. And how? Olive prided herself on her neurotic organization of the bakery's recipes—numbered and color-coded in pastels, according to type of treat and caloric count, for the customers watching their weight—yet she felt nothing but shame sitting on the tile floor of the back room. Surrounded by a circle of recipe cards, none of which contained the steps to make the bakery's highly-celebrated cinnamon roll, Olive began to cry.

"Don't cry," Linus said, pushing his glasses back up his nose. What he lacked in the emotional department, he made up for with his culinary prowess. Olive had loved him ever since that first day at culinary school, when they were taught how to make pear tarts and Linus made crème brûlée instead, because tarts were too "easy." Still, Olive couldn't help but feel her sense of hope slipping through her fingers with the same ease Linus had as he snapped bars of baking chocolate into quarters. Today's special: triple threat chocolate cake.

"Cinnamon rolls or not, I suppose the show must go on," Olive said, wiping her tears with floury hands. Linus kissed her cheek and put a piece of the chocolate in her mouth.

It would only be a matter of time before a customer asked for a cinnamon roll. For the first time in her life, Olive dreaded the sound of the silver bell dangling on the edge of the bakery's front door. She eyed the empty tray in the front display case and sighed. Linus appeared through the swinging kitchen doors, startling her out of her thoughts.

"I'm sure Bethany will understand," he said, placing the finished chocolate cake on the stand next to the cash register. "Recipe cards aren't bulletproof, you know."

Olive put the glass case over top of the cake and admired his handiwork. Linus added a special touch this time—miniature chocolate chips lining the edge of the cake. It looked too good to be true, glistening in its display.

"My mother *never* understands," Olive said. "Besides, before the recipe was hers, it was her grandmother's, and her great-grandmother's before that. Great-Grandmother Bessie would be rolling over in her grave if she knew that I'd lost it." Olive put her chin in her hands. "Can I have a piece of the cake, for my troubles?"

"Ooh, could I have a piece of that cake as well?" The first customer of the day had arrived, an old lady in a pastel jumpsuit with graying hair. Linus patted Olive on the shoulder and disappeared back into the kitchen.

"Certainly," Olive said, attempting a pleasant expression.

"And could I have one of your famous cinnamon rolls?"

"Oh," Olive said, starting to sweat, "I'm afraid we're—our—our ovens are broken."

She imagined Linus at the dinner table that night, teasing her about her inability to keep calm under pressure. *The ovens are broken*, he'd squeak, in a singsong voice. Olive swallowed.

"That's alright, dear! I'll take one of your cupcakes instead. If you want to know the truth, your cupcakes may be more delicious than the cinnamon rolls!"

"You think so?" Olive asked, reaching into the case for a lemonade cupcake iced with a thin raspberry glaze. The woman nodded, smiling as she exchanged her money. Olive, pleasantly surprised by the woman's kindness, felt the spark of an idea. She had been talking for months about inventing The Perfect Cupcake, a Mona Lisa of cupcakes that would make people flock from all over town to come try it.

"This is terrible pillow talk," is all Linus said on the matter. But now, with the cinnamon roll recipe missing in action, perhaps this was the perfect time for a new cupcake.

As a pot of spaghetti simmered on the stove that night, Olive asked Linus the million-dollar question:

"What about The Perfect Cupcake?"

"This again?" Linus asked, pouring himself more wine.

"Think about it. With the cinnamon roll recipe gone, we'll have more time to bake something else in the morning."

"That's true," Linus said, placing a tomato on the chopping block. "This could finally be your chance to set out on your own, like you've said. Why stick to the same recipes Bluebird has used for one hundred years?"

"Because they're good. They're guaranteed to sell."

"Yes, but you're better," Linus said.

"You always say that," Olive said, but she smiled all the same.

On Sunday it rained, which was never good for business. People flocked to coffee shops in the rain, and Bluebird Bakery didn't serve any drinks besides complimentary water flavored with a few strawberries. Olive and Linus stayed home in their tiny apartment kitchen, working on The Perfect Cupcake. Linus thought of butterscotch, dark chocolate cayenne, and pecan praline. Olive thought a simplistic flavor would sell better: carrot cake, classic white, or spice. They decided on carrot cake and soon the counters were messy with mixing bowls, eggshells, and spilled flour.

Olive paced in front of the oven and barely waited for one of the cakes to cool before popping it in her mouth. After two chews, she spat the gob of cake into a napkin.

"Oh dear," Olive said, spitting into the sink.

Linus took a bite and went through the same motion.

"Oh," he said. "The old salt in the sugar shaker phenomenon. I told you I needed new glasses."

They laughed together, even though Olive didn't really feel like it.

Olive doodled on napkins as she sat at the register on Monday, thinking of impossible flavors: coconut lemon cream, cherry berry pie, and peanut butter and jelly. She swept the entire store, looking for the four-by-six-inch piece of cardstock with the cinnamon roll recipe, but it was nowhere to be found. Would it be possible to put up lost posters on telephone poles? *Missing: one family recipe, passed down for two generations. Last seen: unsure.*

"Excuse me," a middle-aged woman said, interrupting Olive's train of thought. She peered at Olive from under the brim of a giant sunhat. "Do you have red velvet cake?"

Red velvet? Bluebird had brownies in the shape of hearts, peppermint meringues, apple turnovers sprinkled with cinnamon and sugar, chocolate éclairs, strawberry tarts and two different kinds of cannoli, but no red velvet in sight. Now that was an idea. Bethany had lost Bessie's red velvet recipe card, and Bluebird hadn't stocked red velvet anything for upwards of forty years. Well, that could certainly change. Olive smiled.

As Olive slid a tray of red velvet cupcakes into the empty space reserved for cinnamon rolls, she felt Linus's hand on her shoulder.

"How are you feeling?"

"Nervous. It's worse than a tasting at a blue ribbon competition."

"Don't worry," Linus said, kissing her cheek and disappearing back into the kitchen before Olive could even blink. "I tasted them myself. That ribbon is yours for sure!"

Olive laughed as she flipped the sign on the door to read, "The chef is in!" As she put a pen to a note card to record her own red velvet recipe, she imagined Bessie would appreciate her resourcefulness. *Red velvet*, Olive began, as the bell on the edge of the shop door jingled.

Crevice
Ladycsapp

The sun stretched higher in the sky as the day approached half past nine. More people and their pets began to gather in the park. I stood and contemplated in front of the pond for about fifteen minutes and continued along the path. Up ahead a young couple was walking in my direction. The man had his arms wrapped around his partner as the breeze seemed to pick up through the leaves of the trees. A wave of sadness struck me as I watched them pass by. I imagined me and my wife linking arms walking along the path of the park when it snowed. I was all I had.

There was a secluded area of the park where willows and pine trees hung over a larger pond and swans swam. I sat on a bench in the shade which was facing the pond. The area smelled of refreshing, damp pine needles and mud. I had never been to that area of the park. Shadow patterns from the leaves of the willows were imprinted into the ground. I looked at my watch and it was almost 10:20 a.m. and this would conclude my walk. Then suddenly there was a faint tapping noise which was getting louder. The noise interrupted his thoughts. There was a slim, tall middle-aged woman wearing a white puff coat and a white beret. She wore black shades and walked with a guide stick. She was nice to the face, but shrugged off the thought. The white she wore was blinding me. She was headed for the bench. I wanted to sit alone. So I grabbed my cane about to leave.

"Hey, wait, don't leave," said the woman wearing the white beret.

"I have to head home now," I said while glancing at my watch.

"No, hold on, I want your company," she said.

"You want my company," I asked.

"Yes, unless there is another person with you," she said.

The woman reached her arm towards me. I assumed that she was trying to shake my hand but couldn't find it. We shook hands.

"Hi, I'm Charlene," she said.

"Hi . . . I'm Frank," I muttered.

"Nobody else with you?" she asked.

"No."

"Okay."

We both sat on the bench together in silence for a few seconds.

"So, what brings you to my spot in the park," she asked.

"I just happened to come across it," I answered.

I wondered how the blind woman was able to know what spot in the park to go to since she wasn't able to see.

"You are probably wondering how a blind woman is able to find what specific part of the park she enjoys," Charlene questioned and chuckled. I furrowed my brows and gave her a side eye. She deeply inhaled and smiled.

"You smell that, the scent of pine trees that is how … this is the only portion of the park that has pine trees," she exclaimed.

"Oh."

"You see, blind people have a strong sense of taste, smell, and touch," Jones said. She reached out to touch Frank's hand.

"Please, don't touch me."

"Sorry."

They sat in silence once more for a few seconds. The splashing from the ducks in the pond broke the silence.

"I come to this park every Sunday . . ." I said hesitantly.

"You do? Me too, me and my late husband used to come here . . . it was a Sunday ritual," she added.

"Oh, I'm sorry to hear, yeah, me and spouse too . . . she passed away about seven years ago," I said.

"Sorry, to hear about that too . . . if you don't mind me asking from what," she asked.

"Cancer."

"Wow, sorry about that."

"Yours?"

"A car accident ten years ago."

There was silence once more. The shadow of the trees hung over our faces.

"That's life people come and go, right . . . we just have to enjoy it while we still can." We have something in common, she said.

"I'm not sure if I am able to fully enjoy it anymore . . . since she passed away . . . she was what made life so beautiful." I said. I suddenly felt warmth within me, it was if I could tell this everything. I was doing most of the telling and she was asking the questions. She took the lead. She reminded me of my wife.

"I understand, it's difficult when you lose a loved one, especially your soulmate, but I assure you that there is still more to life that you still have left to experience," she said.

"I guess you're right, but I'm just not sure, we used to do a lot of marvelous things together when she was still alive," I said.

"Why do those marvelous things have to stop," Charlene asked.

Her eyelashes fluttered behind her shades and her faded pink lips formed a grin.

"Because life isn't the same without her here," I said.

"Yeah, it may not be. What you have been doing most of the time since she has been gone, she pryingly asked.

"Markets. Going for walks here at the park, but only up the playground, then I turn around and head home, same thing all the time," I said.

"So you are saying that you never walked to this spot of the park before?" "Yes," I answered.

"Frank that's doing something different," Charlene said.

She took off her shades and stared at me with her glossy hazel eyes. It was as if she was staring into my soul, but I knew she wasn't.

"You're right," I answered.

"I know that," she said with assurance.

She nodded and we sat in silence once more.

A Plain Room
An Excerpt
Kendra Sitton

Once there were four bare walls, a floor with a multi-colored rug, and a bed with a brass-knobbed frame. The only way in and out was a six-paneled wooden door with a gold knob which was altogether forgettable.

And inside the room was a girl. Really, she was a woman now, but she never remembered to call herself that. She lived a quiet existence inside the plain room. She looked at the patterns on the rug which shifted with magical meaning. She thought with an imagination bigger than where she lived. And occasionally, she had a visitor. And so she was hospitable and kind. But no matter how well she knew them, she never let them touch the bed. Sure, she could tell them about it and they could look at it, but she never wanted them near it. She was terrified they would experience what she had.

You see, each night a trail of monsters got around the bed. It could just have been a nightmare, but the scratches on her arm, the torn bed sheets, the goo curling through her toes, were very real indeed. All her life they came to greet her, to watch her as she slept.

Until one night in a groggy state, she woke to scratch her nose. She ignored the monsters with gray and green and black eyes blinking at her, to move her finger next to her nose where it was quite itchy. But when she approached her face, a whisker got in her way, and when she touched her face, fur met her. She yelped. Patting her face. There was no mirror to examine it, but she was convinced there was a change. She fought screams tearing from her stomach like an avalanche.

There was a hum and purr and growl from the watching monsters. She was terrified and she covered her eyes. Then she realized her hands, not just her face, were transformed. She pulled them back to stare at claws reaching from her once-normal fingers. She screamed then, a hoarse and throaty cry. She spread out on the bed so as not to touch any weapon with the other and screamed until her lungs gasped for oxygen, with the monsters watching by.

This transformation did not happen every night, but it happened often enough the nights she stayed human were a relief, even a joy, but they were not typical. They were so unusual she stopped waking up to check whether her nails were claws and her nose sprouted whiskers. She decided to try to sleep through the night in an effort to make it go away faster., even when the itchiness made her shred the bed in aching twists and turns.

Who would want to visit the girl in the crowded and lonely room?

Well, one day a boy did. Really, he fancied himself a man, but the girl wasn't too sure. She was sad, and let him in quickly after he knocked. Only a few feet in though, to be safe. And when he tried to look at the bed she blocked his view. She was frightened, but she liked him. The next week, they met again. This time, all her friends were over to give an assessment. They teased her and asked when she was planning the wedding.

This was too much, and she almost pushed him outright then so they would stop paying attention to her. But he was persistent and kind. She let him come in the room again and again, but never of course the bed. He looked at her with eyes so wide they could scoop her up.

Normally at this point in the story they would begin to fall in love. And he thought he loved her, but she knew the truth: he loved the human part of her, but what about the monster? Wasn't the monster her too? It would have been fair for her to show him the beast she became and let him decide whether to stay. But she really liked him, and couldn't bear him to be as disgusted with herself as she was. There was no way to move forward without showing him the bed. She liked him on the rug though, on the edges, and in her door frame. Nowhere else.

So, she did the only thing she thought she could do. She kicked him out. She told him not to come back. He asked if they could be friends. She said no.

He listened to her, and left. She tried to pretend he was a monster, but she couldn't do even that. She tried to pretend she was all monster and would have hurt him, but she knew that wasn't true.

She hoped he would leave on an awfully big adventure. There were other interesting places to go. And I don't just mean houses and mansions bigger than the plain room. There were castles and igloos and tree houses to visit. One of her friends slept in a tent and moved to a new place each night. There were wild and wonderful ways to live without her.

He stayed nearby, never daring to touch the door. Soon, she took to sleeping against the door. She could hear him weeping outside and it made her feel close. She never made a sound.

In her big imagination, she dreamed of them laying on the bed together. He was calm and kept her calm, while the monsters crowded around. And still looked at her with saucer eyes when she joined them. She wanted someone with her as she told the monsters she didn't want to scare little kids or stare at people while they slept. To remind her she was not one of them.

Some days, she wanted to tear open the door and pull him inside, to talk and laugh and hug like they used to. But she knew if the bed ever came up, she would have to kick him out then and there. Her friends told her it would be cruel to constantly let him in and out, in then out. Her mind agreed, but at night her heart would weigh down inside her, trying to get her to reach for the door and let him in once again.

Eventually, he did go on an adventure. Now the girl could weep without him hearing her, but the tears dried up. Most night she went back to the bed to sleep, but sometimes she opened the door to look for him. She imagined him touring an ice cave or returning to the home of his mother. A smile touches her lips (when they are there) and she thinks of him.

She doesn't know if he misses her.

Finally, she breaks a wall in the room and builds a small window. She peers through it often. She looks for him, but she also thinks of the new people she sees and wonders what they are like. She hopes he finds someone to fight monsters with, the same hope she has for herself.

The next time someone knocks on the forgettable door, she will open it. Maybe it will be the boy, maybe it won't.

Outsides Match the Insides
Rebecca E Van Horn

I don't know if anyone will ever read what I'm writing, since it's tucked away on this random blog I made, way far away in the outer reaches of the Internet. It's like I've sent a message to deep space, hoping someone will see it (but making sure no one does).

I have a *Picture of Dorian Gray* situation going on here (which I read in my Lit class—the one I got a middling C in, because my lame ass teacher is a repressed biddy). *Oh god*, even having *that* uncharitable thought about Miss Clemens has opened up that old sore on the inner wrist of my left arm—which makes typing this confessional a real bitch. I *think* that's what it's called. I need to get these thoughts out of my head and away from me. But I have no one who would believe me, because I don't know anyone who believes in the occult or in curses—let alone heavenly retribution. *I* don't even believe in that shit.

I don't know why I got this particular affliction. Or how. Maybe it's hereditary? My dad is a total douche, an unethical asshole who screws people out of their business contracts for a living. Maybe the consequences for his bad behavior have skipped him and shown up on me? The "sins of our fathers," and all that. Maybe I can hold this over his head in some way? Like, I could confront him in his home office and angrily roll up the sleeve of my shirt to show him the ropes of flesh that have knotted themselves up the length of my forearm. That *should* fill him with unspeakable, soul-twisting guilt. He *should* slump in agony into his glorified, custom-made La-Z-Boy (that probably cost the gross national profit of Nicaragua) and gulp twelve-year-old scotch as he stares into the darkness. He *should* be afraid that the rot that started within him so long ago has manifested in the physical badges that his son carries around. Fat chance! We're talking about a man who unsuccessfully lobbied to have the local soup kitchen closed down, demolished, and turned into a parking garage, because there wasn't enough parking downtown.

It all started with nothing special, an everyday occurrence that usually wouldn't have bothered me at all: I lied to a clueless substitute teacher so I could get out of class. That night, I noticed a thin white length of scar tissue on my neck and wondered if I had gotten it from that cheap necklace I had stolen from the mall. I stopped noticing the slight pain it caused after about a week, and it faded away.

After that, the scars got larger and stayed longer. One afternoon, I told that anorexic cooze Jasmine that she needed to stop spreading her distinct brand of herpes rot to all of the jocks. I said this in front of her cheerleading team for maximum strategic impact, completely aware that her close friend and secret rival, Kerri, was listening. Kerri adeptly arranged a concerned and outraged expression on her face for everyone else to see, but I suspect she was about to burst with the gleeful malice I knew she really felt. I knew about the complicated rivalry between the two, and how affection and bile can become inexorably intertwined—especially with girls. I twisted the knife that much further in order to elicit a guffaw out of Kerri, one that echoed around the bleachers. *Everyone heard.*

Jasmine turned around quickly, looking for the source of impudence. When I saw that Kerri wasn't able to reconfigure her expression in time, and that Jasmine's gaze had fallen upon her smirk, I knew my *coup d'état* had landed perfectly; I had gotten them both. The simmering, seeping resentment that existed between the two girls was brought to the surface, and they would never be able to go back to what they had before—no matter how impure and juvenile it had been. At least their relationship had been safe and predictable. I killed two birds with one stone, as the saying goes. The impact of the betrayal on Jasmine was sudden, but the repercussions would probably last well into adulthood, and would bankroll the addition to some high-end therapist's summer home.

After the waves of sadistic pleasure wore off from that little miniature melodrama, I knew I was in for it. Indeed, I was out sick for a week because my hand was twisted with dead tissue. I couldn't have taken class notes, even if I had an inclination to (which I usually don't). It doesn't make sense that I was "punished" so brutally for that one, because that's not even the meanest thing that I've done—not by a long shot. But I guess this curse (or whatever it is) hadn't been fully activated before that day. Maybe it was still festering somewhere deep inside me, gathering strength and resources. It was getting to know me from the inside out.

I continued to be me: lying when it suited me, spreading rumors when it amused me, or insulting and belittling people when I felt bored or frustrated. The scars would manifest, stay awhile, and then fade away. I learned to bargain with them, in a manner of speaking. I figured I would say or do something just mean enough to keep me satisfied for a bit while the scars healed up—which they always did.

However, I suspected the day was coming when the scars *wouldn't* heal quickly—or ever. Then, I would go through life with thick, matted cords of flesh covering my entire body, and everyone would either turn away from me or look at me with pity. Those that pitied me would take it upon themselves, through their own sense of righteousness disguised as empathy and compassion, to help a poor bastard like me see the wonderful inner beauty that was disguised by the unsightly mask that I would no longer be able to doff. But they would realize, as I hurt them, that my outsides matched my insides, and no amount of therapy or medication will be able to help. I would finally, at long last, be myself.

This is the point in my account when I insert some hard-won nugget of wisdom. But sorry, folks, I don't have one. In order to evade the scenario I just illustrated, I bottle up my meanness and do small good deeds—not because I love humanity or any of that drum circle stinky hippie bullshit, but out of self-preservation. I am a wolf in sheep's clothing, I suppose.

But then, the other day, something really weird happened. One of the foreign exchange students (a gangly girl—from some obscure European country, I think) told me that I was, "so nice," as I helped her to find a copy of *The Odyssey* in the school library. I looked at her for a long moment, at her gawky frame, her ruddy complexion, her mouth hanging open slightly as she breathed damply in and out. I looked at all of her unfashionable and unbeautiful characteristics. I mused on all of the things that, once upon a time, I would have said brazenly, cruelly and directly into her gormless, bespectacled face. I would have given her something to be ashamed of, some mean, nasty secret she'd be too afraid to tell her parents when she got back home. I thought of all the things I could do.

In the end, I looked at her with soft eyes, smiled slightly and said, "Thank you." She giggled with shy awkwardness and turned to leave the room. Her ruffled skirt was tucked up into her plain, cotton underwear, but I didn't even reach for my phone to quickly snap a picture.

Barrier
David Ngo

Incoming Message from DoubleSpeak Dating Incoporated
Hello John,
We see you have not logged into your DoubleSpeak account for three months. We would greatly
appreciate it if you filled out a survey evaluating your experience with us. Would you like to take it?
Yes.
Thank you for participating in our survey. Please note that all answers are confidential, and will
be used to further improve you and millions of others' experience with our app.

1.   *How did you first hear about the DoubleSpeak Dating App?*

I heard about it from a friend who was traveling on business to Barcelona. He figured that a dating app that could automatically translate someone's messages to your preferred language was more than a novelty—that it'd expand the "lovers' pool" or something like that. Not really sure why he'd do so for a three-day business trip, but I guess he was trying to be opportunistic.

2.   *Why did you decide to use DoubleSpeak over other dating apps on the market?*

Because I wasn't getting any hits on the other apps. Whether that was because of my own looks or the way the apps worked, I don't know; probably the former. Maybe I shouldn't have described myself as a "fresh divorcee."

Eventually, my friend convinced me to try DoubleSpeak. "Expand my horizons," he said. There wasn't any reason for me to say no at that point.

I was lonely.

3.   *What was your experience like, using the app? Please be specific in terms of the people you connected with, and the amount of time you spent messaging them.*

There was only one person that I connected with. Her name was Ngoc, a woman from Saigon. She was wonderful.

We sent each other pictures every day—sometimes of just things like our faces or feet; maybe something interesting that might have happened to us. Other times our families and friends. We might have sexted a little.

She had this blunt charm to her I guess. If I ever sent a message that was worded wrong or sounded offensive … like one time where I joked that I only wanted kids for the tax breaks. She went completely off on me for that. You know, at first I thought she was just being too sensitive.

But then she told me she couldn't have kids.

4.   *Are you currently in a relationship with someone you met on DoubleSpeak?*

No.

5.   *Are there any additional comments that you would like to make?*

After a while, I think Ngoc and I did fall for each other. But you can never be too sure with these types of things. I mean, we never met in person. I was considering it—visiting her in Saigon. But I'd have to learn how to speak Vietnamese or she would need to learn how to speak English fluently. I knew for a fact that neither of us had time to do that. Or maybe I'm projecting that, I don't know. I'm surprised we never brought it up. Ngoc was afraid of it too, probably. Or maybe she didn't care as much as I did. Eventually, I stopped talking to her. I didn't see a future.

And yet it's been three months, and I'm still waiting to not care about her.

6.   *Do you plan to use DoubleSpeak anytime in the near future?*

Yes

7.   *Please rate your experience with the DoubleSpeak App out of Five Stars.*

Three.

Thank you for completing our survey. We hope you continue to use DoubleSpeak to find someone you thought impossible to communicate with.

Xin chào Ngọc,
    Chúng tôi thấy bạn đã không sử dụng Doublespeak trong vòng 2 tháng. Bạn có muốn điền vào một cuộc khảo sát về kinh nghiệm của bạn không?

Amie and Juno
Ash Rinae Stockemer

Amie spent her childhood living at the edge of a forest and watching the trees change colors each fall. There was little time for grown-ups, or school. She told herself that she would uncover the secrets of the trees, and therefore she would never have to grow up. She would never have to die, she would learn to pause like the trees when earth was barren, and she would open up again in spring, good as new, while everyone else got older.

It was her secret mission, bestowed upon her at her mother's funeral. She heard it whispered in the wind, and saw it spelled out in colored leaves, it meant she wouldn't succumb to some fancy-named disease and die so young, like her auburn-eyed mother. She could not forgive her mother, never forgive the conversation in the mudroom where she laced her boots, the words, "I'm sorry Amie, I'm dying. I wish it weren't so." Amie could not forgive her for not finding another way.

Each fall, when the leaves turned orange, she carefully pulled out the old mud-spattered laces from her boots and wove new bright pink laces through each hole. She tied them tight around her ankles, and finished with a perfect bow. Re-lacing boots with so many holes would be an annoying task for many, but for Amie, this was the ritual that officially started Fall, and marked another year on her quest to find immortal life.

At her mother's funeral, they dressed her in fall clothes. Amie insisted upon it, remembering how cold the ground became in the fall. They wrapped a bright red scarf around her neck and put a beanie on her head.

This year, Amie was ten. She was determined to find the secret. She thought eleven was an irredeemable age. She pulled on her gloves, buttoned her coat and kissed her father on the cheek. He grunted, barely aware. Staring blankly at a rerun of last Sunday's game with the volume turned all the way up. She hastily unlocked the shed where her bike lived. "This year's the year," she told her bike, "I have a plan."

Juno was a boy who greatly disliked his name. He couldn't shorten it, unless he went by "J" and that was altogether too jerkish of a name, plus, he felt he couldn't pull it off. So he grimaced when his mother called "Juno, dinner!" or when the teachers at school called roll and looked surprised to see a boy shyly wave his hand and mutter "here."

October was here. His least favorite month. He hated the cold winds, the neighborhood games of capture the flag where he was always picked last, and he hated the impending holidays. Filled with wet kisses from his auntie and too many wedgies to count, he scowled at Halloween pumpkins, declined cups of hot apple cider, and generally avoided other kids, who often became so excited that Halloween was coming that it was all they could talk about.

"Juno!" His mother called, "Don't forget your coat and gloves." She was upstairs, yet somehow knew he hadn't bundled up properly.

He put on his coat and gloves begrudgingly, averting his eyes from the bright red scarf hanging in the foyer, and thought his act of rebellion today would be to leave it behind. Smiling at the thought, he turned the doorknob and pulled open the front door.

"Juno sweetheart, not so fast!" His mother's hurried footsteps came down the stairs. "Let me give you a hug." She pulled him toward her and paused, "Now, please, have a good day at school and don't get into any trouble, Junie."

"Mom, please" He pulled away, "Just don't call me Junie. My name's bad enough already."

She looked at him with a soft expression and pulled down the red scarf from the coat hanger and wrapped it tightly around his neck. "Now go."

He rolled his eyes and stepped outside, secretly grateful the red scarf was blocking the wind. Still looking for rebellion, he set off for school the long way. Perhaps he'd even be late for roll call.

If he walked up the street, past the corner grocer and a little up the hill, he could cut through the forest. There he wouldn't find the neighbor kid running to catch up with him, nor see his old babysitter, who liked to wave at all the children as she got her morning newspaper. No. This was better. No people to yell "Baby Junie, Junie boy!" or to jump out from behind a dumpster just to see if he'd holler.

He stopped at the edge of the forest trail and tried not to appreciate the soft orange glow of leaves that scattered the ground.

Bink Bink!

Juno looked around wildly to see a girl on a bike pedaling towards him. "Hey!" he shouted as she passed, not completely certain why.

The girl looked back at him, then forward again. Then suddenly, she hopped off her bike and bounded towards him.

"What are you wearing?" She said, her eyes wide.

"Uh," he said, "fall clothes, I guess."

"That scarf!" She shrieked, "it's beautiful." She pulled off her gloves and ran her hands along it.

"Oh. Uh . . . You can have it." Juno pulled off the scarf and thrust it towards her, turned and kept walking along the path.

"What's wrong with you?" She said, running to catch up to him.

"Nothing! I'm going to school. Aren't you?"

"Oh no, I never go to school. There's much too much to do right here." She looked around at the forest as if her meaning was perfectly clear.

"What do you mean you never go to school? Are you homeschooled?"

"Sorta. My dad thinks I go to school, but I don't. I'm working on a secret mission instead."

"But don't they call your parents? I mean, won't he find out?"

"He doesn't answer the phone. Or check the mail, or do anything really. Really it's okay!"

"Well . . . What's the mission?" Juno ventured.

"I . . . I could tell you, but you'd laugh. And I really don't have time for, you know, chit-chat." She pulled the scarf around her neck, feeling a surge of sympathy for the boy, whose cheeks were flushed with cold. "Look, if you promise not to laugh, you can come with me."

"How long will it take?" Juno thought of the scolding he would get if he didn't show up to class.

"It should take forever, I hope!" She smiled. "We're looking for the secret to everlasting life."

Juno shrugged. It was rebellious enough to ride off with this crazy girl.

She grabbed him by the hand and got on her bike. "Get in the basket." She ordered, then softly, "What's your name?"

He climbed into the basket. "I'm Juno."

"Juno," she said, kicking off. "I'm Amie."

"Where are we going?" He smiled. He didn't mind when she said his name.

"Everywhere. Nowhere. We gotta find out how they live forever." She pointed at the trees.

"They don't live forever." He said, "They die every winter."

"But they come back in the spring!" She countered.

"I'm from California. There's no winter. Trees don't die." He craned his neck back to look upside down at her to see a smile cross her lips.

"Then we'll go to California!" She shouted, pedaling deeper into the forest.

Two-Body Problem
Rachael Kuintzle

You were so important when I met you. Every time you made me laugh, I felt my brain cells build new transmitters and carry them down their axons to my synapses, hard-coding your voice into my mind. When you challenged my preconceptions, new dendrites budded and branched out, learning you, keeping you, and I wished my hand could grow extra fingers to hold your hand more entirely.

You were the first person I could talk to about everything. My musical tastes stretched like latex to include your preferred genres—alternative rock and classical. You were the first person I moved in with. I'd never before had the privilege of fighting with someone about what brand of paper towels to buy. I entertained thoughts of never leaving you.

Then two years into my six-year neuroscience PhD, you moved 3,000 miles away to become a nuclear engineer in Oakland, California. I understood that there are only so many places one can become such a thing. I was stuck in Boston, chasing my dreams.

It turned out that the fiber connecting us had poor tensile strength, and neither of us was willing to make the professional sacrifices necessary to close the distance. You said that as soon as a good job opened up near Boston, you'd take it in a heartbeat. But you didn't have time to search, and none of the positions I suggested fit your criteria.

At some point after our transition to long-distance, you stopped being my oxygen and started being carbon monoxide. When you said you loved me, it took my breath away in a new sense. My lungs didn't know the difference; they filled and emptied with their usual rhythm. But I was suffocating, and I realized I'd have to find a way to let you go.

The last time I flew to visit you, I remembered a thought experiment I'd learned about in college math: Zeno's paradox. It holds that when traveling from point A to B, you must first cross half the distance, then half the quarter remaining, then half of the last eighth, and so on, forever; thus, you can never reach your destination. When you picked me up at the airport, I felt that Zeno was really on to something.

We called it a mutual decision. The opposite of symbiosis, we separated our lives in order to survive. Your absence crept into the directories of my mind and began deleting files one by one. The image of your face was reduced in resolution. I started to forget about us, through the miraculous and necessary process that transforms lovers back into acquaintances. Receptors at the synapses of cells storing our memories were slowly recycled, broken down for spare parts. Dendritic trees were pruned, neuronal processes retracted as if from an unwanted touch, erasing the evidence of your impact on my life.

But traces of you will persist indefinitely. Memories are tangible things—they live in the organization of our neurons. Strange, to think that my physical brain contains remnants of your influence, like scars. I don't think about you all the time anymore, but our past is tangled up with other circuits in my mind. A song comes on the radio, one that was popular during our relationship, and it's like time travel.

There are certain smells, too, that can still access the emotional network preserving your two-year contribution to my biology. Fewer smells now than before. The aromatic compounds in jasmine used to speak of our walks in spring, when the tangled vines all over campus bloomed synchronously. After you converted me into a coffee drinker, the vapor of my daily dark roast smelled like our morning commute. In the years after you left, the jasmine continued to bloom, and God knows I kept drinking coffee, till new footage was taped over my old recordings. Now coffee just smells like the start of my day, like e-mails and optimism.

But some scents still belong to your memory—curry, because you cooked Indian food several times a week; the laundry detergent you used; your shampoo. The deodorant I wore back then, before I switched brands. I still have a half-used stick in a drawer; I take it out now and then because it scratches a hard-to-reach itch in my brain.

Oh, the power you once had over me! I used to marvel at your ability to rearrange my very atoms. But back then I pretended this was a special truth, when I knew very well that everything in the world has the same power.

Three Vignettes
Jenna Jauregui

Wrinkles

The iron gurgled and exhaled steam as Joanne stretched the dress over the oblong board. Oprah was on TV, pretending to cook something with that good-looking chef she often saw on the Food Network. Bobby Oliver or something. Oprah marveled over the heap of pasta they were making in the studio's pretend kitchen. Pasta sounded good. Joanne was glad she had chosen Italian for the catering—breadsticks, salad, lasagna, and spaghetti from the same restaurant where her daughter had her rehearsal dinner years ago. You could still get a lot of food for a pretty good price.

Joanne tugged at the dress so she could iron the back. Cotton wrinkled so easily, but this particular blue was just her color. She hoped she wouldn't spill any red sauce down the front. She heard the scratch of the doorknob as Tom entered the bedroom. He rummaged in his dresser drawer for a tie clip, his shirt hanging untucked over his flat backside. "Take off that shirt and let me iron it for you," she said, giving her dress a shake before laying it neatly on the bed. "But I've already tied my tie," he frowned.

"Come on, it's not like our kids throw us an anniversary party every year!" she said. With a sigh, she heard the slippy noise of his tie sliding out from under the collar, and he handed her the deep plum button-down shirt she had given him for Christmas two years ago. Purple tones brought out his green eyes. They made him look taller.

She turned the shirt over the board and pressed the iron into the fabric, running it quickly over the creases. The steam hissed and gurgled as she went through the motions, starting with the outside of the collar before sliding on to the shoulders and cuffs. Tom's watch caught the afternoon light as he moved behind her. The surprise glimmer bounced into the mirror over the bureau, and she glanced up to see her reflection, the tissue-paper crinkles that gathered and stretched her skin as she reached up to smooth the frizz from her hair. Ironing ruined her curls. Ironing and draining freshly boiled spaghetti noodles over the sink.

On TV, the audience clapped as Oprah hugged the chef. One time, Joanne had seen a tabloid photograph that showed Oprah without all her makeup. She looked old. Like a real person. It made Joanne feel good to know that TV was nothing but an illusion. Oprah wasn't always so glamorous. They hadn't really made pasta in the fake kitchen.

Still, Joanne thought as she laid Tom's shirt over the faded floral padding on the ironing board, it would be nice if she could iron her birthday suit as easily as cotton.

Old Farts

Judy heard it all the way from where she sat in the living room—a creaking croak that ripped through the silent stretch of air between them. The television was on mute. Colorful images flashed on the screen in a jarring sequence of advertisements. The kind of commercials that come on when old people are watching, on channels like TV Land and Hallmark—commercials for denture adhesive and power scooters and bathtubs with little doors in the side. The black and white closed-captioning text blinked across the bottom of the screen, but she couldn't read it from where she sat, and she was too comfortable on the couch to go get her glasses from the den. That was why Bill had gone into the kitchen—she had remembered the leftover brownies from Tuesday's bingo mixer, suffocating in their Tupperware container and begging to be savored in front of tonight's rerun of *I Love Lucy*.

He was always doing little things like that, offering to bring her book over when she had just snuggled into bed and realized she'd forgotten it. Warming her coffee mug before pouring the hot dark liquid (two sugars no cream.) Leaving a post-it note on the mirror with some lovely message just for her—nearly every day for the past forty-seven years. She was cozy under her quilt, and she watched his faint shadow pass over the kitchen wall as Corelle dishes chinked against the tile countertop.

"What was that?" she called to Bill, though she knew perfectly well what the sound was. "I stepped on a frog," he said, a shade of a smile lifting the corner of his lip as he spoke, entering the living room carrying the brownies in two shallow bowls.

"Sure you did," she chuckled. Just like always. "Come on, it's starting again."

Bill handed her the brownie, clicked on the TV volume, and they both settled into the evening. Dessert was sweet and molten with chocolate. She barely finished three forkfuls before she heard it again. And this time she felt it, too. "Oh!" she laughed, a blush blossoming into her cheeks.

"Excuse you," Bill chastised with a gleeful smirk. The TV audience erupted with laughter and Bill slung his arm over the back of the couch, dropping his hand on her shoulder.

"A girlfriend of mine used to call them 'angel fluffs,'" Judy mused as she cut off a gooey bite with her fork. "I always thought that was a silly name. I mean, really!"

Bill leaned over and kissed her soft white hair above her ear then blew a loud raspberry into her neck, making her yelp in surprise. Revenge came in the form of a floral couch cushion.

Butterfingers

An open bag of Butterfingers candy bars lay next to the other stuff on top of the refrigerator. All day long, the chocolate and crisp wafers were calling to Peggy in their yellow plastic jackets, chocolate coating and peanut butter wafer begging to be unwrapped. But she was waiting for the right moment. The anticipation gave her a smiling feeling all afternoon and evening.

Finally, the grandkids were asleep, and Joe was snoring in the bed next to her. She slowly pushed aside the comforter and shuffled down the hall into the kitchen, her bare feet soundless as her slight frame moved through the dark house. Her toes touched the cold linoleum, and she turned to her left towards the refrigerator. Her arm stretched up towards the top, which seemed to be getting higher all the time. She rose onto her toes and strained as much as her arthritis would allow. Finally, her thin fingers touched the crinkly bag as she groped for a better grip, and she managed to tug the bag closer to the edge. Slowly, making as little noise as possible. Only a few more inches, and then suddenly an avalanche of mini candy bars skittered down the front of the fridge and scattered over the floor.

Peggy yelped in surprise, partly from the noise and partly from the sensation of them hitting her soft noggin of white hair as they tumbled down. A light came on in the hall, and tiny footsteps crept closer to the kitchen. Her granddaughter stood clutching her blanket and mopping sleep from her eyes with her tiny fist. Peggy looked at her from where she sat on the floor, surrounded by Butterfingers.

"Grandma, what are you doing?"

Peggy did the first thing that came to her head. She held out a candy bar, drawing the child closer. "Want some candy, Jessica?" she smiled.

The girl took the candy with wide, inquiring eyes. "Candy after bedtime?"

"Of course!" and flustered, she added, "What are you, the food police?!"

Mother Tongue
Eva Malis

My mother speaks a language of love, and I am not yet fluent.
My mother was never given what she has given me. The youngest of eight in rural China, both parents bedridden and dead by her twenties. My mother was the mother of a household even then, doing the cooking and the sweeping for five brothers and two sisters early into her teens. Bathing her parents and feeding her older siblings as if they were her own to nurture.

When I came along, she had almost given up. We don't speak about it, but I always knew. I feel our secret gripping tight in my chest. To think that I have now relived her past, and she will never know.

Elementary school taught me to be ashamed of my mother. It taught me to color in the circle next to the word 'White,' to hold my Saturdays at Chinese school as a deep dark secret under my tongue. It taught me to dread the question, "what are you?" and to lie when asked. It taught me to hate the unfamiliar curve of my nose, the orange glow of my skin, the confusing angles of my eyes. Elementary school taught me that belonging is for people with only one part to them.

One day, it was open house night at school, and I pretended to my parents that it wasn't. I had to keep up with my lies. I was eight, and I did not know what race was, only that there were no other Chinese in my grade and that Mulan was nobody's favorite movie. I spent the evening drawing pictures of a princess with long brown hair who was able to transform into anything she wanted to be.

Twelve years old. My secret is out. A girl asks me if I am Mexican. I tell her no, but she insists that I look Mexican. I tell her I am half-Chinese. "Why don't your eyes look like this?" I shrug and step away as she draws her fingers up to her eyelids. The girl follows. "Do you eat rice every day?" she asks earnestly.

My mother asks me if I like any boys. I am so embarrassed that I yell, "NO." She tells me that a mother is a best friend, and that I can tell her anything. That nothing can break the bond between us. I've heard it before, but this time I get so mad. "*No*," I say again, and leave the room.

Fourteen. I still have never met another person like me, and have stopped going to Chinese school. Somehow, all my friends are boys. They talk about how "little Asian chicks" are "so hot." I stay quiet, unsure of where to fit into this. Later I find myself making a point to share with my classmates that I am half-Asian after all, basking in the specialness that it brings me.

My best friend's mother dies of lung cancer. We all see it coming, but for some reason he does not give her flowers on her last Mother's Day. On the night that he texts me "She is gone," I open the Joy Luck Club for the first time and cry myself to sleep.

Eighteen, now. First semester in college, sitting on the couch of a Korean boy that I am falling head over heels for. "Hapa girls are so beautiful," he says, and shows me a website titled "Hot Half-Asian Women." I giggle away my confusion. I rest my head on his shoulder as he scrolls through pictures of women that don't look anything like me.

My mother tells me on the phone that since I left home, she does not know what to do with herself. She tells me she is spending a lot of time taking naps on my bed, talking to me as if I am there in my bedroom with her. When we hang up, I realize that never once have I said the words "I love you" to her.

In university, I find myself surrounded with a progressive self-righteousness that I often find silencing. I am told it is offensive to use the word *hapa*, which is somewhat relieving. The next time that somebody asks, I use what is familiar to me, telling them that I am half-Chinese. *What's the other half?* So from then on, I say I am both, Chinese and White. It feels awkward and uncomfortable, telling people that I am whole when I am not yet so sure that I believe it.

My first winter break home from university, I do not realize how much pain the whole family is feeling. The night before I leave for the second time, something breaks, hard. I run out of the house and wander on the dark suburban streets for two eternal hours. Nobody finds me, but I hear my mother's shrieks echoing throughout the neighborhood. I keep on walking, hiding behind gates and trees each time a car passes by. When the cold becomes unbearable, I finally run into the house and straight to the bathroom, the only room with a lock. Seconds later, my mother is pounding on the door with unearthly screams of fury. I huddle shaking in the corner and text a friend, *my mom is about to murder me. please send help!*

In my second year of college, my mother turns sixty and I write her a poem. It is the only way that I know how to say I love you and she frames it and hangs it up on her wall.

I decide to go back to China, and fail to follow through with my daily commitment to studying the language. My pronunciation is natural but my vocabulary is horrendous. I begin to dream in Chinese words that I cannot even recognize.

Sixty, when I am twenty. I cannot stop thinking about death, about how fast to marry in order to bestow grandchildren that she can meet, about the number of years left to walk this world together. Me, her only child, her last one to provide for. Plagued with the inability to return what was given to me.

My mother tells me one day that she is at peace with her life, that there is nothing that she would do differently. We are walking on a local path that is bordered with poppies and tall green grass. For one vital moment, I feel my world stop spinning as I realize that finally, I can be rooted in this. That no matter what happens between us, or how long she stays with me, I can come back to this moment and know that there was nothing else left for me to do. That at least once in my life, there existed a moment where everything was fulfilled.

My mother's hands are withering and her veins are revealing themselves. The gray hairs are spreading from her head but her eyes still sparkle with more life than anyone I know. She spends her mornings gardening, practicing taichi, baking rice cake, bickering with my father. When I am home, I hear the beat of her prompt footsteps rattling the house, announcing her presence and her movement, sending life flowing through the walls of our family's home.

A Simple Peace
Emily La

"Graduation's here now, huh?" The question came from Eirene, who sat across the table from Evalyn. Eirene, dressed in her signature ripped jeans and a crop top as bright yellow as her hair, took a bite of her croissant sandwich. "Y'know," she said, the word coming out muffled among all the ham, egg, and cheese slices in her mouth. Evalyn nodded in response, staring down at her smartphone, her own lunch half-eaten next to her arm. "I feel like we were freshmen just yesterday," Eirene went on, dabbing the corners of her mouth with her handkerchief. She checked her own phone, swiping spam messages sent from their school, and turned it over onto its screen. "Remember when we first met each other in Prof. Taylor's class?"

Evalyn groaned at the memory, tearing her eyes away from her own device, and Eirene snickered. "Don't remind me," Evalyn muttered, taking a long, *long* sip of her green tea frappuccino. Her eyes glared down hard, trying to burn the table, hot as it already was in the 82°F weather. Five minutes ago, she might have thought about how grateful she was for her shorts and stockings. She might even have thought about how particularly fashionable she looked today with her blue ribbon and blouse. But right now, with ½ of her frap practically gone, all she could think about was "Damn Prof. Taylor." She chewed on her straw, all the while swatting her short brown hair out of her face. "Who the hell makes a group project due in three weeks?" she muttered. "I thought we were done for after Kevin dropped the class."

"I mean, back then, I didn't appreciate it," Eirene responded without missing a beat, brushing strands of her equally short blond hair behind her ear. "Like, really did not appreciate it. We had to make up so much work, and Prof. Taylor was kind of an ass about it. But, hey, if something came up with *my* family, I'd be outta there, too." She shrugged and took a sip of her coconut milk macchiato, the caramel and chocolate syrup having melted together into a muddy (albeit delicious) concoction. She continued to do so, drinking her drink with the same rhythm one would breathe air, until she glanced at her wristwatch. She set her drink on the table with just a little more force than necessary, enough to slightly reposition the ham and bacon in Evalyn's ham and bacon panini. "Hey," she said, "what day is it?"

"Sunday," Evalyn responded, taking up that same panini.

"No, I mean, what *day* is it?"

"The 18th."

"Damn," Eirene muttered as she pulled her backpack up into her lap and began rummaging through. She shoved papers everywhere, and Evalyn ate as Eirene threw a graphing calculator beside her meal, thinking fleetingly about how she had to sell her own soon. "Where's my phone?" she spoke to herself, tossing her backpack back onto the ground, only to realize it had been in her lap the entire time. Evalyn raised an eyebrow, but Eirene merely shot her a sheepish smile as she quickly dialed a number and checked in with restaurant arrangements.

"Reservation for tonight?" Evalyn asked, setting her food down, and Eirene nodded. "Father's Day?"

"You know it," Eirene said, but sighed. "I've had so much stuff to deal with, though. I barely managed to get this reservation in. I practically had to *beg* the manager, but my dad has just been wanting to eat here so bad, you know?"

Evalyn nodded because she did know, and if everyone around them had known about their conversation, they also would have nodded because they knew too. Everyone knew. Evalyn's phone buzzed then, and she checked it, also looking at the time. 12:34 p.m. "Did you get everything ready for graduation tomorrow?"

"Nah," Eirene said, putting her phone away, "but it'll be fine. I need tonight to go way better than tomorrow."

"Cool." Evalyn continued browsing through her phone, reading emails and messages from within the last hour. She tapped one with her finger and then stopped. She stared down at the name—*Kaizer*—and remembered him, in his overly large white tank, waving her goodbye that morning with his gloved hand. It was like any ordinary day, but for some reason, seeing his back receding into the distance made her turn around and stare after him. How often was it that they waved to each other and walked their separate ways so peacefully? She wondered. "Kaizer said he wanted to hang at some point," Evalyn said, still looking down, "When are you free?"

Sipping on her drink again, Eirene hummed thoughtfully. A day out with Evalyn and Kaizer sounded fun, but she didn't exactly want to be a third wheel. Not that Evalyn and Kaizer were a *thing*, necessarily, but with the sparks flying among them, from anger, from jealousy, who would want to get in the middle of that by themselves? "Can Christian come?" She knew her classmate would come along if she asked, and if he didn't, she'd just need to add *But won't you come for me, Christian? Pretty please?* That always got him. It almost infuriated her how easily it did, and she bit her straw, sincerely hoping he'd just say yes, so she wouldn't have to resort to that method. But she didn't want to go alone, and she had no one else to ask. And they knew each other decently enough, didn't they?

"Yeah." Evalyn took up her phone in her hands, adding, "It's supposed to rain this week."

"Man! Then how are we gonna go out?" Eirene sighed and ran her hand through her hair, crossing her right leg over her left. "Can I let you guys know later? I'll ask Christian about it when he gets off work."

Evalyn nodded, and they took up finishing their food again before it got cold. "Hey." Evalyn turned her head up suddenly, remembering something. She leaned forward, pressing her elbows on the table, and asked, "When do tickets come out for that thing again?"

Eirene stared at her, holding the croissant in front of her face. "You know," she said, blinking at Evalyn. "I honestly have no idea."

The Eighth Day
Kyle Edward Harris

The annual BBQ is humming. Moe's been throwing the July get-togethers as long as Pan has been his neighbor, although he doesn't remember being invited the first few years. Moe loves to show off his grilling skills and brag about the size of his Bubble. Each year he trades in for a bigger model and each year he invites more neighbors. This year, Pan counts twenty people until he loses interest. He decides there can only be twenty people—twenty being such a nice, round number. Twenty people, twenty chairs, twenty chances for small talk, twenty reasons for Pan not to be there, twenty different dishes on the table: frog legs, frog pot pie, Cajun-deviled frogs, sea-salt-rubbed frog kabobs, barbecue frog salad, south-of-the-border macaroni and frog, frog vinegar slaw, frog puppies, frog paste on toast, frogbread, frog brisket, frog fries, sweet potato frog fries, baby back frog, Mexican-grilled frog with cilantro, creamy frog pudding, pickled frog, frogs over easy, wilted frogs, frog jello.

Pan is stuck in a conversation with the neighbors from the end of the block, a nice enough couple: The Farrows. Mrs. Farrow is wearing a sunflower yellow sunhat; everyone who looks at her squints. Later, in the Bubble, she will complain to Mr. Farrow that all the guests are making faces at her. Mr. Farrow is sporting a Crocodile Dundee cap. That is, a baseball cap promoting the 1986 film.

"Oh, Pan, it is so nice to see you again. Keeping yourself busy? Can you believe this weather, 75° and sunny! Remember last year's plague? Oh, it was simply miserable! It never stopped raining and was a dreadful 65°." Mrs. Farrow tips her hat up slightly to scratch her forehead, revealing her white hair. As if seeing somebody yawn, Mr. Farrow copies her. Pan can't help but notice the white in their hair move around. He wouldn't be surprised if most of the guests here had lice and wore hats to hide them, not to prevent them.

"Yeah," Pan replies. Pan of course wears the Peter Pan cap he bought at Disneyland last year, where he stayed the day before the first plague. If he was going to have a last day, he'd prefer it be at a theme park than alone in his parent's house. Moe joins them and holds out a platter of lemon wedges. He is wearing a leopard print chef's hat with "Blow Moe" embroidered on it. In the corner of the yard a kid is stomping on cornered frogs.

"Charlie! Charlie, you cut that out or you'll ruin your new boots . . . Don't you give me that look!" A woman Pan remembers from plagues past grabs Charlie, stepping on a frog as she does. "Now look what you made me do! I'm so sorry, Margaret, I don't know what gets into him sometimes."

"Don't worry, I think he's simply adorable." Charlie turns his head and smiles at Margaret. A man in a Trojan soldier helmet notices Pan. Pan doesn't remember his name.

"Pan, buddy!" he smacks Pan on the back, "Long time no see!" He sucks on a nearly dry lemon, letting out a loud, long sigh of refreshment. "Ahh, never hits the spot, right, boy-o?" He smacks Pan on the back again and leans in closer to whisper, "You know, let's just say that I heard you can boil the blood out of your liquor if you mix a drop of urine with it." Trojan-man pulls a flask out of his pocket and winks at Pan. Another smack on the back. "Alright then, man! Say, have you met our little

Charlie over there? What a piece of joy, right? Piece of something, anyway. Hey, Charlie, come here, show Pan how you can make frogs squeal!"

"No, no, that's alright. I'd rather just eat them, thank you." A frog jumps by Pan's leg and looks up at him. It grabs a fly from his leg. Pan mouths *I'm sorry* to the frog. The frog doesn't say anything back. Trojan-man has gone to play with Charlie, leaving Pan alone again. Three ladies sit around the table talking about yesterday's plague, the firestorm:

"I think it's just awful that some people can't afford a Bubble. And they expect us to let them into ours. Listen, I don't know about you, but I worked for my Bubble and I'll be damned if I'm going to let some no-good, lazy kid freeload off of me. And who are these parents that let them just roam around like vagrants? I know I would never let my people go!" The frog by Pan's feet seems to roll its eyes and say *Do you happen to have the time?*

"Really? Me and King let people in all the time, if they ask. I don't want to imagine any poor soul out there during the Storm. You see the footage of the houses without Bubbles later and you just feel for them." Pan mouths back to the frog, *I think it's sometime just after three.*

"Serves them right. There's plenty of programs they can sign up for that will get them into a government-run Bubble, but they're too lazy to fill out the paperwork." The frog mouths, *Good luck to you, gray eyes,* and hops off in the opposite direction of Charlie.

A few frogs are inside the Bubble. Charlie tries to step on them, but the Bubble is too crowded for him to really move around; like an upside-down fishbowl with too many fish. With all the colorful hats and shape of the Bubble, the neighbors almost look like the plastic plants and multi-colored rocks inside an aquarium.

"Everybody look up! You can see it. Hotdog, is it weird-looking!" Trojan-man smacks somebody on the back, not knowing who.

"Even after all these years, it still amazes me," Moe says, admiring the sight like fireworks. The entire sky looks like a ceiling that has been painted, haphazardly, a shimmering, green-brown color. That ceiling is quickly dropping from out of the sky. As it gets closer, it looks wavy, like an old dog's spine. Somehow it's active like a beehive, but static; none of the locusts have anywhere to fly to, they're too mashed together.

Pan closes his eyes and waits for the sound. Even in the Bubble it sounds like a gunshot from the top of a bridge. Neither of which Pan has heard, he just imagines that's what the sound of trillions of grasshoppers hitting the Earth at the same time might sound like. The jump of the ground jolts everybody. Charlie is crying. *Holy cow!* mouths a frog before croaking.

Moe opens the Bubble back up, "So, same time tomorrow? Of course, you don't have to leave right now. I can start grilling up these locusts if you want, yeah?"

And Then I Walked into the Sea
An Excerpt
Michelle Tan

Shulman sent me home early Thursday morning when he left for his business trip. He put a hand on my waist as he told me his new emergency contact and then left the office discreetly.

It did not take me long to learn that "business trip" was industry lingo for company-financed getaways with his accountant, who just became his second wife.

Soon after I started covering his desk, we'd developed an unspoken understanding. He would always return to find his write-off forms on his desk beside two ibuprofen caplets and a glass of tepid water. In exchange, I could have some time off.

On these rare vacation days, I always felt like I had to do something I never do. That time I drove down to the beach.

I made the mistake of wearing my work shoes. The deep-blue oxfords with hard soles. As soon as I crossed from concrete to beach, they sunk flat into the sand and filled up with loose grains, so I kicked them off and left them at the edge of the parking lot.

I distanced myself from the crowd and sat down on a patch of cold damp sand, crossing my legs in front of me. The sea rose up to me coolly and grazed my heels.

He said, "What's up girl? You come here often?"

"No," I replied.

"How do you like my place?"

"It's ok."

"Just ok?"

"I hate sand. The texture is weird, and really gross."

He let out an uninhibited laugh and was now inching up behind my knees. I started to notice how my cheeks burnt under the sun. Looking up at the sky, I sighed and uncrossed my legs.

After a while, he asked, "Do you like fish?"

I didn't stop thinking about what happened in the days that followed. I took my time fixating on his charm and the oddly exciting possibility of becoming a pescatarian.

I met Lucy for brunch on Melrose that Sunday, where I told her about my encounter.

"I know it's soon, but I think I'm in love," I admitted. With love, I'd learned it was best to cut to the chase.

Lucy liked to think of herself as a romantic. She wasn't, and she didn't, but that was why I wanted to hear her advice. Even though I rarely listened.

"You know I'm a romantic, *but*—I'm not so sure you should go through with this."

"Why not?"

"I mean, everybody loves the sea, but what do you really know about him? You never even go down there, you talk once and suddenly you say you're in love? I don't want you to get swept up and get hurt again, you know?"

"But I think it's different this time. He seems like one of those old souls. Like, he's always surrounded by people but is actually lonely on the inside. He told me about

103

how he's around people all the time but feels like no one understands him. Just like me."

"Fine, if you say so. And I guess if you're going to be with someone who's just going to come and go, at least this one runs on a predictable schedule." She looked like she was deep in thought.

"But you also have to consider that this can't be... you know... *sanitary*. Who knows what's been down there."

This was true. I knew I could be exposing myself to a number of conditions that may result in the loss of important appendages.

"Can't be much worse than the guys I dated in college. Remember Calvin? The one who showered with dish soap because he thought body soap was overrated?"

"Oh right, *him*. Screw that guy."

Lucy still looked skeptical. It seemed like she was about to say something when the waitress came to take our orders.

I looked for the most aquatic thing on the menu, which turned out to be smoked salmon pizza topped with mounds of oregano. It was disgusting, but I ate it all.

We ate silently. I studied Lucy's face as she picked at her eggs. The sun peeked out from behind her, making a gentle halo around her frame. I couldn't shake the feeling that she looked different from the girl I knew not too long ago.

We were close friends in college. But we had a falling out in the most clichéd sense. It began when she confessed to falling in love with my boyfriend at the time. She promised to distance herself for the sake of our friendship and, to my surprise, kept this promise. Yet I felt very awkward about this, like she had done some big favor for me that I never asked for and could never repay.

Over time our friendship simmered naturally. My boyfriend and I also became bored and restless and eventually split up. It was odd how we went through all that trouble trying to salvage our relationships only to see them dissolve on their own.

We had reconnected online just a year ago after learning that we had both moved to the same city. We met up in a cafe much like this one. Somehow we both knew to keep our reminiscing brief. We talked about our old classrooms, our careers, but we both knew not to bring up what'd happened between us. We got along like before, but it felt like we were starting entirely anew, as different people. Like our earlier friendship had never existed.

Lucy broke the silence by asking me about the new foreign films Shulman wanted to acquire. I'd spent a week sampling all forty of them and was in the process of assigning each of them a 'yay' or 'nay'. I told her about a film from Southern Italy. The whole movie, which was a little less than two hours, showed only goats walking around on a pasture.

She laughed. After catching her breath, she told me that she envied my job. I could tell she meant it. She knew it was my dream job in college. And I could understand how working under a foreign film distributor would seem idealistic to Lucy, the auditor and aspiring romantic.

I sensed a familiar urge to shake her by the shoulders and tell her things I knew I shouldn't. I wanted to say that the menial tasks I faced every day were draining the life from my veins. And that watching countless hours of obscure, impenetrable films, desperate for the sympathy of complete strangers, made me feel sick. And that my boss Shulman took liberties staring at my chest, but only when I wore turtlenecks.

But of course, I held back. I used to wonder if she would be relieved to know that my path wasn't much better than her own. But it seemed too selfish and too cruel to tell someone that you could achieve your dream and still be unhappy.

Shulman looked like a child in the passenger seat of his own car. He snuck glances at me through the mirror but stayed quiet. I stared ahead and sped through the lanes. The car was impressively steady, I thought. My own car would be falling apart at the speed I was going.

He seemed a little bewildered when I pulled over by the pier. As soon as I stepped out of the car, I was engulfed by winds screeching and stirring with the faint scent of salt and the sound of distant waves. Shulman crept up behind me and slid a hand up my lower back.

As if propelled by the contact, I launched forward, kicking off my shoes and running into the sand. I recognized the soft thumping noises behind me as Shulman stumbling in his dress shoes.

That sand.

Under the moonlight, the sea stretched like a black sheet into the seamless horizons. As I came closer, my knees shook from the cold. Shulman shouted my name over and over from afar.

Finally, I stopped at the edge of the sea. He rushed to me in a single sweep, wrapping around my legs.

"It's you. I was hoping you would be back."

Shulman called again.

"Who's that?" he asked.

I knew better than to look back. My entire waist was now submerged, with my shift dress spreading out around me like a veil. I felt myself getting lighter.

"I don't know," I said.

And then I walked into the sea.

Champagne Sparkle
Sarah Kahn

Shifting weight onto her left hip, Tamar reexamines herself: the faded surf logo on her halter top, frayed cut-offs, and high-top Reeboks, brown and dirtied on her feet. She stiffens and the clothes turn plastic like the wrapper of a fruit-filled hard candy. The pink wrapper means "strawberry" not to be confused with strawberry. The white wrapper means "pineapple" not to be confused with pineapple. So she is a luscious bonbon gushing with a gooey "strawberry" center encased in an impeccably-molded and precisely measured edible saucer. All wrapped in pink plastic. But Tamar and her friends wince at the perfectly-manicured trees by Bruner Hall, the way they plop orange softballs in connect-the-dot rings filling the air with fragrance and apparent ease. It is California after all.

Anna chases after Tamar with Saki trailing behind. They pass the biology building and the art gallery before reaching the library, breathless and laughing. They swing open the door. The sensor flashes red then green as each girl swipes her student ID card. "This one!" Tamar signals to a small, empty room and the girls drop into wooden chairs while Tamar scribbles on the whiteboard: *Today's Learning Objective: To Un-Learn.*

"Let's have a debate about God."

"I don't want to have a debate about God."

"Well then let's talk about pros and cons, like, if he exists. I, for instance, don't believe in God. I believe in human connection. You know, like when you see a painting you really like and someone else likes that same painting and you just, I don't know, connect?"

"The two aren't mutually exclusive."

Anna's gaze lingers on Tamar, prompting an explanation.

"As in, God and human connection. The two aren't mutually exclusive. It's like the I-Thou relationship? Every time you relate to another person, you're brought closer into a relationship with God."

Saki stands abruptly and addresses her board of trustees in one long moan: "I have so much work to do. It never stops. If I'm not working, then I'm thinking about the fact that I should be working."

"You *should* just be in a continuous state of work then. Although, the end of mortal man is worms and worms don't care how much money you made or how you made it." And with that, Tamar slides her chair back, the wooden legs screeching against the wooden floor, two like substances colliding and yet repelling one another. She stands in mock pedagogy and snickers into her can of budget beer, sourced straight from the runoff of a snow-capped mountain in the magical winter wonderland of nearly tasteless pee water.

She glimpses down at her phone: four missed calls and a text. Frowning, she walks out of the windowless study room, her feet dragging like soggy toast. Once outside, she withdraws a pipe and watches as little green embers bop and boogie, like little green men, pulsing as one on the glazed dance floor. One man stands alone. Can't catch aflame because he's too burnt out. Tamar presses her thumb to the concavity in the glass and scoops away the burnt remains as her friends exit the library.

106

Her mother received the call when Tamar was at a soccer tournament. She was thirteen and competing against teams from Utah, Arizona, and Nevada. Her team was losing but all she could focus on was the piece of whole wheat bread wedged between her braces and her left molar. She tried to dissolve it by resting her tongue against the metal. One minute on, one minute off. At halftime, Tamar grabbed her water jug from the sideline and trotted over to her mother who stood with an ice-pick at her back. Tamar stiffened in response.

"It's your brother. I'm flying to Indiana and bringing him home tonight."

He was slurring his words but it was only because she interrupted his nap. He was hostile but it was only because the minimum wage-earning incompetent piece of trash was too stupid to add extra tartar sauce to his fish filet sandwich. Open your eyes she said. But instead, he spent six years in an opiate slumber. Sometimes, when Tamar was in high school, she would find the little green men among crushed pills and burnt foil between the toilet seat and the trashcan. And the bathroom would reek of that air perfume, that Champagne Sparkle. And Tamar would cry. It was all very Pavlovian.

From the library, Tamar, Anna and Saki venture to the dried-up lake across campus. On the way, Saki assembles a bouquet of woodland wildflowers and herbaceous plants, a few ferns, and an outrageously large yellow flower that eerily resembles a cheaply-dyed lambswool duster.

"It's really beautiful," Tamar says, fingering the petals.

"*That* one is, but wanna see something disgusting?" Saki plucks a droopy flower from the bunch. Two fingers pinch its head closed and the flower appears perfectly unspectacular. "See how pretty these petals are? Well, now look." And Saki removes her fingers. The petals fall, revealing the hairy black bulbous innards of the flower.

"Why is this disgusting?"

"It looks like a beetle, like a furry, fungus-y beetle."

"Maybe disgust is simply a projection of your own mortality. Hey, anyone want to go Lambda Alpha's tonight?"

And the hills are alive with iTunes Top 100 as they push past hordes of over-made-up girls in micro mini Barbie doll skirts and frat boys, pink as Kirby, ready to float away by the puff of their cheeks. They squeeze past the freshman, flailing their bodies to the beat on top of tables on top of each other. One girl is on her knees frantically swiping her hand across the floor for her missing phone. The strobe lights offer limited assistance. In the jungle of beer-soaked brotherhood, anything is fair game.

Finally, they reach the keg, but Saki is sauntering off with some blond-haired fellow. So Anna and Tamar seek refuge in the Smoker's Den. They amble down a heaving, dimly lit hallway to an open door exposing two parallel bunk beds. Opposite this is the Smoker's Den, a considerably larger room with some shoddy couches, a hammock, a coffee table stickered with skate shop logos, two lava lamps serving as bookends for an Aldous Huxley anthology, dancing bears sharpied around the subwoofer, that Pink Floyd poster of naked, painted women and a bong resting haphazardly between two untucked couch cushions. A scruffy boy in hiking boots hands Tamar the bong as she sinks into the couch. Her breath is visible in a stream of white smoke and she tries not to think of her brother, that he was her age when he entered his first Sober Living house.

God, there must be more than this. And Tamar pulls herself from the couch and walks out of the room. She drifts to the sculpture garden, past the library with its windows highlighting cubicled students hunched over their futures, past the Catholics marching out of Sunday Night Mass, past the track team completing their midnight jog and past all of this, Tamar drops to her knees and surrenders herself at the feet of *The Burghers of Calais.*

Frostbit
An Excerpt
Emma Henson

They decided to build a Death Ward in the hospital at Dong Ha Combat Base on a Monday, closed off a small section of the sick bay with rain-swollen two-by-fours that Tuesday, and placed Bethy in charge of it before the sun rose Wednesday morning.

She didn't have many patients, but they were colorful, and what they were doing, the dying, was sacrosanct. Not in the sense that God presided over them, but that there was some primordial importance to it. Bethy felt like a shitty nun, pressing gauze into their wounds when she should have been singing hymns or burning holy water or whatever it was the religious did when things were of a mortal nature. She wouldn't know.

There was the Lieutenant, Ken Abbot, who had shot spread all through his body from the low bits of his intestines to the capillaries of his lungs. No one knew how long he had left, but it didn't bother him much.

Ray Tennant, an eighteen-year-old enlistee from Alabama, had the bed next to Abbot. He walked point for a foot brigade at Hue, an outpost near the border with the north. He'd missed a landmine, but the soldier behind him hadn't. He laid on his stomach in the warm room, waiting for a piece of the metal to displace and sever his brain stem.

Lance Corporal Vinny Upton had the cot pushed against the far wall and a case of dysentery that wouldn't respond to antibiotics. They'd told Bethy there was nothing to be done for it.

And, at last, there was a nurse. She'd been thrown against the side of a transport bus in an eruption of mortar fire. She'd been brought to Da Hong in a coma and hadn't stirred for the past few weeks. She was strange, pale and female in a room of dark and indelicate men.

"Good morning," Bethy greeted blithely as she opened the curtains.

"God," Abbot said, "how're you still such a cockeyed optimist?"

"Haven't you heard, Lieutenant? It's eighty degrees outside and rum's cheaper than water in Saigon."

"Haven't *you* heard, Bethy? We've run out of bullets," Tennant managed to quip, pulling his face up from the pillow.

Ken Abbott died that night, not painless at all. When Bethy walked into the ward to begin her morning rounds, a new patient was in the corner bed. He was asleep, and she went to wipe the beaded sweat from his forehead with a cool cloth. The covers were pulled up below his chin, but she could see the dented curve of a broken occipital bone. It made his cheek cave inward, turning the left of his face into a blackened valley.

She had just pulled the cloth away from his forehead when he stirred, opening his eyes wide. Bethy paused for a moment, staring at those pupils, one red with the blood of broken vessels.

"That bad?" the soldier asked in a sleep-heavy voice.

"No," she lied. He tried to respond, but the power of the morphine had those eyes closing, his head falling to the side on his pillow.

"You look like you've just seen a ghost," Tenant joked when she moved to change the dressings on his back.

"What if I had?" she asked.

"I'd tell you to get in line. This whole place is full of them."

Dr. Eric Green was a trauma surgeon from Dallas who oversaw the most complicated cases at Da Hong. She marveled at the immensity of his presence in a room as she sat across from him in the mess hall. Part of it was his frame, but it was mostly the power of his voice, the infectious quality of his booming laughter. She finally screwed up the courage to ask about the new patient after he'd recounted the story of a day he'd spent in small claims court in Cheyenne, fighting for rightful ownership of a mounted bass.

"Gabriel Hart," Green explained around a mouthful of dry sandwich. "Got a gash in the left lobe of his liver. I tried to cauterize it, but the bile's still seeping into his stomach cavity. Give him a week, maybe, but I don't like to guess those things anymore."

She was lost in her own thoughts, thinking of the patient's face, feeling strange like she'd seen it before. Shaking her head, searching for a neutral topic, she asked, "Did we really run out of bullets?"

"For a couple of hours," he replied.

"Well, what did the soldiers do?"

"They had a positive attitude adjustment," Green said, face splitting into a toothy grin.

"What do you mean?"

"They decided they positively *hate* this place."

She was changing the rate of Hart's saline drip when he stirred and opened his eyes. She searched his broken face, swallowing the lump in her throat to ask, "Good afternoon Lieutenant, how're you feeling?"

"I've been better," he managed, and Vinny laughed.

"How's the pain? I can speak to Dr. Green if you'd like."

"The pain's alright," he responded, shifting slightly in the bed, trying to hide the grimace that flashed across his features. "But something's driving me crazy. You see, all I can do is look out that window." He lifted a hand and pointed to the single window on the far wall. He could just see a sliver of sky and the very top of a palm tree. "And I just stare at that coconut." Bethy followed his gaze and saw the fruit; it was head-sized, a mottled brown, generally unremarkable.

"Alright," she said. "Would you like me to close the curtains?"

She couldn't sleep that night on her stiff cot, thinking of Hart in his narrow corner bed, of the coconut. She rose from her bed and walked outside, feeling like a specter of a woman in her white dressing gown, walking through the empty halls of the base. Only a soft murmuring from the radio room disrupted the silence of Da Hong. The soldiers were either asleep or on night missions, and the front lot was empty.

Bethy walked onto its tarmac, cool beneath her feet despite the heat of the night. The moon was bright and high in the sky, and she could see the stark profile of the jungle for miles on every side. The black horizon had no depth; it looked almost like she could reach out and grab where the world fell away, pinch it between her thumb and forefinger.

She took off her shoes and walked to the curved base of the palm tree. It was a thin trunk until the top where a section of branches grew outward from the body of the tree. The bark was marred by long spikes of wood, an evolutionary defense that would ruin her hands. She stared at the inch-long barbs, wanting nothing but to hold the coconut in her hands, to tell Hart she'd picked it.

Grabbing the tree like she would a dancing partner, too gentle and willing to let it lead, she hefted herself up with all of the strength in her arms. Her feet scrabbled against the rough trunk, the skin over her inner ankles ripped away by the contact. Arms shaking, she fell and landed unceremoniously in the dirt. A glancing pain shot up from the base of her foot to her calf, and she felt the ridiculousness of it roll over her. She grabbed her shoes and walked back to the quiet of the base.

Dr. Green came to draw blood from where it was pooling in Hart's lungs, but the Lieutenant refused. She thought it might have been brave if it wasn't so pointless.

After Green left, Hart reached for one of Vinny's cigarettes on the side table. She watched his slow fingers try to shake one out of the box, and finally she asked, "Would you like me to smoke for you?"

He said yes, and she walked over to take the pack and the lighter from him. Making a cup with her palm to shield the spark from the ceiling fan, she lit a Lucky Strike. She tried to draw enough smoke into her lungs that her exhalations filled the room with a haze of gray, but she exhaled too hard and started coughing with it. She kept going, her eyes and throat burning, seeking the relief of those moments when the smoke obscured Hart's features, the sight of his ruined face.

He just sat there, breathing, looking out that window at the tree.

It became her morning ritual to wake before the other nurses when the sun had not yet risen but the horizon was the hue of a blood orange, and try to climb the palm tree. On the third day, she managed to make it halfway up the trunk, only to slide back down, ruining her hands on the spiked bark. Bethy showed up late to her rounds, cuffs of her dress ripped, stockings asunder, and Tenant said, "You know, you almost missed my funeral."

Vigil
Bri Wilson

8:07 p.m. The 37. Woman gets off, girls get on.

A Minnesota cold on a San Francisco street. Thin coat, shivering legs. Cold but not cold enough to leave. Never cold enough to leave.

The couple walking home. Blue coat, black coat. Dinner plans that disappear halfway to her ears, pizza in the Mission at a restaurant called . . .

Hands shoved in pockets, knuckles colliding with keys, phone, headphones.

8:37 p.m. The 37. Mother and daughter get off, two men get on.

Sunset. Right leg crosses over left. No warmer.

The old man sits on her bench. He texts, she stares at the sidewalk.

Shivers in her gut, rattling her spine from the inside out.

M&M's? He offers. She shakes her head no like she always does.

The gum islands. A new addition to the archipelago, an electric blue smear bridging the gap between the elongated purple triangle and bottle cap-shaped green trio. Must have happened in the night.

Her legs jackhammer into the sidewalk sea in which the gum islands float.

9:07 p.m. The 37. Young woman gets off, the old man gets on.

Bus stares at her. Orange numbers, hot, steely eyes. Bus slides away.

Still street.

Standing. Heels in love with gravity again. Pull her legs down, down, down, but she marches forward, forward, forward.

Concrete feels like mud.

Her fingers don't feel like anything.

Bus stop. A small house.

This place isn't a home.

The right wall. An advertisement, Geico. Green lizard, thumbs-up. Smiling. Like a human.

Tucked into the frame, a photo. Young girl. Smiling. Like an angel.

When the sun slips below the skyline, her smile is where it goes.

Her fingers pull the photo from its spot. They don't know how to hold it, still, after a month.

Corners tearing, paper crumpling. It had rained that day. She had forgotten. That's why she's cold, her coat got wet.

Photo into pocket. New photo from other pocket.

Crisp, bright. Like her sister's seven-year-old smile.

She took the picture in their backyard. Summer. Playing in the sprinkler. Red and blue swimsuit against the black of her skin. Braids, she remembers how they bounced when she kept telling her sister to stay still, I can't take the picture if you keep moving...

Photo into frame. Two fingers to her lips, two fingers to her sister's forehead.

She gets a kiss every day even if she can't feel it.

Hand hangs in the air. Drops to her side, heavy. So heavy.

Street outside bus stop calls her eyes to stare at the pavement. This is where her sister fell.

A month ago. Warmer. Hand in hand, waiting for the bus to take them home. She got a phone call, work. Couldn't let her sister hear her being fired so she stepped outside the stop, walked to the bench.

Tripped by the curb, the wind, someone else's foot. She didn't see it happen. Heard screams, a dull crash. Hung up, ran to look, heart in throat. The 9:07 p.m. 37 bus backed up, slowly, revealing her sister's body in the street.

She doesn't really remember what happened after that.

Eyes squeeze shut. Open. Hand clutches old photo in pocket.

Feet pull her away, towards home.

At 6:00 a.m., they pull her back to the bench.

6:27 a.m. The 37. No one gets off, no one gets on.

Something's Burning
C.M. Wilbur

"Something's burning" she said, her nose turned up at the end. "Check the oven." "There's nothing cooking," he replied "you're always doing this." "Doing what?" Thick silence. It all started the day she couldn't find her way to work. Nothing looked the same anymore. Two yellow lines became three and the oaks in their fields seemed to move closer around every bend in the road. Her supervisor called five times before she had the courage to tell her she was lost. "What on earth is wrong? This isn't like you." "I've had a lot on my mind. I must be more stressed than I thought. I'm sorry. It won't happen again." "Take the day off, have a drink. Or something." Or something. Shaking, she punched her home address into her GPS. At first it was easy to hide, paying in cash to avoid having to admit she'd forgotten the pin to her debit card again, diligently marking everything in the small calendar she carried in her pocket, names, birthdays, phone numbers. On the good days she would record herself, Turning the keys in the ignition. Putting on lipstick. Lighting the stove. So on bad days she could teach herself again. After a while she forgot to watch and seemed to melt inside her clothes, clomping everywhere she went in shoes two sizes too big. Once he found her in the frozen section of the small grocery store down the street, her left hand gripped tightly around something melting. When their eyes met she jolted suddenly as if she'd been sleeping, all she could do then was cry. Towards the end she scattered Post-it notes everywhere. *Put gas in the car. You have a husband. Eat. The dog food is in the blue trash can.* But when she couldn't remember to do that anymore even her own hands looked unfamiliar. Like claws. And the burning smell wouldn't leave her. Every day or two she'd forget to remember not to notice it out loud. "I'm sorry" she said. Not knowing how long she'd been closing her eyes, "I think something is really wrong." She counted to thirty waiting for his response, but when she opened her eyes, she was alone.

Strangers in a Phonebook
Marina Shugrue

On the day that it finally worked, she wore a yellow raincoat and carried a matching yellow umbrella. The streets of the city were crowded, like they always were, but no one bothered to look her way. If someone had looked, they might have noticed that she held her umbrella away from her body, tilted sideways over her shoulder. If someone had looked a bit longer, they may have noticed the rain never seemed to touch her skin—the water veered off somewhere else. Her clothes weren't wet, her hair maintained its style, and her makeup refused to run down her cheeks. She skipped down the graffitied streets, loitering in the rain while others sprinted to the nearest subway station. Twirling her umbrella, she wandered to one of the city's last remaining phone booths.

After jimmying the door back and forth, she opened the booth and stepped inside. It hadn't been cleaned in a long while, and a cloudy film of dirt and perspiration shielded her from the street. She closed the door, sealing herself inside. From her purse, she pulled out a yellow phonebook, disinfecting wipes, and a purple sack filled with jangling coins. She inserted a few quarters into the coin slot, wrinkling her nose as she picked up the phone. She cleaned the phone with a wipe, but the smell of sanitizer couldn't cover up the smell of urine. With the phone cradled between her ear and her shoulder, she propped the phonebook on her knee and flipped to a random page. 314. She scanned over to the third row of numbers and searched three names down.

Grant Howard. 555-306-1366. She punched in the number. Maybe this time it would work.

Grant Howard jolted awake to a phone call. He fumbled to pick up the call, hoping it was his workplace calling him in for a shift.

"Hello?" he answered. He rubbed his eyes, wandering into his kitchen to make coffee.

"Grant Howard?" A woman's voice. Unfamiliar. A bit static-y.

"Yeah—who is this?"

"Unimportant. I need you to meet me somewhere."

Grant pulled the phone from his ear and stared. There was no caller ID, and the number wasn't familiar. Grant thought back to the past few weekends, thinking that perhaps he'd given his number to someone, but he'd not gone out recently. He spooned a few tablespoons of cheap coffee, listening to the static.

"Still there?" she asked.

He poured in water and turned on the pot. "Yeah."

"And?"

"Thinking."

He heard her sigh, heard fingernails tapping. He glanced at his calendar, each work shift written out in neat letters with a red pen. Grant used a green pen for scheduled plans with friends. He frowned when he realized there were no green marks at all this month.

The woman spoke again. "Are you going to stop thinking soon?"

Grant laughed. "I've got today free. Guess I'm game."

115

He swore he heard her smile as she answered, "Good." The static noise in the background mingled with the dripping coffee, yet Grant thought he heard her shifting papers around.

"I have some questions for you, Grant Howard," she said.

"Okay," he said, pouring himself a fresh cup of coffee.

"Is your address still 345 Foster Street?"

He stilled, his coffee cup halfway to his lips. "How did you know that?"

"Page 314. How long have you lived in the city?"

"Since college. About eight years. And what did you say about—"

She interrupted. "Favorite part of the city?"

"The wharf, I guess. Somewhere along the water."

"How do you take your coffee?" she asked him, just as he took a sip from his cup.

He swallowed, and answered, "No sugar. Some cream. What is this for?"

"You don't ask the questions, Mr. Howard."

"Why not?"

She huffed, "Because that's not how this works. I like things a certain way. I like calling strangers. I like having bright clothes that leave me unnoticed. But I don't like walking in the rain and not getting wet. And I like asking questions and getting answers."

Grant smiled, hoping to catch her. "What's your favorite color to wear?" he asked.

"Yellow," she said. "I'm wearing a yellow raincoat now, actually."

"You know, for someone who likes asking the questions, it's easy to get you to answer them."

She paused, the static seeming louder. "Meet me at the AM coffee shop by the marina. You know what I'll be wearing. You have thirty minutes." The phone line clicked. He listened to the dial tone, half expecting her to pick up the line again, waiting to hear her voice.

Finally, he put the phone down, his coffee cup beside it, and sprinted to his bedroom, throwing on whatever clothes he could find. He only had thirty minutes, and it'd been too long since he'd done anything that wasn't work.

She tried to take her time, but she ended up at the agreed upon meeting spot quite early. There was still twenty minutes until Grant would show up—hopefully. No one had ever followed through post phone call.

She hoped anyway. Maybe that was why she kept making phone calls; maybe the results of her experiment no longer mattered so much as the process.

She had nothing to lose, except her curse.

She lingered outside the coffee shop, wondering if she should go inside or wait for Grant. Pacing on the wooden dock at the wharf, she worried about silly things, like if she looked cute, or if Grant would be cute, or if she and Grant would look cute together, or if Grant was a serial killer, and if she looked like a potential murder victim.

"Hey!" someone shouted. She turned and saw a rain-soaked young man walking towards her. "I'm looking for a woman in a yellow raincoat who calls people and asks them questions. Know anything about that?"

She smiled. "Grant Howard."

He nodded. "That'd be me. Do I get to know who you are, now?"

She shook her head, putting down her umbrella. "Not yet."

He frowned. "Wh—"

She cut him off by reaching for his soaked sweater collar with her dry hands, pulling herself up, and kissing him. He jumped, arms flung out, then realized her kiss was pleasant. He drew her closer, wrapping his arms around her waist. For a moment, he swore the rain stopped, and when she let go, he felt warm.

She picked up her umbrella and held out her hand to shake. "I'm Willow Simon."

Grant looked at Willow's hand, bewildered. "Nice to meet you."

"Thanks for coming. No one's actually met me in real life before." She bounced on the balls of her feet. "It's all very exciting."

"What exactly is this for?"

She shrugged. "Just an exercise in trust."

"Trust?"

"Yeah. Phone a random person, meet them, and kiss them. Simple instructions, really." Willow stuck her hand out from under the umbrella, smiling as drops of rain hit her skin.

Grant watched her. "And I'm your first success?"

She pulled her hand back. "Yes. And likely my only one. People here just don't trust each other anymore."

He laughed. "True. Hey, Willow, wanna grab a cup of coffee with me?"

Grant nodded towards the coffee shop. She beamed. "I'd love to."

If Grant had been paying closer attention, he would have noticed that Willow, standing in the rain, was getting wet, whereas he was getting more and more dry with every drop that fell to the ground.

Student of the Week

An Excerpt

Bryan Firks

Lila opened her eyes up extra early today and saw plastic eyes staring at her. She whispered "Good morning, Beebee" and Beebee said it back with her eyes. Lila was eight now, and as long as she could remember, Beebee's eyes had been open. She thought that was sad.

Lila pet Beebee's hair one, two, three times, put her on the bed, and sat up. Now what? Get off the bed, put on dress number two because today is extra sunny. Say bye to dress one and dress three, don't be sad, there are more days. Put on tip-toe socks.

Now close the door—shhh, slow over the noisy part. Now pass the big bedroom, really slow. Step one fine, step two good. Step three squeaky, hop over. Love tip-toe socks. Wait for loud snore—ew—now tippy-toe into the kitchen.

First, grab Captain Crunch. Find special pink bowl, not the blue one, yes that one. Find milk, sniff first. Yuck! Sour patch kids snuck in again. It's okay, Captain Crunch is just as good without milk.

Can't forget morning jobs. Go into the big room, pick up pillow and put it over couch-rip. Throw empty cans in big trash. Brush chips under couch, shhh nobody knows. Back into kitchen, check ceiling rain cup. More full than yesterday. Hm.

Pick up Smuckers sandwich—only two left in the box already?—throw in backpack. Anything else? She hadn't checked drippy sink yet, but old Hello Kitty watch said it's time to go! Extra careful with squeakies on the front door, worse than the room door. Remember not to use bad arm.

Lila skipped through the yard. The ground made extra-loud crunchies when she skipped. She stopped at the potty house with its broken door. Three knocks on the door for good luck. Just like when Mommy was here, three knocks to make Lila come out when she was hiding.

Lila walked past the big trees, so tall and lonely. This was where she was supposed to turn right, but she didn't. She knew the special way. She kept going through the big trees and found the shiny fence. Nobody knew this, but there was a tiny little hole at the bottom of the shiny fence. Lila could always find it because the big red stop sign was right above it. Too perfect!

She snuck under the hole. It always made her dress look dirty, especially dress number two. Bad arm hurt a little bit, but she made it! She skipped onto the other side. Not as many crunchies over here, though. It was different on this side.

She called this side the Greens. Everything was just so *green* over here. Clean, too. Lila loved walking through the Greens. Every street had a name, and they were all bird names! There was Pigeon Lane, and Bluebird Lane, and Owl Lane.

Things were just different in the Greens, and she liked the different. Just weird things like how they didn't have potty houses! She could spend a whole day walking through the Greens. But usually it was just mornings before school.

Today was a special school day for Lila. She went over to her class line-up on the blacktop, second from the four-square court. That's it! Mrs. Travis's third-grade class.

They lined up here every morning with the whole school. So cold out sometimes! But not today. She was wearing dress number two today.

"Good morning, Lila," whispered Mrs. Travis, smiling as Lila walked past.

"Good morning Mrs. Travis!"

Mrs. Travis always smelled like lemon—her favorite. Remember, arms behind back, walk in straight line. Sit criss-cross-applesauce, hands in lap. Wave good morning at Jimmy, he's looking at you.

It was a special school day for Lila because today was Student of the Week! The best thing every Friday on the blacktop, even if it was cold.

Lila wanted to be Student of the Week so bad. She had the whole pledge of allegiance memorized, and wanted to say it in front of the whole school. She knew it was important to say the first part *Ready, begin* before you start. A lot of kids forget that and everyone starts too soon. She could do it better, if only it was her class's turn!

Oh look, Mr. Cunningham is going to talk. Okay, okay, say *Happy Friday, Mr. Cunningham* really slow like everyone else. Look, he's talking about Student of the Week now. Yes, we know we do it every Friday. Whose turn is it?

Mrs. Travis!

Finally! Everyone is sitting straighter all of a sudden. Mrs. Travis is walking up to the front now in her nice flowery skirt. She always wore nice flowery skirts.

Lila *loved* Mrs. Travis. Her voice was so high and nice and she would whisper when she got close so she wouldn't scare you. She always said nice things about Lila's dresses one, two, and three. Mrs. Travis made Lila want to be *so* good. Made her want to sit up straight and put hands in lap and sit criss-cross-applesauce. Made her want to do pluses and minuses and spelling. She was extra good at spelling, too.

Lila knew *so* much about Mrs. Travis. Knew she was 35 years old, and her favorite color was yellow. Knew she liked planting flowers and wearing flower skirts. Even knew her house number! 12 Bluebird Lane. Lila learned this when they were all writing their house numbers to put on fancy envelopes. Lila's was tricky though, no number on her house.

Mrs. Travis was almost at the front now! Lila wondered who she was going to pick. It *had* to be her. She always walked the straightest and did good at spelling and raised her hand before talking. She loved to talk to Mrs. Travis before school too about her flowers. It had to be her ... but what if she picked Jimmy? He always had his hands in his lap and always tried to get in line in front of her so Mrs. Travis could see him best. No, don't let it be Jimmy.

Mrs. Travis got to the front and took the microphone. Her skirt moved a little in the wind. She said some things about how her class was best and we should all get the award (not Jimmy, he shouldn't) and how she loves us all. But still she had to pick one and that person was . . .

Lila got out of criss-cross-applesauce and walked super quick (don't skip, don't skip) to the front. She *knew* it! She loved Mrs. Travis and Mrs. Travis loved her. She got up there and saw the big flag and Mr. Cunningham next to it, smiling and clapping. Other people were clapping too, so nice! Mrs. Travis leaned down and whispered "Congratulations, sweetie," and handed her a big paper. It said *Student of the Week* in huge letters and her name was right under it! And there was Mrs. Travis's name at the bottom in her perfect printing.

Lila knew everybody was looking but she gave Mrs. Travis a big hug. She felt Mrs. Travis's skirt and smelled lemon, her favorite. Lila took a deep breath. No morning jobs here, no crunchies. She took the microphone, remembered not to use bad arm, and said put your right hand over your heart, face the flag, now *ready, begin.*

The Artist's Canvas
Piper Walker

My body was a canvas that was long forgotten in the corner of a room. Covered by a sheet and a layer of dust, it used to merely exist until I met him. He is an artist. And he saw potential in the canvas that everyone else had passed by, untouched. Others were either unimpressed or intimidated by the canvas, but he wasn't. He saw a challenge and a reward in it; in me.

Gently he set the canvas on his easel and he turned me into the light of the sun. His words he spoke with such care and the dust began to clear. His fingers were brushes he would run across my skin and I would see bursts of color. A deft touch to the inside of my wrist and I would melt, all my colors blending and softening. Colors would streak across the canvas, rich and striking in beauty when he touched my cheek. With every touch to my back hues of red splashed onto the masterpiece he was shaping, painting, creating.

He would speak softly some days as he worked, smudging gentle blues and gray into the art, wondering how everyone before him had seen nothing in the canvas. And on the rough days, when the colors would darken, the clouds would roll in and words of anger lashed like a whip—he was always careful never to let the canvas drop off his easel.

He is an artist and my body was his work. One breath across the skin here, a whisper of a touch there, and my back would arch as if he had demanded it. But of course he had not. The scene he was painting was one of compromise and love. Everything about him was gentle, reverent. I was valued; the canvas his treasure.

Time is what broke us. In time his brush strokes slowed. He would go days between painting and I was depending on him too much. He would go and the canvas would sit on his easel, eagerly awaiting his return. My colors would fade and dull until he returned. Until the day he didn't.

The artist. The man with the gentle paintbrush strokes had left, without a word or explanation. My body, the canvas, sat alone in the center of the room, again forgotten. Until the day I realized I had to be the one to move the canvas, to move myself.

The Clerk
An Excerpt
Jon Goodnick

The sun had now climbed to a reasonable height, signaling the Clerk to unlock the door and wheel out the sign. The sign, decades old and hand-carved from imported maple, read:

APPENDAGE IMPORIUM

We Buy AND Sell;

Trades Also Accepted

At the bottom of the sign, small but distinguishable, was a carving of the Clerk in his late-twenties, smiling impishly, as if the sign itself was the height of absurdity. And it was; his poorly etched face was often mistaken for a wall-eyed actor renowned for his portrayal of Frankenstein's assistant, however, the Clerk did not own a television (he never had), and could not begin to refute or agree with any such comparison. However, the Clerk cherished the sign, not for its aesthetic achievement, but rather the opposite. Its failure to approximate even the slightest amount of artfulness instilled in the Clerk a sense of unwarranted pride, so he continued to wheel it out each morning, the way the Bearded Woman, comfortable with herself, refuses to shave. With the sign planted out front, the Clerk settled in behind the counter and opened his book. This particular book—a paperback of considerable wear, the name on the spine long since scraped away by countless hands—contained a story that the Clerk found effectively distracting. It described the life of a visionary scientist who, through countless impractical experiments, finds a method for verifying the existence of the soul in humans. The story spewed the kind of cloying moralism that the Clerk resented, but found inexplicably absorbing, for he could identify with none of the scientist's conviction. And so the Clerk continued to read attentively, searching not for the key that would unlock his own devotion to a set of steadfast principles (he knew he had none), but instead, he awaited the unavoidable misstep anyone so ambitious as the scientist was sure to make, as they, who like the scientist dared to soar so close to the sun, would inevitably burst into flames. Yet each successive page brought with it the further triumphs of this man of science and inspired such frustration in the Clerk that, when he finally looked up (having had no customers that day), the sky had already begun to darken.

As the Clerk looked ahead in the chapter, searching for a natural place to stop for the evening, the chime from the bell attached to the door alerted him to the arrival of a last-minute customer. The Clerk peeled his eyes from the text and assessed the man who had just entered the boutique, his irritation being transmitted through the intensity of his glare. The man was distressingly boney, a sign that the Clerk understood as an implication of a lack of nutrition, or at least an untreated glandular disorder, both of which, the Clerk concluded, signaled a gross deficiency of finances, making the gangly man's presence all the more gratuitous. His clothes were baggy and faded; his sweatshirt, billowy like a homespun sail, was frayed at the cuffs and insinuated the bluish color it may have once been. His pants—reverse pleat khakis—were stained in a chance pattern that, to the Clerk, had the appearance of a relief map. This was the type of man who would almost certainly browse around, picking up and putting down piece after countless piece, only to leave the boutique without having bought a thing. Torn from his book and now heavy with resentment, the Clerk watched the man survey the store, inspecting only the splintering ceiling and the faulty wiring that had incensed the town's fire marshal for over a decade, following the hazardous bundle of wires to where they disappeared back into the wall. Satisfied, the man refocused his sharp eyes and approached the Clerk, coming to a sharp stop before the counter that separated the two, then, with a few adept twists, unscrewed his nose and placed it on the glass between them. The Clerk looked down, his face wilting from the unwanted patronage, then lifted the nose delicately between the thumb and index finger of his right hand, bringing it close to his face.

"Provenance?" asked the Clerk, inspecting each surface of the nose. The Clerk awaited a response from the man, who shifted his weight back and forth on his feet in a sheepish, involuntary dance, while intently watching each stage of the Clerk's investigation. Yet, he said nothing. Impatient, the Clerk bristled, "Where's it from, fella?"

"Dutch. It's Dutch," replied the man, his voice sudden like a backfiring car. The Clerk (who had been ready to leave since the moment he arrived that morning) picturing a glass filled with a peaty single malt splashed atop a single cube of ice, allowed his mouth to the luxury of watering. After a moment, the Clerk realized where he was and swallowed the daydream.

"You sure?"

"I'm sure."

The man again continued his dance, shifting his weight from his left foot to the right, then back again, which made the Clerk squint his eyes disapprovingly.

"It's mostly Dutch. My mom thinks her granddad was a Pole."

The Clerk set the nose back down on the glass with a fleshy thud and met the man's eyes. They were cagey, taking in more than they gave away, and appeared to be the only thing the man possessed that was of any value. The Clerk wondered if they were for sale instead.

"No. Russian," said the Clerk.

"What?"

"It's Russian. Actually, fella, if we're being technical, it's Slavic."

"Ok," replied the man without blinking. "It's Slavic, then." He placed his hands facedown atop the glass of the ocular showcase, and, with each eye peering up from below at his dry, split palms, he began to force air through his teeth in a muted whistle that, instead of resonating within the yawning space of the boutique, died against the rotting support beams and its porous grain.

"I'm going to take a closer look. A moment." The Clerk bent at the waist, and, disappearing beneath the counter, left the man to continue his dance of rearrangement while he hunted for his examination kit. Beneath a pyramid of dusty thumbs (each well-manicured but shabbily hemmed around the joints in a way that made the Clerk reluctant to display them, as he did not want to jeopardize what little bit of business integrity he had left), the Clerk felt the smooth handle of the case and shook it free, and, standing back up with a wince, placed it on the counter beside the man's nose. The Clerk unclasped the case and lifted the lid, making sure to do nothing but keep focused on his task. This guarded the silent solitude in which the man appeared to be perpetually immersed, though his whistle, subdued and resolute, would let no one forget his presence. From the case, the Clerk first removed his black-framed glasses with their dual monocular loupes and put them on, he then located the pocket scale and caliper, setting them atop the counter as well. As the Clerk began his audit of the nose, the man holstered his whistle and leaned forward, as if waking from a trance:

"A good nose. A good nose this one," the man declared. "Been in my family for years. Generation to generation . . . that sort of thing."

The man drummed his fingers on the glass awaiting a reply from the Clerk, who continued to look closely at the nose, taking its measurements and noting its diminishing worth. A decade ago, maybe two, a nose of these dimensions would have surely fetched the month's salary of a bank-teller or cabbie, but with the industry wavering as it was, it was barely worth the shelf space.

"It's useless, this nose. Couldn't sell it if it came free with Mussolini's molars. I used to move ten, maybe fifteen like this a week. Now, I'm lucky if they even come up in conversation, see, with these—" the Clerk cut himself short, and slowly moved his two fingers along the curve of the nose, while the man, having leaned in even closer, now had his elbows resting on the glass.

The Hunter's Moon
Pearson Sharp

It was the second night of the Hunter's Moon, and freshly fallen snow twinkled under its cold light as I watched the frozen woods from my hiding place. My lungs burned with each breath of frigid air, and inside my fur gloves, my fingers were going numb. It was the coldest night of the winter, and I had drawn the straw to go hunting in the forest.

Already several from our village had died, and my mother was afraid my sister Brighde—barely a year old now—wouldn't see the spring thaw. My father was old, and only having his one good leg, the hunting fell to me and my younger brother, Bran. These were dark times, and our shamans prayed to the old gods, whom they said we had angered. But I didn't think they were listening. Besides, we make our own fates, I thought, and gripped my spear tighter.

A bitter wind scorned down through the dead trees, and I huddled deeper into my hollow between two trunks, pulling my fur-lined hood down over my face. I watched an owl glide through the skeletal branches, vanishing like a snow wraith. I considered turning back, but the faces of my mother and father floated up before me, my mother's desperate eyes more haunting than the glaring Hunter's Moon above.

A cracking twig nearby startled me, and I heard the soft "thumpf-thumpf-thumpf" of footfalls in the snow. A moment later, a herd of wild boar plodded into the clearing. I caught my breath, for these were no ordinary boar. They were enormous, and they filled the clearing with a wondrous light, reflecting the moon off manes of brilliant gold. These were gods of the forest.

My father once told me my grandfather had killed one of these boars, and its meat—filled with the ancient magic of the woods—had fed the village for a month. There was no law forbidding killing the gods, but the shamans warned you must respect the balance of the forest.

The killing of a god was no light thing, and though my mouth turned to ash, I knew if I hesitated, I would return home empty-handed. With the blind resolve that warriors speak of, I stepped out of the hollow and pulled my arm back as my father had shown me. Saying a silent prayer, I hurled the spear as hard as I could.

For a terrible moment, I feared I had missed. But I had aimed true, and I was rewarded with a solid crunching sound as the spear drove deep into the side of a large boar. It squealed in pain and collapsed, as the other boars scattered into the woods. I rushed to its side and wrenched the spear out. I had hit its heart, and it was dead.

I panted with exhilaration as the golden light of the boar slowly faded, leaving behind only a dull, yellow coat. But some light did remain, and I looked up to see a smaller boar watching me from nearby. If I could take home two boars in one night, my village would be safe and fed for months. Without thinking I whipped my spear in its direction, and to my surprise, it landed square in the boar's chest, driving it backward into the snow. The boar grunted and rolled over, dead.

I was elated. I would be a hero. Yet something felt wrong. I had killed two gods, I had taken more than I needed. I knelt beside the large boar and offered a prayer to the spirits. I heard a noise then and looked up, and saw yet another golden boar standing on the ridge above me. It was gigantic, and its black eyes regarded me coldly. "You have taken more than your share, Ardan," it said. "You will kill no more boar this night, or any other—or we shall claim your life in payment." He glared at me, and I could do nothing but stare. "You must promise you will never again kill another boar. Do you swear to it?"

Awestruck, I nodded. "I swear," I managed to whisper. The boar looked at me almost with pity, and then turned and disappeared.

I was shaken, but I mastered my fear. Angering the gods was a terrible thing, but such was the price for a hasty act in a time of need. Lifting the smaller boar, I set off for the village. My kill weighed heavily on my shoulders, but it was heavier still on my heart.

As I stalked back through the woods for home, I stopped, and listened. I could hear shouting, and voices raised in alarm. I dropped the boar and ran, sprinting through the barren trees. It must be wolves, I thought, as I burst through the underbrush and looked towards the village. But it was not wolves—it was the golden boars. The gods were taking their revenge.

Dashing up the hill to the palisade, I saw the boars had broken inside. Men were scrambling for weapons, with the women and children climbing into a stone-walled cellar. I saw my father standing with the other men, and my mother and sister disappearing inside. But where was Bran? A shout drew my attention, and I saw my brother waving to me. "Bran!" I shouted, but as I started for him a giant golden boar—the same who had spoken to me in the woods—stepped in my path. He was bigger than a horse, and glowed with all the fearsome power of the ancient ones. Bran was trapped, and backed into the palisade.

I readied my spear, it was an easy throw. But with spear in hand, I froze as the warning of the old boar rang through my head. I watched in horror then, the giant forest god edging closer, his mouth bristling with tusks the size of swords. Bran's eyes filled with dread, the boar took another step forward, and my insides turned to stone.

Like my brother, the old gods had me pinned. I watched, powerless, as the boar advanced, his breath streaming out in thick white clouds that billowed over Bran. But no, I wasn't powerless. Fear would not rule me—now, or ever. A sudden cry burst from my lips, filled with the rage of all my ancestors beaten back by the cruelty of the gods. The golden boar turned to look at me then, but it was too late. I raised my spear, and with all my might, plunged the point deep into the old god's heart. As I did, a thought flashed through my mind again: *we make our own fate.*

The giant boar reared, letting out a deafening screech and knocking me to the side. I covered my face as his massive body writhed and kicked, tearing up deep furrows in the frosted ground. He shuddered once more, his wild eyes filling with hatred for me as he finally lay still.

In a moment, it was over, and the remaining golden boar fled the village in panic. I tugged the spear free of his body, and breathed in the cold night air. A sense of peace and finality flooded through me, and I felt my grip on the spear suddenly weaken. Somewhere far above, the Hunter's Moon shone down through an icy black sky. "Ardan?" My brother called me. I looked down at him, and smiled.

Lunar Tides
Cloud

The sun set a couple more times, and some stars died in silence. None of this seemed to make an impression on the flower.

"These are dark times Floyd," the flower's girlfriend had once said to him in the distant past.

He had simply attributed this statement to her dramatic nature and whisked it away, but as of late, the haunting words ate away deep at his roots.

Not only was the flower losing his ruffled petals by the week—punchy yellow in color—but his stamen—now a splotch of grease-stained umber dwindled his confidence to a weed. For the first time he was jealous of the trees, the birds, and the slugs—the skies.

Still, this did not stop him from wanting to receive praise from his fellow flowers. He was early to rise before the others, carefully and desperately fixing colorful feathers abandoned by birds to fill the screaming cavities of where once his petals bloomed with blatant pastiche.

When the sky finally graced the earth with drops of glittering dew as the peeking sun licked them with warmth, Floyd would pretend to be asleep, waiting to be awakened by the chorus of adoration from the surrounding vegetation.

"Oh, my! Oh, my! Wake! Wake Floyd—Wake you—you majestic . . ."

In these moments Floyd felt celestial.

When asked by his admirers of how he attained such grandeur, Floyd would pompously speak of the exotic lineage his family of flora had come from and how he was the last of its kind.

"I had two different bees, a hummingbird, and the queen ant herself visit me just the other day . . ."

He would go on, basking in his own idolatry—denying his delusions despite his perfect self-awareness.

"Ahhhh," the other elder flowers cooed in unison with a sarcastic flashing of eyelashes.

Floyd cried himself to sleep that night—in secret.

Under a timid Monday sky, the beginning staccatos of rain infused a vague scent of moist asphalt and dirt into the stagnant air. Devout earthworms quietly tickled along slanted sidewalks marred with speckles of crusted gum—softened now by the rain. Technicolor oil splotches along the streets arrived in the form of ethereal jellyfish.

A frantic exodus. Dramatic. Oozing pinks and swollen bruised blues. A harsh moonlight fell heavily on a squirming colony of worms seeking safe haven. They would not all see the promise of the next day. Some, minced into segments and grounded into pulp by wheels or passerby soles, while others unwilling to venture into the wilderness would drown in their sorrow. And still, others, distracted by the pleasure of loafing in puddles, would dry out with tomorrow's sun—gasping, regretting, paralyzed. These were a stiff-necked worm.

That night, the waning moon retreated under a veil of clouds, and Floyd woke to the sound of a leaking chrysalis hanging from a tree above him that he mistook for the moon.

The flower knew his youth had now passed him. He understood that all things must come to an end. For the first time, he had eternity in his mind. He wanted to be whole.

Straining skywards the flower looked at the pitiful crescent and found comfort.

Inside the chrysalis, the melted organism's subconscious wept. Frightened. Would she be able to keep her memories from her previous life? She thought about thinking.

She had never wanted this change. Had prolonged it—promised even—to someone, reassuring him daily that she would never change—and yet one day she found herself leaving him for no good reason and when she woke up the next day it was all too late.

Hoping to wake any second from this nightmare, only the feeling of helpless suspension grew like a stain to enshroud her with each passing thought.

Time dragged, and with it a deep thirsty darkness intending to stay—not that she could feel. The outside world receded further into the distance—not that she could see. She wanted to say something, but even the thoughts that fed her voice in her mind retreated to someplace she could not retrieve. So she did not bother trying, afraid to further disappoint a lost cause. Her existence became an echo submerged in forever night.

She imagined leaking teardrops, imagined some sense of moisture form where her eyes may have been, felt some sort of gravity pull, as the tears would trickle down, making its way past the eye—escaping into reality. To glimmer. To touch someone, anyone.

Ferrets and Meringues
Emily Crosby

BANG! BANG! BANG!

The repeated clanging of plastic on iron reverberated around ancient walls. Eliza jumped and clapped a hand to her chest. Anne chuckled behind her hand before furrowing her brow and frowning unconvincingly.

"Aaannnne," Eliza shoved her friend, causing her to stumble up against the imposing rock walls surrounding them.

"Sorry, but not sorry!" Anne snickered as she pushed off from the wall to stand upright again.

A cacophony of screeches and sales pitches interrupted Eliza's retort. She spun on her heel and glared at the array of appendages dangling ponchos and selfie sticks through the bars. "Ok but it is actually terrifying. It's like a reverse zoo!"

Anne stepped forward as the line crawled closer to the ticket counter. "Don't worry. Chad will protect you from the scary vendors. Isn't that right, Chad?"

Adjusting his beige cargo shorts and brown button-down, Chad turned from the ancient Latin plaque he'd been reading. "What?"

"That fanny pack of yours looks pretty dangerous." Anne's face was serious. "You'd protect Eliza if one of the vendors tried to snatch her purse, wouldn't you?"

Chad shoved his glasses further up his nose as he fixed his gaze on Eliza. "Well, considering the number of vendors all attempting to outsell each other, the prospects of having one's belongings snatched are actually pretty high in this particular zone, so I'm not sure what the point is in hypothesizing potential situations." He puffed his skinny chest out noticeably. "But I suppose if I were in the vicinity, I might make an attempt to prevent the perpetrator from apprehending anything of importance."

Eliza smiled uncomfortably and moved to Anne's other side. "Dammit Anne," she muttered, eyeing the still-staring Chad. "Don't encourage him!"

Subtly sticking her tongue out, Anne patted Eliza's shoulder patronizingly.

Suddenly Eliza leaped again, uttering a shrill gasp. Spinning on her heel, she tried to slap the young man who'd crept up behind her quietly singing the chorus to "Blurred Lines."

"You know you want it! You know you want it!"

"Oh my god Brit! I hate you so much."

Bearing his teeth in a snort of laughter, Brit pranced away and threw his arm around Chad. "C'mon Eliza, we're here to see how the greatest civilization of all time killed people! And then we're wrapping up the day in the tombs of the people they killed! There's no room for infighting in our little group."

Thoroughly peeved, Eliza rolled her eyes and turned away from the two young men.

"Actually," Chad awkwardly returned Brit's bro-hug as he raised his other hand to point to the Latin plaque. "If you had taken the time to read the plaque, you would have learned that the Romans never killed Christians in the Colosseum. It's a common misconception, though, so don't feel bad."

The other three exchanged exasperated glances.

"Wow, Chad," Brit rubbed his hand through his hair and stepped away from Chad. "That plaque really says all that? I must have been using the wrong declension or something. I definitely thought they crucified Jesus in here."

Chad blanched. "Brit, you don't *use* declensions, and Jesus never even went to Rome!"

Brit shook his head while the girls shook with silent laughter. "Damn, Chad. I guess I'm just too dumb."

Chad looked as though he was about to say something more, but the line began to move once more, cutting off his words. Anne grabbed Eliza's arm, and they traipsed to the ticket counter. Anne paused while the others traded their euros for flimsy stubs of paper that granted them access to ancient history. Inside the Colosseum, the rain was coming down in torrents, and Chad popped open his umbrella as they moved through the gated entrance.

"Wonder what other stick he's got in that sack," Brit whispered to Anne, nudging her and winking.

"Are you still thirteen years old?" Anne forced a sigh and tried not to laugh.

"Nope. I just . . . ." Brit paused and grinned mischievously. ". . . *call 'em like I see 'em*."

"You didn't. Please tell me you did not just make a Colosseum pun."

All too pleased with himself, Brit meandered off, pretending to be interested in what the tour guide in front of them was saying.

Anne rolled her eyes and allowed herself to smile. She looked back through the entrance to the vendors still clambering about on the iron rails, shouting the prices of their wares. A green poncho fell from one of the vendor's hands and drifted to the ground. Its bright plastic reflected the electric lights inside the waiting area. Anne watched it fall and then looked up. Her eyes met those of the vendor's. His eyes were foreign, yet also familiar. Then the man leaped from the railing and was gone. Fresh rain melted ancient mud from the bricks as Anne turned to rejoin her friends.

"Spring break in Italy was definitely the best decision we've made all semester, guys," Brit sauntered past a centuries-old statue of a bare-chested woman and tipped his poncho-ed head to it. "Don't you feel free and alive?"

"Oh, for sure," Eliza agreed. She casually twisted her body so as to close the gap between her and Brit.

"Actually, in order to make the decision to spend our time off in Italy, we first had to make the decision to spend a semester studying in England." Chad's voice cracked awkwardly as he assessed the narrow gap between Eliza and Brit in relation to the width of the sidewalk. "So technically the decision that led to the opportunity to make another decision was the best decision. You have to decide to do something before you can do it, so the initial stages are equally important, if not more important."

"Pretty sure that level of arrogant intelligence is illegal in Italy," Brit muttered to Eliza.

"What?" Chad ducked and wove behind the pair, trying to squeeze himself in next to Eliza.

"I said I'm pretty sure fat ferret pestilence is diesel in Italy."

Chad rubbed his goatee hard as he struggled to make sense of Brit's reply. "Ah, well, petrol *is* hard to come by in Europe." He bent over suddenly and pulled his tan socks back up to his knees, then continued, "Brit seems to think Rome has a ferret problem. But actually, the Romans use ferrets for hunting purposes so it makes sense that some of their descendants would still inhabit the city. In fact, Caesar Augustus himself owned a whole collection of exotic ferrets and was even buried with one or two. Emperor and beast. Isn't it insane how these insignificant creatures managed to exist with and even outlive the greatest civilization in all of history?"

Anne's eye twitched. "Yeah, Chad, the strength of ferrets is pretty crazy."

"Actually, they're not that strong relative to their size—"

She cut him off. "Brit! Eliza! I think I see a bakery just ahead. Let's go get some meringues or something and dry off a bit."

As Chad attempted to direct the conversation back to ferrets, the trio headed towards the bakery, which promised a split second of warmth and satisfaction before they faced the elements once again.

Letting the Spiders Out
For My Grandma
Shayne Taylor

He watched as the spider crawled across the pile of old newspapers in the wicker bin, crosswords filled out in pen. Its macabre, little legs reaching and pining for the arm of the loveseat where he sat.

Rolling the funnies he was reading, the boy made to crush the creature. No, no, grandma said, holding his arm back with an open palm, her rings cool against his skin. Grandma was the woman who slept with amethyst under her pillow. She collected polliwogs from the puddles in the gully and watched them grow legs and took them to the creek when they did. She was the woman who let the boy pop popcorn without a lid, just to see. Grandma unrolled the paper and invited the spider to crawl onto Charlie Brown's face.

She took the paper and sat on the ground, Look, she said. The boy followed and crossed his legs next to her. The spider continued its business, slowly moving one leg at a time, long and articulate. Grandma lay her hand next to the spider and gently it climbed into her palm. The morning light cast sinister shadows under the spider, but the boy felt safe because he was with her. Grandma lived in a house entirely of windows and curtains that never closed, which as he grew up the boy wondered if they were for looking out, or in.

The spider crawled to the underside of Grandma's hand and began to descend on a tether of silk. She held her hand up so they could watch. The silk shone like quartz in the sun. And silently, the spider landed on the back of the boy's hand. Its footsteps reminded the boy of butterfly kisses from his mother. Grandma, with her hand on his back, brought him to his feet and led the boy to the deck. The spider swayed in the wind on its delicate legs.

With the creature in his palm now, Grandma cupped hers under his and guided him to the fig tree. "Thank him for visiting," she whispered. Thank you for visiting, the boy said, and the spider stepped out onto a green fruit. It began crafting a web, and the two watched.

Protected by the leaves, nourished by the gnats, it looking out, and them in., the spider made a home.

The Purple Moose
Donna P. Crilly

The best time to drink is in the daytime because then it feels like a holiday. You go into a dark bar on a bright street and come out a few hours later having forgotten about the sun and wanting to ride out the fun before taking an evening siesta.

When I got started on daytime drinking, the pressure was off because I didn't have to spend all day winding up. I just walked outside my house and, after some convincing, met my friend down the street and had a day. My friend was a few years older, but I always felt like an old soul anyway.

Jess met me at the Purple Moose on Wednesday, when it was almost the p.m. but still the a.m. The jukebox played '80s music. It was dark inside. The walls were black with glow-in-the-dark paintings of moose in various neon colors. Above the bar was a sign that read, "Cash Only." The bartender leaned against the counter with a white rag hanging from his back pocket. Every twenty minutes or so he went outside for a smoke break, and I would either have to wait to order another drink or give up and have a cigarette as well. Sometimes he went out and just stayed there.

I ordered the first round of drinks while Jess was in the bathroom. The bartender grabbed two cans of Tecate and two slices of lime and placed them in front of me. He held up four fingers and said "four." I gave him a five-dollar bill and told him to keep the change; then he went back to leaning against the counter.

Jess came back and said, "Ooh, Tecate. You really know how to treat a lady."

I shrugged. "Tecate, why not-tay?"

We had a couple of rounds before Jess suggested we step it up to something classy, like Stella. I didn't care, as long as it was cheap.

"You're the poorest person I know," Jess said. She always said that.

It didn't bother me that I was poor. I never worried too much about money because I never had it. Everything just worked itself out somehow. The only time it became an issue was toward the end of the month when I was a little short on rent and had to jump down to my mother's house for a few days until things cooled off or I got paid. Jess was broke most of the time too, but there's a difference between broke and poor. She bought the next round, and we went back and forth like that.

"I remember when I was your age, Karlita *bonita*," Jess said. She always switched to calling me Karlita after a few drinks. "I would go to the bar by myself and sit down, and random guys would come up to me, and I'd write them stories on napkins in exchange for drinks." She motioned two fingers to her lips. "Let's have a cigarette."

We placed the coasters atop our open drinks and went outside. The sun waxed onto the empty street. I crouched in the shadow of the awning and lit my cigarette with a practiced swift motion of my Zippo. I handed it to Jess. The bartender stood there not really noticing us, until Jess said something to him and all of the sudden he started telling us his life story about how he was caught trying to cross the border when he was fourteen, but now he's a citizen and wants to bring his family over. His name was Miguel. He was handsome in a way but looked sort of old; he had to have been at least in his mid-thirties.

"What do you guys do? I mean, how did you become friends?" Miguel said.

"We go to City College and write for the school paper," Jess said.

"So you want to be journalists?"

Miguel was talking to both of us, but his eyes were on Jess. Jess just stood there, not even trying as usual, and Miguel eventually broke his gaze to look at me. Unless we're talking about Virginia Woolf or Sylvia Plath or Hunter S. Thompson, I never knew what to say to people I didn't know, and I was glad I had put on sunglasses. Miguel started speaking Spanish to me, and I said, *"No hablo muy bien."*

"Sorry, I thought you were Mexican," he said.

"Only half," I said.

"What's the other half?"

"White."

"Gringa on the inside, Morena on the outside," Miguel said. "How about you?"

"Filipina and Irish," Jess said. She took a nonchalant drag from her cigarette.

"A lot of mixed around here. Beautiful combination," Miguel said. He finished his cigarette and tossed it into the street. "Spanish is so easy. You can learn in one month, maybe two. We should all go to Tijuana to practice, I will show you everything."

"Oh, I go all the time. I have family there," I said.

"Eh, I don't go to TJ anymore," Jess said.

It was apparent Jess had picked up vibes from Miguel, but she was more experienced with being flirted with, so she flirted back in that way as to not make herself seem available, though not shut him out completely. From the shadow of the awning where I stood, I watched them light another cigarette. They were standing directly under the sun. I scanned the block. About a third of the businesses were boarded up—casualties of the recession.

"Can I get one of those?" I asked.

"How about we share this one?" Jess said.

I shrugged and took a step into the light toward them. She handed me her cigarette, and I took a couple of puffs. We passed it back and forth.

"So, what kind of stories do you write?" Miguel said.

"News, features, arts, you name it," I said. "Whatever we see, we write. The City is our muse."

The conversation began to wane, and Jess signaled we head inside to finish our drinks. We stepped back into the darkness of the Purple Moose. I felt a little light-headed from the cigarette. There were only a handful of other people in the bar besides us. I eased back in the comfort of my Stella and my increasingly tipsy state. It was two-thirty in the afternoon when we left.

Sirens
David Alexander

The man was awoken by warning sirens echoing in the distance. Sirens placed some time ago to alert of an impending attack. Weeks prior, when the rumors became the inevitable, the cities of the West began their evacuation. Seeking refuge within the heart of the country. The middle and eastern states became flooded with those who weren't ready to die.

When the reports came, the man began to pack and prepare for his expedition. He thought perhaps Las Vegas, but acknowledge the popularity of that destination and thought better. Nebraska maybe. Any state where people were scarce but welcoming. However, on the day of his scheduled evacuation what unfolded before him was nothing less than biblical. The neighbors he had lived next to, people who once looked after each other and ate with each other, had turned into savages. Screaming and fighting with each other over the little resources available. Squabbles turned into fights. Fights turned into worst outcomes. Those with firearms used them, those with less relented. The decline of society had shaken the man. When other neighbors had come to claim what was his, he defended himself. Somewhere between the fourth and fifth altercation, the man decided not to leave. Why go, when he would find the same chaos anywhere else he went.

When night fell, the man stood at his sink cleaning the blood from his face with sore hands. Outside, he heard another argument. Stepping out to confront it, he noticed it was his next-door neighbor, France. France had been the only neighbor who boarded his home and didn't involve himself in the evacuation.

France was yelling at his wife in his foreign dialect. Not understanding the language, the man could only summarize the situation. The wife was pleading for France to flee with her. France simply shook his head and forced upon her the car keys as he hugged her. The man stayed frozen in silence only watching them. Eventually after some time, the wife stepped into her car, red-faced. She pulled out slowly looking at France, before turning her head and driving away. France and the man stood silently, their eyes following her into the distance, into the dark. They stopped looking once they could no longer see her. With the wife gone the man noticed France was staring at him, the man stared back. The man simply nodded his head and walked back inside.

When the sirens had ended the man stepped outside. The entire sky was blanketed in a dark gray overcast. It had appeared ominous to him, almost fitting in a way. God had provided a perfect setting for the end. He had noticed that France was already outside tending to his garden. France was a meticulous creature and prone to habit. No matter what was occurring in the world, France would be at his garden every morning.

The man called out to France, "Do you want a drink?"

France replied, "Of course."

The two men sat in the house drinking and talking about women, the world and the things they would miss. France noticed the blank walls voided of all pictures. Emphasizing the lack of any familiarity or connection between the man and anyone else. The only item in the house that looked of any interest was a piano. France had never heard it played before in all the years of being the man's neighbor.

When the sun began to creep down, France and the man moved a couch to the middle of the street. They sat and continued with their conversations and liquor. As the time closed in on the attack, the man spoke.

"I didn't want to ask because, to be honest, I don't like prying into other people's lives. But this might be the only time and I feel like maybe you want to tell me. Why didn't you leave when you had a chance? Why didn't you go with your wife?"

France looked sternly at the man and produced a meekly smile, took from his drink and responded, "I have cancer. Terminal cancer. Even if I were to escape this, I wouldn't escape that. My poor wife, God bless her. She'll be okay. She headed to Canada, she has family there."

"And you didn't want to spend your last days with her?" asked the man.

"No, I would have loved to but," France paused. "I don't want you to judge me even though you won't have the time," he smiled. "But you see my life insurance won't pay out if the cancer kills me, but it will pay out for other forms of death. For example, this nuclear blast. My wife and her family will be taken care of. The best I can do for her is to stay here and burn." He took another sip from his drink.

"That's good," said the man, thinking on what he would do in that situation.

"Well," said France, "I didn't ask you because I don't think you want to tell me. But you asked me so I'm asking you. Why have you stayed behind?"

The man stared at the ground, "Seems to me that this is going to happen everywhere not just here. I can run today and make it fine, but I'll probably end up running again. Why wait." the man responded.

France continued, "Then why don't you want to wait?"

The man paused then began again, "To be honest, I don't have much reason to wait. I don't have a family; my parents have passed, and the music no longer plays as sweetly as it once did for me." The man laughed at himself. "I don't know France. Call it depression. Call it loneliness. All I know is that I dictate how I choose to die. This is my freedom. This is how I'm defiant. No man or country threatens my life thinking it's something precious to me." After another pause, "Plus, I'm tired and this seems like a good enough end."

France nodded his head in approval and repeated the last words back, "A good enough end."

When the time came, the sirens rang loud and the two men at the same time cheered to their death. Soon the sirens would stop, the sky would be filled with an artificial light and the ground with fire which nothing would escape. The sirens stopped and only the sound was the wind filling the void. The two men sat waiting for some time with nothing happening. They did not talk nor move. Simply sat and waited and waited. Two men ready to die but unable to. After about an hour the man spoke.

"Looks like today wasn't the day either, same time tomorrow France?" asked the man.

"Of course," replied France.

Golden Seas

I stand in front of golden seas
Watching the suns light fade from me
The dark creeping over
Turning gold into black
I'm careful to notice my feet losing track
They sink into the world
Disappearing from me

I lift my feet up
To stop the engulfing death
If I allowed it too
The sea would take my last breath
Take me deep in
Bury my soul
And look for another
trapped in its world
I free myself
Knowing how hard
The longer I stay

Oh, I wish I could stand longer
Let the sea take me in
To perish my name
To cure my every sin
Yet I continue to move
Preventing its take

Every day, every time, I refuse its embrace
I only know one reason
To continue the fight
For another opportunity
To just see the light.

Uncle Babool
Marcus Rigsby

He was hiding somewhere in the house. Ethan, the youngest of the Hawtrey children, had no doubt. While he did not know what the creature looked like, a tradition of playground lore had taught him something of "the bad uncle's" business. The big children, he turned their stomachs to jelly and sucked them out through the belly buttons. The small children, he stuffed in a sack, which he wore over his head, and dragged them through dark doorways, where living bodies never returned, save for the bones. That night, Uncle Babool had come to call on the Hawtrey children.

From their bedroom, they shuddered at the sound of a glass cabinet shattering in the foyer downstairs. The quiet that followed was enough to freeze their blood.

An upturned desk barricaded the bedroom door, while the children huddled within a blanket fort, armed with a hockey stick, a baseball bat, and a hairbrush.

"What kind of weapon is a hairbrush?" said Harriet, the second eldest, frowning at Ethan's choice of weapon.

"Everyone knows you can't kill Uncle Babool," said Ethan shortly. "But if you hurt him, you can make him go away. When Dad brushes my hair, it hurts plenty."

"What makes you think this Uncle Babool is even real?" said Hans-Peter, the eldest. Despite his skepticism, he had pulled back the blanket walls of the fort to glance about the room.

"You heard the noise downstairs," said Ethan.

"An animal broke in, that's all it was," said Hans-Peter, flinching from the shadows that swayed in the glow of the fireplace.

Suddenly, the doorknob jiggled, and the door rattled. It sounded as though someone was trying to rip it off its hinges. Then silence.

"We should tell Dad again," said Harriet. "I know what he told you, but—"

But even if any of them had courage enough to step outside the fort, let alone the bedroom, Dad would be of no help. Ethan had gone to him already that night to tell him that Uncle Babool was raising havoc in the house. But instead of scolding Ethan for waking him or for lying, he offered these puzzling words:

"You and your siblings must learn to be each other's strength. You won't always have a father to fight monsters for you."

"What do you think he meant by that?" said Ethan.

"Obviously he meant that he's going to die someday," said Harriet, taking a superior tone. "And he wants us to look after each other."

Ethan frowned. "Dad's not going to die," he said. "Why would he?"

"What are you, stupid? Everyone dies."

"Shut it, you two!" Hans-Peter hissed.

A low creak had begun to rise within the walls, a creak which became a voice.

"I see three little weasels hiding in their den," it said. "But they needn't be afraid, not all of them, not tonight. I will make them a deal. Give up the littlest weasel now. If they let me have him, then I'll not come for the second littlest for seven nights. Then I'll not come for the eldest for seven nights again."

Ethan looked from his sister to his brother. He saw practical Harriet turn to cowardly Hans-Peter, and he knew what they must be thinking.

"You won't let him take me," Ethan said. "Uncle Babool never keeps promises. And even if he does, he'd still come for you in seven days."

"Fourteen days for me," said Hans-Peter. "Not that we'd let him take you, I mean," he corrected himself.

"No, of course we wouldn't," said Harriet. "Never in a million years!"

Ethan narrowed his eyes to slits.

"You'd better not," he said, so scared he could cry. "If you do, I'll make you sorry. I'll come back as a spirit and be ten times as scary as Uncle Babool. I won't give you seven days or fourteen."

"Ethan!" Harriet snapped. "You're our brother. We're not letting anything happen you." She sounded as though she meant it this time. Hans-Peter nodded nervously. If he had any objections, at least he was unprepared to voice them.

"Good," said Ethan. "Because all children Uncle Babool takes come back as—"

Suddenly, Harriet and Hans-Peter's expressions melted in horror. Ethan spun around.

A shadow had moved in front of the fireplace and eclipsed its light. The silhouette stood outside the blanket fort, its body twisting from one shapeless mass to another. At last it settled into the form of a man, unnaturally tall. Slowly, he bent down to lift the hem of the fort.

The enormous hand that stretched through was raw and ragged, and a sweet, meaty odor wafted from its flesh. The bloody claws reached for Ethan. Ethan looked for his brother and sister and found them frozen in terror. Seeing that they would spare him no defense, he resolved to fight this battle alone.

He swung his hairbrush over his head, and discharged a war cry that filled the room with a deafening echo. Then he charged straight into the arms of Uncle Babool. The damp appendages clenched him eagerly.

"Ethan!" cried Harriet and Hans-Peter, shocked to their senses and leaping to their brother's aid. What began as a rush to snatch him from the cruel grip of the monster soon escalated to an infantry charge, and the elder siblings raised their bat and hockey stick as they raced to battle.

The Hawtrey children crashed through the blanket walls and tumbled out into the bedroom. Never did their weapons strike the enemy, and the children considered themselves doomed. Yet they were satisfied that they would make a valiant end, despite flopping on the floor like fish.

But when they lifted their eyes, they found no enemy waiting for them.

"Look!" said Ethan.

Spread out in the fireplace was a burning pile of clothing: A tattered suit, the sack that once covered the monster's head, and a rope which he wore for a necktie. The garments writhed in the flames and were rapidly reduced to ash.

From the corners of their eyes, the children spotted a man's shadow scurrying across the ceiling, and then that too was gone.

The Hawtrey children stood and gaped at each other. Until that night, Ethan never imagined that his brother and sister cared enough to risk their lives for him, and in truth, neither had they. It was a lesson they would be glad to have learned when, three months later, their father inexplicably vanished. He left for their inheritance the Hawtrey house, with its dark doorways and voices echoing faintly.

Bea and the Presumptuous Elephant
Kayla Latta

There is an elephant sitting in my kitchen. A bumbling, bizarre, bafflingly big elephant blocking my breakfast. I wait, warily watching from the doorway, wanting to walk away yet wondering where in the world this elephant has wandered in from. It wasn't there when we ate dinner last night. I certainly would have remembered seeing it while eating the overcooked mac and cheese I know Maggie hated. She didn't have to say it for me to know—it was my first time making it on my own and she knew I was trying. No, the elephant had most definitely arrived this morning.

She sits at our kitchen table, in Mom's old spot, drinking black coffee from *my* favorite mug with her trunk. Bea is even scrawled across it in yellow paint, claiming it as my own and yet this elephant doesn't seem to care. I scowl, souring as I suddenly think about the stain I'll surely be left to scrub, but I simply stay silent. Dad pours more coffee for the elephant, who blushes and bats her long elephant eyelashes at him. She looks over at me and beckons me forward with her round foot, but I stay glued to my spot. I most certainly do not trust a presumptuous elephant who comes into a home uninvited and drinks from a ten-year-old's favorite mug.

"Morning, Beatrice," the elephant says sweetly. I glare, glower and grump, keeping my distance from this great, gray intruder.

"Hey Bea, I'm about to make pancakes," Dad smiles. He holds up a pan and a box of Bisquick. "I wanted to have them done before you and your sister woke up, but you're out of bed a little earlier than I had anticipated." Dad glances over to the elephant quickly, then turns back to me and gives me another smile. Dad seems to smile an awful lot around this elephant.

"But it's Saturday," I reply, taking a step backwards.

"Perfect day for pancakes then, huh?" the elephant says cheerily, taking another sip from my mug.

"We eat pancakes on Sundays," I snap. The elephant winces slightly, then looks at Dad.

"Bea, there's no need to be snippy," Dad warns. "I just thought we could mix things up a bit, eat pancakes today and maybe French toast tomorrow. Won't that be fun?" Dad goes back to smiling, but I don't smile back. Instead, I fix my glare on the tactless traitor and wonder how anyone could think it's okay to put a stupid elephant before family tradition.

"So Bea, how is school going? Your dad tells me you're about to finish fifth grade," the elephant asks, cocking her gigantic gray head to the side as if to say she cares. I don't believe her though, not for a minute. So I stay silent, while the sound of batter sizzling on the pan cuts through the air. Much to my dismay, my silence doesn't deter this relentless beast. "Don't want to talk about school on a Saturday, huh? I get that. Well, what about your friends? How are things going with them?"

Since my silence failed, I decide to change tactics. "I don't have any friends," I glower.

My words startle the elephant, who looks down at the table and stops any further questions.

Mission accomplished.

"Bea," Dad sighs, "why don't you wake up Maggie? The pancakes will be ready in a few minutes." I leave the kitchen without a word, walking down the hall very slowly so I can listen to their conversation.

"Maybe going out and leaving them on their own last night was a bad idea," the elephant sighs. "Are you sure they're ready to meet me?"

"You've been in my life for a few months now, they should know who you are. I thought inviting you over for breakfast would be the best way, but—I mean I figured Bea would be ready, she's so mature for her age . . . well, she normally is anyways," I hear a soft thwack as Dad flips the pancake. "She has had to do a lot of growing up since her mom . . ."

"Shhhh," the elephant soothes.

"She takes care of Maggie just as much as I do," Dad continues in a weirdly garbled tone, "which kind of breaks my heart you know? And she wasn't lying when she said she doesn't have any friends. I don't know what she's going to do next year when she goes to middle school, but I'm hoping it'll be good for her. She needs more friends than her seven-year-old sister." Dad and the elephant continue speaking, but I stop paying attention. I don't really want to listen anymore.

I walk into Maggie's room and sit on the floor for a little bit, running my fingers through the soft yellow rug. I don't want to go back out there, but I know I'll have to eventually. After a few minutes, I walk up to Maggie's bed and shake her on the shoulder. She opens her eyes slowly, blinking away the sleep from her brown eyes. She sniffs the air and a moment later she bolts up.

"Pancakes!" she exclaims, before jumping out of bed and running down the hall, her hair a rat's nest and her jammies twisted oddly around her body. I walk out of her room and find her standing in the doorway to the kitchen, just as I had minutes ago.

"Who are *you*?" Maggie asks, confusion and distrust written all over her face. I stand next to Maggie in the doorway and follow her accusing gaze to the blonde woman sitting in Mom's old spot and drinking from my favorite mug.

"Girls, there is someone I would like you to meet," Dad says, he walks up to the woman and puts his hand on her shoulder. She reaches up and laces her fingers through his. "Bea, Maggie, this is Eleanor." They both look at us with hesitant, hopeful smiles.

Maggie turns and looks up at me with wide eyes. "Who is she Bea?" she whispers.

"She's trying to replace Mom," I whisper back.

Maggie reaches out and grabs my hand, holding on tightly with all the strength she can muster.

A Turn for the Worse
An Excerpt
Kyle Campbell

The leaves of the trees swirl and dance, the wind gently pushing them to and fro. As they shimmer a thousand different types of vivid greens; each unique and wondrous emerge. The trees sigh with age, hunched over from time's crushing weight. It is a beautiful place, a clearing deep within the forest. A small brook zigzags and worms its way through the clearing, giving a gentle rhythm to the sounds in the trees as it smoothly and unceasingly serenades anyone willing to stop and listen.

It is a place of gathering for the woodland creatures. Deer graze upon the grass and gratefully drink from the bubbling brook. Squirrels zip along the trees, digging here and there, occasionally pulling from the earth a prized possession left from winter's brief reign. The birds chip and chirp, a symphony keeping in time with the steady flow of the brook.

Sir Richard and his young squire traveled for two days to reach the clearing; the pace had been slow, but there was no reason to hurry. Even so, the trail had made both men unclean, covered in dust from the long road they traveled. Richard pulled at the hood of his cloak, trying to keep it low over his brow.

The seasoned knight took a seat on the ground wearily. His companion, feet sore to bleeding saw the chance to rest his own battered body and joined him, dropping a single pack on the ground with a soft thud.

"Think he'll be along soon then?" asked the squire.

Richard paid him no mind. If he was going to die, he might as well take in the full beauty of his surroundings. He was not frightened, his ill fate was one he had chosen freely, and one he would choose all over again, given the option. A smile spread across his face as his gaze wandered across the clearing, reminiscing on many secret sacred nights.

"My Lord, what do we do now?" concern creeping into his escort's voice.

Richard kept his small smile, "You must learn patience Thomas, I'm in no hurry this day. Why don't you fill our waterskins in that creek there." It was less of a question than a command. He began rummaging through the discarded pack and retrieved a whetstone and a scrap of clean cloth. Swiftly and deftly he tossed the items to his squire and in the same motion brought his blade free of its sheath.

Thomas caught the items clumsily, and gave his teacher a bewildered look.

"After you are finished, clean yourself up, and sharpen my blade for me," said Richard calmly. His sword was already sharp, but it couldn't hurt to distract his distraught student. What was done could not be undone, and no amount of preparation would help anymore.

Thomas nodded grimly, and stood up. He then hurried himself to the brook, the waterskin slung over his shoulder bouncing lightly in every step. Every movement was deliberate, his concentration so focused,

Richard lowered himself onto his back with a contented sigh. The day was nearly clear, a mild smattering of stringy clouds sprinkling across the otherwise azure skies. The sun was busying itself with finding the horizon as quickly as possible. The wind cradled his weathered face, tanned from years of adventuring, rough and cracked from the countless windburns he had received. He stretched his arms above him, muscles moving powerfully, strong and quick. Not as quick as they used to be, he noted. He held his hands up to the sky and inspected them, fingers knotted from countless breaks and fractures during years of training.

Years of training that would soon be tested.

The sound of thundering hooves became audible through the trees, and the woodland creatures fled in a blind panic.

Richard sat up groggily; some time had passed while he had lain, searching the sky, and watching the few stringy clouds reflect the evening sun. They shone golden, like the precious hair of a beautiful maiden, one that Richard felt certain was watching that very same sky, hoping for him to return.

Thomas dropped the whetstone and spun around to face the sound of the approaching hooves. "What should I do sir?"

"Easy, Thomas, just bring me my blade, your part in this is finished." Richard ran his hands through his long hair once to get the tangle of leaves out; he wanted to at least look presentable to his Lord.

The hooves rampaged through the forest, trampling the ground in a terrible cacophonous roar. Twigs snapped, leaves crunched, and branches bent. The steady and measured beat of the trees swaying, wind blowing, and stream flowing were replaced by the shouts of men pushing their steeds to breaking.

Four riders burst into view, their enormous mounts stomping and nickering nervously. The lead horseman wore a brilliant white cloak, beneath the hood of which was a face Richard recognized. The face that was once filled with charity and kindness now bore the sole burden of hatred. As they came upon Richard, they made an uneasy circle and came to a stop. Suddenly the clearing felt full of tension, so much so that even the brook listened intently—seemingly falling into the background.

"Richard." snarled the man in the white cloak. "Shall we finish?"

"M'Lord Fredric," Richard swept his arm out as part of a bowing motion. "Would it not be prudent to take a few minutes to rest? You must have been riding hard to make such good time." Richard grimaced slightly at slurring his greeting.

"Don't you dare mock me with your pleasantries; they won't extend your life any further than the end of my blade." Fredric grimaced as he dismounted; obviously he had strained himself while riding. He gestured to the three men accompanying him, "This time you won't escape, even if out of luck or some twist of the gods' will, you manage to fell me."

In response to his words, the three men also dismounted, their heavy armor clinking and clanging in discordant unison. One of them grabbed the reins of the other horses and began marching them over to the nearest tree to tie them while the other two unslung the crossbows across their backs and began winding them. The crossbows whined in protest at the stress being placed upon them. Two clicks affirmed that they were wound tight, and they each placed a bolt in position, pointing their gnashing teeth toward Richard.

"Is this really necessary, Fredric? I'd sooner let you stab me than be shot like a common pickpocket by those contraptions." Richard allowed himself a small grin. The gods had truly spun fortune's wheel a final time for him.

"Necessary!" scoffed Fredric as he shrugged off his cloak, letting its snowy perfection touch the ground for perhaps the first time. "You dare speak to me about what is '*necessary*' after the crime you committed?" He spat at the ground, "and when I demanded justice, you turned tail and fled like a dog to this . . . this damnable bog! You left me with naught but a note and a promise to be here!"

"I felt it would be poetic if our kinship should end where it all began. Look around you Fredric, do you not recognize where we are?" Richard raised his arms and gestured around him, "In this very clearing I rescued you from those low life bandits who had kidnapped you for ransom."

"That was a long time ago, and I am not here to reminisce with you." Fredric grabbed at the thick blade strapped to his hip and drew it smoothly. "I demand justice! Now, draw your sword so that we might finish this as poetically as it began!"

Richard calmly looked towards Thomas, who was now standing nearby, having realized that the sword was already impeccably sharp. The young squire held Richard's sword reverently in his arms, cradling it as if fearful it would be the last time he might do so. Without a word, Thomas approached and held the sword out to Richard.

"That's a good lad, Thomas. Now stand back, and whatever happens, don't give these men a reason to add your body to the pile they seek."

Thomas nodded slowly, the frown on his face growing longer each passing moment.

Fredric chuckled lightly to himself, "Finally, my vengeance will be quenched!"

The two men faced one another, Fredric with his sword point between them. Richard quickly gave a polite bow and raised his own blade. With a furious yell, Fredric charged toward Richard, brandishing his blade for a swing towards his throat.

Richard parried the savage slash, wincing under the brute strength his opponent exhibited, the steel clanging together loudly as the swords glanced off one another, sparks flying. Fredric brought his sword around and attempted to sweep Richard's leg with the blade, but again, he was stopped short as their metal met. While able to block the ferocity before him, Richard found that he was slowly backing up, losing ground to his opponent.

Fredric varied directions time and time again with each chop, the wider blade carried considerably more weight, which made it harder to block. He had Richard on the defensive and he knew it, grinning wildly, lost in the ecstasy that any moment he might cut into not metal, but flesh.

Coming Home
Mary McQuistan

I muttered a few prayers as I drove past the dilapidated wooden fence framing a graveled driveway. As soon as I parked, my head fell back to rest against my seat.

My stomach lurched at a harsh knocking on my window. My eyes fluttered open, and I glared at a weathered-looking man.

I pressed a button to lower my window. "May I help you?"

"Hazel Peterson?" the man asked.

"How do you know my name?"

"You're here to go through your father's house, right?"

My eyes narrowed. "Do you always answer a question with a question?"

The man chuckled. His smile revealed several stained and blackened teeth, likely from heavy use of chewing tobacco. "You haven't been answering any of mine either, Miss Peterson."

"And you are . . .?"

"I'm Greg Hudson. I was a close friend of your father's."

"I wasn't aware that I would have company."

"He wished that I were to preside over the distribution of his items."

I snorted. Even in death, my father made things difficult. "I guess I can't fight that. Let's get this done and over with." I raised my window and grabbed my cane. I ignored Greg's surveying glance as I stepped out of my car

"Aren't you a little young to be using that?"

"Rheumatoid arthritis. Had hip surgery a few months ago." My hand tightened around the handle of my cane. After shuffling a few steps forward, a screaming pain shot up the left side of my hip, and I hissed out a breath.

"You need any help?"

"I'm fine." I limped up a set of cracking concrete steps and whipped open a screen door. I was greeted by the smell of cigarettes. I walked inside to find boxes upon boxes piled on top of one another. And where there weren't boxes, bulging crates were thrown on top of even more boxes, cutting into the cardboard and disemboweling out the contents.

"There are a couple of chairs right here, if you need to sit a moment." Greg himself collapsed into one of the indicated lazy boys and grunted as he pulled the lever to release the footrest.

I decided to follow suit and hobbled over to the other lazy boy. I felt my body sink into its worn padding.

I surveyed the room, taking note of my father's disappointing skill at interior decorating. The rose-colored wallpaper was unfurling at the corners. The furniture was even worse. The wooden legs of each piece of furniture had rotted with age, and each had collapsed to the ground. In the dimly lit room, it seemed as though I was looking over a battlefield at the twisted corpses of fallen soldiers.

Greg cleared his throat. "I understand your relationship with your father was a bit rocky."

"Guess he told you a few things about me."

Greg shifted around in his chair and ignored my sassy comment. "You could at least have a little respect for the man now given that he's dead. It's not flattering for a woman to be so bitter."

I couldn't figure out if I should be more offended by his misogynistic views or his ignorance. "If your father left you when you were thirteen, you'd probably be a little pissed off too."

Greg studied me a moment, obviously trying to formulate a clever comment to trump mine, but he gave up and turned his attention to the room. His eyes glimmered a moment as though he found a missing dollar. "You were a dancer, right?"

My pulse started to pound in my ears. "What are you talking about?"

Greg cranked the lever down and pulled himself up from the chair to trudge towards the TV. "I got to show you something. Could you open the drawer in that table?"

I leaned forward to a coffee table and opened a drawer. Inside was a cluster of remotes.

"Grab whatever is the biggest one." Greg was rustling around in a box of videocassettes.

"If you say so," I whispered. I grabbed what I deemed to fit Greg's description and pressed the power button. Black and white peppered the screen.

"One minute here." Greg pulled out a tape and blew on it. I grimaced at the dust particles that rained onto the carpet. "There we go, this is it." He pushed the tape into the VCR and the screen changed to black.

"I don't think we have the time for a *Mission Impossible* marathon."

"This is a little more entertaining than Tom Cruise. Just sit back and watch."

I was ready to come up with another sarcastic comment, but my voice caught in my throat at the faint sound of warped piano music.

I turned to watch a flickering image of a group of girls in tutus twirling and bouncing across a stage.

"Where did you get this?" I asked with a steel voice.

"Your dad. He filmed a bunch of the dances you were in."

"That's impossible. This is when," the dancers split in the middle to reveal a figure dressed in stark white, "this is a few days after he left. He never saw this."

Greg collapsed back into his chair. "You thought he never saw this. But he did."

"This was my solo. This was the last time I danced before I started to feel the pain . . ." I turned away from the TV screen and faced Greg. "So you expect me to believe that my father, who left about a week before this dance had bothered to come see this dance?"

"Your father is not so much the evil villain you are trying to make him out to be," Greg said. "He actually made many sacrifices for you."

"Sacrifices?" I laughed. "Not sure if running away from a physically-ailing daughter could be considered a sacrifice on his part." I grabbed my cane. "I knew this would be a waste of time."

"What are you doing?"

"Leaving. You're trying way too hard to redeem my father's reputation, and that's not what I came here for."

"Hazel—"

"No," I pried myself from the chair and tried to make my exit. "You're wasting your breath."

146

"I—"

"Just stay in this rat hole and figure out all my father's crap on your own, okay?" My fingers grazed the doorknob.

"He left because he couldn't help!"

I squeezed the doorknob, but I couldn't make myself turn it.

"He left," I heard Greg grunt as he tried to catch up to me, "because he didn't want you to hate him more. He knew he couldn't help you and he didn't want you to hate him for it."

"So he preferred that I hate him for being hundreds of miles away?"

"He wanted not to be a father who let you down, who couldn't comfort you as you got worse."

"That's the thing, Greg," I was getting uncomfortable with the amount of things he knew about me. "He wasn't even a father, and that's all I needed from him." I pointed back to the TV. "And no sentimental home videos are going to change that." I turned back to open the door.

"Where are you going?"

I looked at Greg Hudson, my father's last attempt to fix his mistakes. "Home." The door shut with an echoing clap.

As I walked down the driveway, I tried to figure out if my cane hitting the ground was louder than my racing heart.

Café
An Excerpt
Karin Erickson

The day Hart had agreed to meet her mother was unseasonably warm, and the sun stared down on the marketplace with relentless attention. Vendors called out from their stalls and dickered with interested pedestrians. She moved through the center of the thoroughfare with an expedient gait driven both by apprehension and a mild, unexpected excitement. It had been a long time since she'd seen her mother, and it was the only time in her adult life she could remember her mother initiating a meeting. She prayed there would be shade for them to sit in and that she would be the one to arrive first at the sidewalk café. As she rounded the corner, she saw that the latter of her wishes was not to be.

Her mother sat at a small table, a cup and an empty plate before her. Hart felt the sight of her in her stomach. Veronica Talbot, overdressed as usual, was a striking figure—a statuesque blonde, as rigid and ornate as the scrolled-iron bistro chairs. Hart forced herself forward. The older woman's head turned toward her as though she had sensed her approach, yet her expression registered little in the way of recognition. As she walked, Hart pushed the corners of her mouth outward in what she hoped was more smile than grimace. Her mother lifted the linen napkin from her lap and placed it on her plate, rising from her chair with a grace that belied her age.

The two embraced before retreating to their seats. "I was beginning to wonder if you couldn't find the place."

Hart stiffened. "I thought we agreed on 10:30, it's only 10:15."

Her mother looked beyond her, signaling to the waitress. When a young, fresh-faced girl in a white blouse and black pencil skirt appeared, the woman smiled and said, "She's here, at last."

The waitress's eyes flicked toward Hart with a nod as she tucked her empty tray under one arm. "Do you still need some menus, Mrs. Talbot?" she asked, placing a hand on her shoulder.

"I don't think so, Lacy" the woman answered. "I'll have a refill, and she'll have a coffee."

Hart observed the crumbs on her mother's plate visible beneath the rumpled napkin. "You've already eaten?" she asked.

"Well, I figured it was getting late in the morning. Surely, you've already eaten by now."

"No," she said. "I thought we'd be having brunch."

"You really should get up earlier in the morning and get your day started," she sipped her coffee. "You know I've always encouraged that."

Hart pulled her bottom lip between her teeth and watched the florist in the stall across the way rearrange blooms. An uncomfortable silence was descending. "How have you been?" she asked.

"Things are pretty much the same as last time I saw you, I suppose."

"It's been a long time since I've seen you."

Her mother's eyes widened with what seemed genuine surprise. "Well, it hasn't been that long."

"Almost two years."

"Nonsense. And we spoke over the holidays." She lifted a delicate hand to tuck a bit of hair behind her ear. Hands so unlike Hart's own large, unmanicured ones.

"These last holidays?" Hart's throat tightened in a familiar way. "I sent you a card and left you a voicemail, but I never heard back."

"I don't think that's true." Her mother paused as though considering it, and then followed, "Anyway, what did you come here for? To start arguments?"

"I came because you asked me to." When the older woman didn't respond, Hart added, "I was glad you asked me to."

Veronica Talbot drank her coffee and nodded. She sat her cup down and said, "Well, you know how your brother is. He thought it was overdue." Then she cocked her head to the side as though something had occurred to her. "Did you say something to him?"

So their meeting hadn't been her mother's idea after all. Hart internalized this new injury and felt anger at her naiveté for thinking it might have been otherwise. "No," she responded. "I didn't." She leaned back and knotted her fingers in her lap as a hot cup of coffee and a small decanter of cream were placed before her. She hoped this would be enough to slake her hunger. The waitress refilled her mother's cup then made her way to offer refills to other patrons as they talked over bacon and eggs. "Anyway," she told her mother, "I was only trying to say it's good to see you."

"Now *there's* a hardworking young woman," her mother said and nodded toward the ponytailed server.

Hart turned to watch the girl and fought her instincts to take the bait. Today would be different. This time their visit would not end with her walking away dejected. This time her mother would learn of her successes and words of praise would be for her. This was the first time in her life that Hart was confident in her accomplishments. She focused on that and felt an upwelling of empowerment.

"Is something funny?" her mother asked.

"Hmm?" she realized she'd been smiling. "No. Just thinking about something else."

"She's pre-med." the woman said with raised brows. "Working her way through school, all by herself."

"Just like I did," Hart said. "Good for her."

Veronica Talbot laughed then—a lilting condescension. "Art school is not medical school, Hart." She shook her head, and her eyes roamed over those feasting on breakfast nearby as though searching to see if anybody else was getting a load of her daughter.

Hart looked down to hide the effect of those words. "I didn't go to art school. I only took a few art classes," she said. "My degree is in design. Interior architecture."

"You know your sister doesn't even know you're an interior designer?" she said. "You really should stay in better contact."

"We talk all the time." Her face flushed. "And that's because I'm not an interior designer." She fell silent and fixed her coffee, pouring a liberal amount of sugar from the dispenser. She could feel her mother judging the calories.

"Honey, why are you getting so flustered?" the older woman asked. "Why must you always be so sensitive?"

Hart sighed, an exhalation of many swallowed sighs. The excitement she'd felt earlier was gone, and she searched for some window of hope she could open again. She had imagined this moment with unyielding clarity since the day her mother had called to ask her here—telling her of the award for her design, her new job, and how her mother would respond with the same exuberance she'd shown for her brother on his graduation day or her sister with all of her pageants. But the moment was tainted, and she thought maybe if they talked about something else for a while, she could steer the conversation back here on a more positive note later on. "You said on the phone that you went to the Bahamas over Christmas?" Her mother brightened at the change of topic and rambled with enthusiasm about her husband and their many travels.

The sunlight crept toward them across the concrete. More people filled the marketplace, and the world was alive with color, overlapping voices, and the throbbing hum of unseen vehicles somewhere distant. Under any other circumstances it might be a wonderful place to sit with her work and people watch. She nodded and questioned in the usual way as her mother animated the importance of her stories with hand gestures and photos on her phone. Hart's thoughts drifted off—the errands she needed to run that afternoon, the nagging pangs of her hunger, and then her current project, an old firehouse a bohemian couple with new money was converting to a residence. She pulled her pencil and notepad from her bag to jot down a quick idea, but stopped and looked up when she realized her mother had gone quiet.

"Am I interrupting something?" her mother asked.

Hart pulled her things into her lap as a student caught passing notes by a teacher would. She apologized.

Her mother wore a convincing visage of having been wounded. "Did you even hear what I was saying?" she asked.

"I just wanted to write something down before I forgot about it," she said, putting things back in her bag. "For work." When her mother didn't respond, she added, "I'm sorry, it was important."

It was almost imperceptible, the roll of her eyes, the slight twitch of a threatened smile, but Hart saw them. Felt them like a knife. "It was important," she repeated.

"Did I say otherwise?" her mother threw out her hands.

An old anxiety began to fester under Hart's ribcage—a familiar visitation of dread. "What were you saying?"

"Nothing important, I'm sure." She elongated the vowels on "important."

This was the moment that always came. And this would be the moment, if she didn't manage to diffuse the situation, that would replay itself in her mind, teasing out the infinite number of ways it could've, or should've, been handled.

Summer Vacation
Arianne V. Advincula

After three hours of driving and a toll road in the middle of the Californian desert, ten pairs of feet waited at a security gate. They handed over cell phones and showed driver's licenses, school IDs, and state IDs to a flat-faced officer in sunglasses. Among the crowd of sneakers and slippers and heels stood a pair of smaller feet. Child's feet. Little Boy held onto his mother's hand, wiping snot onto his Pokémon t-shirt.

His mom presented his Carter's Elementary school ID. A piece of plastic cut into a square he hated. In the photo, a gaping hole stood in the middle of his teeth. The day before picture day, he lost both front teeth. Little Boy pulled at the edge of his shirt; he hated that photo.

His mother took his hand and walked thirty more feet up a sandy hill. There, three more sets of feet waited at a small bench in the middle of nowhere. A woman in high-heels was sitting alone, but she stood to allow an elderly couple a seat. Little Boy looked at the old man. He gave Little Boy a smile with nothing but pink gums.

Little Boy looked up at his mother, trying to ignore the old man. "How much longer?"

Another pair of feet joined the group. Black boots. Officer's boots. He tipped his hat. All these people knew him; they arranged themselves into a neat line.

"Finally!" Little Boy jumped up.

A bus appeared in the distance. It stopped before the line of people. The driver pulled a lever and the door swung back. A different group of fifteen clambered out, covering their faces with their hands, and others with heads buried into another's shoulder.

"It's too hot today," one woman in an orange spaghetti top said, fanning herself with a newspaper as she got on.

Her daughter fell in line behind her, "It's the middle of July, Mami, of course."

The police officer in the driver's seat pulled the red lever back with effort and the door creaked closed.

The seats were torn up leather with the cotton puffing out. The group filed in together, taking their seats, thighs pressing against each other, the women crossing their legs so they wouldn't touch the men next to them. A pocket of sweat built up in between their squished thighs. Little Boy sat on his mother's lap.

The bus started once the two officers nodded at each other. It chugged down the road toward the security gate. The other officer stationed there stepped out, watching the bus as it made a u-turn and started back up the sandy road from which it came. In a few minutes the group rolled along at a full speed of 25 miles per hour, kicking up desert dust behind them.

A man in sunglasses sat next to Little Boy's mother. He crossed tattooed arms over his stomach. The woman in the spaghetti strapped shirt took her daughter's purple-painted nails into hers. Aside from the small movements the people on the bus made as they shifted back and forth, there was utter silence. Little Boy hated this silence. He sat up, trying to find his mother's brown eyes behind her bangs. His mother was looking down.

So Little Boy looked, at the tattooed man, the gaping-hole-smile old man, the spaghetti strap woman.

"Are we going to get Daddy this time?" he asked.

The man with the tattoos next to him, the Little Boy could see, looked up at him from behind those dark sunglasses before his eyes darted away quickly.

The driver looked at the rear-view mirror. "Ma'am."

All the people in the bus crunched their shoulders together, squeezing themselves, especially the women who prayed he wasn't speaking to them.

"Control that little boy. No standing in the bus."

"Honey," his mother took Little Boy's arm.

But not this time. Little Boy pulled back. He looked at the tattooed man who was looking at him again. "No!" Little Boy spun around, crossing his arms like the man.

The bus went over a dip in the road. Little Boy was thrown back into the high-heeled woman's lap. Everyone on the bus shuddered. They sank into their seats. His mother didn't bother to move.

The high-heeled woman wasn't a mother, but she knew kids. She took Little Boy by the shoulders.

"Hey there," she smiled. "How old are you?"

"Six." Little Boy wiped snot onto his shirt right in front of her.

"You have to sit down—"

"Are you here to see your daddy too?"

The entire group shifted back and forth with the swaying bus, folding arms and making themselves tighter.

"No," she shook her head. "My sister."

Little Boy held onto her knees to keep himself from swaying. "Is my daddy coming home this time?"

The woman in the spaghetti strap broke out first. She covered her face with a handkerchief. Her daughter next to her plugged her own eyes with both palms.

Little Boy looked up at the high-heeled woman. She was crying too. Everyone on the bus was crying, shivering shoulders shifting against the motion of the bus, throwing the people forward with their elbows on their knees or back with their heads against the faded windows.

Inside, something inside Little Boy fills up, like a balloon swelling, ready to burst inside of him. It presses against his bones and begins to hurt more than when he crashed his bike into Mr. Johnson's car and lost his teeth. It's dad's fault for getting him that tricycle. It's more embarrassing than that school photo. It's dad's faults for not rescheduling picture day.

He doesn't want to cry in front of everyone. So Little Boy, stuck his finger in his mouth, feeling the empty space of his gaping smile.

The Gray Laundromat
Shelby Grates

The laundromat down the street was gray. Not just in color but in the overall mood, as most laundromats are.

I had passed the little laundromat several times on my Sunday walk, and each time I tried not to be reminded of the pile of my wrinkled clothes worn one too many times each waiting on my closet floor to be cleaned.

One Sunday, when I could no longer ignore the pile leaking out of my closet door, I decided it was finally time to visit the laundromat.

Laundromats can't really help but be gray—the muted, soap residue-covered silver of the machines, the common white textured wallpaper that's yellowing in the corners, the overall mood of doing something no one wants to do but everyone has to do . . . All of these make them gray.

But I quickly realized this laundromat's shade of gray was different. It was quirky, colorful gray if gray could be colorful. It was a gray that was trying hard not to be. A gray that almost wasn't.

A little white wooden "welcome" sign hung on the glass door by curled white wire, with a delicate pink bow glued to the top of the "W." It banged a bit as I pushed it open, waddling through with bags of neglected clothes.

The sign hung there behind the glass as if to say this wasn't just some laundromat but a person's small business. Once I passed that dangling white welcome sign, I expected to find the owner sitting in an old wooden chair with the paint chipping off, reading a book about a family that lived in a house on a sunflower farm or something.

The owner was sitting there in a chair, but not reading a book about a family living on a sunflower farm. At least, not at the moment.

She was a heavier-set woman with hair that may have been bleached a few too many times, pastel blue cotton pants and an oversized blush pink t-shirt. She was sitting there, talking to her few customers as their clothes tumbled.

Maybe it wasn't small talk, because maybe to a small laundromat owner who has clearly had the place for a while, it was just a normal-sized talk about things that she liked talking about.

She talked about what she was making for dinner and about a pan she recommends. She talked about how pretty the seventy-two degree day was. She joked about the mundaneness of laundry, "But hey, we've all got to do it!" She giggled.

She was sort of talking *at* her few customers, as they responded with the occasional quick comment or chuckle, not really wanting to be bothered as they were too busy checking their emails or sitting there in silence.

I noticed a little quarter candy dispenser at the entrance just a few feet from the white welcome sign. It was one of those where you get a handful of probably a few months old Mike and Ikes for a quarter.

I wondered why she put this little candy dispenser there. Maybe it was for the kids that get dragged along to do laundry with their moms, and after they lose interest in watching their soccer uniforms swoosh around in circles through the glass after a few moments, they can exchange one of the quarters jingling in their parents' pocket for some artificially colored sugar.

153

Or possibly she put it there for the adults, the ones that have let their dirty clothes pile up because they're too busy doing the dishes or staying late at work or forgetting to pay their car registration. Maybe she put it in the little laundromat so that when they're sitting there attempting to bury themselves in their self-help book that just isn't giving them the "ah-ha!" or in the warm fuzzy inspired feeling they seem to be searching for, they'll put it down and notice the colorful Mike and Ikes sitting in the corner, just a quarter and a turn of the metal handle away from being in their hands.

Maybe she put it there so that if one of those adults does wander over while their socks and slacks and button-up shirts are tumbling around and they go for some Mike and Ikes, they'll remember how when they were kids they wouldn't eat the green ones, and they'd give them to their little sister. Maybe they'll sit there in that seemingly gray laundromat and divide up their handful of Mike and Ikes and pick out the green ones. Perhaps they'd offer her the green ones and talk to her about how when they were little they'd never eat the green ones and she'll be able to listen for once.

There was an attempt of a mural on the wall, bubbles painted probably by the owner or her niece, the one whose picture is cut out and taped just below one of the brush strokes. They were just blue outlined imperfect circles of various sizes with a little "c" shaped line inside them to give the bubbles some reflective and dimension feeling, I suppose. There was also a orange bottle of laundry detergent painted in the corner, and what I think was meant to be a washing machine, but it looked just like a gray box with a blue circle in the middle.

On the opposite wall of the mural was a poster that read "Voted Best of the Bay 2009" with a clipping of the short magazine article about the "Cleaning Village" posted under it, and I hadn't even realized this laundromat had a name.

This was obviously a laundromat that was giving its best effort not to be gray.

And maybe this laundromat wasn't gray at all.

Maybe what I found most gray about the laundromat wasn't the yellowing wallpaper, the dingy silver machines, the dust-covered dangling welcome sign, the overlooked candy dispenser, the quickly painted bubbles on the wall, or even the people trying their best to ignore the chatty and optimistic laundromat store owner.

What I think I found most gray about the laundromat was something much worse.

The happy little dust-covered welcome sign kept me from going home after my walk to grab my laundry and bring it there to get it taken care of. The first thing I thought of when I saw the candy dispenser was how old and crusty that candy probably is. The first thing I saw when I looked at the hand-painted bubbles was the pencil circle outlines no one bothered to erase. I didn't want to make little conversations so badly that I'd rather drive to some lifeless laundromat where there's no owner lingering. Everyone has their headphones in and I can throw my soiled clothes in the washer in peace while not attempting to explain why I moved north, discuss the abnormally warm day or how I should be washing my delicates on cold.

Maybe the laundromat wasn't gray, but I was.

I brought in my last couple of bags of clothes and started my loads. I had only enough quarters to cover my loads, but I held off on one.

I took a quarter out from my jingling pocket, and went over to the door where the candy dispenser sat. I put it in and cranked the nob and filled my hand with Mike and Ikes. Then I separated them, green in one hand, the rest in the other, and I walked over to the owner, sitting in her chair, and held out my hand.

"You know, I never ate the green ones as a kid."

She reached out and took them from my hand and popped the green ones in her mouth.

"Good, because I myself never fancied the red," she said smiling, "Quite the warm day out, isn't it?"

Cancer
Ileana Lallain

Her eyes trace the lines of his cheekbones, noting the unusual prominence of them. He pushes his hair into his face, turns away from her, and says "Can you stop staring at me, Lyla? It's . . ."

"Sorry." She looks down at the oak table instead. A pause stretches out between the two. The sound of dripping water from the kitchen sink and the ticking of a black and white analog clock on the wall behind her fill the space. "It's been too long," she pauses, clearing an itch in her throat. "Since we last hung out, that is."

"Mm." He agrees softly, staring at a portrait on the wall. It's one of Lyla's family, complete with her mother, older brother, and late father. They smile at him though their blank eyes don't meet his gaze.

"How's homeschool been going?" She looks up at him without lifting her head. Her auburn hair spills over her slender shoulders.

"Fine."

"Is it better than regular school?"

"It's okay."

A pause "Anything interesting happen lately?"

"Not really."

"Oh."

A long moment stretches out between them. The scent of magnolias sneaks into the room from the open window. It stings his nose. "I mean, my mom accidentally spilled orange juice on one of my textbooks. It was such a pain to clean up."

"I can imagine," she says with a small smile. She fingers the edge of the wood table, tracing a random shape with her index finger. "Which textbook?"

"Algebra 2." He readjusts his hair, pulling it down further. He crosses and uncrosses his legs, wiggling uncomfortably in the chair.

"You must be happy about that. Still hate math the most, right?" She looks at him, waiting for an answer that never comes. Another silent moment passes before she clears her throat and says, "Do you want something to drink?"

"Water's fine," he replies.

She leaves and returns a moment later, placing a cold glass of water in front of him. He doesn't even glance at it.

"It's really taking its toll on your hair . . ." she mumbles, staring at the pale white skin of his scalp, prominent beneath the thin, sporadic strands. He adjusts his hair, avoiding her eyes. "How is . . . it going?" she asks, biting her lower lip.

He waits a moment before saying, "I went to the supermarket and saw the weirdest thing: sprayable cheese."

"Oh really?" her voice is lower, emanating from the back of her throat as though it cannot reach her mouth.

"I was tempted to buy some, just to see what it tastes like."

"Hm."

"Have you ever tried it?"

"No."

"Oh."

A pause.

"How long?" she asks.

He tugs at his hair again. "I watched a really lousy horror movie the other day. You'd love it."

"Felix . . ."

"The main character was sooo stupid. I mean, who locks themselves in a bathroom when there's a chainsaw killer chasing after them?" He tries to chuckle, but it comes out choked. "Right? That's sooo dumb right?" He glances at Lyla, then returns his attention to the blank wall.

She just stares at him, silently.

He clears his throat, twice. "It's allergy season you know. Lots of pollen in the air." He clears his throat again and looks up at the ceiling. The arm resting on the table begins to shake. He curls his fingers into a fist.

"How long?" Lyla repeats. Her lower lip quivers as she bites down on it.

He clears his throat and tugs at his hair to hide his eyes. His phone buzzes loudly in his pocket. "That's my mom," he says, his voice lower. "I'd better go now." he stands. The chair scrapes against the wooden floor. The glass of water sits untouched, a small drop of condensation rolling down the side like a tear.

He gets up and walks past the mahogany staircase and to the front door. His shoulders shake violently, sending tremors down his thin white arms. He fumbles with the brass doorknob, struggling to unlock it.

As he exits the house, he says, "Bye, Lyla," never looking at her.

"Goodbye, Felix," she whispers, lowering her head into her arms with a sob.

Symphonic Recurrence
Brienne Flaherty Betín

I'm in a restaurant staring out at the marina when the song comes on. Suddenly it's snowing, and we're walking back through the busy streets at night, where you are holding my hand and I can feel the warmth through my gloves. Your cheeks burn when you turn to look at me, eyes crinkled upward and glowing, and though I can't see your mouth behind your scarf, I smile back. I almost slip where the pavement is all slush and no traction, and your eyebrows turn up with skepticism before—

We're on the beach and you're quiet. I like that about you, but you don't know that yet. I say something obvious, you turn with a half-smile and nod, pick up a stone and skip it across the water. The sand reminds you of something, something methodological, a science project when you were eight. I lift some and it slips through my fingers, a temporary comfort, reminding me of when—

I've told you I'm a champion at mini-golf. This is untrue. I am, however, winning, and you can't seem to find a way of refuting my claim. My ball has just made it over the river and under the windmill when you run after it, picking it up and tossing it two holes back, where it manages not to damage anything—you don't have the best aim—and I take it upon myself to offer you the same courtesy. You're laughing when you offer a duel instead, raising your club. I raise mine in turn, it's only fair because—

The train to the bay up north runs along the coast. We've been playing cards and sharing headphones. We're talking about science fiction when our car slips under a tunnel, the darkness is brief and strange, and you kiss me, and by the time I open my eyes the light has flooded back in, and you have this look on your face like—

We're in an elevator, I'm nervous, and a song is playing. You tell me I look beautiful, I tell you *you* look beautiful. You grin, ask me to dance. I don't reply, but I do push the buttons to every floor before taking your hand. After all, the song just started, and the play can wait—they never start on time anyway, do they? You dip me backwards in a comically exaggerated fashion when the doors ding open, and several spectators look on quizzically, about to ask—

It's raining for the first time in a long while and I can't read past the second line of this book in your apartment. I've been trying for five minutes and nothing translates, there are flowers on the desk and you're making tea, the smell fills the room with a distracting sort of softness, where I can't focus on much of anything but the lean line of your shoulders by the counter, dropping honey into a spoon and—

There is time I must spend away from you. By the time I see you again it is in a forest, and the wind is brisk, and the quiet is different now. You're wearing these ridiculous hiking boots I find oddly charming, and our conversation winds and breaks and stutters to a stop. I'm reminded of the sand and snow and there's a melody I can't get out of my head—the same way I can't get you out—and—

"Babe?" A person I hardly know across the table is gesturing for my attention. "You ready?" The song ends and I select something, looking again toward the water. I should really text you back.

158

Dark Stars
Sam Gross

"I'm tired of trying to see the good in people."

Celia looks up at me, a frown already working its way down her face. She frowns at me more often than she does anything else. She folds in on herself when she sits down, her arms pulled tight across her chest. She reminds me of an accordion binder, hiding secrets between the folds, but easily spilled, easily broken.

She tries too hard. Celia has never been one to do things halfway. It made her easy to talk to in the beginning, until I realized how much I prefer to half-ass my life. Now she frowns at me, her body a paper accordion, folded up in disappointment.

"What makes you say that?" she asks. Celia never does anything without a question first. I hate asking questions, but I hate answering them more.

"I watch the news," I say, because I know it will piss her off. "Shit hit the fan, like, globally. And I'm tired of trying to see past that. Humans are bad, I think it's time we at least acknowledge it."

"There is more than just bad news, Andromeda," Celia says, voice tight, because that response has ruffled her feathers, but she will never admit it. "People do good things. People are kind to one another."

I snort, an ugly sound that scandalized my mother the first time I made it, and continues to scandalize her even after I stopped doing it in front of her. Then I cross my arms over my chest, because one act of defiance is never enough.

"Do you really want to talk about the darkness in humans?" Celia asks, because she thinks I'm transparent, but she's really just a decent guesser. She has to be, but only because she has my life compiled into a neat little accordion binder, sectioned off by different crises. "Or are you just trying to avoid talking about the darkness in yourself."

I snort again, this time as a cover-up for my own transparency. "I'm dark because I'm human. Didn't Socrates have an argument like that? Humans are dark, and I am human, so I must be dark."

"Socrates also believed that people inherit the knowledge of humanity when they're born," Celia says, even though there is something to be said about universal human belief and similarities between cultures.

I remind myself that there is a story about a flood in every religion. A giant creature in every history. An eye toward the sky in every age. I want to lean to the left of the couch I'm slumped on and peer through the window shades, just enough to see if the stars have come out yet.

"Do you think your parents have darkness within them?"

I want to laugh at that, but I'm not sure if the noise that will emerge would be depreciating or just sad, so I swallow the urge and look at Celia's accordion body.

"I think my parents pay you to ask me questions, so they don't have to," I reply, but even that feels like too much honesty. "That doesn't mean they're completely dark, but it certainly doesn't make them good people."

"Do you think your parents don't care about you?"

I think my dad is too busy chasing comets to look at me and see that we're both tethered to an unsteady ground, staring up at a blackness that would kill us both without remorse. I think my mom wants to look up at the stars and see God's face too much to recognize that neither of us is as holy as she'd like to believe. I think my parents spent so much of their time married arguing about science and religion that their divorce has left me with a disdain for both. But I could never hate the stars, even if I hate what they stand for to my parents.

But I can't say any of that to Celia, who will just write little notes about how I'm a surly teenager in her fancy leather notebook and then tell my parents to up my dosage of depression meds. Which, they maybe should, but I'm not going to be the one to tell Celia that.

Instead, I lean to the left and peer through the slats of the window shades to see that, yes, the stars have just started emerging. One winks at me, a secret we can share, even if I'm not really in on it.

"Andromeda?" Celia says, and I have to look back, look away from the winking stars, because nothing ever happens on the ground when my face is pointed toward the sky. My mother was the one to teach me that, glaring at my father as she said it, as though by tearing down our biggest similarity, she can replace everything of him inside of me with her.

She doesn't know it's only driven me closer to him. If only he would notice. But his gaze has been trained toward the stars for longer than I've been alive, and I learned through my mother that love has nothing on the allure of the unknown.

"I think they think they care," I say, because that's just snarky enough to maintain my angsty teenage image, but honest enough that Celia will think she's doing a good job.

"Let's talk about space for a minute," Celia says, because like my namesake, I will never escape the stars; unlike my namesake, I don't want to.

I want to monologue, because she's not expecting me too, and it's nice to talk about something I love, even if my only audience it accordion folder Celia and her fancy leather notebook.

"It's huge," I start, because that's always where my father starts, but that's the only thing I say out loud. Everything else is whispered into the darkness inside my own mind, a prayer I send out to my mother, a secret I share with the winking star. I don't bother to send the thought to my father, even though he's the only one who would truly understand it.

It's huge, unfathomably so, a big emptiness, darkness beyond our Earth. But it's not empty, not really. It's full of so much more than we can know, trapped under the fleeting gaze of pinpricks of light.

It's unexplainable, and as storytelling creatures, we immediately latched onto it, sure that there was a reason it exists. That we exist. Some chose science, others chose to spin stories of gods and creatures made of starlight, cast in the shadow of the moon and a foolish fondness for the depths of space. Some chose both, because there is beauty is learning what is right and what is true, and deciding for yourself where we all fit in the vastness of it all. Where I fit in the vastness of it all.

I don't really believe that humans are only dark. It's a balance, probably, that just got a little out of whack. We spent too long staring at the darkness above us that we couldn't help but try to imitate it. But we kept the tiny patches of light, because we sat beneath the stars stretching billions of light-years from our home, beacons of light in a dark place, and knew that they were beautiful.

But I can't tell Celia that. I can't tell my mom or dad that. I can't even really tell the stars, because they're too far away to hear me. So I sit quietly in my therapist's office and monologue to myself and the winking star and tell myself that someone is listening, even if I know that no one really is.

The Field Trip
Ayla Glim

After half a decade in the orphanage, all Oliver had left of his family were fractured sensations, barely memories at all: the scratchiness of his dad's beard, the rosy, soapy smell of his mom. Images of his twin sister, however, came to him clearly. She had disappeared when they were very young, long before their parents perished, but he could close his eyes and instantly conjure an image of her holding her favorite stuffed bunny.

His last memory of her was near the very spot he stood now. She had laughed and chided Oliver for being frightened of the carnival's mascot, a monkey comprised entirely of gears, shafts, and screws. Oliver shook his head and willed himself to focus on the monkey in the cage before him. He wished his sister was beside him to poke fun of him again, but she had been missing for years.

Oliver shook his head, willing the strange hallucination of the monkey holding the rabbit to fade from his mind. He returned his focus to the stage.

"Listen carefully!" Mr. Sterling, a rotund man dressed in sharp suit and a jaunty hat, was addressing the group of orphans. I've prepared two surprises for you. First, you get the entire Park to yourselves! I've even sent my employees home today. And second: the first ten clever souls to find the monkey's lair will get to go on our secret ride."

The crowd began to buzz. "I thought that was just a myth!" The gawky girl in the front piped up. "No one has ever found it!"

"You are correct, dear," he said, tipping his hat. "Indeed, no one can find the ride—unless I invite them to find it." He chuckled. "Remember, the monkey doesn't want you to find his lair, either. So keep your eyes and ears open. Don't let him sneak up behind you!"

The monkey rattled the bars loudly, causing the crowd to jump and devolve into bursts of murmurs and nervous laughter.

The Park owner produced a large key from his vest pocket. "Alright! It's time to play! I will be unlocking the cage in ten minutes, so you better get a move on. Where you head now is up to you!" He brandished the key above his head. "I'll be waiting for the lucky ten winners. Go on, have some fun!"

The children immediately dispersed, hollers of "Come on, this way!" and "Over here!" echoing from every direction. Oliver wanted nothing more than to go back to the bus, but he knew the matron would never let him. Within seconds, he was left standing alone in front of the stage with both Mr. Sterling and the mechanical monkey smiling down at him.

"Need a hand deciding where to go?" Mr. Sterling asked.

As Oliver shook his head no, a flash of his sister's stuffed rabbit lying at the feet of the Park owner pierced his memory, but it was gone as quickly as it had entered his mind.

He suddenly felt the need to get as far away from the monkey as possible before the cage was unlocked.

Mr. Sterling looked curiously at the small boy as he stumbled away from the stage and down the nearest paved trail.

"That's one of the winners," Mr. Sterling muttered to the monkey.

The monkey nodded.

Oliver just wanted to find a quiet place to hide from everything until the bus driver returned. He made his way down a marked trail until he reached a wide plaza packed with game stalls, prize booths, and test-your-strength machines. The allure of the flashing lights had already distracted several of the children from the treasure hunt, and groups had formed in front of the stalls to compete for bagfuls of candy and other loot.

Oliver continued down the path, hoping to find a less populated area, when something peculiar about the nearest booth attendant caught his eye.

At the same moment, a thought occurred to him: Hadn't Mr. Sterling said the employees were home for the day? Every stall on the boardwalk seemed to be manned.

He took a few cautious steps toward the nearest booth, peering at the figure inside.

Oliver's stomach flipped over as he realized exactly what had caught his attention. The uniformed attendant's movements were identical to the monkey's creaking, mechanical gestures.

The boardwalk employees were not human.

The revelation caused the hair on the back of his neck to stand on end. He tore his gaze from the stall and began to jog away from the plaza, not stopping until the hollering of his peers had faded completely.

After several long, silent minutes, Oliver passed through a cement tunnel studded with bright lights and came out on the other side to find himself surrounded by a cluster of withered, drooping trees. He crossed a wooden bridge suspended over a green, algae-coated pond, hoping to put even more distance between himself and the mechanical attendants, but he was met with a large, forbidding sign: EMPLOYEE RESIDENTIAL AREA. NO GUEST ENTRY. He sighed, wondering if Mr. Sterling had lied and if there were any human employees left at all.

He started to head back towards the tunnel when a voice called to him.

"Hey! Come back, please!"

Oliver stopped, his pulse racing. He slowly turned until he could see the source: a teenage girl in coveralls and long braids, pacing back and forth next to the sign and waving frantically for him to join her.

"You have to listen to me," she pleaded. "You're on a field trip here, right?"

Oliver nodded slightly in acknowledgment, but did not respond. She continued waving, growing increasingly exasperated by his unwillingness to move, before finally rushing forward to meet him on the bridge. "I know you're scared, believe me," she panted. "I am, too. They're planning something in the park, and they're not telling us what's going on." Her eyes were the size of saucers.

Another yell from the employee area reached Oliver, this one obviously an angry male. The girl looked over her shoulder, panicked. "He saw me leave. Just promise me you will *not* go on the secret ride. Okay? Tell everybody in your group!" Oliver opened his mouth to reply, baffled, but he was cut off by another shout.

"What do you think you're doing out here?" A man with a large badge pinned prominently to his coat appeared from behind the employee sign. He narrowed his eyes at Oliver, who turned and began to sprint back through the tunnel, leaving the frightened girl behind. He kept running and running, not looking back, until he made it to the game plaza.

He stopped to catch his breath, a sharp stitch spreading in his side, and rose slowly when he realized that he could no longer hear anyone playing or laughing. He rounded the corner and saw that the entire boardwalk had been abandoned; even the mechanical attendants were no longer stationed in their booths.

Oliver made his way through the plaza, listening for his peers, but heard nothing at all. He decided to stick to the path he was familiar with and eventually arrived back at the entry gates, in front of the welcome stage.

The monkey's cage now stood empty and the door swung freely. Mr. Sterling was nowhere to be seen.

As Oliver got closer, he noticed something small, unmoving, and strangely familiar tucked in a corner of the cage. Oliver cocked his head. Was it there before?

Struck with sudden, fierce curiosity, Oliver crept up to the stage and peered inside of the bars. What he saw took him several seconds to register, and even then, he still wasn't sure if he believed his eyes.

His sister's stuffed rabbit was quietly occupying the dark chamber. He took a step forward, then another, his arms automatically drifting toward the animal. He was inches away from scooping it up and cradling it close, desperately hoping it might hold his sister's smell, when the cage door clanged shut behind him. The velvet curtains swung heavily into place, enveloping Oliver in blackness.

Oliver soon found himself strapped tightly into the front car of a roller coaster, surrounded by the glossy stares of the mechanical booth attendants. As his eyes adjusted to the dim light, he realized somebody else was strapped in next to him. Squinting, he made out the shape of the excited girl from the front of the crowd who had claimed the secret ride was a myth. She stared straight forward, her face a mask of fear. Behind him, he could hear the confused whimpers of other children.

"Welcome, prize winners!" Mr. Sterling's voice echoed through the dark chamber, though Oliver did not see him anywhere. "You are the lucky adventurers who were clever enough to solve the monkey's puzzle. Well done!"

I didn't solve anything, Oliver thought frantically. This is a mistake! "Let me off!" He yelled, but his yells mixed in with those of the other trapped orphans.

"I promised ten of you a ride, and only eight made it all the way to the end," Mr. Sterling lamented. "So, I handpicked a couple of you. I hope you don't mind. It means you get to be a part of Sterling Park history, my friends!"

The mechanical monkey emerged from a corner of the dark room and climbed up to an elevated platform next to the tracks. His perpetual grin had always been sinister to Oliver, but now it just mocked him.

"Have you ever wondered what powered our famous mascot and our new, lifelike employees?" Mr. Sterling asked. "You're about to learn firsthand!"

The monkey leaned forward and yanked a lever affixed to the platform. The roller coaster started to inch forward.

The moment before the coaster plunged over the crest of the first hill, Oliver locked eyes with a female mechanical booth attendant. She clutched a stuffed rabbit in her arms.

The Loveliest Vision in This Dark World
Denise M. Schmitz

She was born in the sea.

Between two forks of coral was an egg that was soft and luminescent and made of jelly. Days passed, and the speck inside the egg grew and ebbed. Weeks passed, and it became a translucent feathery rosette. Then feathers became fins, and the jelly melted away, and she emerged into the salt and the currents of the reef.

As she matured, her fins grew strong, and she became a part of the sea. Her reef bloomed, a lacy frame about a small cropping of rock that burst upwards from the foamy surface of the water. There were fish and crustaceans that flocked among tiny forests of anemones. The sea was warm. At night, the stars danced.

She learned to laugh and to turn in circles and to swim races with the fish. She learned to pull herself up through the coral with her arms and rest on the rock, watching the seafowl above. She learned to breathe air. Her skin became deep blue and speckled with small silver bubbles, and her fingernails were made of white stones made smooth by tumbling through the waves.

The sun was just dipping below the surface of the sea in the distance, and the moon was suspended gleaming in the sky, and as she slept, she dreamed of a face.

It was a face unlike her own. The skin was smooth and bright and slightly speckled, like the shells of the hermit crabs that lived in a cave beneath the rock. Surrounding the face was a beautiful shiny fan of hair that moved just slightly as the mouth breathed, gently, asleep. Then the eyes opened, and to look into those eyes was to look into the sea.

She awoke then, but for many days afterwards, she was in a dream.

Her days were lazy. She glittered and swam and sang. The fish were free and flying, and they were good company. Great groups of them moved in rippling fabrics through the seaweed and the waves. They bred. They laid their cloudy glass eggs. Generations of fish lived and died and lived again. Sometimes she would see a fish that she favored, and she would kiss it gently on the top of its head, and it would not die. In this way she collected a small flock of fish that adored her and loved to follow her through the water, surfing the little vortices in her wake.

She dreamed often. When the sun was out, the water twinkled, green above, hard clear blue below. When clouds draped across the sky, the rain made the tide swell and the waves were icy and gray. And when night came, she saw the face of her lovely creature with eyes that twinkled and swelled with the many moods of the sea.

And so she kissed her fish goodbye and went out to where the sea was deep and her rock vanished behind the horizon.

She had never seen land before. It emerged in front of her and grew to fill the entire world with sand and plants standing on posts. She traced the coastline and found it covered in creatures. In her path she found vast reefs populated by unfamiliar colors and shapes of coral, cliffs that seemed to reach the clouds themselves, fish with iridium skin.

She traveled farther and the water chilled. The coastline became white and surrounded her in loops and ripples. Pieces of ice floated all around, showing timidly above the surface. Birds dived into the water and turned their fluffy feathers sleek. She felt smooth skin against her arm and saw a great whale that looked as though it had been cut from ice, and she swam with it, sprinting, and it smiled at her.

But in all her travels to the far corners of the sea, the creature with gems for eyes appeared only in her dreams. She imagined soft wavy hair reflecting the sun's light and she dreamed of shimmering folds of cloth wrapped about slender limbs in place of fins. She knew that such a creature was born on land and was not of the sea.

So she longed for her home and found herself once again amid the crystalline webs of her reef. Fish circled and leaves waved gently in the current as she lay on her rock, watching a ship balanced delicately on the horizon.

She sang now, and the song in her heart was sorrow and the loss of what she had never known and the knowledge of what she had never had. No voice of the land or the sky or the sea was the equal of hers. She was magnetic and she compelled the distant ship toward her like a tributary pouring into a great river.

Her song grew hopeful as she imagined this ship carrying her beloved. She sang of warm soft lips like coral and eyes like gems and the embrace of the gentle arms that she could almost see, waving the sails in a smiling greeting. But the ship grew nearer and she saw that it teemed with creatures, like hers, but not like hers. They were rough and their voices were deep and loud, and they worked frantically to sail nearer. They could not resist her song. She cried out in anguish as their ship struck her rock, and she despaired of ever being united with her love.

She saw ships often and sang to them always. But her heart broke always as she saw that the creatures aboard were not the ones she was seeking.

They drove their boats to explosion on the rock in their frenzy for the song that was not theirs. Her reef became a derelict garden of splinters.

The approaching ships grew fewer, for her voice was death to them. But she sang, and her voice grew still sweeter as she sang of longing and mourning and the one she could not bear to be without. Her soul ached. Ripples of fish brushed against her face and twirling jellyfish swam all about her in rhythmic motions.

A lone ship approached one day and passed her by. The sailors had learned to fear her, and she saw them working with their ears sealed, safe in their silence. She saw their leader straining against broad twists of rope that bound him to his ship. He alone heard and was driven to mad agony by her song, and she knew his pain when he fought as she had fought her own heart's bindings.

The days were too long, now. Each day she longed for the night.

And as she dreamed she saw the sea in a pair of eyes and heard a voice as lovely as her own calling out, balanced on tiptoe on a spindle high above the deck of a sailing ship, with hair flying in the wind and cheeks like the setting sun and lips like coral.

And she opened her eyes and saw a ship raising its flag just above the horizon, and her heart thrilled, and she sang.

Forgetting
Grace Chao

The week after Grandfather died, Grandmother woke up with only a quarter of her memory left. It had already been failing, and Alzheimer's ran like water in our blood, my uncle said, but this time she could not remember that Grandfather had died. My mother and I were still staying over when it happened. "Where is Dennis?" she demanded, looking through their closet and pulling out suit jackets and wool cardigans and throwing them onto the bed. My uncle and mother had to break the news a second time, then a third time, then a fourth. I kept busy by returning the jackets and cardigans, socks and shoes, into their appropriate places. Grandmother picked a plaid hat off the coat stand and placed it on her head while my uncle, exhausted and balding, lied for a fifth time, "He went away in his sleep. He didn't feel a thing." I stuck my hand out for Grandfather's hat and she wouldn't give it back. She just sobbed anew and started pulling out her hair.

Then she forgot who Grandfather was, only that someone was missing. "The milkman gets an F-*minus* for attendance!" "Daddy forgot to pick me up from school today!" She forgot why she had to get out of bed and what to do while taking a bath. She slipped while getting out of a bath and wore a bandage on her forehead for two weeks. She wanted to celebrate her eighth birthday with Pin the Tail on the Donkey and began requesting that somebody—anybody—take her back home to her parents, but that home was now a Kwik-er Mart that sold egg salad sandwiches for two-fifty. "It's a pigpen for lowlifes," my mother had always called it, despite rumors that an egg salad sandwich inside a Kwik-er Picker Biscuit Sandwich tasted like a salty, bulging slice of heaven.

In January, everyone left and I went back to school. My uncle hired a caretaker named Mary and installed a safety camera in Grandmother's bedroom. "Mary has a family to go home to," my mother explained. From time to time I pulled out my phone and flipped to the fuzzy, soundless screen. The password was *ABCD*. I watched Grandmother wake up, put on her brown slippers, and sit back down on the bed. I watched her pace the room and peer into the closet, now barren except for her own oatmeal-colored sweaters and pull-on pants. "I'm on a mission but I know the end," I told a friend with a laugh, as he bought a round of beers at the Gin and Topic. No one tried to laugh with me.

Grandmother took her meals at nine, twelve-thirty, and five-fifteen, all pepper and no salt. My mother had a fresh cake of her favorite lemon verbena soap sent every other week. I watched Grandmother wake up, look out the window, take off her slippers, and go to bed, until I realized that one day I would watch her go to sleep and not get out of bed. "That's the point," my uncle said with neither a frown nor a smile, but he changed the password, gave me a hug, and told me to enjoy being young.

Maria, the Destroyer
Nadine M Patton

The damn key was stuck in the damn door again.

Maria stared at the doorknob, trying to glare it into submission. After a few minutes of standing in the hallway, she gave in and knocked. Surely, Teddy would hear her, fling open the door, and relieve her of the paper bag burden in her arms.

She waited and knocked again.

Admittedly, the knock was more of a defeated slump against the wood and not the traditional, confident rapping, but Maria felt desperate and haggard. *Come on,* she thought, wishing she could convey her bad mood through the door.

Trying not to growl, she balanced her sack of groceries while using brute force on the door. She gritted her teeth and shoved until the door fell open. She staggered inside, flailing a bit in an effort to keep herself from staggering all over the floor. Taking a deep breath, she carefully set the groceries on the messy counter, then turned to see Teddy sprawled on the couch across the apartment, utterly oblivious to her entrance.

It occurred to her how amazing it was that Teddy always appeared so tired despite doing nothing at all. Limbs dangling off the furniture, he collapsed on the couch like a corpse. Then Maria saw the furious movements of his fingers as they played over the black game controlled in his lap, and her eyes narrowed in disgust. Snorting loudly, she began putting away the groceries she had bought. Even though she was slamming cupboards around and making a general racket, Teddy never once turned his head to look at her.

"I'm just looking for the right job," he'd said that morning, and the morning before, and the morning before that. She wondered if getting to level 37 was somehow involved in the training of this "right job" he was looking for.

She was going to have to say something.

Maria was almost horrified to find that she was afraid to chastise him for his lack of ambition. Not because of the kind of stress that would put on their relationship, she realized. Really, Maria found she was more afraid of the names that he and his friends would come up with for her.

About eight months ago over beers with Eric, Teddy's old roommate, Eric's girlfriend had casually and almost arbitrarily been dubbed, Kara the Bitch. The decision had concluded with celebratory high fives; no one had even defended her. Then Marcus had come to the bar complaining about something or other, and Theresa the Douche was born. Next, Amanda the Nagger of Men, Callie the Psycho, and Anthony the Dumbass had followed.

To be fair, Anthony the Dumbass had been somewhat of a nice surprise, Maria had to admit.

If she started nagging Teddy to get a job, she'd be next. She'd be kicked out of the Cool Girlfriend Club and branded with a horrible new moniker. Had Kara *really* been a bitch or was Eric just unforgivably messy? What about Callie? Was she really a psycho, or had Matt just gotten on her nerves one too many times that night? Maria had never really questioned the Naming before.

She jumped as Teddy let out a string of curses. On the screen, she caught the last few seconds of what looked like his character being blown up after stepping on a landmine. He threw the game controller onto the floor as if punishing the plastic for his man's untimely death. After moping for a minute, he glanced up and saw her standing in the kitchen. He gave her his crooked smile; it wasn't quite eliciting the responses from her it once had.

"When did you get in?" he wondered.

"Almost *fifteen* minutes ago," she wanted to stop. Instead of yelling at him, Maria shrugged.

"I went to an interview this morning," he announced.

She raised an eyebrow meant to convey the sheer disbelief at his statement. Teddy grinned and flopped back onto the couch. "Okay," he amended, "I *meant* to go to an interview this morning."

She nodded and turned away so he wouldn't see the terrible scowl pulling at her features.

"So, what are you cooking for dinner?" he asked over the sound of the game restarting. Sighing, she stared down at the countertop. They'd probably start calling her something like Maria the Destroyer.

She bit down on her bottom lip while stalking into the living room to start up a good fight.

I wonder if I could get them to call me that at work, she speculated indulgently.

Another Nondescript House
Jenna Mohl

There is an unoccupied house, on a nondescript street in a nondescript town, that the children say is magic. Not haunted. Magic. Of course, grown-ups do not believe in magic. They don't believe the children's whispers of staircases that move and enchanted forests full of starlight and fairies and monsters and darkness. These practical men and women do not believe; age and experience will not allow them to. And yet they always find some reason not to buy the house.

Abigail Mason has spent her entire life in this nondescript town, in a nondescript house, with her nondescript family. She and her best friend, Rose, believe in magic. They can feel it as they walk by the house on their way home from school. Abby once described the feeling to her mother as a "warm pull." Her mother responded by saying that only junkies hang out in abandoned buildings.

Abby and Rose are not the only ones to feel drawn to the house; at sleepovers and around campfires, Abby and Rose have heard the other neighborhood children speak in hushed tones of a nameless force that beckons them closer.

However, on the day in which our story begins, Abby and Rose are alone. In fact, there is nobody on the streets at all. It is a Tuesday; the clock reads 11:45 P.M. and a full moon hangs in the sky.

Abby, in a blue hooded sweatshirt and carrying a grocery bag, glances up at the moon and then down at her watch. Fifteen minutes. She approaches the front of the house where Rose is already waiting. Rose paces nervously back and forth beneath a street lamp, her shadow elongating and shrinking on the sidewalk.

"We shouldn't be here. We're going to get in trouble," says Rose once Abby is within earshot. Abby rolls her eyes and pulls her hood back "Come on. It'll be fine." She slips into the condescending voice her older sister uses—the one that makes Abby feel small and defensive. "We're not going to get caught."

Rose glares. "You don't know that!" Unlike Abby, Rose is an only child. She does not have co-conspirators; her daily life is not a constant effort to balance competing for her parents' attention with slipping under their radar.

Abby considers Rose for a moment and then takes a calculated risk. "Well if you don't want to come, then I'll go by myself." She begins to walk towards the door. Rose, her eyes glistening with unshed tears, hurries after her.

Abby feels Rose behind her and is relieved. For all her bravado, she would not have gone inside alone. What felt safe by day no longer feels safe by night. The friendly, gentle tug has turned into an eerie sensation—like the house is watching them.

Rose takes a deep breath as Abby turns the knob back and forth three times before pushing the door open. They step inside. The door clicks shut; Rose squeaks in surprise. When Abby opens her eyes, everything is dark. She begins carefully feeling her way into the house.

"Abby, wait!" says Rose, as she struggles forward.

"Stay there until I find somewhere to light the candles." Abby tells herself she's not scared of the dark, but her confidence dwindles the more she strains to see something, anything. Her eyes create terrifying shapes that seem to move closer and reach for her.

171

She is frozen until she hears it. Rose's scream. Failing to keep the panic at bay, she yells into the darkness, "Rose?"

Rose's answer comes from the left, "Something touched my leg!" There is an edge of hysteria to her voice.

Abby buries her own feelings of fear and begins to move forward again, "I told you to stay there! Give me one second!" She pats her foot around in a circle to make sure that the area is clear.

Sitting down, Abby feels inside her bag for a box of matches and one candle. She strikes the match, lights the wick, and watches the darkness slink away. Her breathing slows and she lights four more candles. Relieved and slightly shaken, Rose picks her way over to the light and sits down.

On the ground around them, they see soda cans and candy wrappers. Rose picks up one of the wrappers and then throws it to the side, "So I guess someone else has been here first. I bet it was Simon and his friends."

Abby shares in Rose's disappointment. This was supposed to be *their* adventure, *their* secret. "I bet they were too scared to come at midnight or during a full moon. Everyone knows that's when *real* magic happens."

At the mention of magic, Abby remembers why they are here, why they deceived their parents and snuck out of their houses late at night. She picks up one of the candles and attempts to light her surroundings. Dark trees with twisting branches seem to touch the ceiling.

Everything is still. Then a grandfather clock chimes the hour. Midnight. Abby is so startled that she drops her candle. Rose stands up beside her and they both hold their breath and count the chimes. One. Two. Three. *Come on*, thinks Abby. The darkness answers back.

Fairies, in little circles of light, flit out of the trees. They pull the curtains away from the windows to let the moonlight stream in. Small round mirrors hang from the branches, glowing softly from the reflection of the moon and stars.

Abby's warm feeling returns, but this time it goes all the way to her toes. The fairies dance above her head. They twirl and skip, running the length of the house, leaving streaks of light in their wake. Abby's eyes are dazzled. There is no audible music, but she can feel the melody in her bones.

She looks over at Rose, but Rose is not in awe. She is not smiling. She is terrified. Abby looks back at the house. Time slows down. The fairies have become sparks and the sparks have become flames. And for one glorious moment, the entire house is illuminated.

And then everything is on fire.

Rose screams for Abby, but the smoke smothers her reply. There is nowhere to run, nowhere to hide. For the second time that night, Abby freezes. She can't see, she can't breathe, and eventually she can't remain conscious any longer.

Abby feels the world tilt. There is a rush of fresh air and then she is outside with a mask over her nose and mouth. She opens her eyes into slits and sees Rose lying unconscious next to her. Everything farther away is blurry, but she can make out the flames. She can hear the hissing of water and the wailing of sirens.

But more than the sounds, more than the pain, Abby is aware of the warm feeling seeping into her body. It gently flows through her, pulsing once and then twice. *Thank you.* Abby takes a breath and by the time she exhales, the feeling is gone. *You're welcome.* She closes her eyes and dreams of dancing in an open space with the moon shining overhead.

Years later, a house is built on the lot and sold to a family of four looking to move out of the big city. The children no longer feel a warm pull when they walk by. They just see another nondescript house, on a nondescript street, in a nondescript town.

Mémère

An Excerpt

Ashna Madni

I arrive at Jeanfreau's fifteen minutes before closing. A gust of cool air washes over me as I enter the store. The owner nods in my direction and I wave back. I am here to buy ice. The ice machine in my grandmother's refrigerator is broken. And she needs ice every night.

My grandmother has scars on her back. Not like the scars on my wrists. She didn't give herself these scars. I've only seen glimpses of them if she ever accidentally leaves the door open while she changes her clothes or tests the water in the tub. But I've never seen the full image. She doesn't show me. She doesn't show anyone. She tries to keep them hidden but I know they exist. I grow more curious about their origin by the day. I don't think they came from a trauma like a car crash, a fire, an attack. It was a gradual trauma. I watched the pain in her back grow more intense as time stretched thinner.

North: Time and Date

In the summer of 2005, my grandparents evacuated their home and came to live with us in Los Angeles. In the fall of the following year, on September 18, 2006, we went back with them to New Orleans to help with their move into the new house. We drove through Chalmette, past their old house on Plaza Drive. It had a faded orange X-code spray-painted on the white stucco wall on the front of the house. Bumpers and side mirrors of cars hung in the gutter like Christmas ornaments. Broken roof shingles speckled the dirt lawn. The whole left side of the house looked like it was melting into the ground. My grandmother squirmed in the passenger seat, groping at her back in a panic.

"You okay?" my grandfather whispered to her. His eyes were two quivering brown pools.

"Yeah, yeah, just a mosquito, I think," she responded, yanking at the back of her shirt.

We continued on down Plaza and took Judge Perez all the way towards Mereaux. The new house looked a lot like the old one, just a little bigger and it had already been refurbished. Compared to the one we had just visited, this was beautiful. It even had a new mailbox freshly-painted black drilled into the lawn out front. My mother, father, and I entered the new house. My grandparents stayed back a minute, and when I glanced back at them still standing on the sidewalk, I saw my grandmother's cries became masked by laughs as my grandfather produced a deck of cards, held together with a thin rubber band, from his pants pocket. When they finally entered the house, they sat down at the kitchen table. My parents inspected the rest of the house. I sat on the spiral staircase and watched my grandparents at the table, my plump pink face squished between the railing spindles. He played Solitaire while she watched with her red, teary eyes and massaged her shoulders and upper back with her hands.

West: Rescue Team Identifier

When I was fifteen, I learned that picking the meat off boiled crabs was a good thing to do if you were an introvert at the dinner table surrounded by a family that was brimming with frustration and anxiety. If you didn't know how to pick crabs, you could get the person next to you to teach you, and then your conversation turned into an instruction manual. After you picked your first crab, the next conversation started more on your end but all you did was repeat the instruction manual you just listened to, and you didn't stutter your words once you began to recite the script. You didn't even need to make eye contact because you were so focused on your task of picking crabs, and the crab masters sitting next to you found it endearing. And then everyone forgot about earlier that day when you all went to go catch the live crabs off the side of some lake in the middle of nowhere when your grandfather couldn't bend down to set up the crab nets without falling over and eventually had to sit in the car while you finished crabbing as he watched from the driver's seat window. And you also forgot about how your grandmother claimed that the reason she wore only cotton shirts now was that she developed an allergy to all other materials, and cotton was the only material that felt okay on her skin. No, none of that was mentioned at the dinner table that night. Instead, all that was mentioned was how to graze your teeth across the membrane of the claw to scrape off all the meat, and how to scoop out the yellow fat and spread it on a Saltine cracker, and how there's really no wrong way to pick a crab—just don't eat anything that doesn't look like meat, including that gross squishy, spirally thing. And so we all sat around the kitchen table and didn't make eye contact and talked about crabs. Those crabs rescued our family that one night.

East: Hazards Present

Toward the end of my grandfather's life, the world became a dangerous place for him. Not many places felt comfortable. There was one summer, after my parents' divorce, when the only time it seemed that he was happy was when he lay in bed with my grandmother and she told him stories that she had already told him a million times before, dreamed out loud for him dreams that had actually happened, which to him were the best kind of dreams. I would sit just outside their bedroom door on the floor with my back against the wall and listen. I had never heard my own parents speak the way my grandparents did. Their voices were hushed as if they were the only two people in the world. His favorite memory-dream was the one when they went peach-picking in Georgia during peak peach season. They shoved their faces into the biggest, ripest peaches they had ever held, and the juices flowed all down their necks and shirts, and some drops even made it to their ankles. They consumed so many peaches that day they couldn't look at another peach for weeks after without getting queasy. Some nights he asked her to tell him that memory-dream over and over, and the peach juices whirled around and around like a cyclone for hours in both of their brains. It was around this time when my grandmother started to take painkillers to be able to lie on her back so that she could keep telling the peach story to my grandfather.

South: Number of Live and Dead Victims Found

175

The night of my grandfather's funeral on August 10th of last year, my grandmother lay face-down on the sofa in her den, her arms tucked in between her breast and the cushion, with a bag of ice on her lower back. The ice was the only thing that gave her immediate relief. She stayed on that sofa for three days, periodically getting up to use the restroom or drink water or attempt to swallow bites of the grilled cheese sandwiches I would cook for her. She could only manage a few morsels before sinking down again into the sofa, her skin fusing with the fibers of the fabric. I replaced the ice pack on her back with a hot water bottle every couple of hours and alternated between the hot and the cold for the entire duration of her silent repose. Half-eaten grilled cheese sandwiches on white ceramic plates surrounded the sofa.

It is 6:15 p.m. when I return from Jeanfreau's with two full bags of ice cubes and a headache. The sweat on my skin has mixed with the condensation on the bags. My grandmother emerges from her bedroom groggy, rubbing her back. Her spine straightens when she notices the ice.

"Baby girl, is that for me?"

"Mhm."

She helps me lift them into the freezer. I shut the door and look at her. Both of our chests rise and fall in syncopation as she and I try to cough up the words, but they aren't coming.

"Can I please see it?" I ask finally.

"No."

I dig the nail of my thumb into my finger and keep it there until it makes a mark.

"But I'm leaving. I don't know what's going to happen." My throat gets tighter and I choke on the words.

"You can't see it." Her nose and eyes are red and shaking.

Before the waves rise in my lungs again, she pulls me into a hug and lifts her shirt out and away from her body and takes my hand and places it gently on the skin of her back. I hold it there a moment. I slowly move it up and down and around, feeling the topography of her scars. I form a sketch of it in my head as my fingers collect more of the image. I can see it clearly now. My hand is a magnifying glass. The X is carved jaggedly across her back from her shoulders to her hips, varying from thick to thin to thick all the way down, setting up her back as the compass. "9/18" sits up north, a lop-sided crab lies to the west, a million little crushed peaches doused in their own juice wrap in an almost perfect spiral to the east, and the number "1" rests down south. She winces as I trace the "1." That part is still fresh.

She lets me remove my hand on my own time. I let my hand fall away after it starts to warm from the gentle friction of our skin. Her hands reach for mine and she places her wrinkled fingers on my wrists. I instinctively flinch. The lines on her hands trace my own lines. No one has touched them so gently, treated them with such care. She lets go and sits down at the kitchen table and gestures for me to join her. She is in my usual chair and I am in hers. She picks up the deck of cards. This time she shuffles, and I watch. But I don't watch for mistakes. I watch her hands. The wrinkles that adorn her skin are little natural scars etched delicately or brutally into her body by the hand of experience. Her skin is filled with lines like reams of poetry, an archive of memories lost, buried, cherished, and bottled. This is my grandmother: lines and lines and lines and . . .

Howl at the Storm

An Excerpt

Kateri Ransom

The first storm of July tipped over the horizon, tumbling towards me. Glowing gray and blue, it stampeded over red rock and dusty yellow sand. Wind scurried past, whispering the promise of rain. The school bus had dropped me off and I was starting the twenty-minute walk back home on the dirt sidewalk of Edgecliff's main dirt road. Edgecliff, New Mexico was too spread out for there to be a reason for the bus to make more than one stop there. One time a boy who had a crush on me made a big deal about how it didn't seem safe to make me walk so far on my own. But Edgecliff is really just a sleepy kind of town. You had a higher risk for sleeping through your fire alarm than getting mugged by a stranger. Edgecliff doesn't have strangers. And the fire alarm thing—it's happened here before.

Most likely I wasn't going to make it home before the storm hit, but I always packed a plastic trash bag this time of year. My dad used to always pack them for me before he got laid off from his security job at the Cottonwood Mall and decided to become a trucker. (They laid him off for refusing to get rid of the homeless people who kept sleeping behind the dumpsters.)

The wind picked up, made my hair fly around all crazy. I took my backpack off and laid it on the ground to open it. I was just pulling out the trash bag when a big black truck came up behind me. It honked. I hadn't realized I'd been walking all in the middle of the road...I'd kind of hoped if I just kept my head down they'd keep on going. Without looking back, I shifted to the right as I shrugged my backpack back on.

"Hey, it's Lala!"

I looked up and there was Ricky with his window pulled down and black square sunglasses over his eyes. His bald, veiny head was sticking out the window, shining under the last bit of sun in the sky. The four other bald heads in the car were in shadow, both from the tinted windows and from the stormy sky behind them. Ricky and his brother, Jimmy, owned the truck so they always sat up front. Miguel, Jake, and Dido—one of them is their second cousin but I always forget who—sat in the back like always.

I waved. I hated the sound of my voice when I talked to any of them. It squeaked.

"Hey, you wanna ride or somethin'? There's room in the back," said Ricky. I thought I heard sniggering from the three behind him.

I looked to the storm coming. There was no way it wasn't going to hit us hard. This was the first time I'd ever been offered a ride by Ricky or Jimmy. Way before they ever bought the truck, they used to give me crap every chance they got, but since they'd gotten either girlfriends or jobs they mostly just ignored me. I didn't hate them like I used to, but I still didn't really like them either. They liked guns and fireworks too much.

I shook my head no.

Ricky leaned forward a little more so he could look back to the darkening sky. He frowned.

"C'mon bruh," said Jimmy, slapping his arm. I could barely see him in there but I could see the ever-present, murderously bored slant to his brows. "She ain't cummin.' Let's get the hell outa here."

Ricky shook his head as he pulled himself back in through the window. He didn't look at me as he sped off but he did flash me a deuce. The wind picked up the dirt from his tires in its own little storm, nearly obstructing his bumper sticker: *"New Mexico: it ain't new and it ain't Mexico."*

The fingertips of the storm had reached the sky just above me. The mesas on the distant horizon were now lost in the mist. The flat land surrounding me on all sides felt like it was the only earth there was, like this piece of desert had been scooped out of all space and time and was flooding with the coming storm, leaving no place for the rest of us to run to.

I whipped on the trash bag and ran. The wind carried the smell of lightning.

I don't know how I noticed it. In the dead, cracked expanse behind Walter Keltner's horse pins lay a small lump, completely alone, completely still. After I stared for a while, I noticed there was something about it that was actually moving, like it was a little sea plant in the touch-pool at the aquarium, but I still couldn't make out what it was. I was drawn to it. The storm behind, like a siren song calling me, framed the thing perfectly as I drew near.

A dead dog—

A wolf dog by the looks of it, once I got close enough to see the texture of its creamy white fur, but there was something else about it that was off. Already the sun had disappeared entirely and the wind had grown so strong that I pulled the trash bag over my head to keep my hair out of my face. Then the wind shifted back towards me like a pine tree pushing over its roots. The smell hit me like a hailstorm of needles. There was nothing fresh about it. The rancid stench of carion was perhaps tempered by the sweet promise of rain on each gust of wind, but it was sickening nonetheless, and that's with the close proximity of Keltner's horse pins.

I could see now. The husky wasn't just dead; it was ravaged. I hadn't been able to tell because it had been lying at an angle where its back was facing me, and its back was the only thing about it that was as it should have been. I approached slowly now, wishing I could just turn back and forget how terrible what I was seeing really was, but it was too terrible to look away now, and too terrible to ever forget.

I came around to the dog's front and examined it. There were only two other parts of its body that remained intact: its bottom legs and its tail.

It was as if the dog had curled up in a frightened little ball and endured its murder knowing there was nothing to do other than wait for the pain to stop.

Part of me felt like I should cry, but no tears came. My eyes were as dry as the wind and the earth.

Until the rain came.

The clouds gave a single breath that loosened a light patter of droplets, but that was all the patience they had. The torrent came down hard like the sky was angry sobbing—ugly, violent crying. Pounding the trash bag into my skull, my shoulders, my back, jabbing at my cheeks. But all I could care about was the thing's beautiful creamy white fur, now graying in the wetness, now matting in the mud. I needed a sheet to cover it with—

No. The wouldn't do anything. I had to find someone. I had to find someone to help me fix this. But what was there to do? What could have harmed this creature?

178

Then a sickening thought: who could have done this?

I looked at those strange puncture wounds. Some*thing* had created those gashes—a tool—wielded by human hands. My head twisted manically as I searched for the tool or any semblance of it. Instead I found the only other clue there was. I found tire marks. There were large heavy tire marks in the dirt, but the ground was so dry and hard that they didn't go deep. The rain was already washing my only other clue away, and fast. I tried my best to commit the image to memory; and then, as the first lightning bolt flashed and the thunder roared three Mississippi's after, I raced for home, leaving the storm behind me.

As if that were possible.

It just so happened that old Sheriff Dominguez lived three doors down from me. I went to him next.

"What you doing out in this weather, Lala? You're gonna get soaked to the bone with or without that piece of plastic. Your mom know you're out here?" he said from behind his front screen door. He still liked to talk to me like I was twelve, yet he was the one walking around his house in his underwear in the middle of the day. Clearly he didn't know my mom very well either.

I tried to tell him the story, but he cut me off.

"Alright, alright, I get it. I'll come out and bury the thing after the storm hits. Good timing, too. Gound'll be nice and soft."

"No, I mean we have to find out who did it," I said, still panting.

"Why would you want to do that? I don't see what difference it makes. The thing is dead."

I could only stare; no words came.

He sighed, "You say it was over by Keltner's place?" he asked.

I nodded, already making to turn away.

"Why don't you just go over there after the storm passes and let him know. He's been trying to get rid of the coyotes nearby 'cause they been causing trouble with his horses lately. I'm sure he'd be happy to bury the thing."

I turned and ran before he finished his sentence, ignoring his last thought. I maneuvered my way through the forming mud pits and rain puddles to avoid slipping entirely.

It must have been Keltner! It made perfect sense. The dog was right behind his property and everyone knew he despised any kind of creature he couldn't put behind his bars—or that threatened what he had put behind them already.

By the time I got all the way back over to his house, the rain had gathered on the ground so much and I'd done so much splashing through it that I was soaked up to my knees. Luckily the lightning was staying far enough away, for now.

But Mr. Keltner wasn't there. I knocked and knocked and knocked but he was either gone, ignoring me, passed out drunk, or dead.

RE: Three Hells
Christopher Shonafelt

Hey Sis!

I'm sorry I wasn't able to meet you while in Washington. Pressing issues at my office in San Francisco required me to taxi back early this morning.

Do you remember flying on those business trips with dad when we were kids? On airplanes? I used to love watching the world fall away below me, and then seeing the clouds and city lights drift by out the window. Now this simple pleasure has lost its charm for me. We all fly somewhere for one mundane reason or another every day, and familiarity breeds contempt, I guess. Plus distance and height are tedious challenges these days, when we can fold and tear spacetime like wet paper.

Anyway, everything's taken care of. My guy will hand you a leather briefcase and silver key. Inside the briefcase you will find three gray orbs about the size of pool balls. They're all labeled and numbered.

In case you were worried, this tech is so new that all of this is technically legal. Our lawyers checked. If anyone is bothered by it, you can always draft some pro-dimension containment legislation (congrats on your reelection BTW)!

I'm not assuming you'll know what to do with them, but maybe you know someone who will.

When I started collecting hells, I felt a boyish excitement. I first saw them on my desk, freshly bottled, and I thought back to the *wunderkammen* of the 17th century. What could better fill the ambitions of Enlightenment man than to own the inferno, to hold hell in the palm of his hand? The European kings could only symbolically hold the continents they'd conquered, as painted maps and globes.

This was new, in a way nothing has been since we crossed the oceans. I think for all the utopian talk of colonizing the solar system, space never truly excited us; that's why we've made such meager progress there the past eighty years.

Besides, the planets are empty rocks. Not populated.

Our contractors were all your guys and gals-ex-marines-capable people. The demons put up a bit of a fight (they were demons, after all), but they had outdated weaponry-swords, pitchforks. Besides, we only interfered with them enough to do recon and plant our containment engineering. We may have shrunk their worlds, trapped them in things the size of children's toys, but as far as they're concerned, things are going they way always have, and literally always will.

Here's a user's guide:

The first hell we captured is an endless maze. A network of circular, rough stone tunnels. Each tunnel is about a quarter mile long, and all of them connect at intersections of four tunnels each. As far as we can tell, all the tunnels and intersections are identical, and go on and on, as far as we were able to explore.

The dead wander these tunnels without direction. They drag their feet, slouched and weary, stopping now and then to lean in rest against the sharp broken rock of the tunnel walls. Sometimes, though, a tap-tapping is heard behind them, back at the last intersection, the tapping of Something. Then they panic, and stumble and run, trying to put as much distance as they can between them and Something, until they become exhausted, slouching and dragging their feet again.

The second hell is traditional, if you're into that kind of thing. It has gibbets and rivers of pitch, shrieking, bat-winged furies, manacles and whips, a hooded psychopomp piloting a skiff across a river, the whole nine yards. Glades of cypress trees and tall walled fortresses beneath an eternal, starless dusk. This is the kind of place where you see well-known historical figures like Nero and Attila boiling in lead.

The third hell is overseen by the Plastic Angel and is called Fake Heaven. He gave our contractors a lot of trouble at first-in particular, his ability to cause a rainstorm of dirty syringes anywhere in his domain. The Plastic Angel initially excited interest when he claimed to be the High King of All Hells, until it was discovered that every arch-demon identifies himself to humans, both dead and alive, as the High King of All Hells. They're all shameless self-promoters, those high-ranking demons.

In this hell the walls are painted blue, with bumpy cumulus clouds. The ceilings are distant and covered in flickering fluorescents. The souls trapped here wear crooked halos and backless white hospital gowns covered in pink dots. None of them retain the faces or bodies they had in life; instead they have one of five repeating, forgettable faces. They're wheeled, sedated and blank, to rooms containing gray tepid swimming pools, old arcade games, the pleasurings of smirking eyeless houris. The souls there enjoy them all, drooling. The ironic, existential nature of this hell's torments-not to mention its early 21st century emo/nu-metal aesthetic-suggest to me that it was crafted from the guilt and anxieties of postmodern sinners, as Hell 2 was built from the thoughts of classical and medieval damned.

I have not included in the suitcase my grandest prize, the most awful hell of all.

The contractors I transported to this one never came back. We only got a little before their reports collapsed into yelled gibberish and then static.

It is an abyss that is nothing except an all-bathing light, light the color of unwashed sheets. The light is alive, they said. It knows you. It feels like a steady drip of lukewarm water, or an eye through a keyhole. It caresses. It feels hateful, and grinning.

Some have guessed at the nature of the filthy light. They say it's the head honcho himself, the prince of this world, the great worm that deceiveth, i.e., the devil.

Unfortunately, we can only speculate.

What will be done with these orbs? The possibilities are as limitless as the hells themselves. Our techies are running the first trials in converting the energy they exude into sound waves. Sonically, hells sound like concrete slabs dropped into oceans of broken glass, and warped, prancing violins. You could use this to build noise cannons for the disruption of riots. They could serve as space-efficient prisons, too-not for everyone, just the people who deserve it. They are out there-the predators, the terrorists. You should probably leave it to the ones whose guilt can't be doubted, though. Not that it's up to me now.

But I digress. I've been drinking.

Understand, this isn't about money for me. I know a woman of your caliber feels the same way.

We can't yet, but maybe one day, when we develop this technology further, we can capture heavens.

You can imagine it, can't you? These wouldn't be gray, they'd be in crystal orbs, or gold ones. These ones (and I'm sure you'd agree) would be open to everybody. You folks may have voted to sell all the old national parks, but what a way to make it up to the public this would be! What's Old Faithful or the redwoods when you can walk a rainbow bridge to platinum castles? We can meet our departed family, talk to our ancestors who first came to this country, tell them what they, with their struggle, made possible. We'll drink wine made of lightning, and apples made of sunlight. Fly through sheets of spring rain, laughing.

By the way, those things, the bottles I mean, are tough, but I'm told they can still crack. Make sure you don't break 'em! Haha.

Thanks & Love,
Your Brother

Moving Day
An Excerpt
Mirt Norgren

The initial thump was the sound that woke me from a light and restless sleep, but it was the scurrying of footsteps along the length of my roof that startled me into an upright position in my bed. I clutched the bed sheet tightly to my throat, as if the very act of covering myself would have the power to protect me from an unseen enemy. My eyes scanned the room in darkness, straining to find some order and an exit through the piles of boxes that were stacked throughout the room. It was my first night alone here, in this the rented house that would begin my life of singleness after eighteen years of being married.

Earlier that day I stood by the door in a state of slight paralysis as I watched the moving truck backing slowly out of the long drive, the last connection to my old home and the life I left there. I remained in that spot long after I could no longer hear the truck's engine, even after it cleared the turn down the hill to the coast. I stood motionless on the porch and wondered if I would ever be able to unpack all of my belongings. I was here, alone, separated from the life I'd known, surrounded by the clutter of almost two decades of living. I barely remembered packing any of it, and the thought of sorting through the mounds of kitchen utensils, books, photos and medicinal potions that were neatly contained in labeled boxes was too much to consider.

The safety of the daylight calm was instantly covered with doom the second I heard the footsteps on my rooftop. I'd forgotten to close the blinds before I crawled into bed and I could make out the outline of the pine trees across the street in the darkness, their long fingers reaching out towards one another in the shadowy park. The sunny charm from the morning was replaced by desolation after midnight; there were no barking dogs, no lovers holding hands strolling. The park benches were void of life, there was no comfort looking in that direction. "Quick Jill, think," I heard myself saying out loud. The phone, I had to find the phone that was somewhere in this room. I'm not even sure why I had bothered with a landline, an old habit no doubt, and now all I had to do was crawl around on all fours and find the cord in the tangled mess on the floor. I ran my fingers along the first cord I touched but it led to a clock radio that I hadn't bothered to plug in yet, a flip flop was next, then a hairbrush. My mind was racing. I heard another scrap along the far-right corner of the roof, the footsteps were getting closer.

The neighbor had warned me that the house had sat empty for a while and that the police had been alerted to a vagrant that had been squatting here. Why wasn't that alarming to me when I heard her say it? Why would that person come back here with my car parked in plain view in the driveway? I never dreamed they would return. My heart skipped a beat as my fingers groped along the carpet but In the next moment my hand brushed up against the handset. I heard the familiar sound of a dial tone and I relaxed a little, "It's okay now," I said to the still nothingness beside me. I started to push the nine and then the one, but it suddenly occurred to me that I might be overreacting. What If it was just a branch brushing up against the house, or the wind, or my imagination. I realized I was out of my element, maybe I dreamed the whole thing. I started to picture myself out on the driveway in my robe, the red and blue lights from a police car flashing, the neighbors peeking through their windows at the spectacle of a patrolman taking down my statement into his tidy little notebook. I couldn't bring myself to do it. I would wait it out, it was nothing. I had to relax.

That was when I heard the second thump on the roof at the far end of the house where the noise had originated from. Before I could think it through, I was dialing the familiar number. My fingers knew the way as if they were playing a tune on an imaginary piano. It only took one ring, for him to answer with a mix of alarm and annoyance, "Jill it's the middle of the night . . . "

I swallowed hard, amazed that I had called him, it was like muscle memory, an impulse, an instant reaction without a moment of forethought. "Blake, I can hear someone walking on my roof."

"Where are you?" he asked. This time I heard concern with a tinge of panic.

"I'm in the front bedroom, the blinds are open, I don't think I should turn the lights on." My voice sounded foreign, as if someone else was speaking for me. I held my breath for a second, he was technically still my husband, but he was a stranger. My back stiffened at the thought of it, this mess that I had created. What was I doing on the floor in a strange house in the middle of the night?

There was a moment of silence and then the words "I'm coming over, stay where you are." There it was, the rescue. The moment came and went when I could have shown my independence, but my fingers dialed the number without my knowing it. My psyche wants change, but my reflex was to turn backwards. One last chance to tell him to stay home, that I would be ok, but the phone went dead. That moment was behind me.

I sat on the floor, in the dark until I saw the familiar glow of the headlight coming up the drive. The light bounced off the ceiling and I caught a glimpse of myself in the wardrobe mirror, crouching there with phone still in my right hand. In spite of myself, I felt relief wash over me. I didn't even think to turn the light on, I just ran towards the door. Blake was already in the house when I turned the corner into the living room.

"You didn't even lock the front door! My God Jill, what were you thinking?"

The blinds were not the only thing I'd forgotten to close before I climbed into my empty bed that night. In the eighteen years that we were married, it had been Blake who locked the doors and closed the blinds in the evenings. He had his ritual; it was his way of sealing out the world, of pulling up the drawbridge and protecting our small fortress. I was too old to forget and too new to learn, what was I thinking moving here?

I looked at Blake and he was standing barefoot in a pair of sweatpants and a t-shirt, his light blond hair was receding, it barely moved even when he'd slept on it. In his right hand was a baseball bat, his weapon of choice in matters of protection. Blake looked a little wild-eyed and I noticed that his hands were shaking but I wasn't sure, maybe it was just seeing me here that was causing them to do so.

"Where did the noise come from?" he asked.

"That way," I pointed to the back of the house and I followed him through the study, past the laundry room, and finally to the door leading to the yard. Neither of us reached for a light. We had no idea where the light switch was in any of these rooms, it was the first time Blake had stepped foot inside this house. We paused in awkward silence but I followed after him, the weirdness of the moment trailing behind me as I followed him towards the back door. Once outside we looked up towards the roof and we could see that the branches from an enormous tree were hanging over the rooftop. It would have been a cinch for anyone to climb up there unseen until we heard them. The tree had blocks of wood nailed to the trunk creating a makeshift ladder. Neither of us spoke for a moment, we just looked up and waited.

"Should we call the police before we go up there?" I asked in a too loud voice.

"No, I can handle this, just wait down here." Blake whispered.

Blake placed his foot on the first block of wood and grabbed the one right above his head with his left hand. He realized he was holding the bat with his right hand as he reached up to grab the next rung on the ladder. "Give it to me," I said, "I will hand it off to you once you get up there."

"I can't see anything," he said as he reached the rooftop. "It's really dark up here." I climbed up to meet him, and the two of us stood on a branch looking down the length of the rooftop. Neither of us spoke for a moment, we just waited for our eyes to adjust to the dimness. In the distance a faint light from a neighbor's porch began to illuminate the outline of the shingles and the branches. Suddenly one of the larger branches closest to me swung wide to the right. I screamed before I saw the eyes that were looking down at me. My left foot slipped off the block of wood nailed to the tree that I was standing on, but I caught my balance as the face retreated back behind the leaves.

In the distance I saw the outline of a huge raccoon running towards us from the other end of the roof. I heard the clunk of the bat hitting the gravel beneath us as it slipped from Blake's hands and in the distance we could see two more faces, both of them wearing the familiar bandit's masks as they moved closer to inspect us.

"Should we go inside?" Blake asked. I didn't answer him, I just climbed down and picked up the baseball bat off the ground. I handed it silently to Blake and we made our way through the dark to the living room. I sat down on the couch and Blake leaned on the arm of a chair on the far side of the room.

"What are you doing here Jill?" he asked.

"What do you mean?"

"I mean what are you doing HERE? There isn't even a street lamp anywhere, it isn't safe for you to be here all alone." Blake started to raise his voice, but he stopped himself and added softly, "Come home Jill, you don't belong here" This was the conversation I swore I'd never have again.

"Thanks for coming tonight, Blake, I'm sorry I woke you for nothing," I stood up and looked towards the open door, "go home, get some sleep." I could see that he was about to say something but I held up my hand and heard myself say "no," a little louder than I meant to. He started to respond, but he thought better of it. Instead he got up from the chair and made his way toward the door, he left without closing it behind him.

I waited until the car had cleared the driveway before I closed the door and turned the lock. My eyes had adjusted fully to the darkness and I was settling into the air around me. Tomorrow I would find the light switch. I heard myself exhale for the first time since I'd arrived here and made my way past the shadows of boxes until I found my bed. I closed the blinds this time and made sure the phone was within my reach. I'm going to need a dog I thought, a big one.

Almost Universal
Bryan Kashon

Momma is the oldest child ('70-). She has a younger sister ('73-), and a younger brother ('75-'86).

Momma said that Uncle Ray was always sick. "But that didn't stop him smiling." She always talked about him.

She told me that Uncle Ray was only four pounds when he was born, like me. The doctors thought his heart was going to stop beating immediately. But it didn't. Momma told me the Doctors gave Uncle Ray two weeks, max. That made us both laugh. "572 weeks, actually," Momma said

Momma always cried when she told me about Uncle Ray. She said that all the time in the world wouldn't be enough to spend with him. I always tried to wipe away momma's tears when she cried, but she would always move too far away.

Momma said that a day lost is a year forgotten. I know my Momma's never forgotten a year.

Whenever she cried, I made her tell me a story.

I remember she told me a story about shoes: every time her brother made her upset she would take his shoes and throw them over the power lines. He would wail like he did when he was born.

"Like me," I said, sitting up. But Momma just sat there, like she didn't even hear me.

Whenever my momma told stories she would get this look, like she was someplace far away.

On the day of his funeral she said she threw his new shoes over the wires.

I remember she was crying, but I didn't dare move. She would have flown away. She used to say if you see an angel cry you leave it alone. Momma said that an angel that can't cry flies away to Heaven. Momma wanted his shoes to be closer to Heaven, she said. So all the angels would compliment him. Momma didn't say anything for a while when she was done talking. We both sat in silence for a long time.

Momma doesn't cry anymore. I wanna ask Momma to tell me another story, but she's busy with my shoes. I wish I would have wiped her tears away.

"So they're closer to you," she said to Uncle Ray.

"So you look good in Heaven," she says to me.

('03-'14).

Landlocked
An Excerpt
EJ Conway

Lex stumbled as Kita bounded up the stone steps three at a time, nearly bowling over other townsfolk gathered at the top of the city wall. She threw out a sorry where she could, but still people—and guards—glared, but did nothing on a day like this.

"We're not going to be late," Lex panted. "Calm down!"

"Shut up!" Kita said brightly and elbowed her way through the crowd to the wall's raised edge and shoved Lex forward so she could have the better view. Behind her, Kita breathed heavily and leaned forward, resting her hand on the stone level with Lex's shoulder. "Whew," she gasped. "Just made it."

Lex panted and reached to wipe the sweat off the back of her neck. "We should've left earlier," she said, reaching to pull her dark hair up into a bun.

Kita swatted the stray strands that found their way into her face. "C'mon, really?" she protested, bobbing away from Lex's hands while her tawny eyes remained focused far beyond Lex herself. "And you couldn't have done this sooner?"

"I didn't expect to *run* to get here," Lex reminded her, finishing with her hair and placing her hands on the wall, standing on tiptoe. "Where am I looking?"

"Over there," Kita said, pointing beyond the tramped earth before the gates and the stretches of farmland to the far lake, glistening a brilliant blue in the still air of the early hour. "See that copse? Keep your eyes on it."

"Okay," Lex agreed, settling back on her heels. "Are we close enough?"

"We'll be able to see everything important from here," Kita said, nodding. "And not, y'know, be shot."

Lex huffed a laugh. "Right. The cannibals."

"*Elves*," Kita chided. "Prefer flora to fauna; can't say I blame them." "An all meat diet, though?"

"Worse things out there," Kita said, shrugging. She leaned into Lex a little more, pressing the latter's chest into the wall. "I think I saw it move."

Lex pushed back against Kita a little. "Sure," she said. "Trees don't move in the south." "I'm sure they don't. Up here, though, we have real seasons."

Lex laughed again and slid her hand over the one Kita still had resting on the wall, her gaze trained on the copse at the water's edge. The two stood there for a minute or so in silence, their breathing evening as they waited. Around them, the townsfolk chatted idly and yawned, blinking in the bright morning light while they casually jostled for a better vantage of the trees.

"You all packed?" Lex said eventually, trying to turn around.

"No, hey! Keep looking," she protested. "And no, of course not. I have a week."

"So you haven't even started?"

"I've *started*," Kita said, "but I don't need to be *done* yet. I'd rather be enjoying the last days I have with you around rather than anything else, much less that."

"Kita," Lex groaned. "Come on."

"I'm not going to see you for a while; I need to make the best of the time I've got while I've got it."

Lex dropped her eyes from the lake to the moss-covered grooves between the stones, frowning. Her hand over Kita's curled slightly tighter, and she felt Kita brush another stray hair from her shoulder and then rest her chin there.

"It's going to be okay," she murmured. "I promise."

Someone gasped behind them, setting off a chain reaction of excited whispers.

Kita's head immediately jerked off of Lex's shoulder while she zeroed in on the trees, which had begun to sway as if in the midst of a windstorm. "Wow," she breathed. "This never gets old. I can't believe this doesn't happen anywhere else."

Whatever wildlife lingered in the trees scattered—the air exploding with birds and the trunks blurred by the movement of rodents and insects alike. They fled from the trees which groaned as they swayed more dramatically, nearly snapping themselves in two.

A small tree at the edge of the group bent backwards enough to skim the ground with its longest branches while an anchoring root burst from the earth in a shower of dirt and tumbled grass. The root placed itself on the dirt and pushed downward as the tree continued to sway as other main roots ripped themselves free.

"Look at that," breathed a man behind them, looming a bit close behind Kita.

"Tourist," Kita muttered under her breath, not quite elbowing him, but leaning back enough that the sharp joint caught him in the stomach when he tried to get closer.

"Oh, sorry," he said, stepping away and trying to get closer to the edge through another group of people.

The townsfolk let out with a sudden cheer as the first tree at last extricated itself and staggered on its root-legs a few paces before steadying itself like some great, many-limbed beast. The roots moved like tentacles, coiling and uncoiling in order to drag the tree forward. And somehow, as tremendously top-heavy as it was, it never seemed in danger of falling over.

"Wow," Lex murmured.

"I told you this was amazing!" Kita said, wrapping an arm around Lex and giving her a quick squeeze. "Look at *that*! And they're just going to go wherever they want to, nothing to hold them back. Just go somewhere nice and warm, the snow and all be damned."

"It's amazing," Lex agreed, but a frown remained in her voice. "But what about that one?"

While most of the trees had been able to pull themselves free, there remained one that struggled still. No matter how dramatically it pitched to or fro, it had only half-freed one root. And the earth, already loosened and tumbled by the other trees, provided little purchase for it to leverage itself free. What little they could hear of the groans seemed more pathetic than those of the trees already freed which, as one, began to move away from the city.

"What?" Lex said, a panic quickening her heart. "What are they doing?"

"Leaving," Kita said. "They can't wait forever." "But without the other trees, won't it die?"

Kita shook her head. "No . . . We'll take it, instead. It loses its magic in the process, but it'll live on in the city, long as it's able." She shrugged. "Doesn't happen every year, but sometimes, there are ones that can't make it. Either too sick or too young or too old . . . Or maybe just unlucky, like this one, who couldn't get out."

In the distance, the trees crested the hill and vanished, a great trench left behind by the churning of their roots. And at the water's edge, the last tree still swayed, one root now free and waving as it lost purchase again and gain on the unsteady ground.

What Happened to Ms. Bloch?
Zoe McCartney

I was waiting for the bus a few days ago after school. It was raining and my hair was soaked. As the bus pulled in, I realized I had forgotten my lucky pencil; Sherlock Holmes. I ran back to Ms. Bloch's classroom. When I opened the door, I saw her sitting at her desk eating her usual bag of sunflower seeds. I noticed her skin looked greener than usual; it was probably all the broccoli she eats. Every day at lunch she would always have twelve pieces of broccoli, a bag full of seeds, and watery soup with small crackers.

"Hanna, you're still here, shouldn't you be going home? It's getting late, that homework won't write itself," Ms. Bloch said as I walked in.

"I'm looking for Sherlock Holmes," I replied.

"Ah, I see," she said knowingly, and nodded her head.

As I walked towards my desk, Ms. Bloch made a squawking noise. Puzzled, I turned to her, but my teacher just kept eating her seeds as if nothing had happened. I blinked, and then remembered that Sherlock was waiting for me. I searched all around my desk, but Sherlock couldn't be found.

"Ms. Bloch have you seen Sherlock Holmes?" I asked still checking under some of the chairs around me. "She was on my table when I left," I added.

"You know, Sherlock Holmes was a man in the books, so for your pencil to be a female, really doesn't make sense," Ms. Block told me nonchalantly, inspecting one particularly large seed before plopping it in her mouth.

"O-kay," I said slowly, what did that have to do with finding my lucky pencil? "So, anyway," I pressed on, "have you seen Sherlock?"

"Yes . . . yes, I have."

"Where is she?" I asked, confused why she didn't just tell me that in the first place.

"Oh, she's in my closet, I'll go get her for you," she said, getting up and walking into her closet, and did a little hop right before opening the closet door.

"Sherlock thanks you from the bottom of her eraser," I told her happy to know Sherlock and I were soon to be reunited.

I heard her rummaging around, and waited a whole minute for her to appear again. When she didn't come out, I looked inside her closet, but she wasn't there. Suddenly, a greenish bird flew out from one of the shelves and strait out the door. Then at my feet, rolled Sherlock Holmes.

Logan's Cove
An Excerpt
Rory Thost

Sarah Bernstein told her mother, who eventually told my father the police chief, that she was raped in a ravine we had forever known as Logan's Cove. The Bernsteins, small and smart and Jewish, moved to our lakeside town six months before. Sarah was their only child and it showed in her loneliness and precision. On that first day, the few kids that had to ride the big, deteriorating bus watched her as she walked to the back, clad in floral and a cardigan and clutching a white lunchbox. We had never seen eyes so brown and big and full of questions never asked. I only heard her speak a few times before the Bernsteins finally moved away, finally giving our mothers and fathers, and maybe even us, what the entire town wanted. The boys on the bus watched as she placed her red bag on her lap and tucked her small-quiet-girl legs against the cheap brown vinyl seats. We concluded that *yes*, she was pretty and *yes*, we would kiss her if given the chance, but *no*, she would never be our girlfriend. At the time, the boys on the bus thought the role of girlfriend belonged to Grace Meyers— the blond-haired, green-eyed eighth grader we had seen become a woman one summer after church camp. Together, but mostly alone in our beds, we had decided that she was *the one*. The one to have our children, the one to kiss at night, the one to make Christmas pot roast, and most important, the one we could cry in front of without feeling lonely and little.

Six months after we decided Sarah Bernstein was pretty with good teeth and soft lips, she was raped in the ravine. During those summers when we were small, the ravine was overgrown and smelled of earth and rain that never came, as if the dense, muddy hills trapped the liquid air, making the green hot and secluded. We loved Logan's Cove more than anything. Right before I left for college, I lost my virginity to Dawn Underwood in that same ravine. It was a Saturday night and we had been at some party and she was half-drunk, whipping her hair, showing me her teeth, and her bra got wet when I pulled it off of her. She cried after it was over and I sat there rubbing her back until she said she was okay, but that she was afraid her father would look at her, *really* look at her, and know. He would smell the sweat she said.

After news broke and the entire town couldn't stop talking about that *vile ditch*, we blamed Sarah for ruining Logan's Cove, for taking away our special place and giving it to everyone. As the developments had cleared more land, as the nice, shiny cars kept coming from the city, and the lake continued to dry up, we felt the little ravine had been left for us, untouched and perfect. But Sarah Bernstein was raped in that little ravine on a Sunday afternoon and our parents, from then on out, forbid us from going.

On Monday, we didn't even notice that she wasn't in school. On Tuesday, Tommy told us she was sick (or something) and that he hoped she was better for his second-period math class. There was a test on Thursday and he intended to cheat off of her. On Friday, Calvin said he heard his parents talking after dinner in hushed voices, saying something about someone *touching* the Bernstein girl. We had not thought of her in that way since the first time on the bus. Suddenly, at the cafeteria table, I thought of her naked stomach and felt sick.

On Saturday, Calvin told us it had happened at Logan's Cove and that at first, she didn't want to tell her parents but they had noticed the wet mud on her jeans and eyes stained from crying when she came home. We went to the empty water park by my house and sat on the tallest tube and smoked a cigarette Danny had stolen from his older brother. We passed it around and smoked the tiny thing till our stomachs shook, looking out at the lake that seemed to be getting smaller as we neared the filter. In talking about Sarah that night, we never wondered who was the man that took her to our special place, not even what he looked like, or what he smelled like, or what his name was, or if we had seen him around town or in the store or at church. Sarah told her parents that she didn't know the man but they did not believe her and insisted to my father that it was probably a high school boy or one of the drunks that hung out at the Mexican food place downtown. I heard my father say to my mother one night when they had been drinking that he wasn't about to make rash accusations and ruin a good boy's reputation in a small town where news travels fast and cruelly. *Like a plague of locusts* my mother added. It had to be one of the drunks he insisted. I said this to the boys the next night at the water park and we agreed, it *had* to be one of the drunks.

Sarah came back to school the next week and was uncharacteristically talkative, answering questions in class, laughing when a teacher made a bad joke, one day telling me that she liked my new shoes. She even waved to me one afternoon when my mother picked me up from school. My mother looked at Sarah standing in front of the plate-glass doors, then at me in the passenger seat, and said quietly, as if not wanting me to hear but needing to say it anyway: *that poor, broken child.*

Against our parents' wishes, that weekend we snuck through the woods to Logan's Cove as the sun was beginning to move behind the hills. The orange light cut through the thick trees and spilled onto the clear water and the green embankments. I remember thinking it had never looked so beautiful. We sat and talked about Sarah and the soon-to-be summer and if we would play basketball in high school. Later that night, I walked into my house right before dinner and my father was on the phone, assuring Mr. Bernstein that he was working on a lead. I looked at his face and I could tell that Mr. Bernstein was crying on the other end. My father never liked the sound of breaking men.

The air grew hot and humid and we began swimming and taking our shirts off after school, only putting them back on for dinner. My sister got a car and when she was in a good mood would drive me and the boys around the lake, blasting Alanis Morissette. Even then, sitting in the backseat, we knew nothing of her pain and anger but as we listened, we sang along, memorizing the words and thinking for brief moments that maybe, just maybe, we knew what it was like to be a woman.

Here. There. Be.

Evan Maier-Zucchino

I come to consciousness before my eyes open. Warmth pours into my body as my fingers caress the grass beneath me. A thrilling sensation courses up my skin. I feel a great urge to do nothing, to lay there against the cool ground for an eternity while I enjoy the solitude of my own mind and the slow course of my breath. Rise and fall. Eternity is a long time.

Sunlight filters through the treetops above, cascading down my face. My eyes remain half-open against the sun's infinite brightness as I grunt to wakefulness and take in my surroundings. Trees surround me. In almost every direction these natural columns stretch, impassable. Before my feet, however, is a gap between two lines of trees spaced a few meters apart, their branches arching over and entwining with one another. The grass below the trees is pressed flat. In the distance a brilliant light shimmers in a dazzling rainbow of colors.

Drawn to the light, I rise from the ground, stretch my tired, aching body, and enter the living tunnel. A breeze sweeps through the air, tempering my sun-baked skin with an enveloping coolness. Light falls upon the ground through gaps in the leaves, clouds of dust giving the rays a physical presence within the shaded forest.

As I walk, I realize that the trees give way to a wide clearing ahead. The gleaming lights rest in its center. They're blinding, as if the sun itself had taken rest upon the ground.

The lights shift.

Slightly, almost imperceptibly.

My feet root to the ground. Air catches in my throat. A hole forms in my chest.

The urge to run overwhelms me.

But I don't.

The lights beckon me forward until, at the edge of the clearing, the lights move once again.

I duck behind a tree and peek out. The clearing is a sea of green, the tall grass swaying along with the course of the wind. A black rock sits in the center, reflecting the sun's beams. Relief flows through my body. I rise from my cowardice to take in the open space.

The rock moves.

The wind slows.

It rises.

I halt, a single tree between me and the clearing.

It falls.

I take a step back.

A burst of air blows the grass flat.

My back bumps into a tree.

He wakes.

His arms, sinewy and large as tree trunks, spread over the grass in a wide arc then extend forward, long gray talons flexing out to rake the ground. His legs push back. Wings, translucent in the daylight lift off his back to bend straight into the air, their tips high above the trees. With the effort of a boulder rising off the earth, he raises his head from the ground. Rising onto four massive limbs, he cranes his neck around to look at the sky. Rows of glinting serrated teeth become exposed as his great jaw widens. His body shakes. A calamitous murmur throttles the space between us.

The sound explodes in my ears. My stomach churns. My mind shatters as if smashed against a rock. I fall to the ground, unable to restrain my convulsing limbs.

Then, as abruptly as it began, the sound stops. I keep my eyes closed, trembling in the grass. When I look up the creature is sitting at ease, his tail flicking delicately with the breeze. An aura of holiness surrounds him as lights dance off his black scales. Wings hang flat, wrapped tight against his round stomach. He lifts himself onto his hind legs. Curving his head around the clearing, he examines his surroundings.

I rush to hide behind a nearby tree before his searching gaze falls on me. I feel it, boring into the tree. He knows. He must.

The ground depresses. A tempest bursts into form, knocking me flat. I lay squirming with my face in the ground, hands over my ears, whispering thoughts of despair.

Nothing.

No earth-shaking roar, no talons, no pain.

I rise from the ground and lean against the tree. Most of the bark is stripped off. Insects throng across its newly exposed flesh. Every tree I can see shares the same fate. The clearing is deserted, the breeze dead.

I glance up. Beneath the clear blue sky soars a shining dot. A thin ray of rainbow light bounces off its hide and strikes me in the face. He drifts through the air, rising and falling with every beat of his massive wings. I smile.

I move towards his resting place. The ground is pressed flat, the markings of each round scale carved into the dirt. A glint of light catches my eye. I lean down and lift the heavy black scale. Its coarseness like a shave against my skin. Holding it up to the sky, its dark sheen transforms into a rainbow of colors.

A distant rumor passes through the clearing. The trees bend and groan.

I pay no attention, my eyes captivated.

I do not hear her enter the clearing. I do not feel the ground shake.

Her shadow falls upon me.

Her hot breath on my neck.

My back slams into the ground.

The scale slips from my hand.

I scramble back and fall over myself.

Rise and fall.

My breath burns in my throat.

Every time I stumble to the ground she takes another step, her inescapable shadow looming over me. Her wings engulf me, her neck cranes like his, and she presses one of her eyes close to my face. It alone is larger than me, and white, pure white, stark against the blackness that stretches across her head. She pulls back. Standing on her two hind legs, stretched to her full height, her wings spread, blotting out the sun. Her eyes gaze at me, into me.

A breeze sweeps over the clearing. The trees sway. My body relaxes into the cool grass. The infinite white sun peeks over the looming mountain.

I close my eyes.

Warmth pours into me.

X-Ray Woman: The Life of a Sensitive
Kimberly Carlson Aesara

Karen hurt her neck. At the doctor's office a nurse placed a heavy blanket over her body. "To protect your sensitive parts," the friendly nurse said. The nurse then went behind a wall and took an x-ray.

Karen liked the heavy blanket. It made her feel as if she were in a cocoon, where all was safe and warm—a place where if she stayed long enough she'd transform into something different and beautiful with wings.

The nurse lifted the blanket off.

Karen lost her breath. Vulnerability filled her chest, her stomach. She felt loneliness spilling from the friendly nurse. The nurse took her blood pressure and temperature, talking the whole time about her youngest child who recently went away to college. "I have nothing else," the nurse said. "I lived for my kids." Tears welled in the corner of her eyes. "You have a nice smile. I bet a lot of people say that to you."

"Thank you. Do you see your children often?" Karen knew that people loved to talk about themselves—and all it ever took was a simple question. She pulled the thin cotton blanket up to her chin, listened and felt.

After Karen was told her neck was "fine, only muscular," she left the doctor's office but didn't go to the mall like she had planned but went home where she slept off the energy of the sad nurse.

She wanted to go back to the doctor's for another x-ray. She couldn't stop thinking about how she felt when she had the x-ray blanket on top of her, warm, safe, protected. That same evening, she took an empty duffel bag and went for a walk. It was cool; the leaves on the liquid ambers were bright orange and yellow. People were outside raking leaves, throwing balls, collecting their mail.

She wasn't like some who heard voices, or heard melodies, or saw color hues surrounding people, or made up stories, or brought everything to a mathematical equation. She wasn't weird like all those people that others talked about. She felt. Physically, the tension centered on her heart, making her weepy, grumpy, withdrawn. Spiritually, she shrank.

As a young child, she felt her spirit soar inside her—stronger than anything else— everything failed in comparison, television, trips to Disneyland, her thoughts, even her dreams.

Year after year, her spirit retreated back into its cave, shadowed and now chained. It wasn't one event, one trauma that was so popular to point at in today's world. It happened with each tear from her sister, every pained look on her brother's face as he cleaned his fishing pole while waiting for his father who'd never come. It happened while sensing misery, smelling of alcohol, seeping out of her dad, hearing stories of an aunt's love for her children who were in prison. It happened to the little Mexican girl who sat alone in her class who couldn't speak English. Karen couldn't concentrate on her teacher, as she sat feeling the dark-skinned girl's isolation. She felt the worthlessness that spilled out of her mother's friends as they talked about men who wouldn't marry them, or their husbands who wouldn't listen to them. She felt and tasted the saltiness of fermented tears from an old woman who lived alone. The childless aged woman would call her over, and while other girls her age were playing Barbies and hide-n-seek, she sat and watched warm slow tears fall from eyes that no longer saw beauty in the world. Slowly, Karen's spirit retreated, needing to protect itself from the world of hate, loneliness, and pain, but leaving her heart, her emotions more exposed, more vulnerable—until there was nothing to catch the blows of the feelings coming to her from others. She was left with a raw exposed heart.

The evening sky was turning dark as it always did. Birds flew violently above her. People were no longer lingering in their yards. Calls for children to come home were heard up and down the street. Not watching where she was going, her ankle twisted and she fell off the curb. She screamed loudly. Luckily for her, a neighbor saw her and rushed her to the hospital.

She lay paying no attention to her swollen ankle, anticipating the x-ray blanket. Then it came—she imagined sun-warmed honey being poured on her chest. The old nurse walked over to remove the blanket.

"One more minute, please," Karen pleaded.

"What?" The nurse looked at her as if she misunderstood.

"Please. I love the feeling I get from this blanket."

"Are you cold? I can get you a real blanket." The nurse smiled as nurses sometimes do.

"This one is good."

The old nurse walked away. As Karen lay, relaxed and almost giddy, she heard the nurse tell the doctor that she thought they might have given her too much pain medication.

Karen stole the blanket. She shoved it in a bag she brought while no one was watching. She felt a bit of guilt about this, so she later donated $100.00 to the hospital, donor unknown.

At first she just slept with the blanket. Sleeping deeply, safely with vivid dreams of living a life full of people who enjoyed the things she could not. Going out to eat. Exercising at the gym. Meeting friends at a bar for a beer.

After sleeping with the blanket for a month, she went out on a couple of dates with intelligent, successful men. Slept with one. After, though, she reached under her bed for the blanket and wrapped it around her.

He laughed and said, "Are you kidding?"

Slowly, as many significant things happen, she took to wearing the blanket more. After work, she came home and cried, for her loneliness, for the lady at work who lost her son, for the custodian's eyes that were filled with self-loathing. Then she'd sit and pull the blanket over her and wouldn't leave the house. One Saturday she wore the blanket, "Just to the market." Sunday, "Just to church." Monday was brilliantly sunny, "I'll wear it just until I get to work—it will protect me from the UV rays."

Now, the blanket was always draped over her. She loved the feeling of it on her shoulders, heavy, dropping down her chest, past her abdomen. She no longer cared what others said about her. She knew they called her "crazy" and "x-ray woman." They said she must have taken some bad acid or maybe something traumatic happened and she just flipped.

What these people didn't know was that she felt their pain still, though less intensely, that she cried nightly for her spirit to come back to her and live as it did when she was a small child, that she longed to take off the blanket and be more like them.

Mommy Loves the Rain
Kikiine

Rain flooded the earth on my walk home from school and I slipped off my yellow firefighter rain boots to rid the pools that soaked my socks. I would have cleaned out the messy mailbox, but I was too small to reach it. There were never enough things to tidy when I came home anymore. All the spoons and forks and knives slept nicely in their drawers, the pictures cuddled the walls in a perfect stack of rectangles, and even the candles on the table sat tidily in their seats, each spaced two inches apart. I know, I measured.

Mommy liked exciting things better, though. Mommy preferred the candles tumbling out of their chairs, pictures rock climbing the walls, and spoons and forks chatting like neighbors. Except we never had any. Every day she would shake up the decorations so I could put them back neatly after school. It was fun, I liked to clean, but ever since the rain started there had been nothing new to straighten. There weren't even dishes in the sink to stack as we hadn't been using any since Mommy went away. But that was okay, I ate at school.

Eight days had passed now since Mommy ran out into the rain. She did that a lot. She often left the house to chase the tails of thunderbolts. Eight days ago, a really big one waved through the air that Mommy just had to go and catch. I haven't seen her since then. Today was Friday, and it was still raining. When the rain stopped, Mommy would come home. She always did.

I asked Daddy once why Mommy always left when it rained. He said it was like when I measured the space between the cups in the cabinets. She didn't *have* to, but she had to.

"Daddy?" I asked, creaking down the steps to the basement, my wet socks leaving puddles to chart my journey. Daddy hadn't left his study for seven days. Or at least I didn't think he had. It smelled funny today. "When is Mommy coming home?"

I thought he would be at his work table, his special knife carving lines into another casket. But he wasn't. In the middle of the floor Daddy sat with his back turned to me, his hand slowly petting something long and brown and wet. Maybe the cat got outside again and was trying to dry off in his lap. "She is home," he said. His voice was soft like when he read me bedtime stories.

"Where?" I asked as I came closer to Daddy. There she was, sleeping on his lap. So it wasn't the cat, it was Mommy. She was wrapped up in a big blanket. "Is she cold?" I asked. Her lips were blue, so she must have been.

"Yes," Daddy said. He pet her hair again. "She went swimming in the river."

"In the rain? Is Mommy sick?" I asked. Mommy always said swimming in the rain would make you sick. "Does she need some medicine?"

Daddy stroked Mommy's hair some more to make her feel better. "Yes," He said, swallowing. "I think she does."

"Okay," I said. "What should I bring?"

Daddy leaned down and scooped his hand around Mommy's head, touching his forehead to hers. He thought about it really hard, so hard that he shook and rocked in place. "All of them," Daddy said, his words crackling like sad thunder. "Just bring all of them."

197

Fallen

An Excerpt

Hugo Alberto López Chavolla

Have you fallen in love? Have you truly fallen in it? As in when the addiction supersedes the need for discretion, the shame of public affection, the logic of your actions and the reality of such a fatal behavior? God, I wish I could forget the many times I have gone through this, the many times I did not learn the lesson, the many loves who never were and are still within me. Why is love such a beautiful dream, yet a painful reality?

His mind rallied with thoughts of suffering from his lost loves. His mind attempted to talk to itself; to teach itself the never learned lesson. He believed that talking to himself as an experienced fellow would facilitate the absorption of his rhetoric. His mind truly wanted, for once, to think before advancing forward with this girl. Just like the ones before her, she was precious. Just like the one before her, she was becoming everything. But, unlike the ones before her, he was afraid to give it all at once.

It has been almost six months. She was everything to you. It lasted almost two years. You two lived together, shared an apartment, chores, laughs, cries, love, hate . . . Yet it ended. The one before her lasted a year and a half. A different story, same outcome. And remember the last one before the last one, before the last one: it lasted three years. In between them you gave yourself a maximum of three-plus months before moving onto a new ship. All of them now rest at the bottom of oblivion. Why would this be any different?

He first saw her at the gym where he attended to escape from the absurdity of life and the nihilistic perception of the days. That day he pressed weight against an iron bar when suddenly his focus weakened for a moment as her reflection past him before the mirror. *She is pretty . . . I wonder if she is new here . . .* The thought lingered for a moment and then he continued with the meticulous routine he had been following for almost six months as the means to distract the melancholy of his last love, but from time to time he would let his sight follow the figure that now decorated his self-imposed prison. *Should I ask for her name? Say hi? No, no . . . Not at the gym, that's really weird . . . but what if I don't see her again? What if . . . I think she is leaving, I guess that's a no.* He stayed for another thirty minutes. He packed his stuff and headed for home to take a shower, eat dinner and go to sleep. As he walked outside he looked around, as if attempting to find this mysterious girl and take a chance, but no luck. Not today.

Why her? Why so sudden and fast? A couple of weeks ago you had sworn you would never go back to that life. To mark your word you insisted: "I am never settling down, never getting married, never again falling for anyone." Remember that? Or are you going to say it as the alcohol? You also said it sober. What changed if anything? What are the excuses this time? Why would you choose to do it again? Think about it: you alone are not responsible for the other's pains; you with her, become part of her pains. You already wasted one to many people's time and tears; you already hurt yourself and others in this mythical pursuit of love. Why do it again?

He saw her again a week later in the same space. His concentration failed once more, but at the same time he thought it would be better to let it go. He grabbed some weights and continued to destroy himself with the hope of forgetting too many things that no longer mattered. *Why did you do that? Why did you tell her you loved her if you didn't?* He turned up the volume attempting to silence the voices in his head and increased the weight on the bar to force himself to grow out of his old self. *It is okay.*

It is okay. You cannot hurt her anymore. The gravity pulled the weight of the bar down; he utilized all his pain to push it up. The song, a familiar tune about lost loves, fed his fury against himself further and the next thing he knew he had been there for almost two hours. He completely forgot to check the time. He would have to shower in a rush and then run to his cubicle in order to get his materials for his class.

Wow! It has been six months today. Exactly six months. This is a new record. You haven't been this free in a while. Do you feel it? You are only responsible for yourself. So, again, why are we so willing to let our freedom go? Solitude is not that bad as a partner. Yes, she is very quiet. A total introvert. However, she never impedes you from going through with your unplanned plans. She does not hurt or gets hurt. So, why? What is it again? I know, I feel it too. WE HAD FELT IT BEFORE. MORE THAN ONCE!

As he walked towards his cubicle, he saw one of his friends talking to a familiar face but he was not paying attention as he was more interested in the music coming out of his earphones. Then his colleague turned and as she saw him she waved. His manners forced him to approach her and to introduce himself to the companion. *Oh dear, it's her!*

Silver Screens
Lindsay Benster

I received an email today, an email plagued with deplorable deceit, polluted with unlaundered misfortune. Plunging across the palisade once guarding my composure, my rationality, my peace, I land on our previous correspondence, dated nearly three weeks prior. Three weeks I had waited. Twenty-fun days of inconscient conversation, checking and rechecking my phone, my laptop, my iPad. Maybe the internet isn't working? I shut off Wi-fi, resorting to the premium of data. Maybe the e-mail application itself is broken? Never mind the endless sea of Groupon, *New York Times* and subscriptions for sites, and products, and companies (and certain people) I failed to recognize let alone disclose my contact information to, flooding my inbox. *No, no, everything's working*, the Genius bar repeatedly and exhaustively assures me, and reassures me, pointing to the stream of messages overcoming said "connectivity" issues.

Five-hundred-four hours scratching phantom itches, deciphering pugnacious apostrophes, counting and recounting my limbs and toes, ensuring my eyes and mind and my mind's eye remain harmonized. Still four appendages, still ten toes. Still eight digits, as two are permanently designated to monitor all forms of L.E.D, at least one at a time, sometimes all three. On this tumultuous journey from anxiety to compulsion, my nerves tingle from disrupted circulation and further from unconstrained anticipation. Only to have my itches lacerated. My inner-monologue abruptly silenced.

Three weeks before, I slumped before my laptop; carelessly, aimlessly, haphazardly clicking through mental tabs—planning out breakfast, constructing my daily itinerary, wandering to distant memories and pondering life's ambiguous questions. As I navigate to the Gmail window, an illuminated band perforated by bolded font, stretching across the uppermost brim suddenly adjourns my daydreaming: "**Everything's Okay.**" The bold words slap my stomach and squeeze my lungs, and through the shock of physical assault, I'm now sitting with an invisible board strapped to my spine, my hands gripping dense spheres of air.

"Everything's okay." I had heard it many times before, usually lacking preface and predictability and always, always eclipsed by a celestial "but."

"Everything's okay . . . but I got a little too drunk and don't know where I am. Everything's okay . . . but I'm feeling a bit sick and have these weird streaks descending my leg. Everything's okay . . . but you might want to start looking for a new car." "Everything's okay" was his ironic, poetic way of disclosing his disastrous misfortunes, his inebriated mistakes, his manner of informing you that everything's okay, but nothing is alright.

Winded from the subliminal marathon of possibilities, I de-claw my right hand just enough to expose what all is okay:

"Hey Linds—Everything's okay but I got into an accident. I was running down a busy street in Shanghai and got hit by a car. My head's pulsating and my arm is spelling out a new letter but I think I'm fine? Will let you know anything as soon as I find it out. Try not to tell Mom and Dad yet, don't want to freak them out. I'll talk to ya soon, love ya."

The initial reading only impressed a pendulous silhouette, a rough outline of "accident" sketched by a misshapen arm—potential concussion? Brain damage? Shattered bones? A secondary deciphering extracted "don't tell the parents." It wasn't until my third reading that I grasped—"I think I'm fine . . . I'll talk to ya soon . . . Everything's okay."

And that was three weeks ago. One week to process. One week convincing family that "Tyler's having an amazing experience in Asia, you wouldn't believe it. I think it's all starting to hit him . . ." One week repeating to myself everything's okay, everything's okay, everything's okay. And three weeks to realize that nothing is okay, nothing is okay at all.

Now I stand, immersed in apple products. Sitting was an activity for the assured, the restful, the serene. Sitting is the first thing they instruct you to do when receiving bad news-you're going to want to take a seat for this . . . why don't you sit down? No, I would not sit. Bad news did not sit well, and neither would I. Feet firmly planted in the ground and my butt far from it, I reflexively tense, from mind to muscle, bracing myself. Exhaling pent up pessimism, in one large puff.

Eyes fluttering from left to right, right to left I become hyper-aware of the harsh edges of Times New Roman. Each letter pointed like daggers, defensively offensive, protecting the phrases and words, rejecting any form of opposition. These conjoined daggers construct words I once knew, but through haziness of emotion their meaning is far lost. I try again, this time shifting my focus from irrelevant technical features to the content itself.

> Re: Everything's Okay
> "Delivery to the following recipient failed permanently:
> tylerbenste@gmail.com"

Delivery failed. Delivery failed? What does Tyler mean delivery failed? Was this "everything's okay" advanced to the next dimension? Contemplating and analyzing Tyler's unique sense of humor my attention averts to the imposter imposing on our confidential conversation. Who is this "Mail Delivery Subsystem"? And through scrutiny and sophisticated comprehension thanks to my collegiate education I recognize the imposter. A familiar name masking an unknown face. Frequently the perpetrator of disrupted communication, lost opportunity, misdirected orders. This time, merciless yet again, unforgiving of my trivial mistake. One slipped finger. Prone because of my jittery composure, my distracted mentality. Perhaps I sneezed. One way or another an "r" was deleted, and the results deleterious.

Anxiously rewinding through the successive levels of inbox, outbox, in-between box, I confirm that my email was never sent. Simultaneously yanked left with optimism and hope, and kicked right with embarrassment and idiocy, I return the ever-so-important "r," and off it goes. Again.

I lean against the wall, my lower half strong with support while the backs of my shoulders melt and mix into the fading paint. Time and sunlight warp around me; kissing my skin, dialing my soul. Stressed, but relaxed. Confused, but assured. Afraid, but confident.

I worry too much, I think. I worry too much, I worry too often, I worry for those who don't worry themselves. As I rotate my heavy head, my eyes freeze on a framed image mimicking my movements. A sharp reflection of light twinkles from a head of fading hairs. My four gray hairs. My four gray hairs sprouted pre-maturely, each born from an "Everything's okay" moment. I failed to pluck them out of myth-based fear and routinely tuck them behind their darker counterparts. But through my expedited aging and thus granted wisdom, I notice they're more silver and less of a gray. And in this world where silver linings freckle the homogeneity of brown, I realize that not all treasures allure; some as unsightly as they are meaningful. They are blind in an unblind reality, silver in a forest of brown. They were born out of worry and watered with stress; I worry, but at least I have ones to worry for.

After an immeasurable amount of time passes, a light humming breaks my trance.

Locating the source of the song I pick up my phone: *Call from: Tyler Benster.*

Sliding aggressively once above, once below, once too quickly, I finally correctly slide to answer: "TYLER! How are you what's going on? Is everything okay??"

"Woah calm down. Everything's okay . . ."

A French Affair in a Roman Bath Room
Alex Dunne

"Fifteen years ago it wasn't like this," was how he introduced himself. We were sitting diagonally opposite in the dimly lit corner of an uncrowded cafe. Outside, the day had begun to ebb into night, the gray sky melting into a deep, buttery blue. Fifteen years ago I was ten, I thought, afraid to meet his gaze.

I wasn't particularly attracted to him, only the way he dressed, so immaculately European. And his shoes—slender but robust, a polished cognac with caramel stitching and a slight sheen. His face was slender too, framed by a widow's peak and tortoiseshell glasses. I could feel him staring at me. His eyes bore into the top of my head while he tore into his quiche. I ordered myself to ignore it, but I couldn't stop shifting in my chair and rereading sentences.

When I finally looked up from my notebook, I could see my entire face reflected in his eyes. It was as if a tiny version of me was trapped there, imprisoned in his pupils. He stared back at me, then turned to face the room.

"Look at them," he said, addressing the scattered coffee drinkers poking at keyboards and tiny screens, "they spend their time with plastic."

I kept my eyes slightly lowered, afraid to look up and find myself gone again.

"I once went two weeks without a phone," I told him.

He opened his eyes wide and his face settled into a smile.

"Do you meditate?"

"Well," I said, unnerved by the question, thinking it may be a test, "I've tried it." I crossed my arms on the table and leaned forward, looking directly at him this time. "Let me guess, you're some kind of a *sensei?*"

He laughed. A rich, handsome sound. He told me how he learned to meditate from a man in Japan whose sole job was to craft the curved spoons used in Japanese tea ceremonies. For twenty generations, this man's family had done nothing but make bamboo spoons.

My eyes scanned the contour of his cheeks and his warm olive hands; I noticed the way his trousers stretched over his knees and hugged his thighs. I'd like to say I sensed then what this man would come to mean to me, but I couldn't stop staring at his shoes.

Later I would tell myself I did it for the story.

And that is how, on a Wednesday night in February, I decided to make love to a middle-aged French man. Actually, I decided I would let him make love to me. I assumed that's what French men did—maybe not all French men, but the wordly, divorced kind with honest eyes and early signs of balding. The kind who, when telling a story about growing up in a rural village outside Bordeaux, looks you square in the face and, raising one hand as if pinching the air, says, "How do you say . . . hétéroclite, what is the word in *American?*"

It happened, of all places, at a Russian Bath House in the East Village. He claimed it was his favorite spot in the city, a place steeped in tradition and tolerance. I thought it smelled like sour feet. I arrived before he did. As I stepped inside, the warmth from the steam rooms rushed to erase the cold, embracing me in a damp, sticky hug. I felt suffocated. A blast of icy air surged to my rescue, and he entered inside.

It happened other places, too—in his Brooklyn loft, on a windy rooftop, pressed against a kitchen sink. When I introduced myself, he'd told me Alex was a man's name. When we made love he would whisper, *Alexandra Alexandra*, and a part of me wondered who she was. Because I really was someone else with him—I smiled with my eyes and let him tuck wisps of hair behind my ears without protest, and not once did I correct the way he said "incongruous" or talk about my fear of bedtime. And when he prattled on about *luxury goods* and the battle of artisan vs. consumer and some champagne that sounds like Cloog, I listened and nodded like a sympathetic bobblehead.

It wasn't until much later that I realized I'd acted exactly as myself—impulsive and self-deprecating and lonely. And I searched for his eyes, but couldn't remember their color. And I searched for something different, something to fill the hole that his affection and intellect had occupied. But I kept thinking of that damned Japanese tea man with his bamboo spoons.

I forget what Dominique said about emptiness, something French. Only afterwards, he winked. Not in the tawdry American way, but by closing both eyes at once, like a slow, calculated blink. And I remembered the way I looked trapped in his pupils, small and scared. Staring up at him with eyes that sought answers, slipping into the crease of his cornea, wet and warm, my own cozy crevice.

I let myself remain there for a moment in the warmth of his memory, then I peeled myself away, letting the cold air rush in and fill the space between us.

Bottleneck
An Excerpt
Austin Shippey

The building was teeming with young pulses, chaotic with the sound of shouting, shrieking, singing, laughing in carefree and confused abandon. The wooden floor, worn in more places than it was polished, was littered with patches of tacky, sour smelling beer which mingled with the smell of youthful sweat and passionate breath. Dancing off the exposed brick walls were laser lights. The pulse of powerful rhythmical bass was felt through the soles of Aaron's shoes. He sipped the last of his warm beer and got to his feet, dizzy with alcohol and tired from the long night. He wanted to go home.

After much squinting through the flashing lights and sorting through a dozen mingling faces, Aaron found two of his friends dancing in the corner next to the speakers.

"*I'm ready to leave!*" he mouthed silently to Kylie.

"*Just a minute,*" she enunciated back, "*I'll gather everyone up! Just wait a few!*"

Aaron went to the bathroom, swaying slightly as he peed. The bathroom was illuminated by a single dull bulb and, like the rest of the bar, had a worn out industrial atmosphere complete with cobwebs, crumbled cement, brown copper pipes, and occasional spots of rusted steel. In the old days the building was a brewery and bottling plant, one of the biggest in Oregon as well as the Pacific Northwest. In the early nineties the owner died of lung cancer and let the company die with him. It remained, rusting and statuary until the property was bought by an investor, probably seeking the sweet profits gentrification can bring.

At first Aaron's friends loathed the idea of the old building being revamped as new residents move into the city, driving up the prices of apartments and causing crime to rise, but soon the bitterness died down and interest began to grow. "What was the big old building in the center of downtown going to be made into?" The interest grew stronger when a free drink was offered to all twenty-one-year-olds.

"I'm thinking it will be a brewery again," Kylie suggested as she handed Aaron the flyer she swiped from the window at her work.

"It could be fun," agreed Aaron. "I'm free that night too."

"Ooh, we'll finally be able to see what it looks like inside," said Emma, and soon the whole network of Salem's twenty-one-year-olds were absorbed. Calendars were marked for the first Friday of January.

As Aaron turned to wash his hands, he heard a long zip from the stall. Out burst loudly the bartender who had served him his drinks earlier, slinging what looked to be a heavy backpack over his shoulder. A brief moment of awkwardly unpleasant eye contact was exchanged, and he was out the bathroom door. "Must be having a long night," Aaron thought.

Leaving the bathroom, Aaron bumped into Kylie and Emma, who were on their way to the ladies room, laughing as they kept each other from tipping over.

"We're almost done, don't worry, we're just gonna say bye to friends!" Emma shouted, a bit louder than the hallway called for.

Aaron nodded.

"Wanna join?" Kylie said with a cackle as she and Emma disappeared into the bathroom.

Aaron saw Gordon and Nick ordering drinks from the now cheerful bartender. He approached them. Draping his arms over their shoulders he asked, "Did Kylie and Emma tell you guys? I'm ready to ditch this place."

"No, they didn't say anything, we just saw them a second ago. They seem to be having a good time . . . though maybe we should stop them from getting any more drinks," suggested Gordon.

"I'm getting tired too. What time is it?" Nick asked, grabbing his fresh bottle from the bartender.

"Almost 2," Gordon replied.

Gordon, Nick, and Aaron took a seat at a long table which looked straight out of a garage sale of worn furniture from the 70s. It was complete with sticky beer stains, used toothpicks, and a chewed wad of gum.

"This place is a bit of a dump," Nick said. "I expected them to do a lot better. They're never going to be popular if they keep this up; Taproot is just a block away. They don't even have any original beers."

"I was expecting a lot better," agreed Aaron.

"I think they just put this night on as a kind of test," argued Gordon. "They probably just had one bartender in to serve simple drinks, you know, just to see the traffic, and I'm guessing it was a success based on how many people turned out, that's why they offered the free beer to twenty-one year-olds. You know, he didn't even check my ID?"

"Well I mean if we're going by free drinks and not checking IDs, he didn't even recognize me. I kept going back, he kept saying *thank you for coming in*, and giving me another free beer. Eventually I just stopped paying for them because I was thinking when the universe gives you gifts, you don't turn them down . . ." Aaron struck a pose of prayer and bowed dramatically. Gordon and Nick laughed.

"Speaking of that, if Emma and Kylie are taking their sweet time, I'm gonna go get another drink." Aaron got up to go to the bar.

"They're probably in there puking!" Gordon shouted.

"Or fingering each other," Aaron shouted back.

"Or both!" roared Nick.

Aaron approached the bartender, still laughing. "Do I get another free one?"

"Did you already get a free one?" the bartender asked, unsure. "Eh, just remember to tip your bartender."

Before Aaron left, he decided to get to know the bartender and ask more about the night and the plans for the building's future.

"My name's Henry."

"Nice to meet you," chimed Aaron, "do you live in Salem?"

"Yep, lived here my whole life."

"I don't think I've seen you around, what high school did you go to?"

"None of them, I was homeschooled. It's not likely you've seen me around." Henry replied.

"How come, do you live in the outskirts of the city or something?"

Awkwardly, Henry pretended to be distracted by a glass and went to wash it.

"Uh, yeah," he said. The demeanor of his face grew to match what Aaron saw in the bathroom: the face of someone very annoyed, or angry.

Aaron was tempted to ask Henry if his father had bought the bar, or if he was going to be an employee when it officially opened, or when the official opening date would be, but the awkward, closed-off nature of the bartender before him as he washed the glass, looking sharply down, made him refrain from asking any further questions.

"His name's Henry," Aaron said as he sat back down.

"Oh, did you ask him about the bar?" asked Gordon.

"No, he got kind of weird. I'm not sure what's up with him. He seems pissed about something."

"I can relate one-hundred percent," said Gordon. "If I was the only guy working here all night I'd be worn out too. I'm glad my uncle's bar doesn't get this busy every night or I'd probably jump off a bridge."

"Well I don't think he should be a dick about it," Nick protested, "the Beanery gets busier than this every weekday. You get used to the flow of it after a while."

Gordon replied, "I can see how you could get used to it after a while, maybe he hasn't been a bartender before."

The conversation weaved in and out. The three's bottles slowly drained. The room began to swim around Aaron. His neck drooped. His eyes got heavy. He awoke with a jolt to find Gordon and Nick walking toward the dance floor, where he assumed Kylie and Emma had rejoined. There were far fewer people now, probably only a little more than a dozen. The bartender—*Harvey?*—was no longer behind the counter. The only others in the bar were two girls sitting in the corner who had been drinking heavily all night, and the blonde of the pair now looked very sweaty and ill. Aaron watched her become distraught, and her friend led her away to the bathroom, presumably to puke. The thought made Aaron's own stomach flinch, and suddenly the sweaty, alcoholic air around him became insufferable. He walked to the back door of the bar.

Upon opening the door, he was met with a blast of cold, fresh air followed by a whiff of sour smoke from cigarettes and weed. Jared and a few of his friends were standing against the building's old brick wall smoking. Aaron greeted them and checked his phone, becoming annoyed at how much time had passed, yet giving up the battle in favor of taking deep breaths of cold, fresh air and attempting to will away the discomfort in his stomach. Pacing around the building, he observed the bare and silent streets surrounding the bar. It seemed the whole city had gone to bed. The city's quiet was pierced by the echoing horn of a train in the distance. The sky was clear and Aaron gazed up at the stars, feeling the weightlessness of the expansive sky above him, compound within him the tiny feeling of being trapped in this small city where nothing but overpriced bars, bland cafes, and lifeless cement buildings surrounded him.

"Maybe I should call an Uber," he thought as he paced the full circle around the building, only to find that his friends were no longer standing by the back entrance, and by the looks of it everyone in the bar had disappeared.

In Baltimore
Blake Lapin

They were up all—night giving and taking pleasure. They rode their motorcycles up and down the streets awaiting morning but thinking they were only running in the night, not towards anything but within. They drank until there was no more to drink and walked long after that when the birds woke and green sparked through the black. Not a sharp tortuous green but a green that platforms all other greens, a type of quiet and ubiquitous green, a green that welcomes the day, their beds and the proximity of sleep.

Rite of Passage
Cameron Geoffrey

It was a dark and stormy night, heading towards a day that would never come. The Santa Sabina Cathedral loomed on the edge of a forgotten forest, its altar dripping with the devoured remains of a toddler that stained satin white cloth. Connor heard the child's screams only moments earlier, but now silence hung on by a mere thread, and lightning provided brief moments of elucidation between claps of thunder.

Windows rattled and the faint patter of something heavier than rain tacked its way through the pews. Connor could not feel his limbs, numbed from the sight of gnawed bone and ruby gruel. He had hunted this beast since it murdered his younger brother ten years prior, but until tonight it always seemed just out of reach. A massive hound stalked the woods behind his village, abducting children and ripping their souls from their bodies through the chest cavity. For Connor, the hardest part was interviewing the parents. Every one of their stories ended the same, their sons eviscerated beyond recognition by a wolf-like creature. Connor felt as if he died so very long ago, he liked to think that he never truly lived.

The mush on the altar was only identifiable as human because a half-mauled buzz lightyear shoe hung off a candle stand, caked in mud and gore that gleamed all too familiar. Connor finally had the courage to look away, holding his vomit long enough to regain his composure.

Not another . . . He thought, as a flash of lightning cast two shadows on the wall. He spun around to catch the predator , but beyond three rows of pews, nothing could be discerned from the void. Every hair on Connor's body stood up on end, scanning the pitch-black church for some sign of the beast, but the very air refused to stir. Hours he stared into the darkness, and just when he started to feel alone again, a tap echoed from nothingness followed by the faint squeal of claws on metal.

The other side of the church was empty, front doors were cracked enough for light to show flecks of blood on a cross engraving. The rain outside intensified to the point where it started to slant, and the wind began to howl like a grieving mother.

Connor once felt that it was his purpose to end the slaughter of the innocent, at any cost. Now, he could only think of trying to save himself.

Comfort was so dissonant, what muscles that brought him here now ached and begged to be anywhere else, to fight or flight for a new day. Connor tried to motivate himself, at first through hatred of the beast, but the ice that gripped his heart could not be melted. He tried to hope next, reminiscing a future that would never be, but gentle taps that echoed between raindrops rippled through his dream. It was night, the beast was coming, and in another flash of lightning, saw the entire church in front of him, splashed in red leaking from massive claw marks that made it look as if the walls were crying blood. But what chilled him to his very core was that the church was empty, the only place he had not checked was behind the altar, and Connor realized in that moment that by turning around he had already sealed his fate.

There was no howl to give the wolf away, but the hot breath on the back of Connor's neck. Droplets of moist blood formed from the mist it spewed, heat from its jaws radiating in all directions as Connor spoke to his pursuer.

"We've been stalking each other our whole lives, yet even now I lack the nerve to look you in the eye."

Connor filled his lungs to their limit with frigid air, taking in the scent of the outside, spring was only moments away. A breath of life, his last, exhaled like so many of his loved ones. Connor clenched his fists, and gathered the last of his strength to turn about face.

There before him was a broken mirror, the reflection of a man lost to madness, matted hair and a cannibal's smile were the only things he saw before the glass shattered.

The 21th Second
An Excerpt
Laura Bouzari

Present Day—July 2015, New York City, NY

"Turn that damn T.V. off Blair!" I barked. That same story aired over, and over, and over again, every hour on the hour. It was as if the stations couldn't get enough: Trump, Trump, Trump, ISIS/ ISIL/ Daesh/ Muslims in general, Trump, Trump, Trump.

Waving her hand back at me dismissively, Blair spoke, "Don't be so insensitive Zaine. I'm sure the stations will air the story. She could be on that raft for all we know." It was as if Blair was talking to the screen. Her body was set in its habitual stance—hunched, elbows to her knees, and eyes glued to the screen. She doesn't get it. Blair's been witness to the mess with my family for the last few years. She believes wholeheartedly that she is helping me, like keeping up to date with news does any good.

Yes, I'm bitter, so sue me.

Dropping my worn and tattered bookbag to the apartment floor, I walk over to our shared bedroom and crash onto my bed. Head in the pillow and arms covering my head, I try to grasp the reality of it all. It's all just too much. The ringing starts in my ears again and the smell of rust and acid grows stronger. It won't stop. A knock at the door startles me up.

"I know you don't want to talk about it, but I think you should watch this," Blair whispered as she nears my bed. She looked at me with clear eyes—the eyes that have not yet been tainted by the reality of what's happening. The bed creaked as she sat beside me. Her long blonde hair cascaded over her right shoulder as she bumped my left arm signaling me to grab her phone.

While gripping the phone in my hand, Blair said, "Start the video at twenty-one seconds."

A white female anchor, dressed in the most exquisite of tailor-made suits made of the finest tweed, was speaking to a correspondent standing in front of what could only be described as a black space. The correspondent dressed in a military green jacket and a dark blue press vest was waving her hand up and down and back and forth. With the sound signal weakening, her arm motions came off even more erratic and incoherent.

"Blair what am I supposed to get from this?" I impatiently asked.

"Wait for it. Just . . . just listen" Blair spoke in a pleading voice.

I unpaused the clip. I wish I didn't.

"Border forces . . . boats . . . migrants . . . no . . ." The correspondent clipped out. What is new about this? Ready to toss back Blair's phone, I heard what I hoped to never hear.

"Capsized . . . forty-three lost . . . seventeen children . . . stop . . ." A frigid shiver shook down my spine. With a death-grip on the phone, my body began to feel comatose. I thought I didn't have another tear left in me.

"Do you think she was on it," Blair asked quietly. "I'm sure she was on another one, right? She has to be. When she called last week she said she was going to be leaving in the morning, right? Yes, she's got to be on that morning boat. Right, Zaine?"

I wasn't sure if Blair stopped talking. Still gripping the phone in my hand, I turn my head and looked her dead in the eyes, "She is gone, Blaire. You know it. I know it. And that's the end of it. Please stop thinking she made it. This is the third capsize in six days. She was supposed to have called once in Lesvos. If she took a different boat, if she missed that morning one day ago . . . she would've called. Please, Blaire . . . please just . . . stop."

"How dare you Zaine! She's your sister . . . *your twin!*" Blair barked. Now standing over me, I saw in her eyes an emotion I wish no one would have to experience desperation. "She has to make it," Blaire cried out.

Unable to look at her anymore, I turn my head in the other direction and stare away—away from this, all of this.

"Wallow all you want Zaine, but you and I both know that this is happening and yes it's scary, but it is terrifying to just give up," Blair spit out. Leaving the bedroom in a storm, Blair slammed the door.

Crash.

"Damn it, Blair!" I get up from the bed and make it over to the dresser. Grumbling as I pick up the fallen books, a golden speck catches my eye from behind the dresser. Dropping the books aside, I crawl closer to the speck. It was the old heart-shaped frame my sister gave me three years ago when I got my university letter when we were eighteen. In a haste to try and salvage it, I try to push the dresser away from the wall to pull the frame out from beneath its weight.

"Come on!" I scream in a huff. My arms strain as I try to push the dresser forward. Switching tactics, I push my elbows to the floor, sit back and use my legs to push the dresser away from the wall. With the little space I just cleared, I stretch my arm between the wall and the dresser and try to grab the frame. I feel the coarse edges of the cracked glass touch the tips of my fingers. Just one more stretch away and that fame was free.

So close.

My fingers extend just a bit further and I feel a sharp scrape against my skin. Pulling back my hand, my middle finger drags once more over the pierced glass edges. Red. All I saw was the red pool of droplets against the tips of my fingers. Pulling my hand up to my face, I became mesmerized by the blood. The cut was deep and the blood collected at the tip was gathering quickly. I look back between the dresser and the wall and see that glint of gold looking back, as if mocking me. I couldn't even get the frame free.

I don't know how long I sat against the wall. It could have been for a few minutes or a few hours. Defeat; defeat was all I could remember. I couldn't even get the frame out of harm's way. I look back at the speck and a flood of memories come pouring into me all at once.

2011, Aleppo, Syria
"*Yell-A[1]*, Zaine! The taxi is outside. We will be late...again." My mom yelled up the staircase.

---

[1] Arabic for "Hurry up."

"I don't understand why you keep yelling, I'm right here." Rolling my eyes as I walk down the final steps. Now, most high school seniors cannot wait for their graduation day. I, on the other hand, think it's just an end to a chapter, not a book.

"Now don't you look gorgeous." My mom smiled up at me.

Unlike my twin, I had my mom's eyes. Looking up at her, I notice a funny look on her face. "Why are you looking at me so weird? Mom?" I asked.

As if waking from a trance, she quickly answered, "Nothing *habibti*[2]. Now come on, we will be late."

Arriving at the school, I see my classmates all fluttering with excitement. All dressed in their caps and gowns wearing the largest of smiles. All the "I will miss you's" and "Please keep in touch" rang around the courtyard.

"Wait, girls, I want to take a picture." Digging through her purse, my mom pulls out her small film camera.

"Aww, mom! Really come on, this is embarrassing. You have enough photos of us as it is," my sister wined out.

"But none on graduation day. You girls worked so hard, let me just have this moment. Just. Just this one moment." She runs over to a neighboring parent and after making him smile and laugh, like she does with anyone she meets, the man came over and took a picture of my family. Giving us one final kiss, sealing a promise of sorts, my mom walked through the auditorium doors.

Dressed in the cleanest of pantsuits, the headmaster's assistant spoke, "Attention students. Please get in your places. We will begin in a few short minutes." The excitement level rose and the getters got worse.

"Zaine! Over here." Pulling my sister along with me, we both walk over to a classmate. I could never remember her name, but I do remember her voice rising when nervous and how she always talked with her hands.

"Can you believe the day is already here!" the classmate exclaimed. Her voice raised a few octaves.

It's just another day. All of us will still be here tomorrow, and the next day, and the next day. Life won't change that quick. Thinking it would be easier to just nod my head and agree, I smile and say, "Well, it was going to come eventually."

What was this girl's name? Rena? Ream? Elena?

"Zaine? Hello, Zaine? Where you'd you go?" The classmate asked laughingly. "Anyway, did you hear back from the states yet? Don't look at me like that. Your sister squealed." I knew my sister couldn't keep a secret.

"Um, no, I haven't heard back yet. It'll probably be a no. I would have gotten a letter by now." Looking away, I pray for a change in topic.

As if the dimming of the lights and start of the choir was the beginning of some magical show, the ceremony began. The "this is it" whispers began to multiply, but all I could feel was the pressure in my right hand. I look over my shoulder and I am met with green eyes that just glow in the dark. Her smile was infectious and her grip on my hand a vice. My sister always made me walk in front of her. I hated being in the front. Then again, I don't like being in the back. But why can't she just stand by my side?

---

[2] Arabic for "Sweetheart."

Peg Leg
An Excerpt
Jason Credo

The whistle of the steam screamed through the café. The smell of espresso danced around the noses of angst-ridden teens and flocks of flamingo-like women, who diligently and deliberately dictated their orders to the barista. By the window, a young woman sat ignorant of the bustling world around her; instead her gaze was to the street. On the table laid a pen, still capped, atop a notebook, still closed. She had intended her surroundings to unleash some sort of inspiration; she had intended for her surrounding to compel her to write, as if the long-dead ghost of Hemingway had chosen to possess her. Alas, such instances only happened in movies, or in the Deep South, where she had read the most hauntings typically occur. She opened the notebook and stared at the first page.

Nothing.

She kept starting.

She checked her watch.

Then kept staring.

The bell atop the open door breaks her trance—her gaze now follows a man, dazed and confused, with a smile on his face and wonderment in his eyes. He looks at the flamingo women and waves wildly; they shoot him a dirty look, flip their hair, and walk away. At the counter, he reaches for the barista's hand and shakes it.

"Hi there! Can I get a large coffee?" the barista took her hand back and laughed nervously.

"Sure . . . that'll be $4.50." she began to wipe her hand on her apron. He gave a name, paid, and proceeded to wait. The writer followed the entire exchange as if it were a nature documentary. The wide-eyed, star-struck tourist in its natural habitat; taking in every inch of wonderment wherever they may find it.

Fascinating, she thought.

"Hello?" The man leaned forward to make eye contact, "can I help you?" the writer hadn't realized that she was staring at him viciously.

"Nope. Sorry." She turned back to her notebook and began tapping her pen to a beat in her head, hoping it would drive him away.

"I'm Daniel." The beating pen wasn't good enough.

"Nice to meet you." She said, still not looking up, praying he'd take the hint and walk away. Daniel leaned forward to look at the blank piece of paper and turned his head slightly, much like a dog begging for treats.

"Are you writing a story or something?" Daniel asked.

"Trying."

"What's it about?"

"Not sure."

"Are you alright?" asked Daniel.

"Yeah, I'm fine. Aren't you late for a walking tour or something?" She finally said, looking up at Daniel. She thought if ignoring the problem wouldn't make it go away, sharp-tongued sass might do the trick.

"Walking tour? I live here," he said, much to her chagrin, "so, what are you trying to write about?"

"Still not sure. Thought I'd test out the clichés, you know?"

"So you went to a café?"

"Yeah."

"Well, that's very cliché."

"That was the plan."

"Doesn't every writer know that clichés don't work?"

"Isn't that, in itself, a cliché?" The writer closed her notebook and looked up at him, triumphant.

"Touché," Daniel smirked.

"So which are you? Aspiring or retiring?"

"Are you saying I might look old?"

"I'm saying that you might be past your prime. Or at least you feel you might be. The option is there, regardless."

"That's a bit presumptuous."

"Well, that's the type of guy I am: presumptuous, obnoxious, preposterous. If it rhymes, I'm that type of guy."

"Yeah. It seems like it." A fender bender outside caught her attention. The men got out of their cars, fuming and foaming at the mouth. Profanity launched from their lips before the door could even open completely. To them, this was an isolated incident that resulted in two men exchanging words, instead of exchanging insurance information. To everyone else, this was a show, universally made solely for his or her entertainment, intervention and de-escalation optional. Videos were being recorded, tweets being sent, and lives were being lived all in a single instance.

"Hey! Hello?" Daniel said while waving his hand in front of her to grab her attention.

"Oh hey, I was just—" she pointed out to the street, but decided to leave it behind. "Never mind."

"Can I tell you something? In all honesty?" he asked.

"In all honesty, I just met you. What can you possibly have to tell me?" She was on the cusp of crass but held back her tongue.

"Why did you let me sit here?" she didn't know the answer to that, "most people would've ignored me or shooed me away, and yet, here I sit."

"Wish I knew . . ." she gave a forced grin.

"I feel like you know the answer."

"I don't think I do." She shook her head.

"Yes. You do."

"So you know me now? Is that it?"

"Something like that."

Meet the Neighbors
Kimberly Zerkel

She asked if I took sugar. I smiled faintly and shook my head no. Then I politely sipped the warm, pink liquid she had poured into a chipped cup for me.

"It's piña colada flavor," she continued. "Anyway. We're all friends here. We say hello in the hallways, you know. Someone's always knocking on your door, asking you to come round for a sneaky glass of wine, that sort of thing. Erica and I do this all the time, you should've come sooner!"

She gestured towards the teapot and plate of pastel-colored cookies.

"We've just been dying to get to know you. We never really see you. Not much gossip to go around these days, though. Sorry to say. You missed it! There was a couple on the fifth floor, must've moved out a year or so ago."

She exchanged a knowing glance with Erica, whose eyes were twinkling. The latter finished chewing and began:

"I never really got to know the girl. She would come rushing in, hair hanging down in her face, carrying one of those huge notebooks or sketch pads under her arm."

"Art school student."

"Never got a good look at her. She looked teeny tiny, just like you. She rarely left the apartment. Depressed, depressive? *He* was extremely good-looking, but the last time I saw him, he had blood streaming down his face!"

I winced while swallowing the dregs of the fruity infusion. I was offered more and somehow found myself not refusing.

"Yes, it was during one of their more heated fights. We were all very tempted to call the police, but Erica was the brave one. We had been listening to plates crashing and feet stomping for over an hour. And the yelling. Already, every other night, the yelling and screaming. Well, Erica finally went and knocked on the door this time."

"He barely cracked it open. He left the chain attached, you see. It was dark but I saw blood just streaming down his face from a cut at the top of his head. She must have thrown something at him. A vase, some trinket, something. She threw things when they fought, we've all heard it at least once, right? He said everything was fine and goodnight, really quickly. His voice was so small and ashamed, I didn't dare call the police."

"When they weren't trying to kill each other, they were up drinking all night. They were dancing in the kitchen. Music blaring. Fall-down drunk."

"Alcoholics," Erica whispered. "And then they would . . . *you know* . . . like animals for hours. The whole building could hear her. Thank goodness no kids."

They were leaning towards me, they were touching my hand or knee when they spoke.

"I never saw the moving trucks, but they must've left a year ago. The peace! The calm! You can't imagine how different life is around here now."

The last sentence struck me.

This was when I realized that they had been speaking about Michael and me the entire time.

He left me about a year ago, sure. That was true. He moved out but only took what he could fit into his leather backpack, the one I bought for his twenty-seventh birthday. The furniture stayed put, obviously. I had, after all, just run out to the grocery store and post office, I hadn't been gone for even an hour. He barely had time to write a goodbye letter, let alone call the moving vans.

Neither of us drank. He liked beer but we never kept it in the house. I sipped champagne occasionally on New Year's Eve to appease friends, but I've never taken to it. No, instead, I would bring home cloudy lemonade from the grocer's for us to share. And he had excellent taste in tea and bought it loose-leaf from a local shop. That was us most days, tea and lemonade. We lived like characters going on some damn picnic in a children's book.

We did dance in the kitchen, on happy days, but to music on YouTube. The speakers on my computer couldn't possibly be that loud. Most of the time, our laughter or steps drowned out the songs themselves.

We were, in fact, very mindful about noise. We kept a small wooden shelf by the front door for our shoes, for example. Michael had spotted it and convinced me of its usefulness as we strolled past it at a sidewalk sale. We had been walking all afternoon and I was too tired for shopping, but a man eventually sold it to us for pocket change, along with some antique spoons and candlesticks that Michael knew I'd like. We painted the shelf pale green and set it by the door so as to immediately remove and store our shoes when home. The rest of the time, we tiptoed around the apartment in slippers his brother had brought back from Japan.

We spoke softly when we received phone calls.

When we worked at our desks, we often wore earplugs.

We were extremely careful when making love. The bed frame I had inherited was old and fragile, so Michael would often slide the mattress onto the floor. It would stay there for days at a time, entire weekends, of course. During one of our first nights in bed together at the new apartment, our focus was disrupted by the clarity of our neighbor's phone conversation coming through the wall. We could make out every word she pronounced and, at times, even the mumbling being made on the other end of the line. For privacy, we invented a game in bed where we had to show our pleasure through facial expressions only. The first time, it made us laugh hysterically. It quickly became one of Michael's favorites.

My favorite was when I would hear his key turn in the lock. I would quickly turn off the light switch and run to the farthest corner of our room. He would say nothing but I could hear him hang up his coat and take the first quiet steps. It felt like hours passed before I would finally sense his breathing and feel shaking fingertips on my face.

And yes, we fought very violently on two or three occasions. Once about his colleague at the bookstore, twice about him moving back to Berlin. These were the only times we screamed. Other times, normal fights, maybe we raised our voices. I could also cry very loudly. I did so the night he accused me of needing too much love. I ran out of words; I opened my mouth and let sobs escape as fat tears slid down through the cracks of my chapped lips.

A month or so before the end, he started coming home later and later. *Drinks with colleagues*, his texts would read. *Dinner at Dad's*. Or, *Helping Justin move*. He'd turn on the light when he got home, leave his shoes next to the shelf, and find me half asleep in our bed, clutching his jade green comb to my chest.

I never threw anything at him and so I do not know how the story of blood running down his face was concocted. But after he left, I did smash the blue-and-

217

white china dishes with a hammer, I flung his great-grandmother's crystal flutes at the wall, I ripped apart page by page the large art books he gave me, I burned the paperbacks and poetry collections in the sink, and I cut his favorite cotton shirts into ribbons before throwing it all into a large duffel bag and leaving it on his mother's doorstep.

So the only blood that ever appeared was my own, scattered little drops on the kitchen tiles and sink. I swept up the bits of broken glass, paper, and ash, and wiped away the stains with a wet paper towel. Then I cleaned and dressed my small wounds before falling asleep on the floor, too tired to put the mattress back on its frame by myself.

Erica added more water to the teapot.

"These infusions are strong enough for two or three goes," she said.

I politely turned down a slice of marbled coffee cake and then nodded along. They'd moved on now and were describing the woman on the ground floor who keeps very large dogs.

How My Parents Fell in Love
Dallas Woodburn

My mother walked out of a grocery store. She wore a red dress and her hair was permed, the way it looks in the photo albums. My father drove up in a car, a fast car, silver, a car that goes *vroom vroom*. He did not know her yet. She was a pretty woman in a red dress with ruffles at the hem. He rolled down the window. He leaned out and smiled at her and said, "Hubba, hubba!"

They fell in love and lived happily ever after.

My mother walked out of a grocery store. She carried a plastic bag, handles stretched taut in her thin fingers. Eggs, milk, strawberries. My father drove up in a car, *vroom vroom*. He liked my mother's red dress and her mess of dark brown hair. He rolled down the window and said, "Hubba, hubba!"

My mother was so startled she dropped her groceries. The milk was okay, but the eggs cracked, oozing yolks onto the sidewalk. My father crouched down and helped my mother clean up the mess. He wore dress pants and a tie, like the photos in his college yearbook.

"I'm sorry," he said.

"It's okay," she said. "It's not your fault, really."

They smiled at each other. He bought her a new carton of eggs.

They fell in love and lived happily ever after.

My mother walked out of the Student Union. She wore a red dress and carried a canvas book bag. My father rode up on a bicycle, glints of silver showing through the chipped paint. He wore a plain T-shirt and his hair hung down over his eyes. My mother—in a rush, distracted, digging through her bag like the nearby beach gulls dug for crabs in the sand—accidentally dropped her coin purse on the sidewalk steps. It snapped open. Coins spilled across the cement.

My father stopped his bike with a *screeeeech* of tires. He crouched down and helped my mother pick up her coins. Their skin touched as he placed pennies in her palm one by one. She smiled at him. *Hubba, hubba*, he thought.

They fell in love and lived happily ever after.

My mother walked out of the rain and into the crowded apartment. She wore a red dress and her silver necklace with the star clasp. A Christmas tree beamed in the corner. People danced, laughed, tilted plastic cups against their lips.

My father noticed my mother as soon as she stepped through the doorway. Her dark hair looked darker from the rain and beads of water trickled down her legs. He didn't know what to say, what he could ever say to her that would be enough.

So, instead, he waited. He stood by the bathroom, under the mistletoe, watching my mother and willing her to notice him.

Finally, she did, but only because she had to use the bathroom. It was occupied so she stood in line beside my father. She, slightly drunk, spilled a bit of red wine on his shoe. He didn't mind.

"Hi," he said, glancing up at the mistletoe above them.

"Hello," my mother said. When she leaned forward to shake his hand, her necklace slipped off into a small silver puddle on the floor.

My father crouched down and picked it up. Their skin touched as he placed it carefully in her palm. She smiled at him.

"Put it on for me?" she asked, pulling up her dark permed hair to reveal the back of her neck. His fingers trembled with the clasp.

"Hubba, hubba," my father found himself saying. My mother laughed.

"Look!" someone shouted. "You're under the mistletoe!"

Later, my father walked my mother back to her dormitory. They fell in love and lived happily ever after.

My mother was invited to a Christmas party by a girl in her Psychology class. She didn't know the girl very well, but it was a Friday night and she had no other plans, so she went. Her dangling silver earrings flashed against her dark hair. She carried a grocery bag, handles stretched taut with the weight of the chocolate cake she had baked that morning and carefully iced with a frosting Christmas tree.

The kitchen was empty save for three frat guys refilling their cups of eggnog, a girl arranging sugar cookies on a plate, and my father, who stood at the sink struggling in vain to wash a red wine stain from his shirt. It was hot in the kitchen and my mother noticed a bead of sweat trickling down the back of his neck.

Suddenly, she found herself stumbling forward, tripping over something in her red high heels—a case of beer, a sack of flour, an empty carton of eggs? The plastic bag lurched from her grasp and she watched the cake smash sadly against the kitchen floor.

My father turned from the sink and saw my mother. To him she was just a pretty woman in a red dress.

And yet.

He hurried over and crouched down to help my mother clean up the mess.

"Are you alright?" he asked.

"I'm fine," she sighed. "Just clumsy. I spent all afternoon making this cake, and now it's ruined."

"I'm sure it's still delicious," my father said, digging his hand into the dark moist cake and bringing it to his mouth, purposefully smearing his face with frosting. He loudly smacked his lips and grinned at her.

My mother laughed. My father stood, then reached down to help her up. Their skin touched. They washed cake and frosting off their hands at the sink. My father poured my mother a cup of eggnog. Their hands found each other again.

Later that night, they kissed under the mistletoe.

They fell in love.

And they lived, happily. Also angrily, naughtily, hopelessly, hungrily. Messily. Ever after. Like saints and martyrs and lovers and children. They lived, and they live. Together still.

The Wishing Tree
Morrisa P Clark

Once upon a time in a small little town with too much quiet and not enough to do was a Tree.

It was an ordinary kind of tree. Big enough to have a few low branches and cast a decent shadow on a summer day. It had leaves in the spring that would burst into colors of red and orange before floating to the ground with the first frost.

What made this Tree special that it was on a walk called 'Lovers Lane'. It happened to be the marker at the end of the path and that is where our story starts.

It happened one day, as these things usually do, that a young girl was walking Lover's Lane thinking of her sweetheart and wondering if he would return her affections. The wind caught at her hair and tugged from it a ribbon moving it to dangle among the Tree's branches. In that moment a thought struck the girl. She tied the ribbon to the Tree and whispered her sweet heart's name. The next day, he asked her to the dance and so the legend of the Wishing Tree was born.

It was a quiet sort of secret that existed only in the small high school. It was whispered about in the halls and soon the story of the Wishing Tree began to spread. As spring turned into summer, the Tree's branches became littered with ribbons of all colors. As summer ripened, the tree looked festive dressed in cotton, satin, and string.

Years went by and the ribbons came and went. Some faded with time or were torn off by winter's harsh hands. Sometimes a crying girl would come and reclaim her ribbon because the Tree had already granted the match to another girl.

Eventually the story started to change. If you wanted to make your relationship last, you had to carve the initials of the couple into the bark.

Slowly the ribbons gave way to initials, and hearts, and forevers, carved by switchblades and Swiss army knives.

Unlike the ribbons, these marks did not make room for new ones so easily. The tree grew little by little each year but not fast enough to offer new flesh for those frequenting Lovers Lane. Soon there was no more room to be had, and so they would cut off whole branches and carve their initials, hearts, and promises into the bleeding circle that was left.

Soon, what was once the lovely Tree at the end of Lover's Lane became the Stump. Soon, it was nothing more than a turning point at the end of a road. Soon, the stories of the Wishing Tree were forgotten.

Now there rests a Stump with rotting scars carved into its surface, and no one ever visits it anymore.

The Tree living inside the Stump remembers every ribbon, every heart, every wishful couple and hopeful girl. It remembers the hands that touched and the knives that hurt. It remembers the limbs torn from its body and its once beautiful leaves that danced in the sun.

The Tree remembers that no one ever thanked it for the wishes it seemed to grant.

The Tree remembers and it waits.

Retention
An Excerpt
Mia Brabham

Everything was spinning. The dark pines looked like they were falling into one another, their leaves even more indiscernible in the lack of light. The forest floor seemed to tilt as her feet moved quickly across the muddy foliage. Mist cloaked the trees, thickening by the minute. Her heart slammed against her rib cage, her pulse pounding in places she didn't know it could. It felt like the wind had been knocked out of her throat and the breath vacuumed from her body.

But she had to keep running.

Her chest burned and her cheeks raged with fever. Everything she touched or brushed against was newly wet, turning her body cold. The scent of rotting bark and sodden silt stung in her nose, the overwhelming aroma of grass only making her feel even more dizzy and sick. The sting of cold spring air whisked across her face, pinching at her running nose and her cheeks blotched with red. She couldn't tell if the tears pooled in the corner of her gray eyes were from running or from fear.

She didn't know how she got here. She kept going over it again and again in her throbbing mind, trying to rake something up. She couldn't remember falling asleep here—or anywhere for that matter. She couldn't remember the day, or the week, or the month. She could barely remember her name.

The blue watch she always kept strapped on her left wrist was conveniently cracked.

She didn't know the time either.

Five minutes. Ten minutes. She had lost track of how long she'd been running. The time was beginning to blend together like the trees. Her mind raced as she continued to rack up thoughts of things she didn't know or understand but wanted to. The only thing she knew was that she was not alone. She was being followed.

She extended her arms into the dark to push through twisted branches that reached out towards her, poking and prodding and scratching. Everything seemed demented and shadowed. Everything mocked her. There was no clear path ahead, or anywhere; just trees and more trees.

Any direction was the right direction, as long as she kept running.

After what felt like another large passing of time, she finally reached an area that seemed more tame than the rest of the expanse—less difficult to navigate. The woods were growing less dense and the ground was becoming more free of fallen branches and underbrush. For the first time since she had been running, she didn't feel confined by hulking trees. She was still out of breath, but somehow, breathing became a bit easier.

There was a good amount of distance between her and whatever or whoever she was running from now. She allowed herself to slow down, and then finally stop running altogether. The burning subsided and numbness began to set in. She could feel it at her fingertips. She hunched over her body, her nails clawing into the skin around knees.

She wiped her nose with the back of her right hand and sunk into a squat, letting her arms overlap on top of her legs. Four or five scratches lined the surface of her skin, revealing slits of bright red. She looked down at her legs. They were sheathed with goosebumps and speckled with dirt and blood. She pillowed her head into her folded arms.

She wanted to believe that she could keep running and that they would never catch her. She wanted to believe that these woods didn't last forever. She wanted to believe that she would find her way home. But the thoughts became even more real each time she thought them. Soft, incomplete sobs began seeping from her lips. She couldn't stop the sounds from escaping.

Something shot through the trees. She instantly straightened up and ran to hide behind the closest tree. She picked up a hefty branch close to the trunk and threw herself against the bark. She flattened herself as still as she could against the bumpy surface, holding the piece of wood close to her chest. In the absence of movement, she suddenly became aware of her entire body. Her wet scarlet hair stuck to her freckled face, fastened by rain, sweat, and streaks of tears. Her light green cotton t-shirt clung to her body. The khaki shorts sitting on her hips were almost unrecognizable with dirt. Her legs were shaking, and the speed of her heart rate had spiked up again. She brought one hand to her mouth to shield the sound of her breathing, and to muffle what was left of her small sobs.

It was closer to her now than it had been before. It was far enough away that whatever it was couldn't see her or hear her, but it was close enough that one small step would reveal where she was. Quiet crunches of leaves from across the clearing were followed by silence. She stayed hidden behind the large tree, tears silently streaming down her face.

The muted hum of the woods was interrupted by the sound of two voices. She couldn't make out what they were saying, but they had deep, threatening tones. And they were still looking.

Her hands clenched tighter around her cracked lips and open mouth, shaking violently. She gripped the wood even closer to her sore body, her unpainted fingernails turning pink from the pressure. When the voices began moving location, she attempted to shrink away from their direction. She stepped to the side, not thinking about what it would do.

A wet tree branch snapped below the weight of her shoe, slicing through the hushed silence of the woods. Her body froze with terror. The murmur of the voices ceased, sending her pulse through the roof. Her nails dug into the wood now, ready to swing if they came closer. Her gray eyes darted around wildly, searching the corners of her vision for the anticipated danger. It was over. She had given herself away.

She assumed they were silently approaching since her back was towards them. It was hard to tell, but she couldn't wait any longer. This was it. She was prepared to jump from behind the tree when a warm hand grabbed her arm roughly. It spun her around, reaching its arm across her body and forcefully grabbing her left shoulder. The branch she was holding fell to the ground. Before she could let out an ear-splitting scream, the other hand covered her mouth. The hand was large and even more balmy than the first.

He whispered into her ear, his breath shaky and urgent. "Don't scream, and don't move."

She kicked at his shins and tried to tear away his arm, which was firmly crushing her chest. He didn't budge. When she tried to scream again, his hand held her mouth even tighter. He shushed her repeatedly, quietly.

He leaned even closer. "I'm running from them, too."

He smelled of wet earth, just like her. She noted the scratches on his arms. The cuts were somewhat similar to hers, but his were bigger and deeper. His arms were scrawny, but they were strong. If she hadn't believed what he just said, she would be in trouble.

She stopped struggling but remained tense. His warm grasp loosened from around her mouth and her body, but he didn't let go.

They waited what felt like as long as she had been running for. They listened closely for noises over the sound of their fatigued breathing and were careful not to move any more than they had been. The voices faded as they hesitantly walked to another part of the woods. The melodic screeching of crickets and the bellowing of frogs rang faintly between the trees. They stood still until those were the only sounds that remained.

As he began to release her, she ripped herself away from him. She looked fiercely at his face. There was a gash on his upper left cheek. He was young—eighteen or nineteen—around her age.

"You didn't have to hold on so tight."

He scratched his head and let out a sigh of disbelief. "Well, you were going to run."

"And?" she asked.

"And you don't have a chance against them." He removed his gaze from the ground and looked at her directly now. "*We* don't have a chance against them."

"How do you know that?"

"We don't know what they're capable of. I mean, look at what they've already done to us. And we're both unarmed."

Her eyes darted to the side and met his again. "Well. We made it this far."

His blue long sleeved shirt was faded and torn in two spots across his chest. Three or four quarter-sized drops of blood stained his shirt.

She turned to walk a few inches away and began to pace back and forth, her face blotchy and hot. The air was stiff.

"I'm sorry I scared you."

She stopped pacing and stared at him, searching for any sign of distrust in his voice.

He extended his arm towards hers. "I'm Jake."

She took another moment before proceeding.

"Emma," she responded. "It's fine."

Another pause.

"Thanks for helping me," she kicked a clot of dirt around, not wanting to meet his eyes.

The corner of his mouth flipped up in response.

She pushed her hair out from her face. "When did you get here? In the woods, I mean?"

"I don't know. The better question is how I got here."

"I was thinking the same thing."

Churches
An Excerpt
Craig Loomis

It doesn't sound like the drip dropping of water, more like someone clicking his tongue against the roof of his mouth, or maybe the slow tap of high heels moving down the hallway. It's not that it bothers me—how could it—just that I can hear it all this way, into the bedroom.

The afternoons are beginning to start earlier and finish sooner. That, and the trees have grown a bigger, brighter yellow-red almost over-night. Between the trees is something like a gray—not even a color really, more like a brooding. The hills seem smaller, softer. All of this I can see from my bedroom window, early on a Sunday morning.

The radio is off and I can hear the faraway dripping, but now comes something bigger, louder, the tumble-scratching of leaves blowing across the porch. A stain of sunlight settles on the sheets, across my legs. I think about shifting to the left, giving the yellow more room, but then the warmth begins to seep through and I change my mind. The distant hum of a machine switches on: that would be the pump in the shed. Ever since I can remember, that same old pump has sung and throbbed and wheezed me to sleep at night. I never thought of it as being a good sound until that time two winters ago when it broke down—something to do with the bearings—and I couldn't sleep. I thought playing the radio would be the same thing, but it wasn't. When I pull my legs up and grab my knees, the sunlight rolls to my feet. The sun keeps my feet yellow and warm, even hot.

Every now and again a cloud wanders by, filling the window, winking out the sunlight. The whirl of the pump stops, coiling back into its silence until next time. Leaves scraping gently along the wooden porch followed by the tick-tock of faucet water. And so it goes.

Finally, I hear the door open and shut. They are back from church.

Micah goes because Mom and Dad go. Of this I am quite certain. Sara is too young to know or care either way. We have never talked about it, this church business, Micah and me. How could we? How would we start? Brothers don't talk about things like that. Talk like that's for school, in front of teachers where it counts.

Everybody said that priests are extraordinary people, they have to be. I mean, think of it: giving up everything like that. And so, last spring I went to Easter services, sitting up close to the front. I went to see for myself. Micah was overjoyed. Sara played with her hair. Not once did Mom and Dad stop looking straight ahead, nodding. On that Easter Sunday with a church so full that they lined the walls, I watched and listened and waited until it was all over before deciding. In the end, I decided that the priest looked very much like the baker over on El Dorado Street. A little younger and not so tall, but he had the same way of perching his glasses on the end of this nose, of holding his arms straight out like he expected you to give him something; he had the same way of staring up at the ceiling, on the lookout for peeling plaster. He spoke softly, almost as if he didn't care if you heard him or not. Secretly, I was disappointed that a priest and a baker on El Dorado Street could be so much alike.

Hearing him coming this way, I turn toward the wall and pretend sleep. The footsteps hesitate, stutter, and then begin again. The bedroom door swings open and would have bumped against the wall if it weren't for one of those rubber doorstops. The door vibrates, the stopper twanging. And then a gap of quiet as he stops to watch me. Finally, his watching over, he says, "You gonna lay in bed all day?"

Of course I cannot answer because I am still asleep.

"You know, it wouldn't hurt if you just once went to church with us. Just once."

I slowly wake, stretching, and say something like, "What time is it?"

Micah is younger than I am but has never once acted like it. He's always liked being the quarterback, the one to score the winning basket. To Micah, playing baseball is hitting homeruns. He hates it when I have to drive him someplace.

And so, after church he's mad. By the afternoon he is okay, but Sunday mornings he's almost impossible. Because he is my brother, he knows I was faking sleep.

"Just once. Is that asking so much?"

Rubbing my eyes, I say, "Yes, well, maybe next time. How about that? Maybe next time."

He sneers at this, "Right. Next time." I can tell he wants to say more, but he never does. When he leaves he tries slamming the door but he's forgotten that it's not that kind of door, and the rubber stopper twangs again.

I sit up and lean against the window and for the longest time watch a line of clouds slide by. Far off on one of the hillsides, I can see somebody walking. He is wearing red, and some kind of blue. There is a dog, maybe two. I watch him walk, stop, walk, stop until he disappears into the pines. The patch of sunlight has slipped off the bed and onto the floor. It is then, right after the walker moves into the trees—the October wind having never stopped pushing leaves back and forth across the porch—that I feel older than eighteen. Right next to this feeling is another smaller one that leans on me like a kind of sadness. So three things: the walker disappearing into the trees, feeling anything but eighteen, and a sadness that has nothing to do with tears but I don't know what else to call it.

It is Sunday and October and Micah doesn't understand why I won't go to church. He gets angry at them for not making me go, for not demanding that I get up and go with them every Sunday. They tell him that I am old enough to decide for myself. They say I'm a man now. He hates that kind of talk. But no matter what they say, when the time comes, Micah thinks I'll be in for big trouble. He thinks I'll pay for all this . . . this neglect. And so, on Sunday mornings, my brother stays angry at a lot of people for different reasons. Today, for some special reason, I feel anything but eighteen and yet nothing like a man, and I wonder where that walker thinks he's going.

Men of Snow
Ryan Inkley

And with a *poof* I'm rolled into life. I'm a three-balled snowman. I'd tell you where I am but I'm still figuring it out. Hands place rocks, *plop plop-plop*, and I imagine air rushing into my powder lungs. I smile because the rocks are arranged in an upside-down arc. A *kerplunk* and I get a sensory overload of smells. I know my nose is a carrot and I don't actually have olfactory glands but the scents are real.

By the time my eyes are placed, I can tell where I'm standing. It's a park and snowmen are scattered across a field in various states of undress. I hear a male voice. But somebody else is here too because I can feel a pair of gentler hands. Not knowing them makes me want to know me. Because I'm round but I don't feel well-rounded yet. Did they name me?

The collecting of snow from the ground has revealed streaks of grass that extend out of my base like a sunburst. The girl says she feels like a TSA agent. I don't know what that is, but they must be the most loving people on the planet because each pat feels like a hug. My edges crumble into little piles they use to build up another part of me. I'm not numb to the voice of each snow globule.

What happens when the sun comes out? I'll melt into a muddle of a puddle. And then that ball of gas will take a drag and puff me out. Instead of being this snowman I will literally be the cloud over my maker's heads. Is that all? An endless cycle of cold, wet, and invisible?

What makes me a snowman anyway? Who decided I wasn't a snow-woman? I'm beautiful and nothing sets us apart if you think about basic snow-being guidelines. Keep your hands on me, makers. I might not be anything tomorrow afternoon. Do you even love me? Next year you won't remember me. Probably because I wondered why I was a snowman.

I'm not even water but I'm already reflecting. Tomorrow there will be nowhere to go but the Troposphere. I guess the only way to heaven is a good scorching. Just like you make your rounds, I make mine. You're 60 percent water. When you die, it's slurped dry from your skin, joining rivers or oceans or Lake Titicaca and then it will make a snow-being. And one day while I am flying, the clouds will break. And then I'll be swallowed, becoming a part of what makes you human. Until I become one myself. A person of snow.

The Island
Jennifer Irwin

Mom forced me to go. Since the divorce, she did everything with her best friend, Becky. My butt tingled from sitting in the car for the eight-hour drive from New York to Maine. Hour three, my Walkman batteries died. My older brother, Ben, was asleep so I gazed out the window dreaming of all the fun I was going to have at college.

We pulled into a dirt parking lot overlooking choppy Maine waters. Buoys dotted the harbor. The air smelled fishy. I peeled out of the car and yanked my hoodie over my head. A layer of mist settled on my sleeves.

"Don't stand there," my mother said. "Help me with the bags."

"Where are we putting the bags?" I asked.

Aunt Becky waved from a lobster boat. The captain tied the lines, and Aunt Becky stepped off. "Welcome!" she said. "Fog's coming, let's get the boat loaded." I dragged my suitcase across the dirt.

"Cami overpacked as usual," Mom said.

"I can hear you," I yelled from behind her.

The captain wore yellow slicker overalls and black rubber boots. He didn't look much older than me. I wondered if he'd already had sex.

With the boat loaded we pulled into the harbor. Ben sat with the captain. I cursed myself for not grabbing that seat first. Water splashed as we moved along the chop. My aunt told us that no one could touch the lobster traps or they could get shot. I zoned out until I heard, "outhouse."

"What?" I said.

"I didn't tell you," Mom said. "No drama please."

"Oh, my God." I crossed my arms over my chest.

"No cars or electricity on the island neither," the captain said.

I contemplated leaping into the icy Maine waters.

We pulled into a horseshoe-shaped harbor. A beach sat between jagged rocks. Behind the beach was a field. Once the boat was parked, we passed the luggage up a ladder in assembly-line fashion. Reality hit hard when I had to pee.

Becky's daughter greeted us with an oversized wheel barrel. Megan had finished her freshman year at the University of Vermont. We weren't close, but we weren't enemies either. I did my best to get along with her since she was like family.

"We're going to have a blast," Megan said. Her thick dark hair was pulled back with a plastic hairband. "A ton of kids are here right now." We passed a well that had a plastic bucket tied to a rope. "This is where we get our water," she said. "We carry it to the house."

"You've got to be kidding me," I said.

She parked the wheel barrel at the edge of the trail. High above, among the fir trees, there was a deck where an American flag flapped in the breeze. "We have to walk the bags from here." She picked up two satchels and started up the trail. I balanced my suitcase on my head and followed.

The house had one main room, a bunk room, guest room, and master bedroom. The master had a composting toilet which was strictly for grownups. Ben and I bunked with Megan while Mom scored the guest room.

"I have to pee," I whispered to Megan. She led me down a path to the outhouse. It had a real toilet seat, and the hole was deep so you couldn't see everyone's poo. Megan instructed me to dump a scoop of lye after I went to stop the flies.

She waited outside on a log. "Let's head to the beach. A few of my friends are down there partying."

Ben spotted us so I told him he could come along. We walked through the field to get to a beach on the other side of the harbor.

A few kids gathered in chairs; most everyone was wearing hoodies. "This is Ben and Cami, my friends I told you about," Megan said. We sat on the sand next to the chairs. One of the guys passed me a joint. I decided it might not be such a bad summer after all.

"Party at Edgar cottage tomorrow," the joint passer said, Dartmouth scrawled across the front of his hat. He was hot, but I acted disinterested.

"Edgar cottage belongs to the island," Megan said. I analyzed her plain but pretty face in the dim light. "We aren't allowed to use it without grownups but whatever." She dragged her hands through the sand.

"I'm Libby," the girl next to me said.

"Hey, I'm Cami." Ben was quiet since he was shy. "That's my older brother, Ben," I said.

"Anyone down for capture the flag?" Dartmouth guy said. He smiled at me. My stomach flipped.

A cooler filled with Budweiser mysteriously appeared in the field grass. Dartmouth snapped open a can. "I'm Rob," he said. "Want a beer?"

The group split into two. One of the guys had a few bandanas to use for flags. The guys sent us to jail where we waited until a teammate tagged us to set us free. The beer and joint had my head buzzing. Megan and I had a laughing fit. The sun dipped to the edge of the ocean and lit up the sky in a burst of orange. We all paused to admire mother nature's gift. Rob wrapped his arm around my shoulder. I felt giddy. Megan nudged me. "We better head back for dinner."

I eased out from Rob's arm. "Maybe I'll see you tomorrow at the party," I said.

Aunt Becky was on the deck hammering at a bell. "Oh, good," she said. "I wasn't in the mood to find you."

Dinner wasn't bad considering we had no running water or electricity. I inquired as to how the refrigerator stayed cold.

"It runs on gas like a car engine," Mom said.

I hadn't seen Uncle Dave since we'd arrived, so I hugged him.

"How do you like the island so far, Cami?" he asked. I wished he was my dad. He cared about his kids. All my dad cared about was drinking and women.

"It's cool," I said. "Thanks for having us." A lump lodged in my throat as though I might cry. I pushed it down. Mom gave a nod of approval over my manners.

After dinner, we played a card game called cribbage which required math, so I sucked. Ben won every game. "I'm going to bed," I said. Mom was half in the bag and doing her embarrassing head bob. "Behave Cami; I don't need a *Lord of the Flies* situation on this island." She laughed, and I died of embarrassment for her.

Settled in our bunks, Megan and I plotted how we were going to steal alcohol to take to the party tomorrow. "Count me out," Ben said. "Mom's been through enough."

"Whatever," I said.

I woke up desperate for a shower. We brushed our teeth with water bottles and spat over the balcony. "What's the deal with the shower?" I asked.

Toothpaste dribbled down Megan's chin. "We have to get water from the well to put in the sun shower."

We carried buckets up the trail. Most of the water sloshed out before I could get to the deck. I begged Ben to help, and he laughed.

"Asshole," I said. I wanted to dump water on Ben's head, but then I'd have to carry another bucket.

Megan laid the sun shower bag on the deck to heat up. We put on our bathing suits and painted our nails. When the water was warm enough, Megan hung the sun shower on a hook. She used half the bag to wash and rinse her hair and then I had my turn. Megan squeezed the nozzle over my head, and I mentioned that I'd seen a bottle of liquor we could pimp for the party. She agreed to distract her mother while I threw it in my backpack. Our plan worked perfectly. After dinner, we told the parents we were going to search for shooting stars. They either believed us or didn't care.

When we arrived at Edgar cottage, the party was in full swing. Other than a few candles, the room was super dark, so I was surprised Rob spotted me.

"You're here," he said kissing me on the lips.

My social anxiety elevated. I pulled the bottle from my backpack and took a swig. Something wasn't right. I swallowed it to avoid making a scene. My stomach heaved like I might throw up. Megan grabbed the bottle.

"Oh, my God," she said. "That's gasoline. My mom keeps it in this bottle in the kitchen. She even drew skull and crossbones on the label."

A burp moved up my esophagus burning my throat. A gasoline odor filled the room.

A Terrible Day and a Tree
Melissa Kandel

From: Henry Littlesworth
To: Marcus Trevan
Subject: Your Job
It's over. Fax Me Up LLC is closing shop, effective immediately. Funny I should write this to you over email, the very thing that killed my fax business.
Well, Rainforest Online Services killed us, too. Damn devil of a company. People should know better than to order fax machines from a website named after the epicenter of malaria and yellow fever. But I digress. Don't worry about securing the Hindler account (obviously). I spoke to Jerry last night and he seemed to understand. I only hope you do, too. Sixteen years as my best fax salesman and wham! All gone. Who would've thought? Also, no need to come to the office to collect your things. I had them shipped to the mobile and Sal is already renting our old space to a nice Korean couple. Vacuum business or something. I wasn't paying attention when he told me. You know how fast Sal can talk and who gives a monkey's sweaty armpit? He overcharged me on rent for years. So, that's it. Nothing more from me. I'll probably take myself up on that one-way ticket to Tokyo even if the damn Japanese subways are a little too clean. Never trust a man who looks too clean unless he's selling you shower heads or bathtubs.
   Have a nice life,
   Henry Littlesworth
   (Formerly) President & CEO, Fax Me Up LLC

And that's how it ended or maybe that's how it began for Marcus Trevan on a terrible day in June. But terrible days tend to arrive wrapped in the ordinary fabric of passing time, without so much as a fine-printed warning one might be headed your way. Wouldn't it be kinder if a terrible day had a Terrible Day Skywriter attached to the front that would scribble in white cloud-ink across the sky? I'd imagine the message might go something like: "Hello, Marcus Trevan. Today is going to be terrible." Then you could prepare. Maybe.
   There's no such thing as a Terrible Day Skywriter. At least I don't think such a machine exists and if it does, Marcus never looked up to see the danger written above. I can guess your next question: How do I know so much about Marcus Trevan's terrible day? Let's add this inquiry, too: Why would I want to write about Marcus in the first place, me sitting here, a stranger hiding behind the comfort of my retina-display computer screen?

I'd rather not say how I came to know about Marcus' terrible day or why I can detail the unsavory events that stuffed themselves inside of it. However, I will reveal this: I'm telling you about his terrible day now because the whole thing makes for an extraordinary story and whether you want to believe me or not, it's also 100percent fact.

Let's get this straight from the beginning: The email from Henry Littlesworth came as not the least bit of a surprise to Marcus. There were definite signs the fax machine industry was fast sliding toward a bleak, black-and-white demise and Jerry Hindler was unquestionably wavering on a five-year contract that might have bought Fax Me Up more time.

After reading Henry's email, Marcus had nothing but time, oodles of it stretching before him on a California road so dry and desolate it might inspire even the crabbiest of businesspeople to write a cowboy song or two. Not Marcus Trevan, though. He was the forty-eight-year-old illustration of an archetypal bore, a company man with no company left to define him. So, who was he on this terrible day?

I'll explain: Marcus was the vaguely underweight owner of a 1984 Chevy Caprice and a slim, graying mustache that clung to his lip for all its dear, hairy life. He had no wife, no kids, no family save a grandmother in the Florida Everglades with a nasty gambling problem—blackjack or craps he guessed—who never bothered to call except when her checking account ran low.

Who else was he? What might describe him? Perhaps his cravings for twig tea with a spot of goat's milk or his ability to recite *Walden* and *The Origin of Species* by heart or his eternal fascination with the life of Fyodor Dostoevsky or the pinstripe navy blue suit he wore each day as he drove to fax machine sales meetings in a car that smelled of cinnamon air freshener and weeks-old sweat. Together, these details might provide a decent depiction of the man called Marcus but if you're looking for the clearest way to understand him, you might start with his mobile home.

The mobile, a four-wheeled, red-striped contraption, was as far from mobile as you could get, rooted to the same spot in the barren underbelly of Silverado Canyon since Marcus found it sixteen years ago. Over time, the mobile became not just the place where he lived but an extension of Marcus' being, the only example of permanence in a life impermanent as the summer breeze.

That's why when he returned from his defunct trip to visit Jerry Hindler and found the mobile missing, Marcus wasn't only missing his house; he also was missing a piece of himself.

We've reached the part in the story where we get to the incredible (but unshakably true) turn of events: The mobile didn't stay lost for long. Not more than five minutes after Marcus stepped out of his Chevy into the empty space where his home had once been, he saw it again, tied with black twine to the trunk of a nearby pine, suspended twenty or so feet above the ground. Unusual? Yes. But still not the crux of the incredible incidents I mentioned. On to those . . .

"What the? That's my house!" Marcus yelled to no one when he found his mobile dangling from the tall tree. He flailed his arms in desperation and shook clenched fists at a blank, misty sky. "How am I supposed to get through my front door?"

"Oh, ssssugar," hissed a low voice behind him. "You need to get out more."

He turned to see a snake, spotted brown and white, shimmying along the dusty ground before him. It moved in a seductive slither—maybe he did need to get out more—up the tree trunk where his mobile was twine-tied and trapped. "You've got to crawl before you can walk and walk before you can swim, ssssailor."

"I'm not a sailor, I'm a salesman," Marcus said, faintly aware he was arguing with a snake. Old, Fax Me Up Marcus might have had a better sense of truth, but new, mobile-homeless Marcus wasn't sure what in the nebulous uncertainty of a talking-snake world could be considered real.

"She's right you know," came a chirp by his left ear. "The business about not trusting snakes is bogus. It's the toads you've got to watch out for and luckily we don't have many of those slime balls in our forest."

This next slice of advice came from a fat, charcoal-feathered goose, waddling by Marcus on its way to the tree. For some reason, it was at this very moment that Marcus heard Henry Littleworth's grave voice inside his head: "What's so special about wild animals? They're a bunch of haughty know-nothings who wouldn't think twice about snatching your house right from under your damn overgrown nose hairs."

"That's not entirely true," said the apparent mind-reading goose to Marcus. "And I ain't no Mamma Goose neither so don't get fancy with ideas about golden eggs or breakfast omelets."

Then the goose, like the snake before her, disappeared into Marcus' mobile home.

"We're taking this sucker back!" Buzzed a bee, whirring frantically in the damp air beyond Marcus' forehead. "You had a good run with her but it's all over now, honey."

One by one, strange animals of the wood—a fox, a beaver, a hawk, an antelope with a missing left antler—leaped, flew, crawled or slinked from some leafy refuge in the Silverado Canyon to Marcus' mobile home.

And Marcus stood there, stupid in his pinstriped suit, hardly aware his mustache was wet and dribbling rainwater down his chin and neck. In all the animalistic commotion, the sky had stewed to a mess of thunderclouds and lightning—there might be a Terrible Day Skywriter after all—and if you believe nothing else of this story, hold tight to one single fact: In the battle between Marcus Trevan and Mother Nature, I most certainly won.

Star Chaser
Taylor Eaton

Every night, I watch the dark sky and whisper prayers to the wind. In those prayers, I beg that the clouds be pushed far away—over the almost invisible horizon—so that the stars can come out to play.

On those nights when the wind complies and the clouds vanish, I gaze up at the twinkling lights overhead, willing my pupils to dilate more. To take it all in, not wanting to miss anything.

When I stare up, I'm not stargazing. Not counting the constellations. I'm watching. Waiting. Ready.

If I stay up most of the night, eyes wide and neck bent back, I usually see at least three or four—they're easy to spot if your eyes are trained. Bright streaks of light, sprinting across the wide night sky, racing from the earth.

Some are too far away—hundreds of miles. But others, when I'm lucky, land nearby. Just a few miles perhaps. And if you know how to read their trajectories in the dark of the sky, you'll know where to find them.

When one touches down close by, I jump in my truck, turn the key until the engine roars, and drive off into the dark.

It's nerve-wracking, chasing after fallen stars. They burn out quickly, you see, once they've touched the ground. Separated from the sky—their freedom stolen by gravity and atmosphere—they don't live for very long on this planet.

So I drive quickly, racing to retrieve the molten fragment of the cosmos before it expires. Most of the time I'm too late. But sometimes, maybe once every month, I make it in time. I see the glow of the star, flickering wildly in the cold evening air and nestled in the crook of a tree branch or in the blades of tall grass in a field.

I pull the truck to a rough stop, not bothering to turn the engine off as I jump from it, running at full speed to the dying thing.

Care slows my haste as I breathe in the scent of the star. Warm petrichor mixed with a frosty, far away smell.

With delicate movements, I scoop the star into a glass jar. The stars always slide in reluctantly, not sure that they want confinement over certain death, but they usually comply. At the bottom of the jar is kindling, to feed the star's fire and keep it burning bright until I can get it home.

The star rides in the passenger seat as I push the accelerator of the truck harder and harder, zooming through the night to get back home. And when we get there, I take the star into the living room. There, I place its jar next to the hundreds of other jars that line the walls, all twinkling merrily, glad to be reunited with one another.

When the sun comes up, I close the blinds and lay on the floor, looking up at my own personal night sky, wondering why anyone would prefer the harsh light of day.

Amna Faruki's Diary
Shireen Hakim

Monday, July 1, 2019

I can't believe I ended up hiding here at Joy's house. We always joked about me using it as a safe house, but I didn't think I actually would need to. Not in such a modern, free country. And as a born citizen. Luckily Joy is woke like me and planned ahead. We knew it could happen since it has in the past. I'm going to sleep now. I'm sleeping on her couch. Her dad, Minister Mulligan, is here, but he's nice. I trust him. I just wear my hijab all the time.

Tuesday, July 2, 2019

I'm the only one in the apartment. Joy is at summer school and her dad is at his church. I stopped going to summer school yesterday, after I came here. Last week, after I read on Twitter that they were moving all Muslims into stadiums, I texted Joy and she said to come over right away. It took me a few days to pack my important belongings, delete my phone history, and get up the nerve to leave home. My family is still at home. I didn't tell them where I was going. That way they wouldn't be forced to tell.

Wednesday, July 3, 2019

Omg. My family got sent to the stadium. Joy gave me a note when she got home from school yesterday. I can't believe it. They're at the Staples Center, that's where Los Angeles County residents had to go. They won't be able to reach me. I threw my phone before I came here. They are probably wondering where I am. I hope they don't think I am dead. I hope they don't die.

4th of July

I wonder if anyone is celebrating in the camps. Probably. We are still Americans. I am celebrating. Joy went with her dad to celebrate at the beach. I'm watching the fireworks on TV with the sound off. If things were normal I would have gone to the beach to watch the fireworks. I just got my license so I could have driven myself.

Monday, July 8, 2019

I didn't feel like writing in here during the weekend. I didn't feel like doing anything. I just lay on the couch. Joy smiles and waves at me when she walks by but doesn't talk to me. The walls are thin so the neighbors would hear us talking. Even if they didn't mean to, they would probably report me. It's better if they don't act like I'm here. Then they won't get in trouble. It's like I don't exist anymore. That's how the government would like it anyway. And a lot of people actually.

Tuesday, July 9, 2019

They show footage of the camps on every TV station. The dictat-president wants to show his followers he's keeping them safe. TV is religion here. I pray.

Everyone at the camp gets electronically tagged so they can be tracked in case they cause an explosion, the news said. What a joke. No one owns guns. They gave them all away because the government said how dangerous they were and accused anyone with one of being a terrorist. Of course the guards at the camps have guns though. Joy's dad is one of the only people that kept one, in case something like this happened she said. We should have known this would happen to us, when they put the Muslim refugees and green card holders in the factories downtown. But who would think they would lock up citizens?

I hope my niece is okay in the camp. I hope she is getting to play and she doesn't know what is going on. Us older people can handle it, but it's not fair to the kids.

Wednesday, July 10, 2019

I use the Minister's old flip phone to play games. I miss my phone but I know I couldn't keep it. It's hard to get rid of the habit of playing with my phone. I write status updates on the phone notepad since I can't post them on Facebook anymore. "I'm playing with Joy's cat, Spence. I'm even quieter than him."

I don't know who would read my Facebook posts anyway. No one in the camps can use the Internet. Well, my non-Muslim friends still have accounts. I'm watching Jessica Jones on TV. She is still cool even without the sound.

Thursday, July 11, 2019

I go to the bathroom a lot here. I'm nervous. I leave the bathroom light off during the day because the fan is loud, but I can still make out my reflection in the mirror. What does it matter how I look? To them I am just brown.

Friday, July 12, 2019

I heard a knock on the door at 10 am. That's strange. No one ever comes to the door. I don't open it. I hope I'm not making any noise. Spence walked over to investigate the noise. He's a black and white tabby. He reminds me of Eileen, my old cat. I'm glad I don't have a cat anymore. I heard of people losing their pets when they were moved to the camps, and that is the saddest thing. I wouldn't be able to handle leaving my cat.

Saturday, July 13, 2019

It's my birthday. I'm seventeen. I wasn't going to celebrate but mom would have given me a gift. She probably was going to give me a car. We could have driven straight to Canada. We should have last year. But I guess now we are a part of history.

The doorknob is jiggling! It's 12:30 p.m. Too early for Joy or her dad to come home. I took their gun from under the couch. The jiggling is getting harder and they're banging on the door! Omg. Soon they will break the door down. How do they know I'm in here?

I'll take the gun, go out the sliding glass door and climb down the fire escape. I will not wait here.

The Lost Names of Kaesong
Kae Bucher

A very long time ago, on the outskirts of the Northern Kingdom, the flowers and creatures would often call to the hill dwellers as they went about their business. But no one bothered to listen, except for one small boy.

"Ruka, Ruka, Ruka," the frogs would call to him as they hid behind green rushes. It seemed that the fun for them was not in the hiding . . . but in the jumping out of his hands once he caught them.

Sometimes while swimming, he would search for freshwater snails, because as it turns out, they were wonderful teachers. He imitated their glistening calligraphy, and the villagers began asking the boy (who had decided his name was Ruka) to paint characters of their family names.

Eventually, the fairy folk of Kaesong became curious about Ruka's friendship with the shelled ones and flitted circles around them like dragonflies. And somehow, Ruka, the village name-maker, became one of them.

There came a time when wave after wave of powerful soldiers invaded the kingdom. The invaders scoffed at the villagers, destroyed their pottery, and sent a decree throughout the entire kingdom that only the holidays chosen by the new emperor would be celebrated.

The village children asked, "What is happening to our kingdom?"

Mothers sadly answered, "When whales fight, the shrimp's back is broken."

Eventually a decree was made that all the families of the Northern Kingdom would be renamed "Shrimp."

Ruka shook his head. "Not even the jungle lion forces his subjects to be called by the wrong name. Why do they want to call us that?"

"Because they choose Power over Love," a giggly fairy explained. "That's why we play tricks on them."

"Well, I'm not a shrimp!" Ruka sighed.

Mother Pearl, his childhood teacher, raised her antennas like eyebrows. "Would you rather go by Snail?" she asked.

"Yes!" he said. "But that would be a lie. I am Ruka and I am a name-maker, and that is all there is to it." Hesitantly he added, "Have the conquerors torn down all my paintings?"

And Ruka's friends grew silent.

Of course, Ruka was no longer able to sell painted names to the villagers beneath the slopes, but he managed to get by in a poor-but-happy way.

"Ruka, Ruka, Ruka," the frogs called his name. And for Ruka, that was enough.

Down in the village, the rulers acted like whales, and that is what the people called them. Overshadowing the people, they forced them to carry precious river rocks from the mouth of the Kaesong to the emperor's palace. When there were no more, the "Whales" told them to dig and find some. The muscles in the villagers' arms and legs and hearts grew thick as snakes.

The villagers whispered about how fat the "Whales" were getting at their expense. The fatter the invaders grew, the angrier the villagers became. Night after night, around the dying embers of their fires, their hisses grew louder.

The men who were called "Shrimp" gathered together and harpooned the "Whales." The villagers pulled out the "Whales'" vocal cords and hung them outside their homes until they began to smell.

The people of Kaesong celebrated their freedom and sent sons up the hills to find Ruka, the name-maker. They asked him to repaint their family names. Ruka was very happy for his people and for his business!

But the celebration didn't last long. One morning, Ruka awakened to a loud banging on his hut door. This wasn't strange. Sometimes the village children pounded a bit heavily in their excitement. But when Ruka opened the door, he saw that this child was different. He wore a scowl on his face and spoke to Ruka as though Ruka was a polliwog, and not the child's elder.

"Are you Ruka the name painter?" he demanded.

Ruka pointed to the banner which hung from the roof of his hut, where his name fluttered like a magpie wing.

"What of it?" the child asked scornfully. "I am not here to play games. I want to know. Are you Ruka the name painter?"

Ruka nodded slowly and noticed how the fairy kingdom grew quiet on the hillside. Even the wind refused to whisper.

"Well," the child said, "my father is the new king, and that makes me your prince. I have come to order you to make family names for all the people of Kaesong."

"You have come to place an order?" Ruka asked.

"I have not come to place an order, I have come to give an order," the child declared.

Still not fully understanding, Ruka questioned, "What names would you like painted, your Majesty?"

"Name, not names!" the child blared. "You are to paint the name 'Whale' for ALL the people in the Northern Kingdom."

"'Whale?'" Ruka asked in disbelief.

"Yes, 'Whale!'" the child said. "For is it not a name of great power? And haven't we ousted the foreign Whales with our own harpoons? And doesn't that make us the greatest 'Whale' of all?"

Then the subjects of the fairy kingdom, who had been holding their breaths to see what Ruka would do, could no longer contain themselves. Their whispers and giggles were heard above the wind's, "Shhhh . . ."

"Are you laughing at me?" the boy demanded, hitting Ruka on the head. "I am Prince Whale, lord of all Created thi—"

He was suddenly cut off as a sprite threw a bucket of wind in his face. The hillside erupted in full-blown laughter and the prince, who was still only a boy, ran down the slopes as fast as his small legs could carry him.

It wasn't until he arrived at the village that he remembered he was a "Whale," and told his father all sorts of nasty stories about the name painter.

As always, the fairies were eavesdropping, and when they heard Ruka's life was in danger, they dumped a large dose of sleeping powder over his head. Hoping to surround him with memories of safer, kinder times, the fairies tucked him within walls of river rock under his childhood hut. Then Ruka proceeded to fall asleep for a very long spell.

When he finally woke up, his beard was long and white and his eyes streamed tears as he prayed about the Northern Kingdom.

His tears streamed . . .

Farther . . . and farther . . . until eventually they found themselves in the Kaesong river.

When Mother Pearl saw them, she hurried . . . at least as fast as a snail can hurry . . . to tell the frogs.

"Ruka? Ruka? Ruka?" the frogs asked.

"Yes, Ruka!" she insisted. "Now, get ready to croak as loud as you can while I glisten out this message. We're going to help Ruka pray!"

Mother Pearl made trails out of Ruka's tears, up and down the bank of the Kaesong. The frogs croaked so loudly that even the river stopped to listen.

Hearing Ruka's prayer, Heaven's great lion shook his mane until the stones of Ruka's hut tumbled down the hill and back to where they were born. The thrones of the Northern Kingdom toppled. King Whale and his son, who were not really whales after all, drowned in the Kaesong River.

Ruka picked up his brush and once again painted names for those who asked, and they all lived happily ever after . . . except, of course, for certain "Whales," who I suppose are better left . . . unnamed.

Lost Footsteps
Hoài-Linh

A burst of laughter sounds from the forest. Behind an ancient tree hides a young girl with golden curls, peeking around the lowest branches. Coffee-brown eyes dancing with glee, she turns and runs further into the woods. Darkness begins to engulf her slim form, and the knight looks on in confusion from the edge of the trees.

"Excuse me," he calls, "but I do not think it wise for you to go any further!"

Failing to catch her attention, he frowns. "Gods strike me dead if I haven't already gone insane," he mutters, unsheathing his sword. "How can she possibly enter the forest alone?"

I will bring her back quickly, he thinks, taking a few slow steps down the fading path. Just as he passes the first few trees, he loses sight of the girl's golden head and stops in his tracks with a frown. Keeping his blade level, he steps over tree roots and overgrown bushes to the left and to the right, squinting through the darkness. Looking further into the trees, he catches sight of the girl slipping in and out of view, turning every few seconds and beckoning to him.

"Might you follow me?" she asks, her soft voice barely audible as a sudden gust of wind rustles the leaves.

Narrowing his eyes, the knight feels himself slowly making his way closer and closer towards the girl, sheathing his sword as he walks. Overhead soft whispers float through the air-tree sprites stirring in their sleep, wondering who dares enter their silent sanctuary. Pushing through the ever-thickening bushes and branches, the knight strains to keep his eyes on the girl weaving in and out of view.

Quickening his pace, his head begins to cloud, disorienting him—all sense of direction is lost and he can only focus on the small figure ahead. Rain starts to fall lightly, decorating what greenery it can reach through the canopy of trees with a glittery sheen.

Suddenly, the girl enters a clearing and stops, turning and smiling sweetly. The knight stumbles after her and breathes in a bitter scent as he trudges into the circle of trees, head slowly clearing with each gulp of air. Unable to balance himself, he leans against a tree trunk, trying to blink away the dizziness.

Vision swimming, he rights himself and turns back to the girl—only to find she is no longer a girl. White, silvery hair has replaced the golden locks; eyes black as pitch stare mischievously at him from under long, ebony lashes; skin pale as the moon shines under the falling raindrops. Xanadus throughout the land, he muses, cannot contain such covert beauty.

"You," he breathes, "are no lost child."

Zipping past him, the delicate tree sprite emits a soft, haunting laugh, and he remembers in a sudden horror the warning of a long-lost memory: no one who enters the Dark Forrest ever sees the sun again.

Lost Regions
An Excerpt
David Scott

Holman kept still as he spotted something coming up through the stairwell. It moved at a steady pace and he saw that it was a small person wearing a cloak, no larger than the size of a child. The darkness was too strong to make out any facial features.

"The Legionaries have singled this building out," the being said with a sense of urgency, its voice noticeably female. "If you want to get out safely, you must follow me."

The nature of the moment demanded instant trust. He wanted to race along with this person, this female being, to flee the scene and escape, but was stuck motionless as the decision hung in the air. Her face remained an unknown, blackness emanating from her hood, and it took the report of several electronic sounds reverberating in the distance for him to realize the need to get on the move.

"Come with me, now," she insisted, gesturing with her tiny arm. "You do not want to be here when they come. You do not want to be in the place where they want to take you."

He found himself following her down the stairwell. Though he couldn't hear her footsteps, he could hear his own as he ran through pockets of crushed rubble and debris. Their flight seemed to carry on and on as they scrambled, ever further into the depths, descending for what seemed an eternity. On reaching the ground floor, they shot through a door that led to a lightless hallway, and from somewhere in the background, the sound of active pursuit was immediate. The Legionaries had entered the building. She led him through another door that led to another hallway of which the entire left side was made of glass, and as he ran, the details of an outdoor atrium adorned with elaborate stonework and indescribable statues were barely visible. They flew through a concluding set of doors and she whispered, "We must hurry!"

They moved through an area that seemed the remnants of some vast welcoming area, a receptionist desk to the right coated with the veneer of wood. Another set of glass doors opened up to the world outside where the cement stopped and a small patch of forest began. It was a small park which formed, in essence, a section of land that connected it to another skyscraper across the way. All was dark save for the continuous, bluish-white glow in the clouds, its source forever rotating from some distant location.

The tiny woman led him through the trees with great speed, though he couldn't help but look behind him. Figures in black were at the door and they looked flustered, uncertain as to which direction to proceed. Holman kept on the move, realizing he'd nearly lost sight of his guide. They made their way past an outdoor pavilion made of wood and bricks, and through more trees until they reached an architectural space identical to that from which they'd just left behind. The two buildings in this fashion, he realized, were like gargantuan sister skyscrapers.

"We have to keep moving!"

Instead of entering this twin building, the tiny woman led him along a cement path hugging tight to the outside wall, and she kept speeding up as if her feet were on fire. They made their way to a street that was positively trashed and Holman had trouble keeping sight of her. But she was visible enough so that he could tell she was leading him through an alley that veered off in a diagonal direction.

For some reason his skepticism returned to take hold of him. He could feel the danger of their pursuers diminishing, but with it he could sense the potential danger of trusting his guide. Why was he allowing himself to believe that she would lead him to somewhere safe?

And yet the alternative did not appear to exist. He simply followed, until they were together, upon yet another desolate street, where individual fires burned far down the way. They went in the opposite direction, along a wide sidewalk, and by a blackened street lamp there ran a cement railing, next to which there descended a set of stairs, an obvious detour designated as access to some subterranean level.

Holman slowed his pace. He needed answers. He tried to speak but she ignored him. Halfway down, she motioned with her hand again, and without questioning he kept going. At the base, the darkness was profound, and they stood together for a brief moment. She produced an object from the inside of her cloak and whispered something. Within seconds a crystal was emitting a soft lavender glow, and Holman was alarmed to find her taking him by the hand, her tiny fingers much like a child's.

Walking hurriedly along, with her pulling him, proved something of an annoyance. She took him through what must've once been a subway station, and then through labyrinthine hallways, refusing to utter not even the slightest hint of information. To his relief finally she began to slow down, where she made for a door that was clearly familiar to her, and she brought him into a room riddled with debris just as everything else had been along the way. It was here that their flight had come to a halt. Holman stood in the center of the room as she closed the door. He watched, observing her in her movements, and she turned around to look at him. And then she let her hood fall from her head.

Holman felt the sting of his amazement. A feeling within the deepest part of his being ignited, beholding the intense beauty of a fully-grown woman, so completely marveling because she was so small. Her eyes were like spheres of wildfire, glossy by the lavender glow, and she expressed an austere look, as if she had known pain and survived to tell the tale. With her hood pulled back, she looked smaller than she had while running, though it was obvious she was no child. She was a woman of apparent experience, seemingly full of knowledge, her eyes illuminating with vitality, her hair long and flowing. Her features were that of a pure and exotic form, shaped to perfection, expressive of the notion that a man, any man, who had ever seen her, would have fallen in love on first sight.

"We are safe," she said. "For the time being at least."

Inwardly, Holman felt himself confronted with the presence of his attraction, and he chased his feelings away, as though he had to snap himself out of a spell. He let the engines of his logic take control as he asked, "Who are you?"

"You must sit down, your energy will not last." She set the glowing crystal down on a nearby table and took Holman by the hand again, leading him to an old and worn out couch, and she looked at him as though she understood his need to know.

"My name, if you must know, is Apatia."

This Guy is Amazing
Patricia Willers

My sister's boyfriend, I mean fiancé, hails from the upper Midwest. Nice guy, normal build—for a farm boy, that is, he's big and tall.

He's a great guy, so sweet, straight A's in school—economics—and he loves to laugh and tell jokes and be with family.

This guy was amazing. He was *so* helpful.

The first time he came down to my parents' house, he was more helpful than all of us combined, and there are four of us! Four kids, almost 100 cumulative years of training, and he beats us to the dishwasher. This guy is amazing.

My other sister has a couple of kids, and you could tell right from the get-go that this guy was ready to start his own family. He could play tag for hours. He wasn't a big reader himself, but my five-year-old niece would bring her books over, climb up on his lap, tell him stories and he would just *listen*.

It's what we all really think we can do, but in fact we're too hyper for it. You think kids can't sit still—try my thirty-five-year-old brother. If he isn't talking—telling jokes, making fun of everyone and everything around him—he's outta there. Can't sit still.

But this guy, he's *amazing*. How many times can you listen to *Chicka, Chicka Boom Boom*, anyway?

And my little sister, she'd been looking for someone for such a long time!

It was nice to see her so happy.

They moved in together; they were living on their own. They didn't even need frivolous things, just movies and takeout and cuddling on the sofa like a couple of happy penguins.

He's an investment banking sort of guy, did I mention that?

Investment banker guys don't get jobs at *normal* places. They're at big banks that we all know and we've all heard pay their employees well, really well.

He'd interview for three at a time and every time just knock it out of the park. Amazing with everything that he does. He had his pick, so he picked one, and got dressed up every morning so happy! He'd take the bus downtown in his new suit just itching to get to work. Then he'd come home and research the stock market and watch his personal accounts. One afternoon alone he made three grand—*wedding money*, he said.

So nice, so generous. He'd had kind of a rough childhood, but he made it through, and he was all the better for it.

One day, my dad said something weird about him. Something wasn't adding up.

In fact, *literally*, something wasn't adding up.

The engagement ring that my sister was wearing—collections called about it.

They'd been having a little bit of trouble, the two of them, you know how young couples are—you think that you have plenty of money and that everything's perfect and you can pay for your car and your cable and get take out and go on dates on the town, but then you understand that one plus one plus all this stuff, doesn't necessarily equal two. It equals a little more than two.

Then the rent check bounces.

So they—my sister and my protecting father too, of course—start to investigate. And they look into the investments that he's been talking about.

And they don't exist. He doesn't have an account with $100,000 in it, of course.

And of course, he didn't make $3,000 dollars in one day.

Of course.

His college degree—nope. There was nothing there either. He took classes, yes, and he got credits, yes, but when it came down to the degree, it didn't exist. He never got it.

This guy got up every morning, got dressed in a suit, and took the bus downtown to a job that *didn't exist.*

I mean this guy, was a*maz*ing! He sat there with my family. He ate spaghetti and salad and garlic bread, and asked so, so politely—to pass the parmesan!

He listened to our stories and shared our life, and he told about his day. And he was lying!

He cleared the table, dish by dish!

He listened to fairy tales with my sweet little niece on his lap. She was wearing a princess dress, Cinderella or Jasmine or Snow White.

Fairy tales?! This was all a horrible, horrible scary tale for my sister. My poor sister thought that she had found someone to share a life with, to work with, to cuddle with, to love.

And it was all a lie!

I mean, this guy . . . was amazing!

When Will True Love Come
Chloe Akemi

As King of the Northern lands, I had everything. Everything that is, except someone to share my life with. Most people saw this as me being critical and selfish, but most women who came for me only wanted riches. Thus far as king, I was going to do something I've never done before. I was going to go out into the lands disguised as one of the common people in search of love.

As I made my first steps through the village feeling like everyone else, no one actually noticed who I was. Stopping at the bakery for some sweets first, I was able to do things on my own and that felt nice. What was even better was that no one was obligated to treat me with respect, they could be their everyday selves.

After the bakery, I was making my way to the town square when I saw a lone woman walking into the forest. It worried me a bit, so I followed her. Even though I spent most of the time in the palace, anyone would know the forests alone would be dangerous.

For a while she was just walking until she stopped at a pond where many radiant flowers grew. Still at a distance from her, I watched as she picked the flowers. She had more purple than any of the other colors.

"Is there a reason for a man to be following me? "she asked plainly, then turned around to face my direction. I didn't even know she knew I was following her. I'd always been the best at keeping my presence unknown. Startled, I stepped out from behind the tree and towards her, hoping she couldn't tell the embarrassment of me watching her. I stepped out from my hiding spot and stopped from the opposite side of the pond of her.

"Forgive me, my lady. It only worried me to see a woman wander off by herself into the forest. They are big and you never know who's out here."

"It's not filled with men like you who follow me?" She teased. I laughed in return.

"I guess I'm showing the part, aren't I?"

"I don't mind company if you would like to stay for a while," she said.

She was so beautiful. Beautiful as a spring morning. I began to pick flowers with her.

"What is your name?" I asked.

"Evangeline." *Evangeline.*

"That's a beautiful name."

She blushed.

"And what do they call you?"

"Phillip."

"Like the King?"

"Yes, just like the King." I only picked the purple flowers as we continued to talk.

"Did your parents name you after him?"

"Yes." I wasn't exactly lying because my father's name *was* Phillip.

"Must be a name to live up to."

"It can be at times."

"I think this is enough," she said. I put the grouping of purple flowers in her basket.

"If you don't mind me asking, why are you collecting so many flowers?" I asked.

"I like to give them to the ones who aren't as fortunate as I am. It seems to brighten up their day and help them go through whatever it is they're going through." How selfless. Not many carry that trait anymore.

"May I come with you?"

"You'd want to do that?" She asked surprised.

"Of course, it seems like a wonderful idea," I smiled, and she blushed in return again.

We made our way back to the village telling stories from our past and getting to know each other as much as we could. Soon after, we began to hand out bunches of the flowers until there were no more. After receiving endless smiles, I convinced Evangeline to go to the Swan Lagoon. We sat against the trees and talked for hours upon hours getting to know even more about each other.

"This was a great day," I said after a long silence.

"Very unexpected, but great." I turned to look at her eyes. "You know, you're very different from everyone else," she said looking back into my eyes.

"How so?" I asked intrigued

"Most men who usually follow a woman into a forest to get what he wants, and he always does." She paused, "Did you get what you came for?"

"If you mean to find a friend, yes I did." Her jaw dropped in awe.

"You want to be friends?" Her smile widened.

"Only if you want to be."

"I would love that, Philip." She said gently.

I leaned in, closed my eyes and my lips met her soft lips. The taste of sweetness and passionate feelings of love swallowed me as I embraced Evangeline.

Has true love finally crossed paths with me?

246

Hope Unchained
Alisa O'Donnell

If she closed her eyes, she could almost believe she was the star of a magic show.

She was led onto the stage bound in chains, and everyone wondered how she would escape them. If she kept her eyes closed, she didn't have to face the reality that she was a patient—and attraction, yes, but a problem to be solved by others. Doctors came from near and far to study her—her case, they said. She was paraded through classrooms of aspiring young people who saw her as a way to instant renown. But none of them really cared about her, not even about her mind.

She was tightly bound, and not only by the straightjacket, for every patient with a mental health condition worth her salt required a straightjacket, whether it was truly needed or not. What no one could see were the chains that kept her immobile. And unlike the Houdinis of show business, she couldn't wriggle free, not from the jacket, and not from the chains.

Each chain had a name: fear, anxiety, self-esteem, approval. Each one robbed her of potential. In fact, that was the latest one that came from wherever they originated, doubt that she had any potential left. Perhaps she should just let them open up her brain and take a look inside. They were dying to, she knew. They couldn't stand not knowing what kind of mental illness or breakdown caused her to believe she was wrapped in chains.

All she knew any more was that the last remnants of hope were quickly fading.

Braeden wiped his sweaty palms on his thighs as he followed the matron through the winding halls of the asylum. He finally had succeeded in getting permission to treat Belinda Byrne. Belinda had become something of a star among doctors who studied the mind. He remembered the first time he'd seen her. He had just declared his intent to pursue psychology when she was brought in as a "guest" to the class.

"Who would like to venture a guess as to what her affliction is?" the professor asked, after briefing the students on her situation.

Several students ventured guesses, but Braeden remained silent. He was enamored by the woman before him. Everything about her was distant and lethargic, but for a moment, their eyes locked, and Braeden felt a physical jolt go through him. Her eyes screamed for help. Her eyes screamed at him to understand.

That was three years ago, and since then, Braeden learned everything about the mind he possibly could. His life, from that day on, was dedicated to helping her. And now he felt so close. An interview with her must result in answers. There was nothing else left to learn, except what she could say.

They arrived outside a room, and the matron banged twice on the door before unlocking it and letting Braeden in.

"You've got one hour," she said gruffly. "But someone will be nearby if you want out before then. Just bang on the door."

She closed the door abruptly, and the clicking of the lock made Braeden momentarily reconsider.

When he turned and looked at Belinda, though, all his doubts fell away.

"Hello, my name is Dr. Braeden," he said. "How are you today?"

Belinda turned dull, brown eyes on him and didn't answer.

"I saw you, once, years ago. You visited a lecture I was attending," he said. "Do you remember? You looked right at me." Braeden focused on her eyes and waited for her to return his gaze. Would it feel the same?

Her eyes slowly focused on his, and it took longer, but suddenly her eyes blazed with the same gold color he remembered.

"Ever since I saw you, I've studied all I can to find a way to help you," Braeden said.

"Why?"

It was the first time he ever heard her speak, and her voice sounded less melodious than he'd imagined. It was rough with disuse.

"When we looked at each other the first time, your eyes begged me for help. I suppose you could say you've haunted me ever since."

"And what do you propose to do?"

"Why can't you move?"

Belinda was caught off guard; her eyes betrayed it. But no one had ever asked her such a simple question before.

"I know you can't see them, but I'm wrapped in chains, I can feel them, the cold metal weighing me down."

"Who chained you?"

A strange look crossed Belinda's face, like a mix of confusion and exasperation. "The world, I suppose, put them on me. But I didn't fight."

"Have you tried taking them off?"

"I don't know how."

"If they aren't physical chains, what do you think they are?" Braeden asked, changing tack.

Though she didn't move, Belinda seemed to shrink into herself.

"Do they have names?"

Belinda nodded, and Braeden waited to see what she might say."

"They all have names, fear, self-esteem, approval . . ."

"So you don't have a lot of self-esteem, self-worth?" Braeden asked, choosing one to focus on. "Why is that?"

Belinda couldn't explain it, but Braeden felt safe. Somehow, it felt like it was OK to talk to him. Taking a deep breath, she collected her thoughts to try to explain.

"My parents were always working when I was a child, so when they were home, they didn't have much energy left to give, and what they did have they gave to my sister. I had a friend in school, but one day a more popular girl noticed her, and she withdrew from me."

"You never made other friends at school?"

Belinda shook her head. "I dropped out shortly after to get a factory job to help make ends meet at home, but the money I brought in was never enough. And the foreman at the factory said my work was always slow and shoddy. He said I was too much of a dreamer to amount to anything."

"Did you dream a lot?" Braeden asked.

"No," she said quietly. "When my parents told me I had to leave school to work, it crushed my dream of becoming a teacher one day. And when my work only drew more complaining and scolding, I gave up hoping for anything better."

"And now? Do you believe you have value now?"

Belinda shook her head, eyes downcast.

"Well, I think do you," Braeden said firmly. "You motivated me to finish medical school so I could help you. And you survived all of that from your childhood, which means you're strong. The matron tells me you've taught some of the other inmates their letters and how to read. Don't you think that has value?"

"I guess so, I never thought of it like that."

"You're strong," he said again. "What do you think would happen if you really put your mind to it and tried to move?"

In her mind, Belinda focused on her chains. She felt them loosen slightly, and her right elbow fought its way out from against her side.

A Sense of Adventure
Cassady O'Reilly-Hahn

Joshua awoke to the sound of rain tapping lightly on the rooftop of his Volkswagen Bus. A short suck of air revealed that the day was fast becoming a cold one. He rolled himself up, taking care to duck before he got to full height, tossed his blankets onto the back seat, and swung the door open. He breathed in the smell of the fresh mountain air as it mixed with the rain and could taste the wet pine on the breeze.

He stepped down into the gravel and took a short few steps past a tree to relieve his bladder. As he walked back, he felt a pebble stuck between his toes and shook it loose. He put on the well-worn electric kettle, and as it boiled he sliced some fruit he had left sitting in a bowl on the seat. The breeze invaded him on the floor of his car, and he threw on a light brown jacket before he poured his tea. He grabbed a few handfuls of nuts from another bag—a mixture of almonds and cashews—before finally eating.

The tea took its time to cool, despite the weather, but Joshua didn't mind. He was going nowhere and had no real thought to get there quickly. The sleep was still in his eyes, and he chanced a yawn that tempted him back to the warm embrace of the blankets. The thought passed through his mind quickly as he sipped his tea.

Today was a good day to be driving. Not for the weather, but for the experience. Joshua loved the rain, and even more he loved how the trees changed in the rain. The wet bark seemed to melt away the decades they had put on, and they looked as though they were sprigs ready to spring their way back to life. When the van sputtered to life, he felt giddy to think that he would get to see Mother Nature so alive.

He pulled away from the bank of the road he had slept on the night before and found a steady pace of forty miles per hour to drive at. Though he was going nowhere, he felt compelled to make a stop at the mountain ranges just along the horizon. The last few days had been made in that direction, and though sometimes the roads turned him this way and that, he always found his way back on to the right path.

Joshua pattered along on his steering wheel to a beat that had festered in his head. It was catchy, but he couldn't quite make out what it was from, so reached into his glove box and pulled out one of many CDs at random. When the noise finally came in, he found that it was *The Wall* by Pink Floyd and felt a sense of bitter irony. The tracks wove their way in and out of the day, and the horizon slowly became the distance, which became the background, and then finally the foreground. By then the day was nearly half gone, but Joshua didn't mind. The sun was high somewhere behind the clouds, so Joshua pulled over and turned off the engine.

He hopped out of the car and drank in the rain on his brow. The mountain stood before him, but he wasn't afraid. It was a great day for an adventure. His socks would be wet by the time he was back tonight, ready to do it all again tomorrow.

Kids World

An Excerpt
Bill Watkins

Sunny in the sleek corner of Lake and Carnival, Roger and Carnell squatted low so as not to be detected. Hell-jets woomped overhead, and inside Roger chuckled.

"They're still going up there."

"Morons . . ."

The rebels laughed at themselves as much as anything else. Aware the *situation* was as moronic as any planes in the air.

"Shhh!"

Grabbing some focus from the cool bright Notvarov air, they minded their radio snow beeping. A cliché of army gear kept them blended with the leaves under a spacy 2050 apartment complex. The "Night and Day" convenience store was still down the street as it had been for seventy years. Only the merchandise changed: drugs of every size, color, and assortment, dressed up as candy to tempt the schoolers coming home from school—

"Wait!" Roger spit into his radio, spotting something across the street. Another uniform, another rebel, this one hiding a pigtail under her helmet.

"Get down, Sabby!"

And Sabrina obeyed, diving into some ivy that barely camouflaged her under the school gate.

Sounds of boots marching, it was drill time for third graders. Sensing a chance before the class passed by, Roger jumped out of hiding, Carnell behind. It was not long before all three rebels crept up bushes and ivy to peek into the school; a world they knew well, resented, and were bound to change.

Click, click, click, the boots scarred the ground, *may have scared a bright green snake*, thought Roger—a fan of Robert Frost poems. The others called him old-fashioned, sometimes labeled him a hopeless romantic. He read paper books, liked the smell of them. The way they brought one in touch with nature in the comfort of a nice indoor reading place.

"Ha!" he whispered, as the third graders passed, a uniformed teacher marching freely beside their goose-stepping rows. All shined in black armor, the kids sprightly, the lone adult sagging under metal.

"Halt!" a far-off order heard and heeded. The world stopped on a dime, as booted eight-year-olds made a hard click Navy admirals would appreciate, Marines scoffing never matched.

"Read the wall!"

Order number two was heeded with a left face to view the hall wall, lights illuminating school and national mottoes:

Listen to Adults
Obey Adults
Have Faith in Adults

Before they yelled out the mottoes on command, Sabrina winced and plugged her ears. The guys would have laughed at her if they did not also feel her pain.

"Company: Quick march, ho!"

And off the kids clicked, marching to a switch produced by their teacher. Bang, Bang, Bang against the roofed corridor walls and ground—anything to make noise and scare the class into submission.

"That's our class," hummed Roger, as the three rebels backed their crouch up through ivy and brush, the sidewalk, then sprinted across the street to the apartment complex nook.

Woomp, Woomp . . . the hell-jet returned above them as they dove low as humanly possible to avoid the gaze of brain readers and scopes.

"Did they see us?" Sabrina muttered, a face full of dirt.

"I don't think so," Roger managed, as all three peeked out to descending chopper noise. "Do you?"

Carnell, put on the spot, smiled nervously, shaking his head.

"Let's go back, then—"

"I'm never going back . . ." Sabrina was lost in her own thoughts, slipping out long enough to mistake Roger's call for home as a return to Monotech.

"*Kids World, Sabrina, Kids World!*" Roger yelled, as if to shake her out of it. Carnell smiled, pretended to smack Sabby on the shoulder. She finally broke out of her trance, wiped a tear, and led the three rebels into a garage under thumping bass music—

"Third-floor party again," noted Roger while he produced a remote control, buttoned a secret door to open from the concrete ground below them. A crude stairway curled below toward far-off orange glow, Roger and Carnell barreling down at a high pace, spurred on by a return of hell-jet noise.

Muffled PA remarks were made from above, and Sabrina paused to turn and listen:

"*Rebels. Somewhere in the vicinity of Monotechnic School on Lake and Carnival—*"

The woomp of blades got close, lights from above invading the garage, as Roger tugged at Sabrina's leg urgently.

"Let's go, Sabby!"

A gunshot blasted a gate open, and the clicking of police boots got loud in Sabby's ear as she dove head first down the secret utility hole to safety. Roger closed with another button, and down they climbed.

Captain Jeremiah Esfuerz mulled over his soup, full of ideas. Ideas! Why couldn't the world above see that these were the thing, not *age*. The U.S. Constitution of the 1780s was the first national document to age discriminate, setting twenty-five as the number of times one must have traveled around the sun before they were ready to run for Congress, *thirty* for the Senate.

Thirty! Though just twenty-four, Jeremiah had heard from his cousin, and read the works of Bill W, enjoyed the comedy of Rick the Comet: all of whom spoke of body parts sagging at that age. Amazing that the authors of the United States' first legal manifesto thought to exclude from the political process anyone with vibrant body, mind, and spirit. You must break down, get old and sag before you are ready to give and participate fully in this land.

Hogwash! Even Jesus, that rebellious rabbi spouting so much truth as to render him dangerous just like the kids of Kids World—even Jesus spoke of putting kids

252

first, "suffer them unto me," "they are the highest-ranking members of heaven," "love a child and love me; offend a child and deal with God's angels that bear His face, who will destroy you."

And yet we haze kids. We haze them because *we* were hazed, and no one seems to have the *cajones*, sagging or otherwise, to do anything about it! Well, enter Kids World of the late 2030's . . . Tired of being bottled up, pushed down, and marginalized, a group of kids led by Jeremiah's Dad, Roberto, went underground, took to hacking, separatism, alternative government structure where they had a part in global decision-making—

"Ah!" Jeremiah let out suddenly, pushing his soup aside in disgust. Then hope flickered as it usually did when he backed up from his thoughts, breathed consciously and opened up to new sets of ideas.

A man may die, nations may rise and fall, but an idea lives on.
—John F. Kennedy

An idea lives on . . . Yes! Even with that preposition ending, the proposition lives, breathes, like Martin Luther King's dream, Gandhi's passive persistent protest—Yes!

Hope gleamed out of the rebel captain now, and he smiled looking up at his humble wall, his humble office carved simply out of dirt, lit simply with bulbs and exposed wires. He read Longfellow, framed behind his desk:

Lives of great men all remind us
We can make our lives sublime,
And departing leave behind us
Footprints on the sands of time;
Footprints, that perhaps another,
Sailing o'er life's solemn main,
A forlorn and shipwrecked brother,
Seeing, shall take heart again.

Legend
An Excerpt
Austin Wiggins Sr.

The stout announcer spoke like a conman in their heyday, "Welcome again to Davis's Arena. Remember that it is because of me, and my father before me, and his mother before him, that you can see this fight. So, remember when the blood spills, I was the one who financed this leisure for you." He paused for a moment allowing anticipation to soak up into the remaining drywall. "Now let's introduce our fighters," he said at last. "Tyson Crews, six-one, with a dynamite haymaker." Tyson seemed taller than what Jaxton stated—his posture was immaculate that he towered over those who towered above him. The crowd yells with blood-hungry anticipation as Tyson entered the ring and he did so with such ease and grace that most missed him even moving at all. To most, he suddenly appeared in the ring.

"Another veteran who needs no introduction, Donna Dawson. The fastest fighter alive." And that's exactly what Donna Dawson was. She wasn't just the fastest female fighter alive, she was unequivocally the fastest fighter that any person, man, woman, in-between, or other had ever seen in the ring. She knew that Tyson's grace was an act, graceful men want the appearance of quickness to intimidate their opponent, they want them to think they possessed the spirit of the jaguar. For a man to be graceful he had to withhold energy; speed however was pure depletion of energy. Donna climbed onto the stage and stood in the corner opposite Tyson.

Jaxton walked to the edge of the ring as the fighters faced each other and rung a solid brass bell the size of his head. They didn't wear gloves; they were to fight until either one of them refused to get back up, or, if one was too stubborn to stay down, until they lost consciousness or died. Donna moved into reach Tyson and delivered a few jabs to his gut. Tyson absorbed the hits and countered with a wild right hook that missed Donna but when she felt the air from the swing, she knew caution would serve her best. Dancing around him mockingly, Donna taunted Tyson with by repeating the same two words and Tyson biting the insult swung at her with less control each time than the last. She taunted, closed in the distance, and delivered a series of jabs to Tyson's stomach, and escaped out of his long reach. She did this over and over again until he made the inevitable mistake.

Tyson with all his power couldn't land a solid, and now after exerting himself in such a wild fashion, his foot speed and hooks slow down. His breath had become shallower. Concerned, Tyson rushed Donna and swung wide and uncontrolled. The grace he had at the beginning of the fight deteriorated while the speed which Donna had shown from the beginning had not staggered or waned. When Tyson got close to Donna, she launched two hooks and an uppercut and Tyson collapsed. Donna watched as Tyson bubbled like a drunk trying to get up and she hoped he would stay down with his face kissing the blue PVC of the exercise mats. Defying even his own expectation, Tyson Crews rose to his feet. Donna leaped to Tyson delivering another right hook to his face. He didn't move this time.

Cheers and primal chants followed the knock-out and some man in the front row demanded Jaxton to pick up Tyson so that Donna could send Tyson to his death. Jaxton, without saying a word denied the request and instead congratulated Donna with a booming voice. She ambled back to the bathroom and as she changed, she said to herself, "I screwed up bad." She opened the bathroom door with her bag in hand and was crouched low, but Marco, with his glass eye, was already there waiting.

"What the hell, Donna?"

"I did what I had to."

"Had to do? We had a damn deal."

"And you promised me I wouldn't have to fake-lose to a shitty fighter. But I had to fight Tyson of all people. So, I changed plans."

Marco shook his head, "You have no idea what you've done Donna, we're both screwed. You'll see." Pouting like a child, the Marco stormed off and joined the crowd in the back most rows, the next fight was about to begin. Donna headed home in the thick of the grime. The wind churned about and grew stronger as the day went. Everything was coated in this grayness that nobody cared to get rid of. It was in the air, the particles that coated the world and tasted look soot and dust and coal. Donna yawned and got a taste of the air but it didn't faze her. She strode over the rubble of disintegrated apartment buildings hardly minding the loose stones that would demand the careful footing of most. Then she went down a long stretch of black and brown colored road, where at the end was a battered building with a once lit neon sign that read "General Store." The building's innermost room was Donna's home but no one else took claim of any of the other rooms.

After bathing Donna laid on her bed made of layers of palm fronds and allowed her mind to wander. That's all there was to do for entertainment that didn't involve raiding other villages or killing passersby. She imagined a place of green, green floors, green on the trees, green on the plants and on the mountains, and she understood this was naivety but she imagined the sky blue anyway. As she thought, her foot and hands tapped about on the walls and the floor. She thought all day without thinking of the consequences of her rebellion at the arena.

She thought of the days prior. Von asked her to pick fruit off the prickly pear so that he could prepare some cheap alcohol for her coming fight, and in exchange he was offering money but he didn't specify the amount. Instead of assaulting Von for specifics she took the offer and the day after she set out in the morning to Von's shack and in that charcoal colored home she found Tyson waiting inside. "He's also offered to help," Von said, I hope that isn't a problem. Donna nodded and explained that she and Jaxton were friends. "Good." He pulled out a tattered sheet of paper and handed it to Donna, "He's a rough map of where you might find the fruit. If you're not back by sundown, I'll just assume you're dead."

They walked silently across the barren, cracked earth and shared no more than occasional glances indicating where they should go next, and all the while their supply of fruit slowly increased. The silence of the desert was complete and even Donna had no intention of breaking it, the quiet laws of the desert seemed more absolute than the laws of her own awkwardness, and so it took Tyson's stumbling words to restore a sense of ease. "You know you're fighting me tomorrow, right?" Donna hadn't known the news but she didn't stop walking or falter on her words.

"Figures they'd pull some shit like this. Are you ready to lose?"

Tyson laughed, "I had something else in mind, why don't we stack things in both our favor. I'll take the fall and we both put our money against me to lose?"

"That'd be too easy, they'd know we rigged it."

"Well it's already being rigged in the first place, I know Marco is planning for you to take the fall and he's working with Jareth and his gang. We'd be better off trying to fight against them than not."

Donna listened to whispers of the wind and breathed deeply, "if this works, I'm getting the hell out of here."

"We'll see when the time comes," Tyson said after picking up a few fruits. "So, we have a deal?"

"Deal."

After her going over the details one last time, Donna went to bed. Jareth would take a day to get into town, everyone would leave her alone until then. Early the next morning, a scratching at the door startled Donna out of bed. Filling what seemed like the entire frame of the door way stood a man in a suit that faded from gray to a greasy black. Behind him were four similarly statured men with their arms crossed and smirks on their face. "You must be Donna, pleased to meet you." Donna couldn't sift through the sentence for sarcasm or authenticity.

"I am, and you are?" Donna said making sure to keep distance from the man.

The man scoffed and the men behind him laughed but the lack of smile lines showed the four men were also intimidated. They were forcing smiles. "Me? I'm Jareth. That's all you need to know. And you, Mrs. Donna, have screwed me out of a grip. You were supposed to lose that fight. Marco promised this money, did he know about it? Because I'm visiting him next. Why'd you do it, Donna? What money did you get?"

"Money? I'm the poorest fighter here. I don't have money just laying around. My pockets are empty and so is my house." Donna moved to the side allowing Jareth to see all her home. The goons behind Jareth started forward but with a swift gesture, stopped them. He shrugged and said, "I'll see you soon. It's not like you can make it out of the city anyway." The group of gangsters plodded along the rubble of the general store and out into the still air.

Donna rushed to grab a backpack and filled it with clothes, and within a few minutes she was out the door. She ran more than walked and if there were people outside she would have looked bizarre. Running in the thickness of the grime, Donna could feel the fine black particles coating her throat, and all could she taste was dirt. It was a minute jog to a small shack on the outskirts of the devastated town. The shack itself seemed like it was built from salvage, complete with a sign taken from a pharmacy that now only read "Jack's Pharm," and the rest of the word had been cut off in the shack's construction. Donna knocked on the door and Tyson Crews opened it.

"They're onto us already?" Donna nodded

"What's your pla . . ." he noticed the bag and shook his head. "You can't be serious. There's no way you can make it to the next town unless you've got water and food, you don't have a horse or anything. You'd starve."

"I'm leaving Tyson, I'd love for you to come with me but I've got no time to lose."

"I'm staying here, that's all I know. Venturing into nothingness like you want is crazy. Here's your cut and good luck." Tyson handed Donna a wad of money kept together with a few rubber bands. Donna looked a Tyson pleadingly but only said,

"Thanks," and she was quickly cloaked in the grit of the world.

Vengeance
Nathan Heard

Easing my cloak back, I touch the quiver strapped to my waist belt. The frigid wind swirls around me. Despite the cold, I don't readjust my cloak. I can't risk losing my shot. My leather coat will suffice for warmth. Dim yellow light from the street lamps isn't enough to expose me from where I'm waiting on the roof of the Standing Elk, the inn I checked in to a night ago. Just hours after Trolan did.

He should be back soon. It's well past dark, and flurries of snow accompany the wind. The beginning of a mean storm. This far north, anyone caught out after dark—in winter, no less—is as good as dead.

I scan the near-deserted street. A few pedestrians hurry back to their homes, but still no sign of Trolan. I readjust my grip on my reflex bow. My fingers are cold, but the wind can't quite numb them through the gloves. I nock an arrow, sliding the groove onto the bowstring. I don't draw it back yet. Trolan hasn't shown; I can only count on getting off one shot.

Nothing left to do, I wait. And with nothing left to distract myself with, the memories quickly resurface.

I was eight years old. I woke up and walked into the main room of our small cottage.

"Happy birthday, Londaen!" Mother smiled down at me. Father grinned as he displayed a long, curved piece of wood. Just what I'd always wanted! My very own bow!

"Thanks, dad!" I shouted, throwing my arms around his neck. I felt his strong, reassuring arms around me. Father spent the day with me as I practiced, instructing me, helping me aim.

"Remember to draw all the way back to your cheek, son!" he would instruct me, playful authority in his voice. "Even if it makes your arm hurt."

By the end of the day, I finally hit the tree I was aiming for. The arrow didn't stick in, falling pathetically to the ground. But I kept training. After five months, I could hit a notch on any tree from a hundred feet while riding on a rickety wagon. I never missed.

And then Trolan came.

It was a year later, a crisp autumn morning; I was barely nine. I was slopping the pigs, Father in the barn piling hay, and Mother feeding the chickens.

Two soldiers cantered up to our farm on their steeds. The horses trotted with an air of authority, but the soldiers were even more impressive than their mounts, with sparkling armor and yellow tunics with white trim and the King's crest emblazoned over the left breast.

Father went to talk to them, sweat glistening on his bare chest as he leaned casually on his pitchfork. I pretended not to pay attention as I continued slopping the pigs, but I could hear.

"Hello, sirs," Father greeted. "What business brings the King's soldiers all the way out here?"

"We captured a criminal three days ago, but he escaped. We've tracked him this far but haven't recovered him yet." He had a deep voice, which seemed strange to me, as he was clean-shaven. I had always associated deep voices with thick black beards.

By Father's tone, I could imagine him frowning. "What's his name?"

"Trolan," the soldier said. "Trolan Ryen. He's average height, well-built. Has facial scruff, blue eyes, blond hair down to his shoulders, deep scar on his forehead. Hard look in his face."

"Do you need anything of us?" Father asked, his voice measured.

"If you haven't seen anything, then no," the soldier said. "Just be cautious for a few days."

"Thank you for the warning," Father said.

"Of course," the soldier replied brusquely. "Take precautions; he's dangerous. Another patrol will come this way tomorrow morning. Let them know if you see him."

"It will be done," Father answered. "If I may, what was his crime?"

"Trespasses against the King. Theft. Murder."

The soldier clicked his tongue at his horse and the two men rode away, his response hanging in the air.

That night, as the sunset merged with twilight, Mother had just finished setting the table. She went to the barn as Father washed his face.

A minute later her scream pierced the calm of the evening. She shouted again, a strangled yelp that was cut short. Father slammed through the door, his bare feet pounding toward the barn. I ran after him, wailing. Father burst into the barn. I heard him shout once in anger, once in pain.

The man the soldier had described dashed out of the barn, holding a bloody hatchet.

I tried to fight him. He simply pushed me to the ground and ran away. I blacked out as my head struck the hard-packed earth.

I'm twenty-one now. It's been a long, cold thirteen years. But I will finally make Trolan pay for his wrongs. My parents will be avenged.

I see him now. He's walking head down, cloak around him and hood over his head. Despite his hood, I'm confident that it's him. I draw my bow back, the wood creaking as it bends under my pressure. I made this bow a few years ago. It's not the one Father made me; that one broke as I grew older. I grew too strong for it, and it snapped. But I've kept a splinter from it. I wear it on a piece of twine around my neck. Mainly to comfort me; it's the only thing from my parents that I still have.

I raise the bow, compensating for the wind by aiming a little too far to the right. At this trajectory, the arrow will fly straight into his heart.

A gust of wind makes my cloak flap again, tugging at my necklace. I feel the splinter of wood as it brushes my chest.

I hesitate. I'm not afraid to kill him. I've been attacked before. I have even killed people before, in self-defense. But I've never murdered someone in cold blood. I'm not a murderer.

But Trolan killed my parents. He deserves to die.

Will that really change anything? Killing him won't bring my parents back. I can almost hear Father's voice, speaking in a scornful, angry tone: "Good job, son. You are a murderer. I'm so proud!"

I shake the thoughts away. Revenge out of the picture, Trolan is still a murderer. He's still dangerous and needs to be stopped. Aren't I doing the kingdom a service? The soldiers would say so.

A young child runs up to Trolan. He laughs as he reaches down to embrace her. His laugh is the joy of a father. My own father sounded the same way when he laughed with me.

A woman walks out, holding her woolen cloak tight around her. Trolan stands up from hugging the child and kisses the woman. Together, they walk toward the inn.

He is completely exposed. I still have a chance. He's a murderer. Of many others besides just my parents. He's dangerous.

Choose. Now.

I have two seconds before I won't have a clean shot anymore. And who knows if I'll ever get this chance again?

Closing my eyes for a fraction of a second, I see my parents' lifeless faces.

I open my eyes, seeing Trolan arm-in-arm with that woman, and holding the hand of the little girl.

I let out my breath and lower my bow.

Laws of War: Declaration
An Excerpt
Darren T Bury

The package on the doorstep was nondescript: simple brown cardboard, clear tape, and a label. As Mason bent down to pick it up, he raised his eyes and found the figure of the delivery person retreating toward the truck.

"Thank you!" he called after the man. Without turning back, the uniformed figure threw a two-finger salute over his shoulder in acknowledgment.

The small box was heavier than he had expected. Curious, he carried it into the house, letting the screen door whisper closed behind him as he looked it over. Setting it on the kitchen table, he called up the stairs to his wife.

"Baby? Are you expecting a package?"

"I don't think so!" came the reply, echoing faintly from the door of the bathroom where she was getting ready.

Mason grabbed a utility knife from the junk drawer in the kitchen, the sharp blade whispering smoothly through the lines of tape. A fine dust coughed out of the box as he pulled open the flaps. He waved at it absently, peering inside. The contents were puzzling. Troubling. But only for a moment. Then the calm took over.

As Natalie came down the steps, she saw him reach into the box, slowly retrieving what looked like a greeting card.

"What is it?" she ventured. Natalie studied his face, searching for some clue. But it was blank. Unnaturally so, as if unburdened by thought. His movements were sluggish, muted. A stark contrast to the tight efficiency his body normally employed.

Mason flipped the card over and read the back. She waited anxiously as he placed it on the table, reaching into the box again.

"Mason, are you alright?"

Her husband didn't answer. His hand came back into view holding something dark. Then the blood froze in her veins.

The matte finish of the weapon reminded her of frozen asphalt. Flat. Cold. Unfeeling.

Natalie felt the hair on her neck stand up. "Mason?"

He finally turned, registering her presence for the first time. Expressionless, calm, she felt his glassy stare pass right through her. The gun floated sideways in his upturned hand, the abyss of the barrel threatening to swallow her life as it swayed lazily in her direction. Then Mason's body rotated, his stance squaring as he faced her.

Her breath caught. "Mason?"

Her eyes followed as the gun drew level. Then Natalie's world went black.

Mack wound his way carefully through the neighborhood streets, windows open. His left elbow rested in the breeze. He decided to try Mason's cell one last time before he reached the house. There was still no answer. Odd, but maybe they were just busy "trying." He chuckled to himself.

Rapid chatter began sputtering from his radio. He wouldn't officially be on duty until he and Mason got into their cruiser, but it never hurt to know if they should be in a hurry. He turned the volume dial on his handset and listened in.

". . . neighbors reporting what sounded like gunshots from 1367 Fairway Drive, need any available units to respond." His blood went cold, then hot, then cold again. He gripped the wheel with both hands as he slammed the accelerator to the floor.

Turning the corner onto their street, he saw the service vehicle he and Mason shared sitting right where it always was. Natalie's car sat in the driveway. The sight spiked his adrenaline. She was normally gone for work early. The tires of his car skittered across the asphalt in protest as he smashed on the brakes in front of his partner's house and leaped out from behind the wheel.

After long enough, every cop starts to develop an extra sense, an instinct, an intuition that shouldn't be ignored. Mack's was screaming as he approached the front door. The hair on his neck spiked as he opened it and called into the house. There was no answer.

He entered cautiously, one hand dropping to the forty-calibre sidearm at his waist, the other to the radio at his shoulder. He clicked on the mouthpiece and announced his presence to the dispatcher. He could already hear the sirens of other units on the way. He drew the sidearm and swept through the kitchen with the muzzle pointed downward, then came around the corner to the base of the stairs.

Natalie lay awkwardly on the hardwood floor, a crimson pool creeping outward from beneath her. He glanced around quickly, ensuring the attached room was clear, then clicked the radio again.

"Officer Roberts requesting an ambulance. Civilian casualty on-site at 1367 Fairway Drive. Female subject, aged mid-thirties. Multiple gunshot wounds." Before he could finish, the air was blasted from his lungs, driving him to his knees. He fought to take a breath through the pain. It felt like someone had stomped on his chest. As the first breath finally came, he lifted his head. Mason was running down the stairs toward him, a gun in each hand.

"Mason?" he croaked between coughs.

His partner reached the bottom of the stairs and stepped carelessly over his wife's limp form. Mason's eyes lifted to meet Mack's.

There was nothing behind them. No life. No recognition. Mack's blood froze all over again. Mason's right arm lifted, aiming the gun in his grasp directly at Mack's head. Instinct took over, and Mack threw himself into a roll back toward the kitchen as shots exploded through the floor space he had just occupied. Mack fired a pair of shots of his own as he took cover behind the wall.

Reaching for his radio again, he yelled into the mouthpiece: "Officer Roberts taking fire! Repeat, shots have been fired. Need backup!"

He heard Mason's footsteps beating heavily at the far end of the hall. Peering around the corner through the kitchen, he saw his partner stride out the front door.

With a groan, Mack forced himself to stand and give chase. Dashing through the door, he stopped abruptly on the front porch. Mason was holding position in the middle of the driveway. The street in front of the house was filled with white cars and flashing lights. Officers had taken cover behind their vehicles and were screaming instructions. Mason stood motionless, arms hanging at his sides. Mack could see blood dripping from his left hand.

"Hold your fire!" Mack held a hand out toward his fellow officers, his sidearm pointed directly at his partner. "Mason, don't do this! Drop the guns!"

Mason turned towards him, the same dead stare meeting Mack's gaze. It made

Mack's stomach feel like it was trying to claw its way out through his throat. Whoever he was looking at, it wasn't the cop he knew. It wasn't Natalie's husband. It wasn't his friend.

"Drop 'em *now!*" he shouted.

Mason blinked once, then began to lift his left hand.

The Spine of the Beast
Jon Vreeland

I remember when the bigger house in the better neighborhood, the swimming pool, the three cars and two gas-guzzling trucks, the nosey neighbors, all destroyed our Spring Breaks and Summer Vacations to Catalina Island. Every year, we and our precious boat, our fifty-foot Baby Darlin' ventured twenty-six miles into the Pacific Ocean, to the home of the last roaming herd of American Bison for weeks at a time, until one day it came to an end.

I was sixteen.

And as a teenager, everything and nothing matters: the smallest comment or incident sets you off with undeterrable justification for uncouth behavior, the teenagers' God-given right to justly do wrong.

"What are we going to do for summer if we sell the boat Papa?"

"We can make the boat payments as a family; I'll take care of the gas, *that* costs 500 bucks alone," he suggested to Mama, Sis, and me.

Silence.

"No really, what are we going to do, Papa?"

They laughed.

Mama tried to explain but I still didn't get it. "Honey, it's just way too expensive, we just can't afford it anymore."

I remember when Mama told me that taking the boat to Catalina was her favorite thing to do in the world. It was mine and Papa's, no doubt. So why we got rid of something that made us all so happy was beyond me. The whole idea of *life* was beyond me as we lived in our two-story house on the California shoreline, in a town called Gospel Swamp, a place with no swamps and not many churches. The town later evolved into a city so my parents moved up the coast to Long Beach and bought a one-bedroom condo off Ocean Boulevard—a sweet little life for the Retired.

"Sorry son, you always said 'when I'm eighteen I'm out of here."

"I know you'll do fine honey. Keep in touch now."

A year later, I still hadn't found a place to live.

I needed a home; a family with fresh new careers, two small children, a false sense of hope lived in ours. At nineteen years old, I'm on my own. I am who I am, a man lingering around his parents' place in another city, a creep in the dark. Who I am hurts pretty bad most of the time.

Except for the other night.

I was over at a friend's house playing cards; won $300, treated myself to the Harbor House Cafe in Sunset Beach, and another twelve-pack of beer from the right 7-Eleven. I parked my beige Volks along the crest of Shoreline Village in Long Beach, found a place to take a leak. I whistled through the stench of my beer-battered lips, cracked a beer, lit a cigarette. I headed for my destination, the whistling now singing, a song I've heard a thousand times before.

"Twenty-six miles across the sea, Santa Catalina is waiting for me."

The lyrics sodden my brain. I stumbled along the docks, the harbor lights melted into the fog. I lit another cigarette, followed the trail of tall black lamps with sallow lights. The boats rocked gently, like oversized children being swayed to sleep, rows and rows of them. And upon my right on the third floor in condo number 301, my undeterrable justification.

"Twenty-six miles, so near, yet far. I'd swim with just some water wings and my guitar."

I hopped the fence with my nine-pack, headed down the dock to where Papa keeps *Lil'* Baby Darlin', the eight-foot dinghy from *Big* Baby Darlin'. (Papa ties it to his neighbor's boat; Papa doesn't have to pay for the slip. Smart). I lifted up the gas tank and grabbed the keys. I unlocked and untied the boat, coiled the lines. I rowed into the fog, letting the misty morning cleanse my face, my body, my soul.

I couldn't see ten feet around me so I started up the eighteen-horsepower motor. I let it idle a bit, then motored slowly through the milky fog. The harbor's pale breath stroked my cheeks as I followed the songs of the sea: the faint howling wind, the occasional distant fog horn. I heard the splash of water slap the sides of boats, the choir of barking sea lions, the seagulls cry. Then a red light cut through the fog, the barks grew louder; the next thing I know I'm near the sea. I take a two-minute leak off the side of my vessel with a beer in one hand my junk in another, a cigarette swung from the songs of my drunken lips.

"Forty kilometers in a leaky old boat, any old thing that'll stay afloat."

I laughed. I laughed at my own self. I laughed at my 8-foot rubber boat with an 18-horsepower engine. Still, I motored through the morning fog, out to the Pacific Ocean to follow the 8 o'clock Catalina Express out of Long Beach Harbor, a 100-foot ship with hundreds of passengers, twenty-six miles to the island of Catalina. Sure, it was crazy, but I missed the island, the people on the island, the strangers I know by their smiling face. That is all that mattered as I busted through the fog a tad off course, but not bad, not bad at all.

And I let the world know.

Hear me, world! I'm your new master! I'm a sailor, a pirate! I'm the god of the sea! Hear that! I'm the god of seventy percent of this world! Obey me, fish! Obey me, birds! Obey me, hags of the sea! The land is for animals, the rest may come with me to roam with the Bison on the green hills of Catalina! We will dance! Then I fell on my ass and broke my cigarette, so I finished coasting to the edge of the harbor, arriving at a quarter till 8.

I waited for a half an hour or so, drank more of my breakfast. Then there it was, slicing through the sea of cargo ships outside the ports. The 8 a.m. out of Long Beach. I twisted the throttle, tore across the ocean, across the orange stripe the sun painted on the sea. Not five minutes later I sped behind the 100-foot Catalina Express, a daily charter boat to the Island. I followed in the goddamn rubber dingy, the throttle at full-speed the entire time. I tried to keep up, and for the first half I did, but the swells got bigger, and the sky never cleared. Then the ocean blew cold breaths of fog until it totally returned. I kept up for another five miles or so until the air thickened more, then completely swallowed the ship, leaving me alone at sea.

The water rolled higher, the skies grayer, a rumble of thunder warned of a storm ready to take me out, end it all for me. I rolled slowly over another swell, back down into the cleft of the next towering wave that almost broke. There was no lightning and no rain, but the thunder roared aggressively. And I laughed. And I sang.

"Twenty-six miles across the sea, dada da da da dada . . ."

I rolled over the next wave, high through the pallid misty air when the fog suddenly thinned. Then, up ahead my favorite spot, the island of Catalina, waded like a giant green monster in the middle of the ocean. A whirl of dust from a large stampede of Bison, thundering along the spine of the beast. There was no lightning, no storm at all. It took me two more hours to get to the Ismuths' shore, the shore of my new home.

To Make the Selection
An Excerpt
Brian Bosen

Sean set his beer on the roof of the cab and opened the driver-side door. The engine cranked up and started on the first try. He yelled out a "woo!" and stepped out, leaving it running. He checked the hitch and eyeballed how he would line it up with the trailer. He got back in and started to back the truck up. The open beer can on the roof clunked down over the windshield and rolled off the hood. Sean hit the brake. "Dammit!" He laughed at himself and backed up again.

Kayla and Brock came outside and got into the truck. She was wearing her black dress with the red and gold flowers on it.

"Why'd you bring the suitcases? We are bringing the damn house." Sean finished hitching the trailer as Kayla loaded the luggage and got Brock situated in the small backseat.

"Don't swear in front of Brock. It'll be easier when we get there if he has everything he needs and can just go straight in."

Sean looked over his shoulder at Brock sitting in the small backseat. "You got any space back there?" Brock nodded once. "Okay, let's go!"

"You should let me drive."

"Why? I like driving."

"Cuz you've been drinking."

"Nah." Sean put the truck in gear and it gurgled forward off the dusty lot, towing the aged trailer-home behind it. "I only had one."

"Two."

"One."

"Dammit, I saw you."

Sean smiled. "Hey Brock, your mom can't count. They wouldn't accept *her* if she was going in today." Kayla hit him in the shoulder. "Ow! Damn!"

"Don't swear."

"I'll be able to pass the numbers portion."

"I know, baby."

"I only had one! The other one spilled."

"Cuz you got drunk off o' one and couldn't hold onto the second?" Kayla huffed.

Sean and Brock both laughed. "Ya. Sure. That."

They drove along the small road through rocky desert. The heat on the pavement caused the horizon of the cloudless sky against reddish-brown landscape to ripple. The truck had no problem hauling them around the occasional windy bend, though most of the road was straight and the red-rock outcroppings dwindled as they got further from where they had been living the past several years.

The road eventually brought them into an agricultural area, and up ahead, along the road on the other side, a figure waved arms to flag them down. Kayla was asleep, Brock silent and bored. Sean squinted and looked on as they approached the figure. A man. He appeared injured. Sean slowed the truck and pulled to a stop on the side of the highway. He got out to say hello as the man limped across the road toward the truck. He wore a security uniform and had a bruised face, bloodied lip.

"You alright, there? What happened to you?"

"Please. My name is Deven." He put his arm on the bed of the truck and leaned against it, breathing heavily.

"You need some water, Deven. I've got some here in the camper." Sean led Deven to the side of the trailer and opened the door.

Brok roused his mom. She rubbed her eyes and realized her neck was sore from the position she had been sleeping in. "Honey, what is your dad doing?"

Brock, still bored, "He's helpin' a guy."

"What guy?" She sat up straight.

"Some guy."

"Kayla undid her seatbelt and opened the truck door. "Who?"

"I dunno. Some guy on the road. He looked hurt. He waved us down. Dad said to wait here."

"Who? What?" She didn't wait for an answer. She told Brock to stay in the truck and she walked toward the trailer. She entered the door and found the two men seated at the small table. Sean was handing a fresh towel over and took a bloody one from him.

"Deven, this is Kayla." Sean motioned to her, still holding the red-stained towel. "Kayla, Deven. He got banged up in a crash. Couple miles up the road, he says."

Kayla moved into the kitchen and stood behind where Sean sat, putting a hand on his shoulder. "Nice to meet you, Deven." She didn't know what else to say. The door opened and Brock stepped inside. Deven looked at the boy then back to Sean and Kayla.

"This is our boy, Brock," Sean began, again motioning with the bloody towel in his hand. "We're heading to The Selection. It's, you know, the big day." Brock mumbled a hello and Deven's eyes again darted back and forth between the boy and his parents. Sean continued, "Is there a place we can take you along the way?"

Deven immediately shook his head and sat up straight. "No, no, we must not go there. We must go the other way. In fact, we should turn your vehicle around now and leave immediately. We really should go *now*."

Sean and Kayla tilted their heads and looked at each other. "No, we've got to get there by four. I mean—"

Deven cut in. "This is your son?" He pointed a jagged arm at Brock. "This is your son?!"

Sean patted Kayla's hand and took over. "Yeah, The Selection is today. Well, this evening."

"Then get him out of here. Please, we must go. Now."

Kayla gripped Sean's shoulder. "Sir, you *know* we can't skip it. *No one* is allowed to miss it. And we must get moving."

"He is thirteen now, you want him to live to be fourteen? Fifteen? We must go!" Deven fidgeted somewhere between choosing to stand and remaining seated. Brock shifted by the door but said nothing.

"Sir," Kayla was getting nervous. "It is nice that Sean here pulled over to help you but I am sorry we can't do anything more for you." She noticed Deven's uniform for the first time. "Who are you, anyway?"

"Where were you headed?" Sean asked, his tone much calmer.

Kayla didn't wait for an answer. "Where were you coming *from*?"

Deven's breathing audibly increased. "They aren't doing a selection. They just choose *everyone*. Well, everyone gets in now."

"You work for the . . ."

"I do. I *did*. I quit this morning. A bunch of us did."

"You quit?"

"So, wait, there is no selection?" Sean glanced over at Brock.

"Not like there used to be. Now please let's go and I will tell you everything."

"It used to be barbaric." Sean said the last word softly, wishing he hadn't said it at all.

"Now, it's worse." Wind from a passing car gushed outside. Deven opened a space between the blinds and craned to peer through.

The silence lasted a full minute.

"Why'd you quit?" Brock asked from the doorway.

Deven stiffened. He looked out the blinds again and let his hand that was holding the towel to his head drop. "I . . ." He looked back at Brock again, then down at the table at his bloodied hand. "I did something I should not have, a bunch of us were asked to . . . we were ordered to . . . and . . ." He averted Sean and Kayla and instead looked over at Brock. "And, I couldn't stay."

Kayla stared squarely at Deven. "What did you do? Why'd you leave?"

Sean put a slow hand up. "Brock, why don't you go into the bedroom and find Deven a new shirt. Long sleeve, if we have it." He slid the glass of water closer to Deven's hand. "You should finish that. Kay, let's you and me speak outside."

"Wait," Deven quickly said, "Please, please stay. Don't leave me with—" but Brock returned and Deven silenced and looked down. He finally reached for the water while Brock placed a t-shirt and windbreaker on the table.

"Ok, Brock, take your mother outside and go back to the truck. I'll be there in a min." Kayla glanced at Sean and mouthed the words *what are we doing?* before she followed Brock down the step and outside. The screen door slapped shut behind them.

"We really shouldn't be waiting around out here."

"Look, I'm gonna take you to the nearest building and let whoever's there patch you up and take you to wherever you've got to go. But, I agree, it's time we got on the road." He stood up to go.

"Wait. My friend."

"It's Sean."

"Sean, you can't bring your son there."

"Are you gonna tell me why not?" Sean realized he was looming over Deven and sat back down at the table.

"The Selection has changed. They no longer want the boys for training."

"Then, what do they want 'em for?"

"They don't."

Sean and Deven heard cars pull up outside. Doors opened, feet on the gravel roadside, and stern voices barked. Deven grabbed Sean's arm with surprising strength to keep him from making any movements and put his finger to his lips. Sean heard Kayla's voice but couldn't make out the words. She sounded confused, trembled. The other voices were strong, sharp. Deven tightened his grip and whispered to lock the door through clenched teeth and wide eyes. Sean shook free and peered through a corner of the blinded window. More muffled voices and then Kayla's voice broke loudly. She was yelling Brock's name. Car doors slammed shut and Sean jumped toward the trailer door. "Kayla!" The door flung open and he was met with the butt end of a rifle.

Pieces of Paige
An Excerpt
Kitty Knorr

I am glad it is illegal to fall in love.

I am also glad I am not the nurse behind the counter. It must be awful dealing with Vessels all day, dealing with women like the one talking her ear off right now.

"When I was sixteen I fell hard for Blake Kennedy only to have him cheat on me with Chrissy Cochran and dump me for Sarah Schmidt, later that year I lost my virginity to Josh Melendez . . . you know he was cute but everything about him was disappointing . . . by seventeen I swore off men until Randy Jenkins asked me to the prom, sex with Randy was better but I'll admit I can't remember it all too well," the stranger exhaled.

I could not care less about this woman's glory days and apparently the nurse feels similarly, their conversation carries with one-sided effort.

"I was eighteen when the Civil War started," the stranger continued. "My high school teachers walked out on strike, instead of graduating, girls my age were thrown into vessel programs. We had no clue what we were in for, at least you have a clue, you now that sweetie?"

Was she talking to me?

"Hello?"

I guess she was.

"Hello yes I'm sorry," I spoke like a robot.

"At least you know what you're in for."

"Yeah I guess so," a depressed robot.

"I don't know about that, after all these years I still think ignorance is bliss. Always had been, always will be," the nurse sprung up and off her chair. "But maybe I'm old-fashioned."

No please don't leave me alone with this talkative psychopath, I thought to myself.

I watch the nurse disappear behind a large white door before quickly redirecting my line of sight down at my lap, successfully avoiding eye contact with the loud woman. I found solace. A moment passed. Maybe she won't try to talk to me.

"What's your name sweetie?"

Damnit.

I hesitated. Do I tell this strange woman my real name?

"Paige," I told her the truth.

"Paige? Pretty name. I'm Tilly."

"Nice to meet you."

"Likewise."

"How far along are you?"

"Five months."

"Ah that's exciting."

"Is it your first pregnancy?"

"Yes," I lied.

"I knew it. I have a good sense about things like this. When I was a kid my family grew up in a Brownstone next to a little old woman who lived alone. Mrs. Ming, yes, I think it was Ming. Anyway, she claimed to be a psychic and would read tea leaves for a living. Kind woman, always invited my sisters and I over. She'd bake cookies and told us never to get married. When I was twelve or eleven, she said I was psychic just like her, at the time my sister was eight, Mrs. Ming claimed it was too soon to tell but I think she didn't want to make Kathy feel bad," Tilly exhaled.

I didn't know what to say to this woman, to this stranger. I suppose I could ask about her sister, that would be the polite thing to do, right?

"Is your sister a Vessel too?"

"Oh, heck no."

She sighed and the cogs of her mind began mashing together, I sensed another short story manifesting. Five seconds past before Tilly started rambling again. My prediction proved accurate, maybe I was the real psychic between the two of us?

As she spoke, Tilly walked towards me and then away. She leaned on the sign in sheet and then dramatically shoved her weight into the center of the room. Every plot twist in her life's story became coupled by an impressive animation of sorts, Tilly's energy compensated for her height and small deposition; this woman was a spitfire. I hope there were nurses in the back watching the waiting room security camera because it was quite a spectacle. My obstetrician's office housed Tilly's one woman show, complete with a one-woman audience.

While annoying, it took my mind off things.

Instead of overthinking my inevitable pregnancy complications, I was too busy wondering if this woman has ever considered seeing a therapist.

Turns out her sister, Kathy, is a therapist.

"She died."

"Oh, I'm so sorry."

"Things happen. She was found in Duke River. The jury is still out on whether she fell in or jumped. I have my theories, which were different from my mother's, who died shortly after."

Once again I wasn't quite sure what to say, so I just repeated myself like a ninny, "Oh, I'm so sorry."

"Don't be sorry, I'm sure you know how high suicide rates have climbed since the King's RRL was put in place."

"Yeah I suppose."

"Well sweetie, look I'm sorry, here I am talking about mothers and sisters, I don't mean to make you feel bad."

Where was the stranger going with this?

"I can't imagine what's like to be a Vessel."

"Well I know nothing different, which makes it easier I guess."

"How sad."

I looked at her blankly.

"King Bruno enacted the Relationship Restriction Laws (RRL) on my third wedding anniversary, the next day my husband and I found ourselves divorced."

I continued staring as she continued moving her lips. All at once Tilly became overwhelmed with emotion, naturally I assumed she was seeking sympathy yet my every condolence was ignored or shut down.

"Don't apologize . . . no I don't need a tissue . . . no you don't understand."

For as long as I've been alive marriage has been illegal, as romantic relationships are a proven waste of time. "Lust derails societal progression": a favorite phrase of

King Bruno's when publicizing the RRL. Tilly's generation experienced a massive dip in population between Civil War casualties and a high suicide rate.

"Society must first be destroyed before it can be rebuilt," chanted Bruno supporters.

Bruno protesters were killed.

The population dipped even lower.

May 14, 3303 marked the end of the Civil War.

Quite some time has passed, but really nothing changed.

Today is like any other day. It's a Tuesday afternoon.

I sit in a waiting room with a loud, sobbing stranger; Tilly managed to move herself to tears by her own life story. Anticipation clouds my thinking until I can't hear her sniffles over my heartbeat. Suddenly there's a break in the blankness of the waiting room walls and the nurse reappears.

"Paige?" she calls my name.

I stand and grab for my purse.

"It was nice to meet you Tilly."

"Pleasures all mine," Tilly exhales through her sobs.

I disappear with the nurse through the white, sterile, passageway.

"I'm sorry about that," she apologized.

"No, it's not your fault."

"We called office security on her a while ago but no one has shown up yet."

The nurse and I dance with small talk as I set myself up on the table, she told me the doctor would be in shortly and left me alone, I sat with my thoughts like usual.

Directly across the room, a poster decorated the wall:

"THANK YOU FOR YOUR SERVICE. THE WORLD IS A PERFECT PLACE BECAUSE OF PEOPLE LIKE YOU."

Now if I was King Bruno building a modern utopia, I would outlaw alcohol, not marriage but then again, what do I know? I thought about Tilly and hoped she'd make it home safely. Selfishly I really hoped she'd be out of the office by the time my appointment ends and I wouldn't have to interact with her again. I thought about her wild days as a woman before the incrimination of love, all of which were interrupted by an urge to pee.

Chasing Ivy
J. Evan Ramos

The curls of her green hair spiraled around the left edge of the diner's menu. Fluorescent lights clarified the exact hue, jungle, a descriptor that fits her. She was contemplating between sausage and bacon, brown eyes swelling with hunger, but I knew she'd order both. I would have guessed her hair was blue because I've only seen her in darkness. They don't exhibit Monet in low light; such art deserves illumination. She had to be seen. And I saw her, in a way that I shouldn't have, in what felt like a different dimension, a reality detached from *that* place.

"I'm having both. I'm just so hungry after tonight."

"Well, we're in the right place. Glad you didn't stand me up this time."

When she gaped her mouth in sarcasm, I noticed her faux dimples, scars from long removed piercings. "I was loaded. Didn't think you'd come."

"Of course I'd come, you know I'm into you."

She shredded her napkin with the prongs of her fork while nodding. The light jumped off of the metal, illuminating the ink flowers brushed into her skin.

I just wanted to feel in between her fingers, see if the ink felt soft like petals. But, I couldn't touch her. Not in this plain of reality, never in public.

I don't remember the process of making it into bed. The tour of my place was short—living room, patio, kitchen, reptiles, and art. She lingered on my crested gecko, Suca, waving hello with a single finger. I'm certain Suca would climb her hair like vines, sleeping within the safety of her curls. Then, she stared at the comic book panels framed on my wall, feeling the thick black ink on her fingers. "Wait, you're actually an artist?" Her face was so close her fake lashes almost brushed against the dried ink.

"I wasn't lying."

Then, we laughed while fumbling over the couch and waltzing through the bathroom into my room. In my bed, I was naked; she was topless, green hair spreading like water over my sheets. She crawled over me, slipped part of me into her mouth. It was better than any *dance* we'd ever had, even the times I'd almost get off in my pants. This time, the lights were on illuminating in the silence. This time it felt real.

The two of us sat in the booth built for four. My hands were drawn out across the dark table, wood grain rippling black. Her hands were in mine.

"It's better here," she confessed. "I just like how we can talk, you know? It's so loud in the club, and I just have to worry the whole time."

I held the oversized glass as if it was a trumpet and sipped the beer that tasted like a meadow. We laughed as she did the same with hers. "I didn't know a half yard was this big, but I have to get another one? I have to get the full yard, right?" I took a bite from my burger while she stole a few fries. "That's how they get you. That's good marketing."

"Get it. I'll get one too. I have to go to work tonight, but I really want to get sloshed. Wish I didn't have to go, but January's been so slow."

"Yeah, it has been." I thought about missed calls and text messages left unread. "Everything's been slow."

I thought about telling her that life's messy, that everything's dying and the only structure is chaos. Telling her that there's nothing beautiful, but we tell stories to create something good where there isn't. I'd say our greatest evolutionary feat was when we learned to narrate the bullshit of life into something that gives us hope. I'd agree that of course it's complicated, and we should be able to see each other more outside of *that* place. I thought about how quickly the tone changed when I told her I wanted to be her boyfriend someday, but I knew that we had to get our lives together first, go on a few dates, feel that meeting outside of *that* place was normal.

But then, her fingers pulled at the tip of her green swirling hair, causing a spiral to bounce. A moment that meant nothing but was beautiful because she was beautiful, and I was with her.

While her friend waited to drive her to the club, our kiss was sweet, soft, and slow with a patience I've never had with her—one I'd never have again.

At Midnight on March 3rd
Lindsey Sacco

Benjamin Douglas died, and at the same time, Scout Bram was born. There was no funeral, no hospitals. Just a broken-down gas station bathroom; abandoned phone numbers declaring "good times" over a mirror that reflected shattered tiles, a toilet missing its seat, and Benjamin. No. *Scout.* "My name is Scout." He tests the name against the muted sound of cars breezing by on the freeway, screeching against puddles of rain. The shape of the lie is a new one—it always takes a few go-rounds to get used to the feel of it.

It might've been ten minutes since he's moved from this position. Posture stiff and knuckles red, wet against the edges of the sink. He's been staring at his reflection in the splintering glass of the mirror he just punched for however long he's been standing there, looking for some semblance of himself. He's changed plenty before, but never this much. *Say it again,* the voice in the back of his head, the one he wished didn't sound so much like Finley the further away he got from the bed he vacated five hours ago.

"My name is Scout Bram. *Scout* Bram." The tremor in his voice is going to get him killed. The bleach in his hair only went so far and his hands were shaking too much to hold onto the electric razor that he had just used to shave one side of his head. "Not Benjamin." Benjamin held too much weight now. Too many emotions that he wasn't supposed to have. *You won't be around long enough to love someone—don't pretend like this can change.*

So here he was, six months into a relationship with someone who *cared* about him. Someone who was ready to accept him with whatever he threw at him, but he just couldn't do it. He couldn't stay Benjamin long enough to see this through. Because even if Finley loved him and said that nothing would shake him—how do you tell someone that you watched your father get killed by a loan shark and now they were after you? You don't. You run.

There was no room for other people on the run. It made things messy. So, it had to end. And when he got into the car afterwards, he hated himself a little more. He didn't have to be *cruel.* He was trying to keep Finley safe, really. If someone got wind that Benjamin Douglas—born Jackson Graham—was there, everything would be over. The men after him would find him and finish the job, and "take care" of Finley just for the fun of it. That's how he found himself here, a rest stop that never got renovated. It wasn't hard to break in. The lock was rusted anyways.

He repeated the name over and over as he finally steadied his hand enough to shave the other side of his head. "Scout Bram, Scout Bram." As the bleached strands hit the floor, the only part of him he could never change stared back through the cracked glass of the mirror.

He looked just like his mother. His eyes a dark green color that a drunk girlfriend once called magical, and freckles creating the facade of a tan only across the bridge of his nose. When he was five he tried scrubbing the freckles away, and the color contacts he wore in three of his previous identities never worked. The last pieces of Jackson he could never get rid of. But he's long since accepted that.

Anger was still coursing through him as he threw the razor into a corner and reached for the hair dye he bought when he paid for gas with cash at the last stop. His father's addiction was what got him into this mess. He put his entire family in danger without a second thought. If things were different, maybe he'd be able to have a regular life, a time where he can be remembered. But now he must live in a reality where he's nothing more than a stare and a *you look familiar.*

By some miracle of nature, the sink still had running water, and sticking his head under the spray, he took the time to remember the past six months. The happiest he's been, he had a life. And was remembered for something. He thought he could get used to a life like that. And then a black car started showing up down the street, in front of work, everywhere. He might've been overreacting, but he can't take anything lightly.

Suddenly, his head whipped up and he opened the door. Was the black car there? Had he been followed? The route he took was impossible—he rolled a dice, which decided how many exits he'd take—but if someone knew his car, then it was all over. The cold post-storm breeze plastered wet strands of hair against his ear as he looked at the empty parking lot. He was alone. Like usual. As he shut the door behind him again, he couldn't help but feel disappointed.

He was wasting time and he knew it. Trying to talk himself out of whatever decision was coming next. In this highway limbo, he could still be Benjamin, and maybe even make his way back on the highway. Find his way back to the place he called home for so long. But once he left this bathroom, everything would be different—had to be different. He sighed and turned around.

Kicking the small piles of hair into a corner that was more spiderweb than tile, Benjamin Douglas took one last look in the mirror before Scout Bram stepped out of the bathroom.

Future Adrift
Kelly Alicia Lewis

Once upon a time, Elizabeth lived in a modest village on a farm with her widowed father. One day, she finished daily chores early and the last meal of the day was prepared and stewing steadily in a pot over the fire, so with nothing left to do she decided to take a stroll to witness the evening sunset. Whilst on her walk along river Thames a horde of men riding horses, kicking up a great cloud of dust appeared, and as they neared she stepped back against the shoreline and recoiled a bit in fear for she didn't know what to expect or how to react as she rarely encountered strangers, and her Pa warned her about the vile obscenities that roamed the earth. To her dismay, a courteous young champ took notice of her frightened state and with a snap of his fingers and a barked order he sent the troop of men a hundred yards up the stream to tend to the horses and give them rest in order to exchange a few words in private with the timid lady.

After the men retreated, the lad called out from atop his horse, "Good afternoon my lady, you ought to back away from that river, for I must confess if it was to sweep you up and take you away, I'd be deeply sorrowed." To which she smiled in relief and replied, "Indeed," in a docile manner as she stepped forward and out of the rivers danger. Together they sat in the marsh for what seemed like an eternity. They exchanged pleasantries as the sunset and well into the evening. The persistent kiss of the nights cooling air urged them to regretfully part. The young champ was none other than Prince Arthur, who would soon become King for his father's health was deteriorating rapidly, and he vowed that night he would return for her. Prince Arthur pulled from his satchel a golden ring as a token and reminder that he would return when he was King and she would be claimed his Queen.

That evening, she recited the day's happy engagement to her Pa and spoke of times in the future that would relieve him from the laborious farm duty once she was made Queen. Her father spoke not a word as she told the tale, and then he overturned the table in a fit of rage as he upturned everything and destroyed their main room, before breaking down into to a fit of hysterics as he banged his fists against the wall and revealed, "I have no choice but to send you away at once to your Aunt Olga's in Russia." Grounding his forehead against the wall, he continued, "You wear the devil's mark about your neck as did your grandmother and mother," he choked out on a sob, "Thou shalt not endure execution by flame or hanging if I can help it!"

They rode all through the night as her father went from traders and merchants, begging and bartering the meek belongings he had to secure her a spot aboard the next ship at earliest dawn. It was imperative that she departs without haste, for should the Prince discover he was bound to brothel a natural-born witch she would be destined an untimely demise.

Out in the Baltic Sea, Elizabeth grieved day and night as the mice scattered and scrounged all about the bottom of the old ship where she took solace and refuge. It was June 6, 1682, according to the calendar that hung on the wall that she discovered the truth of her mother, left her father, village, and future as the Queen of England all behind and set sail to save her life to the mysteries of Mother Russia where she would

277

learn about her inherent powers that marked her throat, which her hands continuously clasped for fear of discovery and execution.

The Hermit Healer
Camille S Ross

"I will get better, Mama."

The timid voice of her son was strained and it made Agnus' stomach churn in fear. It had not yet been a full week since she had buried his father. There wasn't even time for her to mourn his death.

"Shhh," she said soothingly, pulling the cart where her son lay bundled in a torn blanket. "We are almost there."

Timm weakly lifted his head. "I'm scared."

She was, too. It was a chance—her only chance—to save him. The sickness that took her husband was unknown to the villagers. The only hope she had left was the hermit—an old man from stories.

"He can help us, Timm," she assured him.

One of the wheels ran over a rock. It jerked the cart, pulling on her already sore and tired arms. Timm moaned and she cursed herself for not seeing the rock. Agnus pulled the blanket up closer around him and trudged on.

With the brook on her left, she weaved the small cart between the trees and thick brush. If the stories were true, the brook would lead her to the strange recluse. Looking up from the ground she saw that the sun had set and the evening light was fading. She strained for a sight of the hermit's dwelling.

The light was gone and darkness fell around them.

Agnus stopped the cart. Had she missed something? Worse yet, had she made a fatal mistake and the hermit was just a tale spun around mugs of ale? Her heart caught in her throat as she thought of her son. Had she only brought him here to suffer a final night? She leaned into the cart, wrapping her arms around Timm. His head dropped on her shoulder with a sigh. Sorrowful peace flowed from him—a peace she yearned to have.

"We didn't make it, did we?" he asked.

Caressing his tangled golden hair, she replied, "We will rest a moment. Are you hungry?" She reached into her apron pocket and pulled out a small piece of bread.

A twig cracked and she spun around. Her eyes strained into the dark woods and saw movement coming towards her. She seized a thick, wooden rod from the cart.

"Mama . . ." Timm's voice trailed off.

The dark shape was slow and round, and it reminded Agnus of a time she encountered a bear. It stopped, just shy of the moonlight coming through the trees. Her heart pounded in her chest. Any moment she expected it to rise and growl, ready to pounce.

"Are you real?" The sound of an old man's voice startled her just as much as a bear charging her would have been. She grasped the rod tighter.

"Who are you?" she said, her voice unintentionally shrill.

"Ah, you are real." The man cleared his throat. "I believe you already know who I am, otherwise you would not be here."

"It's the wizard," Timm whispered.

Still, that did not put her at ease. She watched him carefully as he moved towards them, aided by a staff. The moonlight revealed a hunched-over man with gray hair and beard. He gestured with his staff, and said, "You are very desperate to journey here. Why have you come?"

"The stories say you are a healer," she answered, apprehensively. "I heard tales of an old man who used magic to heal and restore the sick. I knew I had to come so you could help him." She glanced down at Timm's pale face and saw that he was staring up at the stars, his eyes drooping. She turned back to the hermit with pleading eyes. "I would do anything for him. Please, what must I do?"

The old man circled them and then rested his hands on his staff. "Your sole task was to bring him to me for healing. You are a woman of courage for making that journey on your own, unsure of where it would lead you. But you believed the tales and followed your aching heart. Your love for your son is strong."

A tear slipped down her cheek. "He is my only child. He is all I have left after his father died from this same sickness."

"You possess such fortitude in this trying time," he said gently. "You will need to find even greater courage and strength with what is to come."

Her hand found Timm's and she clasped it tight.

The old man continued, "I do not have many years left, and soon what I know will die with me. I need a successor, otherwise what I do for you will be the last."

"Then you can heal him?"

"I can. But only if you let me take him with me. Alone."

A Social Order
Cori Amoroso

Once upon a time, in a place called Nowhere, during the era of Ubiquity two women were having tea and scones in an elegant and dainty café.

"It strikes me as odd that the color of money is green," Aye Whole said as she bit into a lemon scone.

"I think it would be much prettier if it were rainbow colored, don't you?" said her friend Fallow Weir.

"I think money would be much more pleasantly held in my hands if it were the color of gold for the rich like us and brown for the poor," replied Aye.

"But brown is such a plain and ugly color," Fallow replied stirring her tea.

Aye nodded and said, "Exactly. That is why money for the rich should be different from money for the poor."

Fallow Weir stopped stirring and replied, "Just how rich are you, Aye?"

"Well, I come from money. I always have money. My house is very expensive and everything I wear costs a lot of money."

"Oh, you are made of money aren't you Aye," said Fallow.

"I certainly am. And do you know what else?"

"Please tell me. You know how much I rely on your wisdom," replied Fallow.

"People with money generally know more and do less," said Aye.

"I never thought of it that way," Fallow replied.

"It's the way of the world. Money prevents the rich from doing anything. On the other hand, the poor must always do more and work more so they can be less poor, and if they rest even just a tiny bit, well they become even more poor."

With a look of sadness, Fallow replied, "That is an awful fate. I am glad that we are not poor."

Aye gave her friend a smile and replied, "But do remember that there is a hierarchy with the rich as well."

"There is?"

Aye leaned toward her friend, "Your family is rich, which makes you rich. But my family is richer and that makes me richer. So, it would not be odd for me to say that I am better than you in that respect. There are shades of gray even with the rich."

Fallow took stock of this information. If there were shades of gray between the rich, then she, Fallow Weir, was of the lower shade. "Well, what about Clara Upancoming?" said Fallow. "She was once poor and now she is quickly having lots and lots of money and perhaps doing lots and lots less. Just like us. Why if she keeps doing nothing, she might soon be richer than you."

Aye shook her head. "Pish posh. Someone like Clara will never be better than us because people who come from money and have done nothing to earn their money will always be better than those who have to work for it."

Aye and Fallow heard the chime of the cafe door and saw Clara Upancoming enter with a friend.

"Oh, my. Look at Clara's transformation," said Fallow in amazement. "She looks very well rested indeed and her clothes look very expensive. And she has that purse you've had your eye on for weeks."

Aye haughtily tilted her head up so high that her nostrils faced the ceiling when she saw Clara approach their table.

"Hello ladies," said Clara. "I'm so glad to see you because I am looking for volunteers at the soup kitchen on Homeless Road. What are you doing a week from today?"

Before Fallow could respond, Aye replied, "We are busy doing absolutely nothing that day. So, we decline your invitation." "That's a shame," said Clara. "We could really use your help. If something changes you let me know. Now if you'll excuse me, ladies."

Aye watched Clara take the table next to theirs and eyed with resentment the smart, beautiful, elegant and very luxuriously expensive purse hanging on Clara's arm.

Fallow whispered to Aye, "I think it would be an enlightening experience to volunteer at the soup kitchen on Homeless Road."

Aye snorted, "The rich do not involve themselves with those on Homeless Road. Clara, on the other hand, despite her new money will always be poor and that is why she's compelled to be there because inside, she's still a dirty and stinky pauper. What's inside eventually comes out." Aye, with an air of triumphant superiority leaned back on her chair. But moments later, she felt a cold breeze pass through her and the climb of a sneeze. "Ahhchew," Aye's nose exclaimed and out came a murky, greenish ooze mercifully caught by her napkin.

Fallow heard the sneeze and looked up. "Are you getting sick Aye? You don't look so well."

"It's probably from the bits of dust Clara dragged in," Aye replied folding her napkin and taking a bite of her scone.

With shock and horror Fallow stepped away from the table, covered her nose with a napkin and said, "Aye, you have poop all over your mouth."

"Impossible," replied Aye. But now that she thought about it, the scone did have an uncanny bitter, putrid taste. Aye wiped her mouth and what she saw on the napkin looked like what came out the other end when one suffered from a rotten stomach. Aye suspiciously picked up one of the lemon scones and it morphed into a smelly clump. She picked up another and another and each lemon scone turned into crap at the touch of her hand. The stench traveled throughout the cafe causing a wild chorus of "that stinks" and "get that smell out of here" from diners.

The ruckus brought out the proprietor who witnessed his customers on the verge of vomiting. He followed the origin of the horrible smell and saw Aye. "We don't allow your dirty kind here. You belong on Homeless Road."

"I most certainly do not!" screamed Aye with tidbits of pooh still stuck on her teeth. "Your pastries are made of crap."

"We serve no such thing in this fine establishment," said the proprietor. "You're the only one here with turd in her mouth—you—foul-smelling, disgusting heathen. Now get out." He grabbed an umbrella hanging from a coat rack and with the adeptness of a swordsman, wielded the umbrella on Aye. "Get out, get out, get out," he said poking Aye toward the door.

Aye clutched her stomach and used her arms to thwart the pokes. "There's been a mistake. I'm rich. This cannot be happening to me," said Aye as she fell on the pavement and sullied her fine clothes.

With the source of the stench gone, patrons gave the proprietor a round of applause.

"It's a crime that someone like her could get into a place like this," said a plump woman with a mouthful of raspberry tarts.

A confused Fallow turned to Clara and said, "It strikes me as odd that someone of Aye Whole's money and social status could suddenly transform into a—well into a shit monger."

With a look of pity, Clara approached Fallow and replied, "Not that odd."

The Woman
Phoebe Jane

The woman sat on the side of the road for some tie. She was dressed in rags and her hair was matted. A small bowl sat before her with light gold inlays. For many days she had come, watching and waiting. Hoping that the kindness of the people would shine through.

A little boy had come every day. It was apparent from his manner of dress that he did not have much. However, each day he would come with a bit of hard bread and a small pan of thin soup. The soup had but scraps of vegetables and warm water but every day he came, his mother watching from a short distance.

An older man walked by every day pulling a scrap of fabric over the woman's shoulders. The days were warm and bright but the nights were chilly and the man saw the woman never leave her porch. He brought fabric in the hopes to keep the cold off her bones. She suffered enough living on the street. And so it was as the days rolled by with the woman subsisting on the generosity of the townsfolk. Women brought her water, men brought her food, and all types of people pulled from what they had to drop a coin or two in the bowl set before her.

One day a man known in the city as Tashi approached the elderly woman. Tashi was the nephew of the town's leader and made it his business to speak about the town and report his findings to his uncle. He was tired of seeing the dirty creature spending her days on the corner. *People giving her food and water was their business but money?* He had watched as person after person left money before the woman. This enraged Tashi. *Why should she be freely given money?* As Tashi saw it, it was all such a waste on a useless beggar. When Tashi could no longer contain his thoughts, he approached the woman with a skip in his step, calling to her.

"Excuse me."

The woman did not even look his way.

"Excuse me!" Tashi was even louder but the woman still did not respond. This infuriated the man almost as much as the donations given to the woman.

"Hey, you. Are you deaf or something?"

The woman slowly looked in his direction, her eyes planted on the ground.

"You need to leave. You can't just sit her begging. You need to get to moving."

Still no movement from the woman. Fine, if she will not move on her own, I will force her out, he thought. Tashi grabbed the old woman by the collar and pulled her to her feet. "I will not allow you to continue to prey on the good people of this village. It is time that you leave."

"No," cried out the small boy. He had walked by with the daily bowl of soup. It was particularly thin that day but he still brought a portion of his family's meager meal.

A crowd of people had started to gather. "Tashi! What are you doing?"

The senior man looked at the man attempting to drag the woman to her feet.

Tashi was not used to being challenged.

"Hold your tongue, old man, or you will be next."

"That woman has done nothing to you."

As the crowd became more vocal, Tashi became even more enraged.

"Has done nothing to me? What about what she is doing to all of you? It is not for you to provide for this woman. If she wants anything, then she needs to work just like every person in this town. Anyone who has anything that they want to say about it may need to take it up with my uncle."

The townspeople grew quiet at the mention of the leader. He was not known as a merciful man and he took his nephew's counsel quite seriously.

During the silence, Tashi dragged the woman to her feet and started to push her away.

"Get out and don't you ever set foot back in this village. Should you return, I will be sure to have you beaten within an inch of your life."

The woman limped away silently. The little boy chased after her.

"Here, you forgot your bowl."

"Did I tell you to bring her the town's money?" Tashi bellowed at the child.

With these words, the woman turned to look at the man. She emptied the bowl allowing all the coins and bills to fall. Now empty, she tucked the bowl in her rags and shuffled away.

As she made her way out of the town, Tashi continued to berate the people.

"How dare all of you speak out against me? I am protecting all of you and the interest of our village. She was taking advantage of all of you."

"It was none of your business."

Tashi looked trying to determine who spoke out against him.

"Whatever happens in this town is my business and if you all have so much money for beggars than you will have no problem paying the extra tax to be levied."

Extra tax? It was the taxes that had been such a burden on the people. The leader insisted that taxes be paid and yet the people never saw the benefit of these payments. Their roads were uneven, homes were falling apart and there never seemed to be more than enough to eat. However, the leader and his family seemed to be living quite well.

"And anyone who has more to say can see their taxes doubled."

The crowd was silent. Some of the villagers looked at each other in sadness and disbelief but most looked at the ground, dejected.

Slowly, everyone began heading home.

At the outskirts of the village, the woman continued to amble along. Once she was far outside the village limits, her back began to straighten and her rags began to change. Within moments the visage of the beggar was gone. In her place walked a regal woman wearing garments of gold who disappeared into the woods.

In the initial days that followed, the townspeople would look out for the woman. When they realized she would not be returning, the little boy stopped bringing soup and the old man kept his fabrics at home. They now had even more pressing issues at hand.

Tashi had kept his world and reported back to his uncle of the town's insistence on handing out their money to an outsider.

"They insisted that they had more than enough to give to this beggar woman! If they have extra money to give away, then it should fall into the town treasury."

The leader agreed and sent his nephew out daily to collect an increased tax throughout the town.

Some time had passed when travelers would start passing through the village. These strangers paid exorbitant rates to stay in the town's inn and drink of their wine. Stories were handed out of a monarch from faraway lands who was known for destroying whole villages. These visitors were on the run from the one known as Akira. It was said that she would destroy each village that she came across if she felt they were not worthy of existence.

All of the tales worried the townspeople but not as much as it worried the leader and his family. Secret councils were held as they tried to make plans to deal with the trouble that could be making its way to the town.

"How do we know these tales are true and not just rumors created to force us to leave?"

The leader looked at his nephew. It was true that there was not much proof of the validity of the stories but the crowds had increased. Each day more and more people passed through the town and their explanations all sounded familiar.

"That is not a risk that I am willing to take for the sake of our people. We must evacuate."

Back and forth the council made plans to not just evacuate but which families should be left behind as a sort of decoy for the murderous monarch. Their conversation was held in such a deep intensity that they never noticed the woman standing at the door.

"Excuse me."

Everyone at the table to see the woman dressed in gold. She looked more regal than any queen or ruler that had been seen in centuries.

"I'm apologizing for disturbing your meeting. It seems you were making plans to leave?"

The entire group turned to look at the leader. He nervously stepped up. The smile on the woman's face left him feeling unsettled. It sent chills downs his spine as if he was staring into the eye of death.

"Who are you and what are you doing here? This is a private council."

"Oh, I can see that. It does not matter. I should not be long."

"Well, I ask again. Who are you?"

"I am Akira, goddess of the northern shore."

Goddess?

"From the looks on your faces, I see that my reputation has proceeded me. No matter. I was sure those worm-like monarchs and leaders who abandoned their townsfolk would make their way through here. They will not get far. Soon they will pay for their misdeeds."

"Misdeeds? What do you mean? And who are you to judge rulers?"

The woman sighed.

"Did you not hear? I am the goddess of the northern shore and I make it my business to ensure that the residents of the villages are treated well by their leaders. Every village is surveyed and the fate of the people is judged."

"You never surveyed our village."

"Oh, but I did."

The woman smiled and pulled from her garments a stone bowl with gold inlay. She placed the bowl in front of Tashi and looked at the man with light in her eyes.

"Now what did you tell me about setting foot in your town again?"

Heaven's Headquarters
Dana Lee Burton

"How did I get here?" Ethan, a man with silky brown hair, green eyes, and a slim physique, realized he fell asleep on an elevator. He doesn't recognize this elevator, which has ornate, gilded walls, and he's mystified as to how he ended up inside. Last thing he remembered, he was walking down the street. He suddenly realized that the elevator had no buttons! The elevator kept going up, and Ethan had no idea where he was going, so he started to worry. Suddenly, the elevator stopped and the elevator doors opened. Ethan stepped out cautiously.

Ethan walked into a reception area and looked around to figure out where he was. The walls and floors were cloudy white. There wasn't much else there except a lot of doors and a pearly, circular desk at the center. A perky, blonde secretary popped up behind the desk and watched Ethan. Ethan, not knowing what else to do, went up to the secretary, who had a nameplate that read: Hailey. Before Ethan could ask her anything, Hailey chirped, "Welcome to Heaven's Headquarters! Please fill out these forms." She slid a white clipboard with a couple of crisp papers on it to him.

Ethan felt totally confused. He had no clue where he was, and yet this woman seemed to have been expecting him. "Forms?

Hailey simply explained, "Yes, to show us what would make your eternity the ideal level of blissfulness."

Ethan started to think that he either got too drunk at dinner or else someone had slipped something into his drink. Either way, he thought that maybe he had blacked out and had booked some spa getaway in his haze. That didn't seem like a smart idea, so he tried to clear this up with Hailey, "Look, I'm not sure how I got here, but I gotta leave. I got work in the morning, so"

Hailey interrupted him, "Work? No, you don't work in Heaven. It's your time to relax."

Ethan got a little annoyed by this. He knew that companies often had their secretaries try to save their sales, but she didn't seem to get it, he really didn't have time for this. "Relax? I got a big presentation in the morning. So, can you—?"

"

? Are you holding me hostage?"

"Oh, boy!" Hailey sighed. She coolly hit a pager button on her office phone and spoke into it, "Peter, can you come to the Pearly Gates please?"

A handsome man with a nice suit and a clipboard in his arm appeared next to Hailey instantly. Ethan had to blink. He couldn't explain how the man, who he could only assume was Peter, could appear from nowhere unless Listen," Hailey looked him square in the eyes and talked in a very serious tone at this point. "You're not going back to work. Or your home or anywhere else. You're dead."

Whatever response he had expected to hear from her, it wasn't that! The ease he felt from what he thought was a logical conclusion to this situation had vanished, and if he hadn't booked a luxurious hotel in a drunken haze, then he didn't know what else would bring him here. The fact that she mentioned that he was dead now sent him into panic. "Is that a threatit was some kind of theatrical ruse to scare and confuse him. Peter glanced at Ethan and then regarded Hailey, "Who's this? Let's see . . . ah, Ethan Miller. I told you already that he is most definitely welcome here!"

Hailey calmly revealed, "I know, but he hasn't accepted."

Ethan, in addition to feeling a little scared, grew frustrated by the lack of answers. He had a right to know what was happening! He shouted, "Who are you?"

Peter smiled gently and introduced himself, "On Earth, I'm known as Saint Peter."

Ethan rolled his eyes. He didn't believe that was his real identity, and he resented the task he now had of figuring out who these people were. He remarked to Peter, "Saint Peter, huh? What are you guys, the mob or something?"

"Wow! Peter seemed bewildered by Ethan's response, but he kept his composure. "You weren't kidding about this man! Better send him to the Big Guy."

"Who? Where are you taking me?" Ethan decided he wasn't going to let them take him anywhere and prepared to put up a fight.

Peter snapped his fingers, and Ethan instantly disappeared! Ethan reappeared in a huge office. It seemed to be empty except for the same cloudy walls and floors and a big, wooden desk with a computer on it. Whoever "the Big Guy" was, he wasn't in the office right now. Ethan looked all around him in utter confusion "Okay, what the hell just happened?"

At that moment, a very tall, clean-shaven man with gray hair and a light gray suit walked into the room. The man reproached him gently, "Sir, we don't swear here." Ethan jumped at his sudden approach. The man kindly instructed, "Go ahead and have a seat."

A cushy chair appeared before the desk right behind where Ethan stood. He reluctantly took a seat. He needed answers, and he figured that they must lie with this man. "You're the "Big Guy?"

The man replied, "I'm known by many names. A higher power, Nirvana, Inner Peace, Mother Earth (somehow) . . . but you probably refer to me as God."

"Oh, you're God? Yeah right!" Ethan wondered what was wrong with these people. They were either giving him their nicknames or else he had come across a very delusional cult.

The man seemed unruffled by Ethan's disposition. He probed, "What makes you doubt me?"

Ethan couldn't believe that this guy had really believed that he was God! He had to put him in his place, "God isn't some businessman! He has a really long beard and a robe . . ."

The Big Guy chuckled, "You mean like this?" He snapped his fingers and, to Ethan's astonishment, he changed into Ethan's description of God. "Yes, this look was all the rage when the Bible was written, but we've made some updates since then." The Big Guy snapped his fingers again and changed back into the outfit he previously wore.

Ethan still didn't totally accept their claims that he had died or that he was speaking to God, and he didn't want to feed into that delusion. He had to try to get home. "Look, I don't wanna be here, in 'Heaven,' I want to!"

"No?" the Big Guy remarked. "Would you rather be in Hell? It's not as fun as rock stars make it seem. Here, have a look."

The Big Guy turned his computer monitor around to face Ethan. An automated voice greeted him, "Welcome to Hell Dot Com! I'm Jaime, your virtual host. Let me give you a tour!" The screen changed into a red office with a blonde man in a pepper-gray business suit sitting at a dark, wooden desk. "This is Lucifer's Chamber! He decides how cruel of an eternal punishment a sinner gets." The screen changed into a room with some fiendish monsters standing in front of some sharp rocks. The monsters smile and wave to the camera. "This is the physical pain and torture chamber where sinners go to receive a Hell of a lot of, well, pain and torture." The screen changed to a completely empty room with a small green couch and a wide screen television "This is the viewing room where sinners are forced to watch their worst nightmares over and over again." The screen changed to small, rundown town. "This is Sinners' Living, the living quarters of sinners. Their homes turn into whatever they would consider the most unbearable living conditions." The screen changed to a door with the number 666 on it. "This is Area Six Six Six, where the most evil sinners go. It is so gruesome that we cannot display it on the web." The screen changed to a room full of what looks like operators and telemarketers. "This is the communications room where our "devils" tempt ordinary people to commit a sin." The screen changed to a picture of an empty reception desk. "That ends our tour of Hell Dot Com. We are currently seeking a Hell Secretary if you're interested. See you in Hell!"

The Big Guy turned the computer off and swiveled it back so it faced him. Ethan now felt very much perplexed. Ethan supposed that the Big Guy thought that this presentation would convince him that he had died, but he wasn't buying it! "I can't be dead! The world couldn't go on without me!"

"You don't think so?" The Big Guy reacted. "Well, I can show you that's not true either. Oh, Joseph!" He pushed a button on his phone to summon him. A young man with a gray suit and a white tie, black hair, muscular build entered and looked to the Big Guy to await his instructions. The Big Guy directed Joseph, "Show Ethan his world without him. I gotta go. I'm helping my son throw a party tonight! Hope to see you there!" The Big Guy winked and disappeared.

Joseph grumbled, "Thanks a lot, now I'm going to miss that party!"

Ethan could care less about this man's desire to go to some party. He didn't know what they wanted with him, but it seemed like he had no choice but to play their game. He scoffed, "So, who are you? Saint Joseph?"

Joseph forgot about the party and pleasantly answered Ethan, "No! My name is Joseph Love. I was a soldier in the Revolutionary War."

Whether it was real or not, Ethan grew curious about Joseph's backstory. "Oh, you got killed in battle?"

Joseph told him, "No, after we won, my friends and I had a party and I died there."

"How'd you die?" Ethan asked him.

"I don't know." Joseph shrugged.

This notion triggered a thought, and again, whether it was true or not, Ethan was owed an explanation. "Wait a minute, how'd I die?"

"No one in Heaven is supposed to know," Joseph educated him. "If they think about their death, they'll never stop dwelling on it. Though the last thing I remember is swimming, so I think I drowned. But who knows! Anyways, you think the world can't survive without you, huh? Who depended on you?"

Right away, Ethan came up with, "My fiancée, Diana Shaw. She's in love with me, so there's no way she'll survive without me!"

Joseph's mouth twitched, but he hid his grin. "Is that right?" He snapped his fingers, and they both disappeared.

Note to the Reader

We hope you enjoyed our publication! If you have, we ask that you please consider writing a brief review for the book on Amazon.com. In your review, be sure to mention the title of the writing (or the name of the author) that you enjoyed the most—we will take reader reviews heavily into account when it comes time to decide who will receive our first solo-author book deals later this year!

About Z Publishing House

Begun as a blog in the fall of 2015, Z Publishing, LLC, has since transitioned into book publishing. This transition is in response to the problem plaguing the publishing world: For writers, finding new readers can be tremendously difficult, and for readers, finding new, talented authors with whom they identify is like finding a needle in a haystack. With Z Publishing, no longer will anyone will anyone have to go about this process alone. By producing anthologies of multiple authors rather than single-author volumes, Z Publishing hopes to harbor a community of readers and writers, bringing all sides of the industry closer together.

To sign up for the Z Publishing newsletter or to submit your own writing to a future anthology, visit www.zpublishinghouse.com. You can also follow the evolution of Z Publishing on the following platforms:

Facebook: www.facebook.com/zpublishing

Twitter: www.twitter.com/z_publishing

Author Biographies

Arianne V. Advincula: Arianne is a Chapman University graduate who works in the Japanese video games industry. Her short stories are published in several journals. You can find her on Twitter: @ariadvincula.

Kimberly Carlson Aesara: Kimberly is the author of the award-winning novel *Out of the Shadows*. Her short stories have appeared in the *Sun*, *Toyon*, and the *Hot Air Quarterly*. She writes in the early mornings while her son and daughter sleep.

Alyssa Ahle: Alyssa Ahle is a budding author and playwright from San Clemente, California. She studied communication studies and creative writing at Chapman University. As a writer, she aspires to draw attention to the overlooked beauty and humor of life.

Chloe Akemi: Chloe Akemi is an aspiring author living her dream in Southern California. She spends her days not only writing but also thinking of how to better the world one step at a time. She believes in not only spreading love but also kindness as well as it's what we all need.

David Alexander: David is a Southern California resident who's writing is inspired by the endearing strength and fears of the human spirit.

Cori Amoroso: Cori Amoroso received her BA in English literature at California State University, Los Angeles. She's a copywriter, a dreamer, and a crazy thinker because that's just how her noodle works. She hopes to publish her book, *Mrs. Badley's Order*, but for now you can visit her blog at www.lafemmeroar.wordpress.com.

Lindsay Benster: Lindsay is a recent graduate from the University of San Diego, where she earned her bachelor's in behavioral neuroscience. She currently helps conduct psychiatric research at the University of California, San Diego, while maintaining her passion for writing through freelance opportunities.

Brienne Flaherty Betín: Brienne Flaherty Betín is a recent graduate, social realist, and avid fan of all things fiction. When she isn't tucked into a corner with a book, you will, in all likelihood, find her at the beach, in the sun, or petting a stranger's very cute dog. Interested in speculative science fiction, Brienne typically writes works that address contemporary issues under outlandish and fantastical frameworks, and always with an upbeat inclination toward romance and hope.

Michaela Bishop: Michaela Bishop is junior English major with a creative writing emphasis at Dominican University of California in San Rafael. She is currently a student editor for her university's literary journal, *Tuxedo Literature & Arts Journal*. She enjoys reading and writing fiction in her spare time.

Brian Bosen: Brian Bosen is thirty-three years old with a master's and bachelor's degree in English and is currently living and teaching in Vietnam. He studies Spanish, German, Vietnamese, and Esperanto. His short story "Flash Mob" has been published in the December 2016 issue of the humor and pop culture site Acid Logic, and his stories "Mr. Ichabod Lester Kransten" and "Fixing a Leaky Pipe" have both been published in the 34th issue of *Occam's Razor*.

Laura Bouzari: Laura Bouzari is a current master's of science candidate in journalism at the University of Southern California. Born to a Persian father and Syrian mother, it was only after moving from her hometown in Dhahran, Saudi Arabia, to Southern California that Laura found storytelling as her niche. In 2015, she was awarded first place for her creative nonfiction, "Vise," by the Community College Humanities Association. Laura also holds a BA in English literature from the University of Southern California.

Mia Brabham: Mia Brabham is a word-loving content creator. She has a YouTube channel, "Yours Truly, Mia;" a 365-day blog, *A Year of Lessons*; and a podcast, "The Last Lap." Mia is currently working in Los Angeles. She hopes to become an award-winning writer and TV host. Find her on Twitter @hotmessmia.

Kae Bucher: Kae Bucher is a Central Valley poet and storyteller whose work has appeared in the *Rappahannock Review*. A social justice advocate, Kae is currently working on her first chapbook, two fiction manuscripts, and a novel in verse. You can find more of her writing at www.bucketsonabarefootbeach.com.

Renee Bulda: Renee Bulda is a writer who does not have a lot of time to write. She started writing when she was young, inspired by the books she read. She enjoys fiction and fantasy and is in the process of writing a full-length novel, which she will publish someday.

Dana Lee Burton: Dana Lee Burton has been writing for most of her life. She blends different genres together and puts creative twists on the expected. With her degree in theatre and work in stage and screen acting, she knows how to keep the audience entertained and engaged. She currently lives in California, where she spends time with her family while she works on building her dream career in the arts.

Darren T Bury: Darren T Bury is an author from Northern California, where he lives on the coast with his gorgeous wife, a forty-pound pit bull, and a twenty-pound cat. He is currently polishing his first sci-fi/action novel, *Laws of War: Declaration*, with a psych-thriller, *Miss Remembered*, in the works.

Morrisa P Clark: Morrisa P Clark is a transplant from Alaska to California who has been writing all their life. They enjoy the sun and their cat, who is a strict commentator on all of their writing.

Kyle Campbell: Kyle is currently studying geology at California State University, Fullerton. He lives happily, collecting rocks and minerals from each of his adventures across the world.

Trish Caragan: Trish Caragan is a current undergraduate majoring in creative writing at University of California, Riverside. She enjoys reading and writing romantic teen stories. Trish knew she wanted to write romance novels after reading *This Lullaby* by Sarah Dessen, her favorite author and biggest influence. Her other favorite authors are John Green, Jenny Han, Stephanie Perkins, Huntley Fitzpatrick, Fitzpatrick, Morgan Matson, Laurie Halse Anderson, Nicholas Sparks, and many, many more. When she's not reading or writing, she's either talking to friends or listening to upbeat pop music. One day, Trish hopes to write books that will impact people the same way that Sarah Dessen's novels have impacted her.

Avery Cardosi: Avery is currently a sophomore at Chapman University, where she majors in creative writing and Italian studies. She has a strong passion for creating stories that explore themes of social dysfunction and include a superfluous amount of commas. She hopes to continue to write short stories, novels, and poetry as she pursues a career in screenwriting.

Ariel Castagna: Ariel Castagna is currently pursuing an MFA in creative writing from the California Institute of the Arts. Her work has been published in multiple issues of the *Aerie*. She once ate so many Peppermint Patties that she broke out in hives. She says it was worth it.

Grace Chao: Grace Chao grew up in the Bay Area, graduated from Stanford University, and lives in San Francisco. She spends Sundays watching movies at the neighborhood theater over coffee, eating dinner next door, and listening to Beach House and reading investigative journalism at night.

Hugo Alberto López Chavolla: Hugo Alberto López Chavolla is a graduate student at the University of California, Merced. He is passionate about learning, writing, and literature. His writings focus on the sentiments of love and uncertainty, accompanied by the nihilistic essence of the unstoppable time and the approach of death and oblivion.

Leah Francesca Christianson: Leah Christianson's work has appeared or is forthcoming in *TriQuarterly*, *Sliver of Stone Magazine*, *Storm Cellar Quarterly*, *Sundog Lit*, *Westwind Literary Journal*, and other publications. She earned her BA from the

University of California, Los Angeles, and is an MFA candidate at Miami University.

Ethan Chua: Ethan Chua is a Chinese-Filipino spoken word poet and fiction writer. He is the recipient of the 2017 Geballe Prize for short fiction, and his work has been published in *DIALOGIST*, *Strange Horizons*, and *Hobart*. His graphic novel, *Doorkeeper*, published by Summit Books, is available in Philippine bookstores.

Cloud: Cloud was born under the sun. He thinks of avocados, his brother's dimples, and snow.

EJ Conway: EJ Conway is a recent college graduate hoping to find her footing in the writing world. Along with migratory trees, she enjoys writing about bored necromancers at their day jobs, wizards with bad tempers, and dragons.

Jason Credo: Jason Credo graduated from San Diego State University and has always had a passion for writing. His aim is to continue writing about the world around him and hopefully, one day, write for television. Jason currently resides in Los Angeles, California.

Donna P. Crilly: Donna P. Crilly is an emerging writer from Oceanside, California. She holds a bachelor's degree in journalism from San Diego State University and currently works as an editor in New York. Donna's creative work has appeared in the *Aztec Literary Review*, and she regularly publishes in *Uncle Jam Quarterly*.

Emily Crosby: Emily Crosby is a lifelong resident of California, and she enjoys the beaches of San Diego as well as the mountains of the Sierras. She will graduate university with an English degree and a high school teaching credential. In addition to all things literary, she passionately pursues traveling and ballroom dancing.

Alex Dunne: Alex Dunne graduated from Stanford University with a BA in English. She recently moved, on a whim, from New York City to Amsterdam, where she continues to chase down writerly aspirations and dogs that belong to strangers. She hopes to one day stumble upon the meaning of existence. Although she is not terribly clumsy.

Taylor Eaton: Taylor Eaton is a California native living in San Diego with her fiancé and their dog. She enjoys traveling and nerdy sci-fi shows. She writes across many genres and specializes in flash fiction (super short stories). You can find more of her stories (for free!) on her site: www.littlewritelies.com.

Karin Erickson: Karin Erickson is a freelance writer and editor from Sacramento, California, where she writes for local businesses, newspapers, and magazines. Her short fiction, poetry, and creative nonfiction have appeared in over two dozen literary publications, including *Tule Review*, *Sacramento Voices*, the *Walrus Literary Journal*, and *Calaveras Station Literary Journal*. Erickson is currently working on a novel set in both the Sierra Nevada foothills and the San Francisco Bay Area.

Bryan Firks: Bryan Firks is a filmmaker whose short films have appeared on Virgin America flights, Amazon.com, and in festivals across Los Angeles. His short stories have been published in art journals like *Westwind*. A rather serious Lego builder, he hopes to keep constructing brand new worlds from scratch.

Cameron Geoffrey: Cameron Geoffrey is a sardonic optimist who uses writing as a coping mechanism for the crippling anxiety of applying to medical school. It doesn't work.

Ayla Glim: Ayla Glim graduated from Humboldt State University in 2013 with a Bachelor of Arts degree in English. She matches cats and dogs with their forever families through the Companion Animal Foundation and resides in Arcata, California, with her boyfriend, their dog, two cats, and two cockatiels.

Jon Goodnick: Jon Goodnick is a writer and teacher living in Los Angeles.

Shelby Grates: Shelby Grates is a senior studying sociology at the University of California, Los Angeles. When not writing papers, she's working at the small American office of an organization which provides aid to families in Southeast Asia. While passionate about her work, she plans to invest more time in writing creatively post-graduation.

Sam Gross: Sam Gross has been writing since she learned how to do it and reading even longer. She's been featured in Concordia University's *Aerie* and Z Publishing's *America's Emerging Poets* series. She's always looking for the opportunity to say something with her work, even if she isn't always sure what it means.

Shireen Hakim: Shireen Hakim writes for HelloGiggles and is from Los Angeles, California. Her award-winning story, "Rabbi the Rabbit," is published in *Out of Many, One: Celebrating Diversity*. She has written for the NaNoWriMo blog.

Kyle Edward Harris: Kyle Edward Harris's work can be found in cul-de-sac and the *Northridge Review*. Kyle Edward Harris resides in Southern California, roaming thrift stores and movie theaters.

Nathan Heard: Nathan has loved writing and storytelling from a very young age. Now starting his junior year attending Pepperdine University, Nathan pursues a degree in creative writing and history. He is currently working on his sixth novel manuscript and self-publishes poetry and short stories at www.nathanheardwords.com.

Emma Henson: Emma Henson is a coastal transplant from Sarasota, Florida, currently studying in California. When not writing, she can be found consuming any and all media created by HBO, petting her dogs, and eating breakfast food. Her writing has previously appeared in Best Teen Writing and *Discourse Magazine*.

Amethyst Hethcoat: Chapman University graduate and California native Amethyst Hethcoat examines distance in modern relationships, oftentimes through dark humor and tongue-in-cheek observations. She hopes you find her work enjoyable, if not, disturbing. Previously published in *Calliope*, *Crab Fat*, the *Fem*, *Literary Juice*, and the *Metaworker*.

William R. Hincy: "Some people run from their demons; others sit down and have cocktails with theirs." William R. Hincy is a man who does and writes about the latter. Having become a writer after deciding it was the only sensible thing for a problem drinker to do, Hincy has now published a novel and numerous short stories.

Hoài-Linh: Hoài-Linh is a college student pursuing a career in the math and sciences while also harboring a hidden passion for writing and creating new worlds to lose herself in—worlds in which she can live vicariously through her characters.

Ryan Inkley: Ryan Inkley grew up in Orange County, but he doesn't surf, and his life was nothing like *The OC*. He lives in Los Angeles, where he works at an advertising agency proudly writing ads that people skip or fast-forward through.

Jennifer Irwin: A native New Yorker and captivating storyteller with a flair for embellishment, Jennifer Irwin currently resides in Los Angeles with two cats, a dog, and her boyfriend. After earning her BA in cinema from Denison University, she worked in advertising and marketing, raised three boys, and ultimately became a certified Pilates instructor. While she has written screenplays and short stories since her college days, *A Dress the Color of the Sky* is her first novel.

Phoebe Jane: Phoebe Jane is a rock star project manager by day and a technology addict, book dragon, and monster maven by night. She has been writing since she was twelve years old, but it was only seven years ago when she decided to take her writing seriously. After being called to task by Dean Koontz and Orson Scott Card, she began harnessing those demons of doubt and made a commitment to post her work to the world. Since then, she has written several stories and is currently finishing two novels, *The Queen* and *Carriers of Light*. She publishes book reviews, flash fiction, and project excerpts at www.phoebejanewrites.wordpress.com. In addition, she publishes recipes, photos, soccer posts, tech reviews, and other quirky tales that interest her at www.iamphoebejane.com.

Jenna Jauregui: Jenna Jauregui had fun experimenting with writing in college. Now she teaches writing to middle school students and goes by her married name, Jenna Murphy.

Melissa Kandel: Melissa Kandel is a nationally published author of fiction and nonfiction whose writing has appeared on popular blogs and major media outlets like *Forbes*. Born in New York, she lives in Newport Beach, California. Melissa holds a BA from Columbia University and a master's degree from Northwestern University's Medill School. Find her on Instagram: @melissakandel.

Sarah Kahn: Sarah Kahn graduated Stanford University in 2017 with a bachelor's in philosophy. She currently attends seminary in Jerusalem, and after learning glassblowing and mysticism in Northern Israel, she will return to California for a real job. Just kidding, she will return to California and keep writing.

Marina Kapralau: Marina Kapralau is a University of California, Los Angeles, alumna and a literature/editorial writer living in Los Angeles with her husband. Born and raised in Southern Ukraine, she is a travel junkie, a photography enthusiast, a professional writer's block martyr, and a hopeless romantic aspiring to win a Hans Christian Andersen Literature Award.

Bryan Kashon: Bryan Kashon was born on a mountaintop (or as his parents say, the St. Jude's Children's Hospital in Denver.) When not lounging about or trying to astral project to talk to the figures dancing in his peripherals, he loves to act, write, and hang out with his girlfriend and daughter.

Sheryl Kay: Sheryl Kay was born and raised in Southern California, and she so is generally insufferable and is far too fond of the beach. An aspiring novelist and professor, she is distrustful and disdainful of the rain, the cold, and people who shout things from moving cars.

Kikiine: Caroline Riley is a cheerful illustrator who sometimes dabbles in prose just for the heck of it. She loves cats, Thai bubble tea, and comics. Bringing stories to life, whether it be visually or verbally, is one of the greatest treasures she can give.

Michele Kilmer: Michele is a fiction and screenwriter who lives in Oakland, California, with her fire captain wife and two cats.

Kitty Knorr: Kitty Knorr is an aspiring twenty-year-old author from Carlsbad, California. Knorr enjoys creating science fiction short stories, writing poetry, long walks on the beach, and getting caught in the rain. She thanks Z Publishing for giving her this opportunity as the first step in her writing career. You can find more work by Knorr on her blog: www.kittyknorrpoetry.wordpress.com.

Rachael Kuintzle: Rachael Kuintzle is a Ph.D student in biochemistry and molecular biophysics at the California Institute of Technology (Caltech) in Pasadena, California. Her creative writing has appeared in University of California, Santa Barbara's literary magazine, *Spectrum*, *Caltech's Totem*, and other publications. Rachael's prose often uses scientific imagery and metaphors.

Emily La: Emily La graduated summa cum laude from University of California, Irvine, with a BA in English and an emphasis in creative writing in 2017. Currently, they are pursuing an MA in Asian American studies and working on a book series with their partner. Their writing has been featured in university publications and conferences.

Ladycsapp: Cynia Sapp is a recent California State University, East Bay graduate who majored in English with an option in creative writing. She has a passion for writing, language, learning, drawing, and helping others. Originally from Morgan Hill, California, she dedicates her achievements to her family, friends, teachers, and acquaintances.

Ileana Lallain: Ileana Lallain, pseudonym Celeste Stranburk, is an aspiring author specializing in tragedy, fantasy, and supernatural genres. She loves cats, anime, rhythm games, has eclectic taste in music (including many songs in foreign languages), and is an avid reader.

Priscilla Lam: Priscilla Lam has always had a passion for all things literary. A native of Southern California, she enjoys reading modern American literature and writing short stories. When she's not writing, she enjoys spending time with her dogs, painting, daydreaming, and determining what the stars have in store for her.

Blake Lapin: Blake Lapin is a current undergraduate student at Claremont McKenna College studying literature and politics, philosophy, and economics (PPE). He has poetic aspirations.

Kayla Latta: Kayla Latta is a fourth-year student at the University of California, Santa Cruz, pursuing a degree in literature with a concentration in creative writing. When she isn't writing or studying, she works as an editor for *Red Wheelbarrow*, an arts and literature anthology on campus. She hopes that after she graduates, she can spend the rest of her life writing, drinking tea, and being surrounded by cats.

Natasha Lelchuk: Natasha Lelchuk is a graduate of Reed College and the University of California at Irvine. She teaches high school English in Los Angeles County.

Kelly Alicia Lewis: Kelly Lewis is a blogger, self-proclaimed poet, aspiring novelist, and serves as a board member and publicist for the California Writers Club in the Inland Empire.

Craig Loomis: Over the years, Craig Loomis has had his short fiction published in such literary journals as the *Iowa Review*, the *Colorado Review*, the *Prague Revue*, the *Maryland Review*, the *Louisville Review*, *Bazaar*, the *Rambler*, the *Los Angeles Review*, the *Prairie Schooner*, *Yalobusha Review*, the *Critical Pass Review*, the *Owen Wister Review*, *Juxtaprose Literary Magazine*, and others. In 2013, Syracuse University Press published his short story collection entitled *The Salmiya Collection: Stories of the Life and Times of Modern Day Kuwait*.

Ashna Madni: Ashna Madni is a senior undergraduate at the University of Southern California pursuing a double major in English (creative writing) and social sciences with an emphasis in psychology. An aspiring author, Ashna loves to read and write several kinds of fiction but finds particular interest in the genre of magic realism.

Evan Maier-Zucchino: Through writing, Evan Maier-Zucchino endeavors to blend magic with reality, the surreal with the concrete. Having graduated from Chapman University with a BFA in creative writing, he plans to continue mastering the craft of storytelling while taking the time to enjoy music, sunsets, strawberries, and the warm company of his friends and family.

Eva Malis: Eva is an artist, activist, and storyteller who grew up in Valencia, California. She spent the most recent years of her life in the Bay Area, organizing grassroots social and environmental justice campaigns. She uses storytelling as a community healing practice and to craft movements for justice.

Zoe McCartney: Zoe is an artist based in Los Angeles, California. She enjoys researching anomalies, learning new magic tricks, and hiking to places where the Los Angeles skyline can't be found. To see more of her work, visit www.zoemccartney.com.

Mary McQuistan: Mary McQuistan was born and raised in Nebraska before she decided to become an English major in California. After graduating with a bachelor's degree in English, she decided to remain in California to explore writing opportunities.

Anna Miles: Anna Miles, a Los Angeles–based writer and theater maker, holds a BA in theater and creative writing from Northwestern and an MFA in acting from Brown. Her work has been published in Prompt 2013, The Ms. Millennial Project, and on her blog, Pretty Little Loudmouth. She does most of her writing backstage at her performing job at Disneyland.

Jenna Mohl: Jenna Mohl is a recent graduate of the University of California, Berkeley, where she earned a degree in English literature. She currently lives in Southern California with her family and her two perfect dogs.

Dani Neiley: Dani Neiley graduated from Chapman University in 2016 with degrees in English literature and screenwriting, and she currently works as an assistant editor for a publishing company. She has been published in *Bartleby Snopes*, *Drunk Monkeys*, *Calliope*, *Polaris*, and *Green Blotter*. She loves movies and can beat anyone at Boggle.

David Ngo: David Ngo is a writer and avid moviegoer with a strong disposition for sarcasm. He has written various short stories, poetry, and short films that mostly explore the dynamics of modern love and modern death. In his spare time, he listens to sad music and lies in the grass.

Nicolette Nodine: Nicolette Nodine is currently a student at University of California, Santa Cruz. She is journalistic in training and creative in heart. Pursuing a career in journalism or environmental law, she is also working on her first nonfiction book.

Mirt Norgren: Mirt Norgren is an Cuban-American writer, photographer, and graphic designer. Mirt's observations on life, love, recovery, and spirituality are often expressed in the form of essays or short stories. Mirt lives in Southern California with her husband and two dogs.

Alisa O'Donnell: Alisa O'Donnell has been writing since she was a child. She has participated for several years in National Novel Writing Month and has several manuscripts in various stages of editing disarray. She lives in the Central Valley, California, with her husband and cat. Follow her blog at www.alisagramann.wordpress.com.

Jeanne O'Halloran: Jeanne O'Halloran is a California-based poet, illustrator, and short storyist. She uses poetry and illustration to advocate for mental health and women's issues. O'Halloran spends much of her free time traveling. Her favorite location is Connemara, Ireland.

Cassady O'Reilly-Hahn: Cassady is a writer based on the outskirts of Los Angeles County with an affinity for composing poems and short stories. He received his bachelor's in English literature from California State Polytechnic University, Pomona, in the summer of 2017. Cassady runs his own blog, where he posts content four days per week.

Nadine M Patton: Nadine Patton was born in Oklahoma and currently lives in San Diego, California, where she is finishing up her last year of medical school. She enjoys painting and writing in her spare time.

Moira S. Peckham: Moira is an anthropologist living in Berkeley, California. Her work has been featured in the *Berkeley Fiction Review* and the notebooks she keeps next to her bed. She likes stories with dragons but doesn't write them because she fears their power. She loves archaeology and wishes magic really existed.

GC Philipp: Giulia-Christina Philipp is a twenty-four-year-old Italian writer who recently moved to the United States in order to get her BA. She is now working on her MA in comparative literature. Her icons in the literature world are Bukowski, Murakami, Chekhov, Nabokov, and Gogol.

Cam Plunkett: Cam Plunkett studied creative writing and economics at the University of Southern California. He now lives in Virginia with his fiancé and dog.

Maya Rahman-Rios: Maya Rahman-Rios has been writing fiction since the age of six. She works in beauty and skincare marketing, and her favorite things are lipstick, bad reality TV, and petting other people's dogs. She lives in Southern California with her boyfriend. Follow her on Instagram: @missmayaya.

J. Evan Ramos: J. Evan Ramos is a Puerto Rican writer and artist who was born and raised in San Diego, California. He received his MFA in creative writing at San Diego State University. In his free time, Evan enjoys skating, racquetball, and anything Nintendo.

Kateri Ransom: Kateri Ransom has always lived in California but calls New Mexico her second home. She holds a Bachelor of Arts in English literature from University of California, Santa Barbara, and also studied creative writing throughout her academic career. She currently lives in Santa Barbara, California. She works in mental health, teaches dance, and hopes to make YouTube videos about topics in literature. Feel free to find her on Instagram, Twitter, Goodreads, and YouTube. And look out for her new website.

Lila Riesen: Lila is a recent graduate of the University of Zurich with degrees in English literature and English linguistics. Her short stories have been featured in *Calliope Literary Magazine* and the *Zurich English Student*. She has taught fiction workshops at both University of California, Los Angeles, and the University of

Chicago. Currently, she lives in Huntington Beach, working tirelessly on her next YA novel.

Marcus Rigsby: Visions of shadow beings and malevolent animals haunted Marcus's childhood bedside. Today he writes about the parallel worlds where mythologies and children's nightmares originate. You can read his recent works of magic realism, surrealism, and fantasy in the *Northridge Review*, the *Mochilla Review*, and *In-Flight Literary Magazine*.

Taylor Rivers: Taylor was raised in Vallejo, California, but now attends the University of Southern California. His work has been featured in University of Southern California's *Palaver Arts Magazine*. Taylor is currently working toward a bachelor's in theatre arts and plans on becoming a professional actor, writer, and theatrical director once he finishes college.

Camille S Ross: Camille Ross is a spouse of a navy sailor and is a stay-at-home mother to three active boys. She lives in San Diego, California, but was raised near Oshkosh, Wisconsin. She enjoys spending time with her family, exploring the local area, and experimenting with photography.

Lindsey Sacco: Lindsey is a twenty-three-year-old from the North Shore of Massachusetts, now living in Los Angeles, California. A very recent graduate of Elon University in North Carolina, where she studied creative writing and theater arts, she is a self-proclaimed "literature nerd" and has an extensive collection of books that follow her wherever she goes. If you give her the chance, she'll talk your ear off about *Alice in Wonderland* and Marvel comics—especially Captain America.

Alicia Eileen Sage: Alicia Sage is a middle school English teacher and a creative writer. In her spare time, she enjoys watching *RuPaul's Drag Race* and making up songs about her cat. Her influences are modernist and postmodernist writers like Ernest Hemingway, Chuck Palahniuk, and Virginia Woolf.

Denise M. Schmitz: Denise M. Schmitz is a PhD student in astrophysics. She writes mostly papers on cosmology and occasionally writes fiction.

David Scott: David Scott is the author of *Fourteen Tales* (2017) and *Delicate Soul* (spring 2019). When he is not engaged in perfecting his craft, his time is divided between studies on the paranormal and the tutoring and mentoring of student writers throughout the northern California region.

Pearson Sharp: Pearson Sharp is a published author and investigative reporter living in San Diego. When he's not writing, he's planning his next trip around the world.

Dean L. Shauger: Dean L Shauger is a reservist and aspiring writer. He currently lives in Southern California with his polydactyl cat. He can be reached on twitter and instagram: @SimpleChimp.

Austin Shippey: Austin Shippey is a twenty-one-year-old, two-time self-published author whose books have been sold across the United States, and his writings appear in several magazines. His future aspirations feature a successful career in crafting unique visions into profound and meaningful stories. He lives between Oregon and New Orleans and is currently seeking literary professionals who can help make his dreams flourish. Many thanks to Gordon, Emma, and Kylie for helping me in my nightmares and in reality.

Christopher Shonafelt: Christopher Shonafelt is a writer from California with a special love for stories of the horror, science fiction, magical realism varieties, poetry of all kinds, and occasionally appearing on stage. He lives in Orange County. He can be reached at christophershonafelt@gmail.com.

Marina Shugrue: Marina Shugrue is a young adult fiction writer based out of beautiful Southern California. She writes a mix of fantasy, horror, and mystery work. Follow her on Twitter @MarinaMShugrue or on Instagram @marina.shugrue for pictures of her cats and books (and sometimes both).

Kendra Sitton: Kendra Sitton works full-time as a news writer on the overnight shift. During the day, she can be found serving as a freelance reporter, writing poetry, engaging in creative projects, creeping on Twitter, and sleeping. Contact her at kendra.sitton@gmail.com or @PSKendra.

Ash Rinae Stockemer: Ash Rinae Stockemer is a California writer who grew up in Colorado and moved to California to attend Chapman University. She lives in Laguna Beach with her Australian cow dog. She writes creative nonfiction, short stories, poetry, and someday hopes to complete her novel.

Michelle Tan: Michelle Tan is an avid reader, writer, and filmmaker studying film at Washington University. She travels between her two home cities, Los Angeles and Beijing. She loves to explore narratives in various genres, mediums, and cultures. Her favorite writers include Haruki Murakami, Akiko Itoyama, Ha Jin, and Gabriel García Márquez.

Shayne Taylor: Shayne Taylor is a graduate of the University of California, Santa Cruz Creative Writing program. He is a professional river guide on the American rivers and professional ski instructor in Breckenridge, Colorado.

Rory Thost: Rory Thost spent his formative years in Texas and Southeast Asia. He works in documentary film and lives in Los Angeles.

Anresa D. Tyler: Anresa D. Tyler was born and raised in Watts, California, by a single mother and is one of three children. She graduated with a bachelor's degree in writing from Maryville College in Tennessee and won Best Dialogue for its literary magazine. She is currently working on her first fantasy novel.

Rebecca E Van Horn: Rebecca observes the world around her and writes about those observations, late at night, with the curtains drawn. She is a senior in the Dominican University Adult Completion program, where she has sought refuge from an adulthood spent in retail and caregiving for elderly and crabby people.

Jon Vreeland: Jon Vreeland is a writer and poet. His book *The Taste of Cigarettes: A Memoir of a Heroin Addict* is now available at all major book outlets.

Piper Walker: Piper Walker is a middle school teacher who likes to write in her free time. She currently lives in California and hopes to someday write a novel of her own.

Bill Watkins: Bill grew up addicted to sports and alcohol until twelve-step recovery found him in 1995. Since then, he has explored the world and other dimensions for truth. He has been publishing and distributing poetry (www.travelingpoet.net) and humor to inspire young people and old to better lives than his own.

Mark Westphal: Mark Westphal is a writer and music enthusiast from Southern California. He draws his influences from food, music, and *Jojo's Bizarre Adventure*.

Austin L. Wiggins Sr.: Austin Wiggins Sr. is a writer from Indio, California. He is a husband, father, and disciple of literature. He runs the literature blog www.Writingsbyender.com and is a cofounder of the literature magazine *Beautiful Losers Magazine* (Belomag.com). *Bonds That Bind*, his debut short story collection, is available for free on Writings by Ender.

C.M. Wilbur: C.M. Wilbur is a doula, homesteader, and writer living in the foothills of the Sierra Nevada. She has found comfort in words for as long as she can remember and writes in hopes of making others feel less alone.

Patricia Willers: Patricia Willers is the author of "Case by Case Basis" (short stories, 2016) and "Wandering Canalside" (2013). Her writing includes fiction, short stories, travel writing, beer writing, and more. Currently, she writes and teaches English in Davis, California, and spends evenings and weekends tweeting about books, beer, and writing.

Bri Wilson: Bri Wilson is a senior in the Alonzo King LINES Ballet BFA Program at Dominican University of California. Originally from Michigan, she enjoys spending time outside when not dancing or writing. Her work has appeared in the *Tuxedo Literary Magazine* at Dominican University.

Dallas Woodburn: Dallas Woodburn has published hundreds of stories and essays in magazines, newspapers, and journals, including *ZYZZYVA*, the *Nashville Review*, and the *Los Angeles Times*. Her short story collection *Woman, Running Late, in a Dress* (Yellow Flag Press) won the 2018 Cypress & Pine Short Fiction Award. Contact her at www.dallaswoodburnpr.com.

Kimberly Zerkel: Kimberly Zerkel is a writer and translator. She resides in San Francisco.

Made in the USA
San Bernardino, CA
21 August 2018